Gift of War

Other Books by Dorothy Tinker

Peace of Evon
Book 1 of the Peace of Evon series

Short Stories by Dorothy Tinker

"Infinity Hotel"
featured in *Eclectically Cosmic*
"Dreaming of the Chaos"
featured in *In Medias Res: Stories from the In Between*
"Swelling Tides"
featured in *Riding the Waves*
"Embracing the Storm"
featured in *Riding the Waves*
"Return to the Light"
featured in *Out of Many, One*
"Master of My World"
featured in *Eclectically Heroic*

Book 2 of the Peace of Evon series

Gift of War

Dorothy Tinker

Balance of Seven

*To those who would reach
for the dream of their hearts,
even when others claim it
impossible or impractical.*

Contents

Kensy

Map of Evon

Fayral
Kensy
Northeast Forest
Cosley Estate
Main Highwayman Camp
The Eternal One
Tauresian Sea
Cautzel
Zhulan
Tarsur
Pecali
Helloase
Schönestadt
Calny
Machtstadt
Parshen Gut
Ciudad Ocultada
Pretty Pauper
Friedlichoase
Chanser Estate
Wildestadt
Hacienda Sageo
Central Rebel Camp
Baylin
Caypan
Lefas Estate
Pecalini Sea
Main Highways
Ghost Trail (when not following Main Highways)

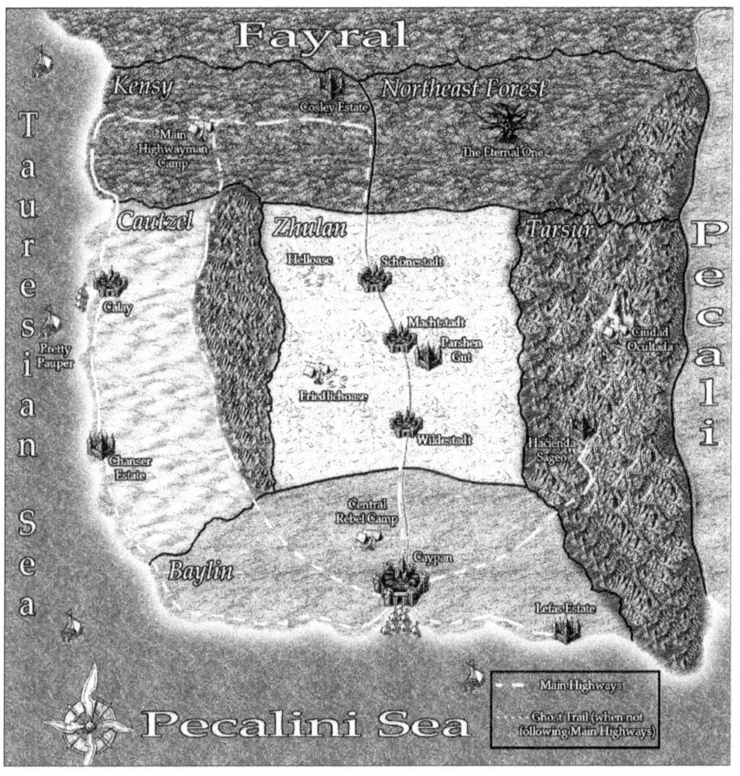

Prologue

30 Early Autumn, 224th year of Evon
Tapestry Room
Pocket Realm of the Fates

"This is unacceptable!"

The harsh words were spoken by the Crone, a darkly colored being who resembled a female human elder in shape. She glared at the Tapestry of Mortal Life, in front of which she and her two sisters sat. Its abstract weave of multicolored strands would have appeared meaningless and without design to most beings, but to her discerning eye it mapped out the lives and interactions of all mortal creatures.

However, it was a singular, striking interaction, represented by the tangle of a multitude of threads, that had caught her attention and driven her to anger.

"War has become intractable! He interferes with the humans too directly!"

"You repeat yourself, Findi," breathed Neris the Maid. Though exactly the same age as the gravel-voiced Crone,

Dorothy Tinker

Neris's appearance was that of a young human female on the cusp of Coming of Age. The variety of colors that composed her soul and formed her skin were pale and light, and they drifted across her being like wind-chased clouds.

"Such complaints hold little meaning without solutions, Sister." The pale Maid shook her head lightly. "So what would you have us do? We have already shown the Kensian Seer everything we can without giving away Peace's true soul identity."

"Not that she would pass along such information, even if we did."

Tapeta the Matron spoke the admonition firmly and precisely. The colors of the Matron's being—as numerous and distinct as those of the soul-strands she wove into the Tapestry of Mortal Life—shone bright and vibrant. While Neris's soul colors danced wildly and Findi's churned with the slow subtelty of a sleeping dragon's breath, Tapeta's soul colors progressed across her skin with the steady and purposeful surety of once-famous dwarven furnaces, lost millennia ago to the last outbreak of Chaos.

Nowadays, the surety of her soul's movements were only matched by the flow of her fingers among the weave of the Tapestry.

Tapeta paused in her weaving just long enough to trace a single soul-strand as she continued her reproof. "The Seers of the Caler line have always possessed a discretion few can rival. Only this one's Healer counterpart, the one some mortals call Old Iron, could possibly surpass her in prudence."

Findi offered only a rasping growl in response. Focusing once again on the disturbing interaction displayed in the weave of the Tapestry, she separated out two strands dangling from its unfinished end. Fingering them, she growled harshly.

"War is causing too much damage with his conduct—damage we cannot undo."

Pulling the soul-strands taut, she slid her Double-Edged Dagger across both. They snapped away from the Tapestry with ease, belying the violence that had killed the two mortals they represented.

"There is no reason I should be removing these souls from the Tapestry so soon." Findi ground her teeth and tossed the dissolving strands into the mass of soul material that represented the Cycle of Incarnation. "War's actions have consequences that reach far beyond his dispute with Peace."

Neris sighed breathily. "Yet only War has the ability to remind his twin of her true place."

The Maid paused briefly in her spinning and fingered the pure purple soul-strand that flowed from her Spindle to the Tapestry alongside a slew of variegated strands that appeared murky and indistinct in comparison. Such a pure color was rare on the Tapestry. With the recent events surrounding the physically incarnated demigoddess the purple strand represented, Neris could only believe that such purity and rareness led to greater danger, not good.

The Matron's strong, smooth voice cut through such thoughts. "Until War accomplishes his task, we can do naught but weave what we See and hope the Tapestry does not fall completely to Chaos."

Tapeta lifted her chin and eyed the small tears that had already appeared in the Tapestry's weave. The tears were signs of Chaos, which had led to her and her sisters' doubts over the outcome of the season. Tapeta was certain the Chaos would only increase before the season finished, but they, the Fates, could not See into Chaos, nor could they predict its effects.

Dorothy Tinker

Findi growled. "I may not have a solution for War's behavior, but there is something we can do to mitigate the more widespread consequences." She reached for several soul-strands laid out nearby and plucked her fingers along six of them: white, black, pink, red, silver, and yellow. "Besides, the other demigods need something to keep themselves busy."

Tapeta and Neris nodded and returned to their eternal tasks. They would await the arrival of the juvenile deities and hope they could stem the Chaos that threatened the realm they ruled.

~~*~*

Main Highwayman Camp, Kensy, Evon
Mortal Realm

Mama Caler sat on a log in Main Highwayman Camp, her hands limp around the bowl of stew Cassidi had given her. Her silvering brown hair hung down her back and around her shoulders as she stared sightlessly into Cassidi's cooking fire.

Only minutes before, she had touched both the disguised king, Ferez Katani, and the hidden heir to the duchy of Kensy, Gemini Cosley. She had hoped to affirm to them the necessity of their present companionship. It was a pairing she had Seen every time she touched young Gemini, even as far back as her Naming Day.

Instead, she'd managed to do the opposite. Though she had only Seen peace every time she touched Gemini previously, the Fates had been frighteningly indecisive this time. The images they had shown her painted two futures: one of peace, to which she was accustomed, and one of utter Chaos.

Mama Caler closed her eyes, calling forth the images the Ladies had chosen to show her.

Soldiers and rebels standing side by side, a feeling of pure peace stilling their blades.

A woman bearing short, dark hair and a bloodstained bodice and skirts, lying dead.

Brothers, separated by ideals, embracing each other, their swords scattered across the ground.

A dark, winged behemoth diving toward palace walls, its mouth agape in anger.

A red-stained winged horse lying on its back, a red sword hanging upright above its belly.

Mama Caler shivered and opened her eyes. Many of the images had been actual Sights, she was sure, but the last was more symbolic. Even stained red, the Seer recognized the winged horse and sword of Evon's flag, though the image had been upside down.

If that last is true, then the fate of Evon may lie in something worse than just another war.

She sighed and glanced toward the Healer's tent, where she had left Gemini and the king. *And the only thing standing in the way of that fate might just be the companionship of those two.*

Young enough to still be considered children by some, both were already experienced enough to garner the respect of those who recognized their achievements: Ferez, the youngest king of Evon and the one who had negotiated for an end to the decades-long war with Fayral, and Gemini, better known to most of the country as James Caffers, unifier of the rebellious groups of Evon. Both were powerful warriors who only wanted peace for their country. They wouldn't give that up for anything.

"I only pray it's enough to hold back the Chaos the Ladies have shown me."

Sour bitterness crept up Mama Caler's throat. She swallowed it down and sat up straight. Digging into her stew, she buried the bitterness in the warmth and spice of Cassidi's cooking. Unfortunately, no matter how hard she tried to reclaim her usual buoyancy, she couldn't ignore the doubt that dragged at her.

One

2 Mid Autumn, 224
Evonese Highway

Last Chance nickered wearily as her master finally guided her off the highway. The soft light of the forest day had long faded to the darkness of night, and the mare could barely make out the deer path she was following. Even the dark stallion in front of her was invisible in the darkness, only his quiet nickers and the rustle of his passage assuring the mare he was still there.

Last Chance kept her head low, her exhaustion and the darkness threatening to make her stumble and lose her way. Long days hadn't been rare during the war, but even then she had never been forced to travel from dawn to beyond dusk with only a single meal halfway through the day.

A light pressure on her nose alerted her that they had reached their destination for the night. Darkness hid the differences in their surroundings as she staggered to a halt.

Dorothy Tinker

Only the sudden lack of plants pressing in on her from all directions proved that they had stumbled upon a clearing.

A crackling above her, followed by a heavy *whumpf* and a slight shaking of the ground beneath her hooves, announced the sudden presence of the dragon, and she stepped warily away from the sounds. On her back, her master shifted in the saddle and laid a hand lightly against her shoulder, murmuring soft words in a tone that sounded as tired as she felt.

Suddenly, light overwhelmed the mare's eyes, and she jerked her head to one side, blinking against the glare that filled the clearing. Once she could see through the brightness, she found the dragon tending a small fire, the flickering light of which barely illuminated her red and purple scales and the wings that hung half-furled around her. The stallion, whom Last Chance had been trying to avoid as much as she could, was easing his way through the trees on the other side of the clearing.

And approaching the mare with a smile was their human companion, eyes focused solely on Last Chance's master. Last Chance snorted softly and lowered her head in search of grass. *I don't understand Ferez's newest friends.*

Oh, she understood the reason he traveled with them. It had always hurt him to see his people suffer during the years they'd traveled around Baylin before they'd joined the war effort. But Last Chance couldn't fathom the reason for the human female's deception.

Or how she's managed to convince the entire country she's male. She glanced at the girl, who was leading Ferez toward the fire. *Her gender seems obvious to me.*

Last Chance didn't even think her old friend of eight years would be too upset if he learned the truth. She thought he liked the girl too much to care.

She snorted again. *He might even be relieved to learn she's a girl.*

Not that the humans cared if males mated with other males. The humans had odd customs like that. It was only her friend's title that would restrict him to finding a lifemate among certain human females.

Last Chance huffed. *Humans are strange creatures indeed.*

"You seem to be keeping yourself entertained."

The nicker was soft, but Last Chance wasn't expecting it. Snapping her head up, she eyed the black stallion wildly. *When did he—*

The thought disappeared as exhaustion suddenly dragged at her. With a snort, she staggered to one side.

"Easy," a soothing voice cooed. Something solid pressed along Last Chance's right side. *"I believe water, food, and sleep would be best, aye?"*

The mare swung her head to the right and found red eyes staring at her. She considered refusing the offered assistance, but she was already using the dragon to keep herself on her hooves. She nickered a reluctant agreement.

When warmth pressed along her left side as well, Last Chance whinnied sharply, jerked her head around, and bit at the stallion's neck. He jerked away from her, and though she staggered in that direction, she would rather fall than have him so close to her. His whinnied response was half pained, half indignant.

"Quiet, Shadow!" the dragon hissed, reaching her head around in front of Last Chance to address the stallion. *"Leave her be. She is not accustomed to traveling for so long. You cannot expect her to deal with your flirting just now."*

"I wasn't—" the stallion began, but something—Last Chance could never be sure what passed between Ferez's new

friends—interrupted him. He snorted, tossed his head, and wandered over to an open portion of the clearing to lie down.

"There," the dragon cooed, her voice once again soothing. *"I will help you to the river, and then you can hopefully graze some before sleep claims you."*

Last Chance eyed the stallion one last time before turning her attention back to the dragon. The dragon led her to the other side of the clearing and through the trees to a large river that Last Chance hadn't realized she'd been able to hear.

She drank her fill and ate as much as she could before sleep came too close. Half leaning on the dragon, she wandered back into the clearing. Under the dragon's persuasion, she settled herself on the ground with her rump toward the fire and let herself slip into a heavy sleep.

~~*~*

Gemi watched as Flame coaxed Last Chance into settling down to sleep. The pale mare's reaction to Shadow's attempt to help had been surprising, but the stallion loved to press his attentions on every mare he met. Despite Shadow's continued insistence that he hadn't been flirting, Gemi suspected the black stallion had simply pushed Last Chance too far.

"She mus' be more exhausted than I thought." The words came from her right, where Ferez leaned against his saddle and bags. Gemi turned to him, startled. She had thought him already asleep after eating the travel rations she had provided.

"Oh?" She kept her tone light despite her curiosity. Ferez's eyes were closed, and his sandy hair fell across his forehead as his head nodded toward his chest.

Ferez hummed for a moment before jerking his head up

and meeting her eyes, his own half closed. In the flickering firelight, she could just see a sliver of silvery blue.

"She doesn' usually let others so close to her."

Gemi frowned, considering the mare's reactions to each of her bondmates. "I thought that was just a result of Shadow's flirting."

Ferez blinked at her slowly before shaking his head. "I don' know abou' flirtin', but I was talkin' about how close she let Flame get to her." He chuckled weakly. "Stallions're another story altogether. She holds a special . . . wariness for them."

Gemi frowned, and Flame crooned softly. A twitch of Shadow's ears was the only indication that he was still listening and that the king had caught his attention.

"How so?" Gemi asked, speaking the question on all three of their minds.

Ferez waved a hand lazily in the air. "When I brought her to the Royal Stables, the stallions there weren' exactly . . . welcomin'." He paused a moment before adding, "There were several attacks durin' the firs' few months I worked wit' her. It reached the point where she could ne'er relax 'round any o' the other horses at the stable for fear they'd attack her."

By the time Ferez finished speaking, Shadow had his head raised and his ears forward. *I don't remember that.*

You did not recognize her, either, did you? Flame's snort was soft enough to not wake the mare she had curled around.

Gemi considered her bondmates' words. "Was she not born at the Royal Stables?"

The king offered a small smile and a shake of his head. "Yeh might've noticed Last Chance has a very distinctive coat."

"Aye. I'd worried about you traveling anonymously with

such a noticeable mount. Clever, rubbing dirt into her coat to darken it."

Ferez nodded, his eyes closing as he did. "The white coat is specific to Pecali. As far as I know, she's the only one of her breed here in Evon." He paused, a frown tugging at his lips. "Well, perhaps there are some in Tarsur, but I wouldn' know.

"Anyway, when I was ten, I found Last Chance on a Pecalini trade ship that had docked in Caypan's harbor for the sevenday." He sighed. "She was gray then, no' that I could tell her color from the dirt. But the dirt couldn' hide the sores on her legs or the way her ribs stood out against her skin. I begged my father to buy her off the ship, if only to save her from such a life."

"Was she raised on that ship?" Flame whined. She nudged the white mare's neck gently with her snout, her desire to comfort the mare pulsing through the bond.

Ferez shrugged when Gemi repeated the question. "Master Ekin—he's the Animal Mage who runs the Royal Stables—he was ne'er able to learn all o' Last Chance's history. The one thin' he was certain about was tha' she must've been raised by a powerful Animal Mage for her to resist Animal Magic as well as she does."

Gemi nodded. Ferez had already explained how he'd only survived as long as he had on the highway five days ago because of Last Chance's ability to deceive Charlen.

"Finding her like that," she murmured, "it must have taken a lot of work to get her to trust you."

"Aye, but it was worth it." The king opened his eyes and focused his gaze on the mare. "Wit' her, I've always felt I can go anywhere, as Frenz Kanti or myself, an' I'll have nothin' to fear. I wouldn' trade her for any other mount in Evon."

Gemi's lips twitched into a smile. That was a feeling she understood well, no matter that her own companions were connected to her more permanently than Last Chance was to Ferez.

"So sentimental," Shadow nickered softly, but his thoughts churned against Gemi's mind.

Suddenly, Ferez jerked upright. Gemi stifled a chuckle as he blinked and looked around. "I think it's time for sleep." She helped Ferez lay out his bedroll, and the king was asleep in minutes.

~~*~*

Ferez woke suddenly to something wet dripping onto his face. Wrinkling his nose, he batted at the air above him in the hopes of knocking away whatever was dripping on him. When his hand slid into and caught on something fibrous, a gasp reached his ears, and he opened his eyes.

He blinked. James was leaning over him, his long, wet hair caught around Ferez's fingers. The boy's amethyst eyes tightened and his mouth twisted. Touching Ferez's hand, he helped him untangle from the black strands.

Once free, James leaned back on his heels and ran a hand through his hair. "Didn't mean to startle you," he muttered. "Just wake you."

Ferez sat up. "By drippin' water on me?"

James ducked his head and wrung the long strands of his hair, squeezing excess water onto the ground beside the king's bedroll.

"Sorry—I hadn't thought about that."

Ferez watched as James continued to comb his fingers through his hair and squeeze out excess water. "Why do yeh keep yer hair so long?" he suddenly asked, thinking of the boy's expression when Ferez had only accidentally caught it. "Surely some'un has used it as leverage in combat."

James rolled his eyes, and the king was certain he wasn't the first to ask the question. "Rarely, actually. Most people don't think to use it in the middle of a fight, probably because they aren't trained to."

"But it has happened?"

James sighed and nodded. "A couple times, aye."

When the boy didn't elaborate, Ferez added, "So why keep it long?"

James glanced at him, eyes widening. "I—"

He frowned, his eyes darting to the side, where Ferez could see Flame tending the fire. The dragon crooned softly, and the boy's cheeks reddened. Ferez raised his brows, wondering what reason the boy had to be embarrassed. James briefly met Ferez's eyes again before shrugging and ducking his head.

"My mother had long, black hair."

The boy didn't elaborate but began to toy with the loose strands of hair. The king didn't know if James was expecting to be teased, but he certainly didn't find the words humorous or absurd.

His own mother, Queen Falen Katani, had died giving birth to him, so he understood the desire to hold onto any connection he could find. At the same time, he had never had the chance to know his mother, so he could only imagine the pain James felt from losing his mother after being raised by her.

"Nothin' to be 'shamed of," Ferez muttered, patting the boy on the shoulder.

As he climbed to his feet, James lifted his gaze to stare at Ferez, his mouth slightly agape. Ferez ignored the look as he stretched and began to put away his bedroll.

By the time he'd finished gathering his things, James had recovered. Ferez was preparing to saddle Last Chance when the boy pressed something into his hands and propelled him toward one side of the clearing.

"You'd best bathe and change before we head out for the day. We'll be entering Zhulan today, and this could be our last chance to bathe for the next two sevendays. We certainly won't be able to bathe in private."

Ferez blinked down at the pile of cloth James had handed him. Glancing back over his shoulder, he realized the boy was wearing a different set of clothing than he'd become accustomed to seeing on him.

"I canna wear my plainclothes?"

James paused in leaning over his saddlebags. Turning his eyes back to Ferez, he straightened and nodded to the pile in the king's hands. "These are better suited to Zhulan's desert climate. More than that, they'll mark you as a nomad."

Ferez frowned. "Wouldn' it be better to wear plainclothes an' blend in?"

The boy smiled and shook his head. "Unlike the other rebellious groups, the ways of the nomads are millennia old. They're proud of their heritage in a way most people don't understand. Most would rather risk persecution than forsake what they are, and one of the reasons I relished becoming a nomad was that absolute refusal to bend to fear."

Ferez stared at James. "So . . . the clothes are a necessary part o' learnin' how they live?"

James's smile gentled. "The treatment of nomads in the cities isn't all that bad, Ferez." The king simply raised an eyebrow, unimpressed. "Most people don't attack nomads on sight, and the guards no longer arrest them without some provocation."

Ferez twitched. "No longer?"

The boy shrugged. "There was a time when guards would arrest a nomad the moment he entered the city, but that was years ago. Now . . ."

The boy frowned and waved Ferez toward the sound of rushing water. "Go bathe and change; we've already dawdled longer than we should have."

That was when Ferez realized that the clearing was no longer depending solely on the fire for light. Instead, a soft light had begun to pierce the high canopy, declaring the sun already risen. Ferez hurried out of the clearing to finish preparing for the day.

He kept the bath short. Despite James's threat that this was most likely the last time they'd be able to bathe for the next two sevendays, the king couldn't stand the vulnerability of bathing within sight of the Northeast Forest. As soon as he'd spotted the thick fog that crept over the San River's eastern bank, he hurried his movements and pulled himself from the water as quickly as possible.

However, that speed meant he was faced with the new pile of clothing that much sooner. His worry that they wouldn't fit—James was smaller than him—was apparently baseless. Both the trousers and the tunic, which was softer and lighter weight than Ferez's own tunic, were loose fitting. The trousers brushed the tops of Ferez's shoes, and the tunic's sleeves reached just past his wrists. He frowned and plucked at the sleeves. *This is better suited to being out in the hot desert?*

He didn't have time to worry about it, though. There by the river, he could see the sky above the Northeast Forest lightening. Ferez stopped playing with the tunic's long sleeves and turned his attention to the remaining articles of clothing.

Immediately, he was puzzled by their purpose.

There were three pieces remaining: a large square of cloth, a long, thin piece of fabric, and a circlet of cordage. The square was simple and unmarked, but the long, thin piece was dyed a deep purple at both ends, several shades darker than James's eyes. Both seemed to be made of the same material as the tunic—a shiny, billowy fabric. Shaking his head, Ferez decided to question James about the remaining pieces and ambled back toward the clearing.

As he approached the clearing's edge, he called out, "James, I can't—"

A sudden flash of light caught his attention, and he jerked his gaze up and stared. Within the clearing, James—at least, Ferez assumed it was James; his distinctive hair was hidden beneath billowing cloth—seemed to dance from side to side. His hands moved as quickly as his feet, and Ferez thought the boy was shadowboxing until he noticed the curved blades hovering over James's knuckles.

The king was suddenly reminded of the conversation he'd had with his dukes on the boat ride to the *Pretty Pauper*. Tern had suspected James carried a pair of the blades Kawn had called scharfmonde: twin moon blades. Since then, Ferez had noticed the sheaths James wore at his lower back, but he had never seen the actual blades before.

He gaped as he watched James practice. The boy's movements were fluid, which didn't surprise him, but he was accustomed to seeing that fluidity with a sword, not with . . . boxing blades. It was the only comparison Ferez could find as he recalled the one boxing match he and his father had attended years before.

When the boy pivoted on one foot and brought up one hand as though to block while the other sliced low, Ferez winced. Such a blow would slice open a man's stomach! James must have caught sight of Ferez then, as he paused and grinned. Swinging his hands down and behind his back, he quickly sheathed both blades.

"Need help?" he asked even as he wiped his forehead with a corner of the large cloth that covered his head. The cloth seemed to be held in place by a ring of cordage like the one Ferez held. The king also noted the long, thin fabric tied around the boy's waist, the ends dangling in front of one thigh.

"Here," James said and held out one hand.

Ferez jerked his gaze back up to the boy's face and flushed as he handed him his extra pieces. The sudden warmth of his face confused him, but he ignored it in favor of James's explanation.

"This," the boy said, holding up the large square of shimmering cloth, "is a kopfabdeckung."

"Kohp-fahb-deh-koong," Ferez muttered.

James blinked and then grinned. "Something like that."

He tugged on his own square cloth. "It's pretty self-explanatory, I think. For nomads, it's a necessity since it protects the head and neck from the constant sunlight. Believe me, you'll be glad to have it."

He then tossed the cloth over Ferez's head and quickly secured it with the circlet of cordage.

"An' the belt?" Ferez asked. He eyed James's as the boy finished affixing the kopfabdeckung to his head.

"It's called a statusgürtel."

"Shtah-toos-ghewr-tehl."

James chuckled and nodded. He wrapped the belt around the king's waist and knotted it above one leg. "It declares a nomad's clan as well as the status of . . . certain individuals." He chuckled. "And we'll have to get you your own once we reach camp so people don't start getting the wrong idea about who you are."

Ferez frowned. "Why's that?"

The boy grinned. "Most statusgürtel are only dyed at one end. Double dyed represents members of the häuptlinge's families."

"Hoypt-ling-uh?"

"Aye. The leader of each clan is called the häuptling. My vater—my father—is Häuptling Hausef Kanten of the Katze Clan. Hence, my double-dyed statusgürtel."

Ferez chuckled. "So I'm no' the only one in this group who's royal?"

James rolled his eyes and turned to his stallion, who had ambled over. "It's really only a technicality. I sort of saved his eldest son's life, so he adopted me in return."

Ferez blinked. "How'd that happen?"

James glanced away from the saddle he'd just settled onto Shadow's back and waved Ferez toward Last Chance. Once Ferez had begun preparing his mare for travel, the boy answered.

"It's how I met the Katze Clan, actually. On my first night in Schönestadt, I overheard a woman begging the innkeeper to help her injured son. He refused, so I offered my own assistance."

The boy tugged on his saddle before swinging himself up onto Shadow's back. "It wasn't until we'd arrived at their camp that we learned the two had been the wife and eldest son of their clan's häuptling. Hausef offered us a place to stay for a while and then adopted me once he'd decided the debt wouldn't be satisfied by anything less."

"Bu' they are your family." Ferez didn't doubt it. Despite the objectivity of his words, there was a tenderness in the boy's voice that the king couldn't mistake.

"Aye," James murmured. After a moment, the boy

motioned to Ferez to hurry. "Up with you now," he insisted. "We're already late enough."

Ferez chuckled and finished tacking Last Chance. As soon as he'd mounted up, they left the clearing for the Evonese Highway once more.

Zhulan

Map of Zhulan

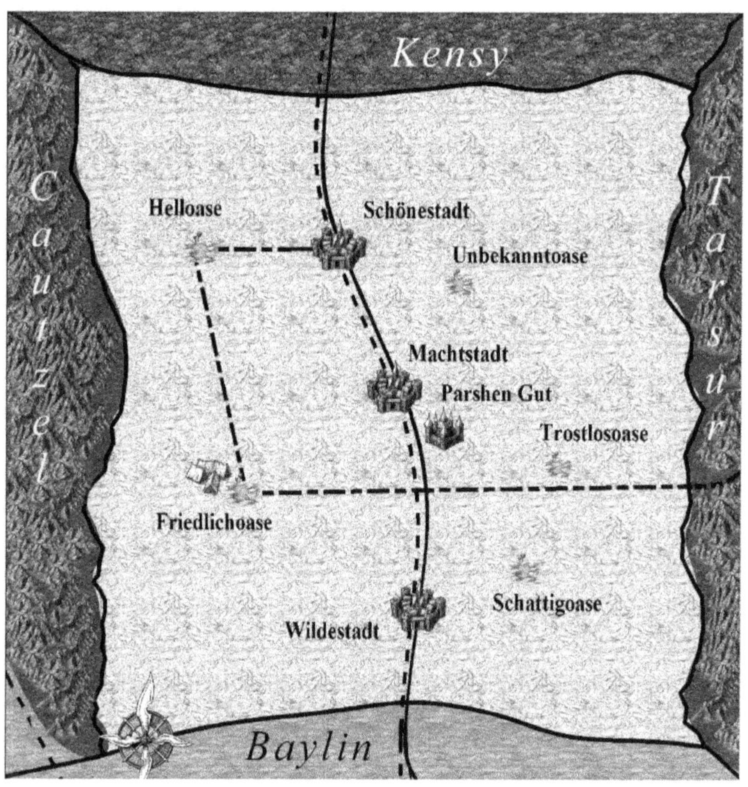

Two

4 Mid Autumn, 224
Zhulan, Evon

Two days later, the sun was just brushing the western horizon when Schönestadt came into sight. The city, Zhulan's northernmost, was large and brightly colored. To Ferez, it looked as if a giant dragon had sprawled across the San River.

Ferez chuckled softly. Before this season, he never would have considered comparing anything to a magical creature except perhaps the winged horse depicted on Evon's flag.

It seems James has done more for me than simply reawaken my concern for my people.

The king turned to comment on the city's beauty but hesitated when he caught sight of the city's gate.

"Seems a bit crowded for sunset."

James shrugged. "Few people travel between Zhulan and Kensy these days, so most people who actually use the northern gates are farmers and villagers who live along the San River north of the city. They usually travel at night to avoid the heat of the desert sun."

Ferez frowned and asked why they had traveled during the hot day, then. James shook his head.

"I always travel by day for the journey to Schönestadt. Once there, we can explore the city for as long as you're willing to remain awake before we claim our beds for the day. We'll leave for Helloase tomorrow night."

Helloase, Ferez knew from James's stories, was the oasis where the boy's clan stayed during this time of the season.

Ferez shook his head. "An' yeh do that every season." It amazed him how strict James was with his routine. After so many years, it was only Ferez and his men who had forced the boy to change anything.

As they came closer to the city, they began to pass other travelers, many of whom cast them odd looks before hurrying past. One man spat on the ground and raised a fist toward them before his companion grabbed his arm, hissing something in his ear as he pulled him away. Ferez turned in his saddle to watch that particular pair.

"Just ignore them," James muttered. "Things have gotten better in the last few years, but there are still those who hate nomads."

Ferez nodded slowly as he turned back around. After the amity he'd seen the Kensians offer the Highwaymen, it was disconcerting to be faced with hatred from Zhulan's citizens when they considered him a nomad.

I once thought the rebellious groups were all the same, but even the provinces' peoples treat each group differently.

Ferez was distracted from such thoughts when they reached Schönestadt's north gate. The horses snorted as they pushed through the crowd, tossing their heads and nudging people aside when they wouldn't move.

They were just coming level with the city walls when a shout on the other side of the gate drew the king's attention. Someone yelled something that Ferez couldn't understand (he thought the harsh words must be Zhulanese) before swinging a fist at a uniformed man. The scuffle that broke out drew the presence of several other uniformed men—the city guards set to watch the gate.

As the crowd around the horses churned and pushed back from the conflict, Ferez tugged on Last Chance's reigns, already planning to help break up the fight. A hand on his arm made him hesitate, and he glanced at James, who shook his head.

"Don't," the boy warned. "No one will thank you for interfering."

Ferez grimaced, recognizing the truth of James's words. He had become accustomed to helping in any fight he witnessed while in Kensy, but if others in Zhulan thought he was a nomad, such help would no doubt be spurned. Instead, he allowed Last Chance to push through the crush of bodies alongside Shadow until both horses could walk freely through the city streets.

"How do yeh do it?" Ferez asked once they were free of the crowd. When James frowned, Ferez clarified. "Shift yer attitude. In Kensy, the fightin's open; yeh're always involved when there's conflict. But here . . ."

He gestured back toward the gate, from which shouts could still be heard. He suspected more people had become involved in the fight.

James shrugged. "It's a necessity, is all. I—"

"Verdammte nomaden!"

The coarse words were accompanied by grasping hands, and Ferez yelped as he was suddenly dragged from the saddle.

~~*~*

"Frenz!" Gemi gasped when her friend disappeared from Last Chance's back. At the same time, the mare swung her head around and, from the following cries, bit at least one of the attackers.

"James!" Flame growled as Gemi swung off Shadow's back. *"Be careful! There are two dead nomads hanging from the gallows!"*

An image flashed through the bond, so vivid through the dragon's eyes that Gemi paused to control the sudden urge to gag.

"Flame!" Shadow chastised, even as he swung his head around to nip at several people crowding too close. *"Not all of us have stomachs of iron."*

Flame's protest sped through the bond, but Gemi shoved the mental awareness of her bondmates to the back of her mind just as she shoved through the crowd to reach Ferez. Several people tried to grab her by the arms or shoulders, but these river-dwellers were obviously neither guards nor boxers, so she easily slipped through their weak grips.

By the time Gemi reached Last Chance's other side, Ferez had regained his feet and was evading the wild swings of a particularly large man. By the stranger's stance, Gemi would have thought him a boxer, but he didn't use the economical jabs that she was accustomed to seeing from a master boxer or a nomad.

She was just reaching for the man's arm in the hopes of

pulling his attention away from Ferez when a shrill voice cut through the noise of the crowd.

"Oi, herren!"

Gemi stilled, as did most of the people surrounding her. The voice had sounded like a child's, and a quick glance around revealed a young boy standing on a stack of crates to one side of the road. The boy raised his hands, from which several small pouches dangled.

Cries exploded from the crowd. When two more children clambered up behind the first, several pouches clutched in each of their hands, the crowd surged forward. Even Ferez's attacker stomped toward the children, one hand clapped to his belt.

As the children disappeared into an alley on the other side of the crates, a tug on Gemi's statusgürtel made her jerk around and down into a crouch. She blinked when she found herself eye level with a young girl, whose hair and face were both dark with grime.

"Kommt!" the girl commanded. "Afore they realize they ain' gonna catch the others an' come back for ye."

"Follow her, James!" Flame growled as the girl disappeared back into the crowd. *"There are guards converging on your position from both the gate and farther into the city."*

Gemi nodded and grabbed Ferez by the wrist. As she pulled him after the girl, Shadow nickered, *"We'll rejoin you later,"* and shoved Last Chance in the opposite direction.

Gemi had already lost sight of the girl, but Flame directed them to an alley across the street. Several turns down the alley, Gemi and Ferez found the dirt-streaked girl leaning against the wall, her gaze sharp.

"Took ye long enough," the girl hissed. She bounced on the balls of her feet and glanced back and forth down the alley. "Thought ye'd been nabbed by the wachen."

Vah-kin? Gemi wondered but then shook her head. *Guards, of course.*

Normally, by the time she reached Schönestadt, she would have already shifted her thoughts to the mixed language most often spoken in Zhulan, but traveling with Ferez seemed to be affecting her schedule more than she'd thought.

Forcing her thoughts into Zhulanese, she asked, "If the nomaden are in so much trouble, why are the schlingel willing to help us?" The schlingel, Gemi knew, cared for naught but gold and their gangs.

The girl snorted and rolled her eyes. "Wille's got nuttin' to do wit' it, Violettauge Nomade."

Gemi frowned. It wasn't often she heard that nickname, despite her unmistakable purple eyes.

"Was a request from Dame Clarimonde. The gang to find ye today an' send ye to her has their debts paid in full." The girl's gaze sharpened as she added, "Ye will tell her Ratte sent ye?"

Gemi nodded. Dame Clarimonde was one of Schönestadt's most powerful moneylenders, and Gemi knew the frau often accepted repayment in tenders other than coin.

"Danke," Gemi replied, but Ratte had already stepped past her and Ferez and was sprinting back toward the highway. Gemi shook her head.

"James?" Ferez spoke then, and Gemi turned toward him. "Eh . . . shling-ehl?"

The word held such confusion that Gemi laughed. She answered the king's question as she led him farther away from the highway.

~~*~*

Ferez shook his head as James compared the schlingel to Caypan's street runners: children who lived on the streets and often became thieves in order to survive. It took some work to understand the boy's words and not just because he was now interjecting Zhulanese into his description. Ferez had known Kawn his entire life, so the mixed language wasn't completely new.

What the king was having difficulty with was the boy's current accent. From the moment he'd begun speaking with Ratte, James's voice had changed, becoming deeper and brisker. The sudden change from the Fayralese accent to which Ferez was accustomed was astonishing.

There's still so much I don't know about him, Ferez realized as they stepped around lazing animals and piles of refuse and ducked under clotheslines. *I wonder if he changes so much for every province.*

A hand on his chest halted his steps, and he glanced at James curiously. The boy nodded toward the portion of alley in front of them. Peering through the growing darkness, Ferez made out a door guarded by two hounds and a small pack of rats. It was such an unlikely combination that Ferez knew there had to be an Animal Mage within.

"Do yeh think it's safe to pass them?" he whispered.

"That's Dame Clarimonde's haus."

Ferez frowned. It took him a moment to realize that was the name Ratte had mentioned.

"Yeh mean tha's the door we want?" When James nodded, Ferez shook his head. "Isn' tha' dangerous?"

James chuckled. "Hardly. You see the falken?"

He pointed up, and Ferez lifted his gaze to the edge of the roof above the door to Dame Clarimonde's home. A flock of large birds, their hooked beaks and long talons looking sharp, crowded along the ledge and circled the alley.

Entranced, Ferez nodded.

"Most Tieremagier wouldn't attract so many falken unless that was their Kräftetier. And the only Tieremagier I know with such a Kräftetier are my familie."

Ferez jerked his gaze back down to James. Before he could ask what he meant, James stepped toward the animals. They focused their eyes on him, but none moved to attack as he passed them and reached for the door. With one hand on the handle, James glanced back at Ferez and beckoned.

"Komme, Frenz. They won't—"

He cut off with a grunt as the door was suddenly wrenched open and he stumbled through the doorway. A hand grabbed James by the neck before the door slammed shut, leaving the king alone in an unknown alley in the dark of night.

~~*~*

Raymond growled as he slammed the stranger back against the closed door. It was bad enough that the stadt was filled with feinde at every turn with the wachen hunting down nomaden and the river-dwellers openly attacking them. But it seemed that even Dame Clarimonde's haus, a nomade safe haven about which only the Kreis should know, was at risk of being discovered.

Knowing he had to remove the threat before it could harm his charge, Raymond braced a forearm against the stranger's chest and reached for his scharfmond with the other hand.

"Raymond Schmidt! If you pull your scharfmond, I swear I'll tell Ulla. Don't think I won't!"

The words stilled both Raymond's thoughts and his motions. The voice was familiar, and he pulled back enough to get a look at the person's face in the lamplight. The light revealed round cheeks and a small nose, all framed by the shimmering silk of a kopfabdeckung, but it was the narrow eyes flashing violet that jerked Raymond to awareness.

"James?" Raymond took a step back to let the boy breathe. "How did—"

He was interrupted by a rattling of the door's handle and a hissed "James!" Immediately, James turned and pulled open the door, dragging in another mann dressed in the clothes of a nomade. When Raymond caught sight of the double purple of his statusgürtel, he growled.

"James, who is this?"

"A freund." The boy frowned. For a moment, he peered up at Raymond narrowly. "What's wrong?" he finally asked. He glanced around. "And where's Zuk?"

Raymond slammed his eyes shut. With James's arrival, he had temporarily forgotten his failure, but James's words renewed the ache in his chest. He tossed his head back toward one corner of the room.

"The bed."

He kept his eyes closed as James brushed past him, but a gasp had him turning around before he thought better of it.

The boy had pulled back the sheet to reveal Zuk, Raymond's best freund and charge. His hair was sweaty, his face was pale, and the bandages that covered his chest were stained brown. Only the soft rattle of his breath and the slight rise and fall of his chest assured Raymond that his freund still lived.

"Oh, bruder," James whispered and dropped to his knees. For a moment, his hands hovered above the bandaged chest before he pulled them back and raised his gaze to Raymond. "What happened?"

Raymond grimaced and dropped his eyes to the floor. "He insisted on trying to save the two Falken."

"Falken?" James asked. Raymond glanced at the boy and saw him blanch. "You mean the two nomaden hanging from the gallows?"

Raymond grunted and nodded. "I tried to tell Zuk it was suicide to try to stop the hanging, but . . ."

He closed his eyes again and swallowed back the bitterness climbing up his throat. A hand squeezed his, and he opened his eyes to see James staring up at him with wide eyes.

"It's not your fault, Raymond. You can't expect to protect him from his own stubbornness."

The man snorted and felt his lips twitch. He bit them then, afraid he would start laughing and not be able to stop.

Once he felt more in control, he grunted, "Maybe not." He shook his head. "And I don't blame myself. I blame those verdammte Schlangen."

James stilled and narrowed his eyes. "What have the Schlangen done now?"

"They killed Volker and Wilhelm!" Raymond spat. "They killed them and left statusgürtel on their bodies. Now Othman's on a rampage, hunting down all nomaden in retaliation."

As James groaned and dropped his head into his hands, his companion glanced between them. "Volker an' Wilhelm? Yeh mean the governors o' Machstadt an' Wildestadt?"

Raymond turned and frowned at the stranger. With his accent, the mann was obviously not even a Zhulanbürger, let alone a nomade. However, James had vouched for him and even dressed the mann in his own statusgürtel, which meant Raymond could trust him . . . even if Raymond didn't like placing such trust in an ausländer.

"Ja, I mean the gouverneure. Volker and Wilhelm accepted us nomaden, and they were eager to renew the old alliance when the erstehäuptling approached them. With them dead . . ."

"The likelihood of renewing the alliance again is almost nonexistent." James sighed and shook his head. "I assume that's what the Schlangen were after, too. Anything to hurt the Vereinte Clans, even if the increased hatred includes them as well."

Raymond snorted. "Not that the Gift Clans have ever cared what the river-dwellers think of them."

"Gift Clans?" James's freund asked.

James grimaced. "He means the Schlange and Skorpion Clans. When they refused to accept my vater as erstehäuptling, they became known collectively as the Gift Clans." Wrinkling his nose, the boy added, "Although, in this case, I prefer the Fayralese translation of Poison Clans."

Raymond snickered and began to tease James about mistaking Zhulanese words for Fayralese. He was interrupted by the soft scraping of the room's second door opening.

~~*~*

Ferez turned toward a door he hadn't noticed before and nearly flinched as he met the hard gaze of the woman standing on the threshold. She was tall and thin and had an equally thin face and severe features that made him want to duck his head, though he was sure he hadn't done anything of which he should be ashamed.

"Herr Caffers," she spoke, her voice sharp. "I see you received my message."

James stood and offered the woman a small bow, which

was greater formality than Ferez could remember the boy offering anyone since they had first met.

"Ja, dame, danke. A schlingel known as Ratte was insistent that her help would repay her gang's debt to you."

The woman inclined her head slightly. "She spoke true. I believe the life of the erstehäuptling's son is worth such a payment." More softly, she added, "And I feared you would be arrested if you attempted to take refuge with Arvin as you usually do."

James straightened and frowned at the woman. "What's happened to Arvin?"

"He and the rest of the public Kreis have been arrested for conspiring against the gouverneur." Her nostrils flared. "This katastrophe has only increased Othman's paranoia and his belief that he is the finest gouverneur Schönestadt has ever had."

"Is he a bad governor?" Ferez asked, concerned.

The tall woman turned her sharp gaze on Ferez, who swallowed. The urge to hide returned as she inspected him.

"And who might you be?"

"Dame," James replied, stepping closer to Ferez. "This is Frenz Kanti, a freund." The boy turned to Ferez and added, "Frenz, this is Dame Clarimonde, one of the most powerful moneylenders in Schönestadt."

Ferez nodded and bowed to the severe woman. "Pleasure, madam."

A sharp nudge to his ribs startled Ferez into straightening. Turning, he found Raymond frowning at him.

"It's dame," the other man grunted.

"That is quite all right, Herr Schmidt. Herr Kanti is obviously not a Zhulanbürger. We have forgiven ausländer for worse."

"Dame—" James began, but Dame Clarimonde shook her head.

"Now, Herr Caffers, I do not know what Herr Schmidt has told you, but your bruder needs the attention of an Heilemagier as soon as possible. I would have had mine attend to the young mann, but Othman commandeered all available Heilemagier when he first learned of the murders of the other gouverneure."

James nodded and glanced at Raymond. "Your pferde?"

The man shook his head. "Gone, of course. Zuk insisted on riding them when we tried to stop the hanging. They ran when Zuk was injured and we were nearly captured."

"They ran?" Ferez asked, surprised. He'd understood from James's stories that the nomads were exceptional warriors. He would have expected their horses to rival those of the crown, not run at the first sign of trouble.

Raymond nodded. "They're trained to avoid capture. If they can't remove their masters from trouble, they'll go for help. By now, they should have made it to the oase and alerted the erstehäuptling to the situation."

James nodded. "I figured as much. We'll have to travel two männer to a pferd, then." He glanced at Ferez. "Do you mind? I know I told you we would explore the stadt tonight."

The king shook his head. He wouldn't be the one to prevent James's brother from reaching a Mage Healer. He just hoped Last Chance agreed.

"I've already greeted your pferde in the stable, Herr Caffers, in case you wish to leave now. I believe my Tieremagier is having them fed and cleaned as we speak."

"Danke, dame. Do you have anything we can use to carry Zuk to the stable?"

Dame Clarimonde stepped back from the doorway and

spoke sharply to someone who stood beyond it. Whoever it was murmured a response before the sound of hurried footsteps echoed down a hallway.

Several minutes later, two men entered the room carrying a stretcher between them. They were accompanied by a small, harried-looking man, who stepped up beside Dame Clarimonde and began to whisper hurriedly.

They were just getting Zuk settled on the stretcher when Dame Clarimonde suddenly snapped, "How dare they!"

Ferez snapped his head around. The dame was glaring down at the short man, who dipped his head in a quick nod. "I convinced them to wait at the front doors for you, dame, but they don't appear to be very patient."

"Dame?" James whispered. "What's wrong?"

The dame shook her head and motioned toward the small man with one hand. "Tell them, Cort."

Cort nodded again. "There are wachen at the front doors, demanding entry. They claim someone informed them of nomaden taking refuge here."

"It would seem your window for leaving is quickly closing," Dame Clarimonde added. "Hurry to the stables now and hope they haven't considered surrounding the haus."

Gripping Cort by the upper arm, she dragged the man from the room. As she left, Ferez heard her hiss, "I will give them a proper tongue-lashing for taking such liberties. Then, I will discover which pathetic little wurm is handing out secrets of the Kreis, and I will have his head for this."

"Kryse?" Ferez asked James as they followed the two men carrying Zuk out of the room. He had heard the word earlier, but it seemed to carry more significance than he had attributed it.

The boy nodded, his eyes never leaving his brother's body. "The Kreis is made up of those river-dwellers who actively accept nomaden. Some, like Arvin, whom I usually stay with, are part of the public Kreis. They don't hide their involvement with the clans from the rest of the stadt."

James finally turned his gaze to Ferez, his expression grim. "But Dame Clarimonde is part of the private Kreis, those who provide their aid in secret. If the wachen know she's hiding nomaden, then there must be a traitor among the Kreis."

"And they'll regret their betrayal once Dame Clarimonde learns who they are," Raymond growled.

Remembering the urge to hide that Dame Clarimonde's gaze had evoked in him, Ferez nodded. He didn't doubt the dame's abilities in that regard.

~~*~*

Gemi was impressed by the efficient commotion that filled the dame's stable when they arrived. Shadow and Last Chance waited in the open area between stalls, two stable hands checking the straps on their saddles and bridles. Several other männer were putting away grooming supplies and feed buckets, while another, whom Shadow identified as the Tieremagier, stood in front of the pferde and quietly gave orders.

As the männer carrying Zuk set the stretcher down, Shadow nudged the Tieremagier and tossed his head. *We need to leave.*

The Tieremagier nickered in reply and then turned and offered Gemi and the others a small bow.

"Herr Caffers, Herr Shadow has informed me of the urgency of the situation. Both pferde have received food, water, and grooming. They should be prepared for the nacht's journey."

"Danke," Gemi answered. Turning to the männer who had carried the stretcher, she waved them to the pferde. "Get him up on Shadow's back. And be careful!" she added as they bent to the task.

"Don't worry, Drache Krieger," one of the männer soothed. "He's not the first injured nomade we've dealt with."

Gemi nodded and watched as Zuk was lifted onto Shadow's back and tied into place.

Once her bruder was secured, she turned to his protector. "Raymond—"

"I'll take him," Shadow interrupted.

Gemi turned and stared at the stallion. Shadow never volunteered to carry someone without Gemi being able to ride with him.

He dipped his head. *"I'm sure Raymond would prefer to keep Zuk close. And . . ."*

He hesitated, one ear flicking toward the mare. When he continued, his tone was softer.

"Last Chance doesn't know Raymond. I doubt she'd be comfortable with a stranger riding behind her master for several hours."

Gemi felt her jaw slacken. *"Are you being considerate of a mare?"*

"James!" Flame growled, her presence suddenly heavy against Gemi's geist. *"You must leave now!"*

An image of Dame Clarimonde's front door passed through the dracheband. Two wachen restrained the struggling frau while several others shoved past Cort and into the haus.

"The stable doors?" Gemi asked, blinking away the image.

"The guards are entering only through the front doors, but you know it will not take them long to reach the stable through the house."

Nodding, Gemi turned back to Raymond, who was watching her with raised brows.

"Take Shadow. He can follow Flame's direction out of the stadt. I'll ride with Frenz just in case we become separated."

"Convenient," Shadow snorted as the three humans mounted. *"Did I even need to volunteer?"*

"Now is not the time, Shadow!" Flame snapped. *"You must leave—before the guards just down the street come into view of the stable."*

"All right, all right," the stallion nickered before trotting through the now-open stable doors.

Three

Flame Tongue drifted closer to the ground as Shadow and Last Chance galloped west, away from the city walls. It had been tricky navigating the two horses through the city streets without incident. The city guards were out in full force, no doubt seeking nomads, and the setting of the sun had not lessened their determination.

Neither had it significantly reduced the city's crowds. With the desert climate, a Zhulanbürger, either river-dweller or nomad, was as likely to be active during the night as he was during the day.

So it was that, despite the horses' initial speed to avoid the guards, the trek out of the city had been slow. It had taken nearly an hour for Flame to guide them to a hole in the city's western wall that remained unguarded.

Flame growled as she circled lazily. That lost hour would cost them dearly come sunrise. With two riders each, the horses would not travel quickly enough to arrive at Helloase before the sun became too hot.

"James," Flame mindspoke as the horses began to slow.

When Gemi indicated she was listening, the dragon explained her worry. *"I can fly ahead with you and Zuk instead, and we can return later to finish the journey with the others, if you wish."*

Gemi shared the idea with the others, who quickly agreed to Flame's suggestion. When Gemi asked for Flame to land, the dragon crooned and descended.

Once she had landed, Zuk was carefully transferred from Shadow's back to hers. As soon as he was secured with rope, Gemi swung up into place behind him.

"Let's go," Gemi mindspoke.

The dragon launched herself into the dark sky and propelled herself west. Helloase was due west of Schönestadt—nearly a full night's journey for a horse. However, Flame no longer had to worry about keeping pace with a horse. Trilling, she stretched her wings to their fullest and flew hard.

She had traveled about the distance a horse would have covered in an hour when reluctant pleasure began to seep through the dragonbond.

Pressing part of her attention through the bond, the dragon crooned. Gemi had her head lifted high, one hand pressed against her kopfabdeckung to prevent it from flying off. The smile that played on the girl's lips was reminiscent of less stressful times, and Flame pushed herself harder, unwilling to deny her bondmate—or herself—the joy of the flight.

Flame's wings were just beginning to burn from the extra strain when the light of several campfires caught her eye. Drawing Gemi's attention toward the ground, Flame reached out with her magic, seeking the familiar mind of one of the clan's Mindspeakers.

"Isa!"

There was a brief pause, confusion stirring against

Flame's mind before the Mindspeaker's familiar magic pressed back.

"Flame? What's wrong?"

Flame restrained a snort. Of course Isa would realize something was wrong without the dragon having to say anything—they were a day early.

"Fetch Mandel, Isa! Zuk is injured!"

A huff echoed through the mental magic. *"Again?"* But Flame could feel the woman's determination and knew she was already running to find the Mage Healer.

The moment Flame's talons dug into the ground in the middle of the camp, Gemi swung off her back, calling for anyone nearby to help. Several men had already begun to pull Zuk down by the time Mandel, Isa, and the rest of Gemi's family appeared.

A hand on Flame's snout distracted the dragon from the activity on her back. Snorting, she nudged the man and offered a greeting.

"Gute nacht to you too, Flame," the Animal Mage replied. *"It seems I once again owe you dankpflicht for saving my son."*

Flame turned her head to view the man through one eye. *"Do not say such things, Hausef. You are family. There are no debts among family. You taught us that."*

The man shook his head, but the smile he offered was wide and familiar. *"Perhaps not, but this seems to be a habit I must speak with Zuk about."*

Flame snorted in agreement as Hausef turned his attention to Gemi.

~~*~*

Gemi was hovering around the männer pulling Zuk from Flame's back when a hand on her shoulder startled her. She jerked around, already halfway into a crouch by the time she realized the hand belonged to Hausef Kanten, her vater.

He smiled gently. "James."

"Vater," she answered, straightening. When the mann spread his arms, Gemi stepped closer, accepting the hug and burying her face against his shoulder. "Es tut mir leid," she apologized softly.

"Nonsense," Hausef answered and pressed a hand against the back of her head. "These are stressful times. All of us are ein bisschen jumpy, I think."

Gemi nodded against his shoulder. Despite the pleasure she'd felt during the flight, worry for her bruder twisted her gut, and her instincts were still sharp from the attack in Schönestadt and everything that had happened in Kensy.

"I—"

"Bruder!"

Suddenly, small hands tugged at her tunic and statusgürtel. Pulling back from the embrace, Gemi glanced down to find her younger bruder and schwester crowding close.

"You all right?" her bruder asked.

Gemi smiled and dropped to her knees, laying a hand against young Lorenz's cheek. "I'm well, Lorenz. I'm just worried about Zuk. That's all."

"Zuk'll be all right, bruder," Ava replied, though the hand she clenched in Gemi's tunic belied her apparent certainty. "Mandel will take care of him."

"Of course he will," snapped an older voice.

Recognizing her Tante Isa's scratchy tones, Gemi stood to greet her tante, mütter, and older schwester.

"Mandel would be offended to hear we might doubt his magie."

"*Worry does not necessarily constitute doubt, Isana,*" Flame chastised. With Zuk finally removed from her back, the drache stretched her wings and hissed as the muscles twinged.

"Flame?" Gemi asked worriedly.

The drache shook her head. *"Nothing a little rest cannot cure."*

"Surely Zuk's injuries didn't necessitate you straining yourself, Flame," Hausef added.

The thoughts bounding through the dracheband in response to Hausef's worry surprised Gemi into giggling. When her familie eyed her curiously, she shrugged.

"Flame and I haven't had the chance to enjoy a proper flight in a while. We decided to take advantage of the long journey."

Ulla, Gemi's older schwester, snorted. "Then you strained yourself for the fun of it?"

"Like I said—"

Panic suddenly flooded the dracheband.

Gemi gasped and closed her eyes, reaching for the source. Fear washed over her like a torrent of cold water when she touched Shadow's geist, and she reached for Flame's neck without thinking.

"James?"

Gemi paused just long enough to glance back at her familie, who watched her in confusion.

"We have to go. Shadow—"

"Go," her vater interrupted, nodding. "Do what you must."

Gemi nodded, swung herself up onto Flame's back, and clung to the drache's neck as she launched herself up into the sky.

∗~∗~∗~∗

Shadow sighed as Flame took off for Helloase. *Well, this journey's going to be long and tedious.*

Of course, he'd be able to speak with his bondmates at any time during the trip if he wanted. They'd long ago discovered that distance had no effect on the bond.

But it didn't seem right to talk to them when another horse was traveling with him.

And I don't want to risk offending her by talking to her.

Shadow snorted softly. He had never felt this torn concerning a creature other than his bondmates, let alone a mare.

Then again, I've never met a mare quite like her.

Shadow snorted again and tossed his head. *Why did Ferez have to tell us her history?*

"Are you all right?"

Shadow nearly stumbled when the soft nicker reached his ears. Ignoring the question from the human on his back, Shadow swung his head to stare at the pale mare through the dim light of the Gemini moons and the stars.

Almost a minute of silence passed before Last Chance huffed.

"It seemed as though you might need to talk. Sorry." She shook her head.

"Wait—but—"

Shadow didn't know what to say. He had expected total silence from her, but now . . .

A sudden tug on the reins at his nose jerked his attention up to Raymond. "What's wrong with you, Shadow?"

Snorting, the stallion swung his head around and nipped the man's leg, too annoyed to keep the bite gentle. As his rider yelped, Shadow turned back to Last Chance, surprised to see that she had stopped. When he vaguely heard Ferez ask

Raymond if he was all right, he realized it was more the king's idea than the mare's.

Taking advantage of the pause in their journey, Shadow nickered, *"I didn't think you'd want me to talk to you."* When Last Chance turned her head to watch him with one eye, he added, *"You seem to take offense at everything else I do."*

The mare continued to watch him silently before swinging her head around to eye her master. Shadow heard the king chuckle before he raised his hands and murmured, "Jus' don' take too long, Last Chance. We've a long night ahead of us."

She dipped her head before turning back to Shadow. *"Did you mean it, then?"*

Shadow tilted his head, unsure what she meant. The mare huffed again.

"When you offered to take both nomads, you said one of your reasons was my comfort. Did you really mean that, or were you just saying it?"

Shadow flicked his ears in surprise. *"Of course I meant it. I know what it's like to travel between Schönestadt and Helloase with strangers on my back. At least when I did it, the Animal Mage was semi-conscious and his companion was female."*

Last Chance snorted and pawed at the ground. *"You say that as though females cannot be a threat."*

Shadow whinnied in surprised amusement. *"Hardly. With bondmates like mine, I'm the last stallion to claim that females cannot fight. But Mina Kanten is neither large nor a warrior. She wouldn't hurt a beetle, and her concern for her son endeared her to James immediately."*

Shadow tossed his head. *"On the other hand, her lifemate's sister, Isa, is a fierce warrior. She alone could deter an attack on their family."*

Silence followed his assessment of the Kanten females.

Shadow shifted his weight, suddenly aware that he could scare the mare away again if he wasn't careful with his words.

Think before you speak, Shadow. It was something he'd never had to worry about before since his bondmates could hear his thoughts as easily as his words.

"You're not like any other stallion I've ever met," Last Chance finally said. *"Most think I can't be a warhorse because I'm a mare."*

Shadow swung his head from side to side. *"They're fools for thinking so. I saw you fight in Puretha and on the highway. You can take down a human as easily as any stallion."* After a brief pause, he added more softly, *"And probably better than most warhorses I grew up with."*

Last Chance eyed him silently for a little longer before tossing her head and turning west once more. When Shadow nickered questioningly, she replied, *"Let's continue this conversation while we travel. We do have a long journey ahead, aye?"*

Warily, Shadow agreed and trotted to catch up with her, ignoring the muttered complaints from his rider. Once he was level with her, they settled into a quick, steady clip that they'd be able to continue for several hours and would hopefully let them reach Helloase by sunrise.

"You were raised as a warhorse, aye?" Last Chance asked after they'd traveled for several minutes in silence.

Shadow snorted, startled. *"What do you mean?"*

"You fight like a warhorse. I noticed it in Puretha, but I didn't think much of it then. However, you don't act like most warhorses I know."

Shadow snorted. *"Considering some of the horses I met in Calay, I'll take that as a compliment."*

Last Chance nickered amusedly. *"So who trained you?"*

"What makes you think I didn't pick up my training along the way? My bondmates and I have been traveling for years."

The mare snorted. *"The way you fight and react speaks of*

formal training. Besides," she added, *"you mentioned that you grew up with warhorses."*

Shadow lowered his head and cursed silently. Seven years of hiding his upbringing as a warhorse to protect Gemi's true identity and he'd thrown it all away on a compliment.

"You can trust me, you know," Last Chance nickered softly as Shadow continued to silently berate himself. *"I would no sooner give away the secrets of you and your bondmates than I would give away Frenz's."*

Shadow hesitated. *"I . . . do trust you."* Shadow wondered if the mare could hear the surprise behind his words. *"We've only been traveling together for less than a month, but I . . . we can tell how close you are to Frenz. And we've come to consider him a friend."*

Shadow swung his head away from the mare and muttered, *"That's why I've tried to stay away from you mostly. I was afraid everyone would think I was just flirting like I usually do. And with your history—"*

The stallion stopped his words short. *Why can't I just keep my mouth shut?*

"Frenz shared how we met, then?"

The nicker was quiet, but to Shadow's surprise, he could hear no anger.

"Aye," he answered, eying her warily through the darkness. *"That first night by the San River."*

Last Chance bobbed her head but didn't respond for several minutes. When she finally did, it was with a low nickered *"Thank you."*

Shadow tossed his head. *"For what?"*

"For being considerate." She turned one eye toward him. *"I'm not used to that from stallions."*

Shadow snorted. *"Aye, well, to be honest, I'm not used to being considerate of anyone but my bondmates and those we consider family, so I think we're both running new paths here."*

Last Chance released a sharp whinny of laughter that seemed to startle both their riders. *"I think we'll get along all right now that we know this is new for both of us."*

Shadow nickered his own amusement.

The two horses continued in silence until Last Chance mused, *"So . . . you never did tell me who trained you."*

Shadow eyed the mare. *"You're not going to let that go, are you?"*

"Nay, not when your style reminds me of—"

A sudden yowl split the air, silencing whatever thoughts she had about his fighting style. Shadow halted, and not just because Raymond had pulled tightly at his reins. He knew that yowl. He'd heard it several times before, but he had always been in a large group with multiple Animal Mages.

Never had he heard it when the cry meant true danger.

~~*~*

A second yowl broke over Last Chance just after the first. Immediately, Shadow nudged her shoulder and whinnied, *"Run! Now!"*

As she tried to move forward, her reins pulled tight and Ferez whispered, "What was that?" The words brimmed with terror, and Last Chance knew her master was thinking of the attack on the highway.

"Katzen," was the nomad's reply.

"Desert cats," Shadow supplied shortly. *"And it's a mated pair, so we have to run!"*

He lifted his head behind Last Chance's. She couldn't see what he was doing, but Ferez yelped and her reins suddenly loosened.

"Come on!" he whinnied and nudged her again.

With her head free to move again, Last Chance quickly

broke into a gallop. Shadow was instantly beside her, his nose at her shoulder, urging her into a canter.

"No matter what you hear, just keep running!"

"Why are we running?" she snorted as she sped up. *"If there are only two of them, surely we can take them."*

The fingers tightly gripping her mane and the knees squeezing her sides told her that Ferez would not be willing or able to fight, but Last Chance remembered the wildcats from Kensy. Surely two cats would not be too difficult to defeat.

"Maybe if this were any other province," Shadow answered. *"But these cats make the ones in Kensy look like street cats."* Last Chance twitched her head and stared at the stallion in horror. *"We wouldn't stand a chance against one desert cat, let alone a pair."*

Last Chance grimly faced forward once more. If they couldn't fight the cats, they would have to outrun them. Bowing her head, she focused on covering as much ground as quickly as possible.

The mare wasn't sure how long they'd been running before another yowl sounded, louder than the first two. Last Chance tossed her head, hoping to glimpse the source, but Shadow nipped her shoulder.

"Don't look! Just keep running!"

Last Chance snorted but kept her eyes forward. From the movement on her back, Ferez hadn't been given the same advice.

"They're gaining on us!" Ferez shouted, and the near hysteria in his voice made Last Chance's heart ache. "How are they gaining on us?"

"Because they're katzen," the nomad shouted back, "and we don't have nomadic pferde."

"What does he mean?" Last Chance gasped. *"Because they don't . . . have nomadic horses? What difference . . . would that make?"*

"Nomads . . . train their horses . . . for speed . . . and endurance," Shadow answered. *"A nomadic horse . . . might be able . . . to outrun a desert cat . . . but that . . . is not a bet . . . I would make."*

"We can't outrun them?" Last Chanced whinnied. *"Then why . . . are we bothering?"*

"Because . . . the longer we put off . . . a confrontation . . . the more time . . . Flame has to get here."

Last Chance tossed her head. She didn't reply, but she doubted the dragon would be able to reach them in time. She had left them about an hour before with the desire to return the injured nomad to his camp as quickly as possible. That she might cover that same distance quickly enough to save them seemed impossible.

Still, Last Chance was unwilling to deny the stallion his hope, so she attempted to stretch her legs farther and move them faster, but her muscles already burned. Her sides heaved and her chest hurt, but such concerns faded as she became aware of the soft, steady *whumpf* that was now audible above her heavy breathing.

"Just keep running!" Shadow whinnied once more.

In the next instant, he was no longer level with Last Chance.

Fearing the worst, the mare swung her head around to see what had happened. She stumbled to a halt when she saw that Shadow now stood toe to toe with a monster.

~~*~*

Shadow's sides heaved as he found himself nearly eye to eye with the giant cat

Giant dead *cat,* he amended, but the thought didn't make him feel much better. He'd never been this close to a desert cat, and even dead, the creature terrified him.

Trying to tamp down that terror, Shadow examined the beast. It looked to be larger than he was, though Shadow didn't know if that were true or just a trick of the way it had landed. Its eyes, still open, stared emptily at Shadow, and the scharfmond buried deep in its skull was proof that it truly was dead.

When Raymond had given Shadow the signal for the about-turn maneuver, the stallion had thought the nomad was crazy. Yet training overrode instinct, and Shadow had told the mare to keep running before he stopped and used his momentum to turn himself toward the cat.

For a split second, Shadow had been sure he was going to die as he watched the desert cat hurtle toward him. The sudden flash of metal in the moons-light had been little comfort until the cat skidded through the dirt, right into Shadow's front legs. Unwilling to be so close to the beast, Shadow had danced back from the cat's corpse.

"Shadow?"

The stallion snapped his head around when he heard the nicker. Last Chance stood bodylengths behind him. He couldn't tell at this distance or in this lighting, but he thought horror might fill her eyes.

Suddenly, relief flooded through him—relief that it was he, not she, who carried Raymond. Although she might know the about-turn maneuver, she would not have recognized the signal when the nomad gave it.

Shadow had taken a single step toward her when a sudden, desperate yowl pierced the air. Cursing, Shadow swung his head back around, seeking the yellow eyes of the remaining cat. He'd nearly forgotten about it, and fear filled him once more as he realized that the still-living cat was the female mate.

There was a reason mated pairs were much more dangerous than single cats, and it had nothing to do with numbers. When one of a mated pair was killed, the surviving mate usually became more desperate, willing to do anything for food and revenge.

That this cat was female meant it was larger and that much more dangerous.

"Shadow," Last Chance nickered tiredly. *"I don't . . . think I can . . . run anymore."*

Shadow huffed and silently agreed. His own head drooped even as he sought the live cat, and his body already felt too heavy now that he stood still. Reaching through the bond, he questioned Flame about her whereabouts, but silence was his only answer, her attention solely devoted to the flight.

Sudden movement on his back—accompanied by Ferez's shouted "What are you doing?"—quickly drew Shadow's attention back to his surroundings. Swinging his head around, he snorted when he realized Raymond was dismounting.

"Idiot! What do you think you're doing?"

He reached for the nomad's shoulder with his teeth, but the man deftly avoided the bite and reached for the dead cat.

"If we have to fight the other katze, I won't face it with only one scharfmond."

As Raymond wrapped his hand around the handle of his blade, a yowl cut through the desert night, and Shadow finally spotted the remaining desert cat. It broke into a run, heading straight for the vulnerable nomad.

Whinnying sharply, Shadow threw himself in front of Raymond. Praying that his death wouldn't hurt his bondmates too badly, he turned toward the cat and screamed.

Four

"*S*hadow!" Last Chance screamed when the stupid stallion moved to protect the nomad.

Idiot, idiot, idiot!

Suddenly, her voice was drowned out by a sound so deafening that she closed her eyes, dropped her head, and flattened her ears back. In the next instant, the ground rocked beneath her hooves, and she was nearly knocked to the ground. Dust filled her nostrils, and she snorted and shook her head, trying to dislodge it. Coughing from above informed her that Ferez was in a similar predicament.

Once she could breathe, she opened her eyes and peered through the dust cloud that surrounded them. She was startled to see the dragon crouching in front of Shadow, her wings thrown back and her teeth sunk into what remained of the second cat. A low snarl, which Last Chance had originally attributed to the cat, emitted from the dragon's maw.

"Flame! James!" Ferez shouted, and Last Chance finally noticed the girl scrambling down from the dragon's back. As soon as her feet touched the ground, the girl threw her arms around Shadow's neck.

"Don't ever do that again!" Last Chance heard her gasp before Shadow staggered and dropped to the ground.

~~*~*

When Gemi found herself on the ground, she nearly laughed.

"Hardly funny," Shadow nickered tiredly, but the affection pressing through the dracheband was enough to make her grin.

"Maybe not," she pressed back through the dracheband, *"but we're alive."*

She quickly sobered as she remembered Shadow's last thought before Flame landed on the attacking katze. Slapping the stallion lightly on the neck, she added, *"And no thanks to you."*

"Dummkopf."

The insult made Gemi blink, and she tilted her head up to find Raymond and Ferez leaning over her.

"You should know better than to suddenly put so much weight on a pferd who has just finished running for his life."

Gemi sighed as the two männer helped her up. To her surprise, Last Chance nudged Shadow and helped him climb to his feet. Gemi brushed the stallion's geist questioningly, but he nudged back with a muttered *"Later."*

"Are they both dead, then?" Ferez asked, indicating the katzen.

His voice held a wariness that worried Gemi. Glancing at his face, she saw that his eyes were wide and his face pale, so she stepped closer to him and laid a hand on his arm.

"Are you all right?"

He dipped his head more quickly than she liked and indicated the katzen once more. "They're dead, right?"

"Ja," she answered, even as Flame crooned an affirmative.

"Can Flame tell if they had cubs?" Raymond added.

Ferez turned his wide-eyed gaze to the nomade. "Would we have to worry about cubs if they had them?"

Last Chance nickered and nudged Ferez, but the king didn't appear to notice.

"Ja, of course," Raymond answered with a frown. "They are our clan's heiligetier—our sacred animal," he added, most likely mistaking Ferez's sudden stiffening for confusion. "We cannot just leave them to die."

"Flame says they didn't have cubs," Gemi interjected before Ferez could finally react. She wasn't sure what he would say, but she didn't want to risk him insulting her clan in his fear. "And even if they did, none of us is in any condition to go searching for their den."

"Flame—"

"Is just as exhausted as the pferde," Gemi interrupted Raymond. "She pushed her wings and her Luftmagie to their limits to travel as quickly as she did."

"Looft-mah-ghee?"

Gemi turned and smiled at Ferez. Apparently, she'd managed to pique his curiosity enough for him to ignore his fear.

"Air Magic," she clarified. "Drachen can use many of the old magie that humans haven't been able to access for centuries."

The king nodded slowly, and Gemi was thankful to note that his face was returning to its natural color.

Squeezing his shoulder, she added, "We should start moving again."

Ferez glanced back toward Last Chance, who was leaning her head against his back. "Bu' the horses are exhausted."

Gemi sighed. "And Flame says we won't be able to reach Helloase before sunrise as it is. The sooner we leave, the sooner we can all have water and rest."

"What about the katzen?" Raymond asked.

"What abou—?" Ferez began, but Gemi squeezed his shoulder again and shook her head.

"Flame will take care of them. Kommt!"

She steered Ferez west, waving Raymond to follow. Shadow huffed and nudged Last Chance, and the two pferde followed as well.

When they were far enough away from the katzen, Flame released a breath of fire, setting the two creatures ablaze instead of leaving them for the scavengers. Once done, she joined their group as they slowly journeyed west.

~~*~*

The desert sun had long since risen when the six companions finally arrived at Helloase. Several nomaden shouted greetings as they passed through the camp, but none of them had the energy to respond. Their sole focus was the spring in the center of the oase.

As soon as they reached the water's edge, drache and pferde collapsed to the ground and lowered their muzzles into the water. The three humans were quick to follow, and soon all six had drunk their fill and were quite ready to fall asleep where they lay.

"James," a voice called out, pulling Gemi from the edge of sleep. "Bruder."

The voice was accompanied by twittering and the feeling

of many little weights landing across the front of Gemi's body. Opening her eyes, Gemi smiled at the little desert sparrows that now covered her, signaling the arrival of her little schwester, Ava.

Rolling over and forcing the sparrows to take off and resume their roosting on her back, Gemi lifted her head to smile weakly at the young girl.

"Hallo, Ava," she greeted.

Ava giggled and greeted Gemi. "Guten morgen, James." She quickly peered around at the six companions, most of whom hadn't responded to her arrival. Shaking her head, she added, "Although I guess the morgen is not that good for any of you."

Gemi simply shrugged in response as she attempted and failed to suppress a yawn. "Where's Vater?" she asked once she could focus on her schwester once more.

Ava nodded her head in the direction of Mandel's tent. "I think he's sitting with Zuk. I can fetch him if you'd like."

"Ja, bitte. I'll try no' to fall asleep 'til he ge's here."

Ava giggled again and turned around, running for Mandel's tent. On her way, she passed an older nomade, who walked toward them at a leisurely pace. Gemi groaned and dropped her head as she recognized the nomade as her older schwester, Ulla.

I don't think I can handle any of Ulla's taunts right now.

"Guten morgen, James," Ulla greeted.

Gemi grunted. "Wha's good about it, exac'ly?"

The fräulein sniffed softly. "Well! You're grumpy this morgen."

A snort from Gemi's right alerted her that Raymond was still awake.

"James's always grumpy 'round yeh, Ulla," he grumbled. "No' that I blame him," he added more softly.

A brief pause followed the mann's assessment before Ulla asked, "Is that true, James?"

Gemi sighed softly. She loved her schwester dearly, but the older girl could be condescending at times. She never let Gemi forget her single jahr majority, something the younger girl had lost patience with after the first season.

Ulla huffed suddenly. "Well," she said, her voice strained. "If you really feel that way . . ."

The fräulein trailed off and sniffed.

Gemi jerked her head up at the sound of tears. "Ulla?"

Her older schwester hung her head and turned around.

"Aw, Ulla," Gemi repeated, wishing she weren't so exhausted. Ulla was already walking away, and Gemi knew she would have to talk to the fräulein as soon as she woke later that täg.

As she contemplated what she could say to Ulla to assure her schwester that she didn't hate her, Gemi felt the sparrows on her back shift. When their twitters rose in volume, she lifted her head once more and watched as Ava and their vater approached. Their worried frowns were enough for her to know that they had seen Ulla.

"Es tut mir leid for upsetting Ulla, Vater," Gemi said, apologizing before either could speak.

Hausef frowned. "What happened?"

"Is my fault, 'm 'fraid," Raymond muttered before Gemi could answer. "Didn' realize she'd take my words so hard." When Hausef continued to frown at the mann, he added, "I told her tha' James's always grumpy 'round her."

"An' I said nothing agains' it, so it's both our faults," Gemi amended.

"I see," Hausef replied slowly. "The two of you will speak with her later to clear up any misunderstandings, ja?"

Gemi nodded, and since her vater didn't stare at

Raymond overly long, she assumed the other mann did as well.

"Before then, you two need sleep, as do the rest of your companions."

Gemi watched as her vater looked over their small group and saw his surprise when his gaze hesitated. Assuming he'd spotted Ferez, she muttered, "Tha's Frenz Kanti."

"A freund of yours, James?" He continued to stare as Gemi gave an affirmative answer. "It seems he's a heavy sleeper."

Blinking, Gemi pushed herself up and looked over Shadow and Raymond, who lay between her and Ferez. Sure enough, the king lay on his back, his head lolling to one side and his face relaxed.

Gemi chuckled tiredly. "Still no' used to our traveling schedule."

Shadow snorted, barely lifting his head to join the conversation. *Not that he's experienced much of our normal traveling schedule.*

Hausef chuckled and finally returned his gaze to Gemi. "Let's get you three into beds before the rest of you fall asleep, shall we? I'll have Mina make up another bed in our tent for your freund here."

Gemi offered her vater a tired smile. "Danke, Vater. Hoped you'd say that."

"Of course," Hausef answered with a nod. "He is a guest of the familie."

He turned and called several others to come help the three humans to their respective tents.

~~*~*

Ferez woke slowly, opening his eyes to reveal light-colored

fabric hanging high above his head. He didn't remember falling asleep, but he felt much more comfortable than he would have expected for the desert, which was the last thing he remembered clearly.

Maybe arriving at the oasis wasn't a dream, then.

A gentle tugging on his tunic finally pulled Ferez's attention away from the drifting fabric that seemed to glow softly. Tucking his chin down, the king was surprised to find a small boy seated on his chest. He'd been so comfortable that he hadn't even noticed the weight of the child, whose hands plucked gently at Ferez's tunic. Despite the gentleness of the boy's touch, his brow was furrowed, his small lips tightly pursed.

"Hello," Ferez murmured curiously. The child lifted his gaze to Ferez's face, but the small hands didn't still their persistent tugging.

"'Allo," the child answered shortly before turning back to his work. Ferez blinked, suddenly uncertain. He was accustomed to children who were more excitable.

"Lorenz," a new voice suddenly hissed softly. "Are you in here?"

Turning his head, Ferez spotted another small figure ducking through what appeared to be the tent's entrance.

"Ja, I'm 'ere," the boy on Ferez's chest answered softly. His fingers continued tugging as the new arrival drew closer.

"Herr Kanti," the second child, a girl by the sound of it, chirruped as she knelt by Ferez's head. "You're awake."

As Ferez nodded, the girl turned to Lorenz and tugged on his sleeve. "How many does he have left, Lori?"

The boy wrinkled his nose and stuck his tongue out at the girl, his hands finally stilling.

"Ava," he whined. "You know I 'ate tha' name."

Ava giggled. "True, but I also know that you tend to grow the seeds instead of just removing them if you're left on your own."

"I do not," Lorenz denied, even as his face reddened. He caught Ferez's gaze and ducked his head. "Not on people, I don'."

Ferez smiled and gently patted the boy's leg. "I'm sure yeh don'. Although," he added with a soft chuckle, "I am curious what it is yeh're talkin' about."

Lorenz nodded quickly and tugged once more on Ferez's tunic before holding one hand out in front of Ferez's face. Blinking, Ferez focused on the hand and realized the boy held a sprouted seed in between two fingers.

"They're senf seeds," the boy explained. "They ge' blown abou' by the deser' wind, and they grow on anythin' they land on."

"Including animals and humans." Ava plucked the seed from the boy's fingers and buried it in a pot of dirt Ferez hadn't noticed. "I've heard it's really painful if they manage to start burrowing into the skin." She plucked the sleeve of her own tunic. "It's one of the reasons we wear long sleeves and kopfabdeckungen."

"But ever'one needs deseedin' ever' once in a while," Lorenz added as his fingers began tugging at Ferez's tunic once more. "'Specially after a long journey."

He twisted and tugged on the fabric for another minute before releasing a cry of triumph and holding his hand out for Ferez to see. This time, the sprouted seed seemed to writhe within the boy's grasp.

"Tha's the las' one. I'd've pulled it sooner, bu' they tend to grow faster when I'm around." The boy dropped his gaze and buried the seed in the pot of dirt.

"Because yeh're a Plant Mage, aye?" Ferez confirmed, remembering what James had told him about his youngest brother. "The only one in yer family?"

Lorenz blinked before nodding and smiling shyly. "James told you abou' me?"

The king chuckled. "About all o' yeh, actually." He turned his gaze to the girl at his head. "Yeh're his sister Ava, then? An Animal Mage?"

The girl dipped her head before tapping Lorenz's leg and motioning him off Ferez's chest.

"You can meet the others, too, now that Lorenz has finished deseeding you. James and Vati'll want to know you're awake, but introductions will probably have to wait until after James finishes apologizing to Ulla."

"Apologizing?" Ferez stood and stretched. "Wha' for?" He noted that Ulla was the name of James's older sister, the only Mindspeaker among the siblings.

"For thin's said an' unsaid this morgen," Lorenz answered. Gripping the man's hand, he pulled him toward the tent's entrance with an unnecessary "Komm."

Ferez chuckled as he stumbled after the two children, one hand reaching up to straighten his kopfabdeckung. As they left the tent, he nearly halted, startled to see that the sun was already dropping toward the horizon. However, the children didn't give him the chance to pause and instead dragged him away from the tent.

They passed several other nomads, all of whom were dressed in the same type of outfit that Ferez and James had been wearing since they'd left Kensy. Even the boy's younger siblings, Ferez realized, wore similar outfits.

Lorenz tugged him along until they reached a group of nomads seated near a cold fire pit. As they approached, Ferez recognized James kneeling in front of a young woman about their age.

That must be Ulla, he thought as he watched his friend plead with her.

~~*~*

"Bitte, believe me, Ulla," Gemi begged, all too conscious of the other nomaden surrounding them. "I didn't mean to hurt your feelings; I was just tired. You know how I get when I'm tired."

Ulla sniffled and swiped a hand under her eyes. "Slow to react," she mumbled. "Quick to anger."

Gemi grimaced but nodded. Most who knew her knew her temper was closer to the surface when she was exhausted, though anger really wasn't what had gotten her into this mess.

"You're my schwester, Ulla. I love you. You know that, don't you?"

Ulla sniffled again and lifted her head to meet Gemi's eyes. After a moment, she nodded.

"Ja."

Gemi smiled reassuringly. "Good."

But Ulla sniffled again and frowned. "I still don't get why." Gemi must have looked puzzled because Ulla added, "Raymond's right: you usually are grumpy around me. I want to know why."

Gemi's cheeks heated. She really wished she didn't have to have this conversation in front of so many people, even if they all had known her since she was ten. But the clan was the familie, according to nomade tradition. It was the one thing about life as a nomade that she still found disconcerting.

"Well . . ." Gemi whispered. She wasn't sure how to

explain to Ulla without upsetting her schwester even more. "You remember the first time we met?"

Ulla sniffed and wiped at one eye. "Of course I do." Her voice still sounded choked up.

Gemi felt her lips twitch as she remembered her first meeting with the Katze Clan. "Do you remember that first conversation we had?"

To Gemi's surprise, Ulla blushed. Shifting her gaze from Gemi's, she muttered, "I guess I deserve that."

Gemi blinked at the unexpected reaction. "What?"

Ulla sighed and sat up straighter. "I guess I can be a bit of a gör, sometimes."

Gemi gaped at her schwester as those around them chuckled. "I would never call you that."

Ulla smiled softly. "I know." The smile widened into a grin. "You'd probably prefer 'brat' or something else from your native tongue."

Gemi groaned and dropped her forehead onto Ulla's knees. "And that's why I'm often grumpy around you." When Gemi felt Ulla's hand gently touch the top of her head, she sighed. "I take it I'm forgiven, then?"

Ulla's chuckle was answer enough, and the fräulein slid her hand under Gemi's chin to lift it.

"Of course, bruder," the young Geistmagier whispered. "I forgave you a while ago."

Gemi raised an eyebrow. "And the tears?"

Ulla grinned. "I just wanted to see if you could actually explain it." She shrugged. "You got your point across, at least."

Gemi sighed and rolled her head back. She might have responded, but she caught sight of a double-purple statusgürtel to her side and quickly swung her head around to the wearer. Ferez stood there frowning as his gaze moved back and forth between Gemi and Ulla.

Gemi's cheeks burned. She didn't know which was worse: the possibility that Ferez had heard her pleading with her schwester, the teasing that followed, or the position that Ferez had found her in, with her head practically in Ulla's lap.

And why should that bother me? she wondered, even as she pulled back from Ulla. *We're schwestern. It's not as if we're interested in each other in more than a familial way.*

Despite her self-assurances, the heat in her cheeks didn't abate.

Hoping to distract herself, Gemi scrambled to her feet and grabbed Ferez's hand. "Let me introduce you to my familie."

~~*~*

As Ferez watched James lay his head in Ulla's lap and listened as they referred to the first time they met, a growl swelled in his chest.

Biting his lip to keep the sound from escaping, Ferez frowned at them. This level of intimacy hardly seemed appropriate for such a public place. Of course, he still had a lot to learn about the nomads and such might be normal within the clan.

Not to mention, they're siblings, Ferez thought, chastising himself for the sudden anger.

The anger didn't ease, though, until James jumped up and grabbed Ferez by the hand. The king didn't have time to wonder over his shifting emotions as the boy began introducing the small group that surrounded them.

"Frenz, this is my schwester, Ulla."

The young woman James had been apologizing to stood

and nodded before bending and brushing off her trousers. Ferez couldn't see how they needed that much cleaning.

"My mütter, Mina," James continued, turning to a woman seated to Ulla's left. While Ferez had been distracted by the conversation, the boy's younger siblings had joined her—Lorenz in her lap and Ava kneeling by her feet.

"A pleasure, madam," Ferez greeted, offering her a small bow.

"Hardly necessary, young mann," Mina dismissed with a wave of one hand. "A freund of James is a freund of the familie."

"You are too trusting, Mina," someone accused in a rough voice.

Ferez turned toward the speaker and clenched his jaw to keep from gaping. The right side of the woman's face shone fierce and beautiful, and her right eye watched him assessingly. The left side, however, glistened and ran together like molten wax. Her right eye narrowed as he stared.

"He is a stranger."

Mina huffed, and Ferez dragged his gaze away from his accuser's scars. When he looked, James's mother was shaking her head. "I trust my son not to bring with him someone who might mean harm to the clan. Surely you cannot fault James's judgment, Isa?"

James's aunt, then. Ferez glanced at the scarred woman. *I wonder . . .*

Isa scowled. "It is not his judgment I'm questioning."

"Tante," James interrupted sharply. "Frenz has been traveling with me almost since the beginning of the season. He's a freund."

"He doesn't mean any harm, tante," Ava twittered. "He's just curious." She flashed Ferez a smile he couldn't help returning.

"Bitte, freund, forgive my schwester."

Ferez glanced at the man who'd spoken and nearly bowed a second time. He didn't need to see the double purple of his statusgürtel to recognize him as the clan's leader. The way he held himself was too reminiscent of Ferez's own father for the man to be anyone else.

"Frenz," James spoke with a quick squeeze of his hand. "This is my vater, Häuptling Hausef Kanten, Erstehäuptling of the Vereinte Clans."

Five

Once introductions were complete, Hausef led the familie
back to their tent. Now that everyone was awake, there
was no reason not to finish the conversation there.

As Hausef let the entrance flap drop behind the last of
his children, he took a moment to observe his familie and
their guest. Mina settled atop their bedding, Ava and Lorenz
leaning against her. Isa took up position beside one of the
tent's support poles. Hausef sighed. His schwester's crossed
arms and sharp frown signaled that she still wasn't
comfortable with his and Mina's easy acceptance of the mann
who accompanied their wandering daughter.

As Gemi and her companion settled near her bedding,
Ulla stopped in front of them and planted her fists on her
hips.

"What I don't understand is why, after six jahre of
traveling alone, you suddenly have a human companion you
insist is trustworthy."

"Ulla!" Hausef frowned at his oldest daughter. She tended to take after his schwester in many ways, but he hadn't expected her to be so suspicious of the newcomer.

"But, Vater," Ulla complained, glancing at him over her shoulder. "Flame says the mann's geist is off limits. I want to know why."

Hausef sighed and rubbed his forehead. *Well, that explains both Ulla and Isa's dislike.*

Both were Geistmagier. To be told not to touch the geist of a stranger with their magie, even if they had not planned to do so, would only increase their curiosity.

"This is not how we treat guests, Ulla." He shook his head. "Especially ones accompanying familie."

"But—"

"Nein, Ulla!"

His oldest daughter pursed her lips and crossed her arms, looking much like the gör she'd called herself earlier. When Hausef didn't relent, she huffed but nodded and turned to her own bedding.

Suddenly, Isa's mental voice drifted through Hausef's geist. *"Ulla might have approached the subject in the wrong way, but it is curious that Flame would insist the mann's geist remain untouched when the circumstances are so unusual. We've never even heard James mention him before this season."*

Hausef turned his frown on his older schwester.

"Tante." Gemi sighed before Hausef could chastise Isa. "Would you let me explain before you spread rumors throughout the geisternetz?"

To Hausef's amusement, Isa's right cheek darkened, and she glared at Gemi. She was still present enough in Hausef's geist for him to hear her terse *"I am not some gossiping old busybody"* before she subsided with a soft huff.

"Bitte, James," Hausef said once it became apparent that Isa refused to respond out loud. "I believe all of us—"

He stopped and turned as a rustling indicated that someone else was at the tent's entrance. When Zuk stepped through, the entire familie called out greetings, while the youngest two quickly scrambled over and latched onto their bruder's statusgürtel.

"You feelin' better, bruder?" Lorenz asked. Ava twittered the same in the animal tongue.

"Ja, much better," Zuk answered with a soft chuckle as he tweaked his youngest siblings' kopfabdeckungen. He looked to Gemi and added, "I hear I have you to thank for that. Again."

Gemi only shrugged. Hausef knew she believed that the gratitude was unnecessary since Zuk was her bruder. Then again, she hadn't expected anything in return the first time she'd saved his life, either; it was simply the girl's nature.

A chuckle drew Hausef's gaze to Gemi's new freund. The mann was smiling at Zuk, who stared at the mann in turn. "I understan' the circumstances were similar as well."

Hausef glanced at Gemi with one brow raised. She was blinking at her freund, but the smile that soon followed told Hausef that the unexpected words were not actually unwelcome.

She's told him about that?

"I suppose," Zuk muttered. He turned to Hausef and asked, "Who . . . ?"

"Zuk," Gemi answered. "This is Frenz Kanti. He's a freund of mine."

Herr Kanti snorted and shook his head. "So yeh keep sayin', James, but I don' think yer family's acceptin' that as yer only answer." Gemi frowned at the mann, who added, "Don' know why you canna jus' tell them I'm a farmer from Kensy. Wha's so wrong with that?"

Gemi rolled her eyes. "It's not so much your identity they have questions about but rather the breaking of my habits."

"An' it's no' like everyone in Kensy didn' have the same questions. I've learned tha's jus' one o' the hazards o' travelin' wit' you."

"And just why are you traveling with James, Herr Kanti?"

Hausef rolled his eyes. *You're relentless, Schwester.* The thought earned him the barest ripple of a mental shrug.

"Please, call me Frenz," the mann replied with a smile. "I'm travelin' wit' James to Caypan wit' a reques' for the king, so I'll—"

"A request?" Ulla interrupted. "James doesn't . . ."

Hausef pursed his lips to keep from chuckling as she trailed off. He wondered idly if someone had mentally chastised her or if it was only the glares aimed her way that stilled her tongue.

Frenz nudged Gemi. "I think now migh' be a good time for an explanation."

To Hausef's surprise, his wandering daughter chuckled. "You do realize they'll require a much longer explanation than most of the people you met in Kensy, ja?"

Frenz shrugged. "Better to have it all out now, aye?"

Gemi shook her head before turning her gaze to Hausef. "I met the king earlier this season."

~~*~*

Ferez listened as gasps filled the tent in the wake of James's declaration. The family's surprise was quickly followed by a barrage of questions.

"How did you manage that?"

"Does he know you're the Drache Krieger?"

"Does he know we support him as king?"

"He didn't hurt you, did he?"

"Is he handsome?"

"What's he like?"

"'E's kind, ja?"

The last came from young Lorenz, who now knelt in front of Ferez and James. The boy's lower lip was caught between his teeth, and his eyes were so wide that Ferez feared the child would start crying in a moment.

James reached out and tugged on Lorenz's kopfabdeckung, offering him a small smile. "Ja, Lorenz, kinder than you might imagine for a noble." The small boy grinned. "He's also courageous."

James lowered his voice and whispered conspiratorially. "He rowed a small boat past a line of known pirate ships to investigate a scuffle aboard one that was considered extremely dangerous."

Several whistles greeted James's words, and Ferez felt his cheeks heat. Thankfully, no one seemed to notice.

Hausef was the one to encourage the tale. "This sounds like a story you should tell from the beginning, James."

James nodded and began to tell his family how he'd arrived in Calay to find the Tauresian Pirates and the king's men threatening war upon each other. Although Ferez knew most of the story, he found that he was just as enthralled as the rest of the boy's audience.

When James mentioned Mock being upset with him for fighting with a wounded shoulder, Ferez straightened. He never had learned why the boy had still been wounded then but healed when they'd next met. Apparently he wasn't the only one who was curious, as both of the boy's parents questioned him about it.

James ducked his head, his cheeks turning a dull red. "The injury was from a fight in Baylin. One of the rogues caught me in the shoulder with a poisoned blade."

Ferez winced. He didn't have to be told what kind of poison he meant. One of the things Baylin's rebels were known for was their use of anti-magic poison, even if the poison wasn't restricted to that group. The thieves in Caypan also used it, though more sparingly.

"Flame let you fight with the poison still in your blood?" Isa asked.

James's cheeks darkened, and he dropped his chin to his chest. "I wouldn't let her bite me."

Ferez blinked. *How would that have helped?*

Isa sighed. "James—"

"Don't, bitte," the boy pleaded. The shame in his voice startled Ferez, and the king gripped James's shoulder tightly. "I already received a scolding from both Flame and Lakina. I don't need one from you, too. Bitte?"

Isa sighed again, and Hausef asked James to continue his story.

When the boy began to describe Ferez during their first meeting, the king was overwhelmed with the sudden desire to hide. The boy avoided an actual physical description, thankfully, but the detail he provided about the power Ferez had exuded when he rebuked Seyan brought heat to his cheeks once more.

To hear James praise him as a worthy king to his family in the next moment only made it worse.

"And what did he do when he learned you were the Drache Krieger?" Hausef asked.

James shook his head. "He didn't find that out until later, and I didn't learn about his reaction until Kensy." More questions broke out then, but James raised his hands. "Are you going to let me tell this story or not?"

The family fell silent once more, their anticipation palpable. Ferez suddenly wondered if James often told his family stories of his adventures. He soon realized he must have since they began asking after specific pirates when he mentioned the attack on the *Silent Raider.* James shook his head.

"Tælen and Voz are all right, though I believe there were several in their crew with major injuries. I understand Dayphin was planning to send his Heilemagier over to the *Raider* to help out."

Isa snorted. "More likely, he took the magier over himself."

James shrugged. "Knowing Dayphin and Tælen, that's probably true, but I couldn't tell you either way; I had to leave the port not long after the battle."

He described the pirate council meeting then, which Ferez found interesting since it was information he hadn't heard before. When he then mentioned how Seyan had called him out and forced him to run and leave Calay, Ferez grimaced.

I'll have to do something about him once I return to Caypan. I can't risk him threatening our peace after everything we've done.

"And after all that," James said with a finality that cut through Ferez's thoughts, "the king simply wanted to talk."

Lorenz gasped. "An' 'e wen' into Kensy with only four other nobles?"

When James nodded, the small boy whispered, "Bu' tha's even braver than rowin' to a dangerous pirate ship." His face shone with such awe that Ferez shifted uncomfortably.

"Or even more foolish," Isa added. Lorenz didn't seem to hear her. Shaking her head, James's aunt turned to eye Ferez.

"I still don't see how any of that would lead to you gaining a human companion, James."

"Mostly circumstances o' chance, actually," Ferez answered, suddenly tired of the woman's suspicion.

He knew they were only worried for James's safety, but surely the boy had long ago proven himself capable of judging whether someone meant him harm. And if James wasn't a good enough judge of character, surely Flame was.

"And what circumstances would those be?" Isa asked, her right eye sharp. The look was disconcerting in the half-melted face, but Ferez had faced scarier things—like the knowledge that Lakina had been the Mage Healer to find him after his father's death.

"I was lookin' for some'un to travel wit' to Caypan, an' I jus' happened to stop in Puretha on the same day James spoke wit' the king an' his nobles. I caught him . . ."

Ferez glanced at James. "How long did yeh say it was? An hour or so after they left?"

James nodded. "Seine Majestät had expressed an interest in his people and a concern that he had neglected his duty to them. I felt that since I had met him and discovered he supported my work, I had no reason not to help someone bring his concerns to the king.

"Granted, of course, that he could keep up with me on the road and in battle."

Ferez glanced at the boy in surprise. Ferez remembered

the traveling requirement. James had been rather firm about not slowing his pace for Ferez.

However, following him into battle had never been mentioned.

Then again, he probably didn't expect as much fighting as we've seen this season, and he had already seen me fight.

A low whistle from the tent's entrance drew Ferez's gaze to James's older brother.

"You're a fighter, then?" New respect filled Zuk's words.

The king dipped his chin. "My farm's in Kensy. My father an' I both fough' to protect our livelihood durin' the war."

"And he's rather talented with his blade," James added.

A snicker from James's older sister earned her a glare from the boy. "He's a talented swordsman and tactician. His skills were invaluable in bringing down the rogues once and for all."

That had all the adults straightening. "Completely?" Isa queried.

James grinned and nodded. "The rogues won't be causing any more trouble in Kensy."

The woman hummed softly before turning her piercing gaze on Ferez once more. He didn't know what she sought, but after a moment she nodded and turned to an empty set of bedding and sat down.

"Well, that is good news," Hausef finally said. "Hopeful, even." He shook his head, then turned to Ferez with a wide smile.

"And I find myself curious what concerns you're taking to the king, if you don't mind my asking. It must be important if James is willing to let you travel with him, even if you are a talented swordsman."

Ferez chuckled, having expected the question some time ago. *Curiosity is something everyone has in common, I think.*

"I'm bringin' him a reques' for a new duke for Kensy."

~~*~*

Gemi winced as concern filled her familie's eyes. Even young Lorenz seemed to understand the significance of Ferez's chosen request. He gripped her tunic in one hand.

"But isn't—?"

Gemi quieted her younger bruder with a quick tug on his kopfabdeckung and a small shake of her head.

"I thought there were rumors that the old duke's heir still lived," Hausef quickly added, no doubt to cover the boy's slip. "Is that not true?"

Ferez eyed Hausef curiously before shrugging. "Perhaps, bu' no one knows where she is. An' I'm no' the only one who thinks it's abou' time Kensy had another duke." He offered a rueful smile. "The Highwaymen take care o' people, bu' they canna provide the order a duke could."

Gemi grimaced. The words were reminiscent of Geoff's in Puretha. Gemi couldn't decide if she would rather curse or thank the mann for providing Ferez with such rhetoric.

Magie pressed against her geist then, just hard enough for Gemi to hear a soft, worried *"James?"* from her tante.

I don't want to discuss it, she projected before shoving her tante away like she would Flame and Shadow.

At least they know when not to press something.

"Enough!" she snapped when it looked as if Isa would say something aloud. The frau pursed her lips and eyed her narrowly but, thankfully, remained silent.

"James?"

Gemi closed her eyes and sighed. She focused on the

pressure of Ferez's hand on her shoulder and imagined its warmth soaking into her muscles until she relaxed under his palm.

"Es tut mir leid," she murmured, opening her eyes to meet his worried gaze. "I guess I'm still ein bisschen tired."

He still looked skeptical, but he nodded and didn't press.

Gemi turned to her vater. "I want to know more about what's been happening here in Zhulan that has the städte in such chaos."

Hausef nodded and motioned to Isa. "Why don't you explain, Isa? You're connected to the geisternetz, after all."

Her tante sighed. "It's been almost nine täge since we learned of Wilhelm's death. Volker was found the next morgen, and those nomaden still in the städte have been in hiding ever since."

"Then there are Geistmagier still in the städte?"

"Ja, in all three. Several were arrested when their safe häuser were raided by the wachen, but they're still connected to the geisternetz."

Ferez leaned forward. "Are there any still free in Schönestadt?" Isa frowned but nodded. "You should warn them tha' the guards'll probably come lookin' for them."

Isa shook her head. "Those who are still free are hiding with the private Kreis. I doubt they have anything to fear."

Gemi glanced at the king as he shook his head. Before he could reply, she gripped his shoulder and gave him a quick warning glance. This wasn't news her familie should hear from a stranger.

"That's not completely true, tante. It seems there's a traitor among the Kreis. I believe Dame Clarimonde was arrested just as we left her haus."

Mina gasped, while Hausef and Isa simply shared a glance.

"Very well," Isa answered, her lips tightening. "I'll share the news over the geisternetz, whatever good that might do."

Her eyes lost focus, a sure sign that she was communicating with the other Geistmagier who belonged to the Vereinte Clans.

"The situation is worse than we thought, then," Hausef murmured. "Volker and Wilhelm will surely be replaced with river-dwellers unwilling to speak with nomaden, let alone renew the alliance. And if Othman is hunting down the private Kreis as well as the public, then it will not be long before the wachen find all of the nomaden and our allies in Schönestadt."

He shook his head and sighed. "I do not know how the Vereinte Clans can survive this katastrophe intact."

Gemi bowed her head. She hated hearing her vater lose hope, but the situation was dire. Even she couldn't see a way to fix what the Schlangen had wrought.

Here, Ferez and I just attained victory with the Highwaymen in Kensy, and we arrive in Zhulan to find that the nomaden face much worse.

Gemi had a brief thought of Mama Caler's words and the speculation Ferez had made about the identity of whatever force threatened the peace they both sought. She sighed softly. She didn't think it mattered if it was behind this katastrophe; they would have to think of a solution either way.

The sound of a throat being cleared broke the silence that had followed Hausef's lamentation. Gemi blinked and looked to Ferez, who watched her expectantly.

"There is somethin' we can do, aye, James?"

Gemi stared at the king. She had the impression she wasn't the only one, but most of her attention was on Ferez.

"What do you mean?" she asked once it became apparent he wouldn't elaborate on his own.

Ferez glanced around the tent before turning back to her. "Well, yeh told me the king wasn' the only one among the nobles yeh met who seemed amenable to yer work."

Gemi frowned. Ja, only Lord Lefas had spoken vehemently against Ferez's decision to accept her work, but she wouldn't have said any of the herzöge, except perhaps Lord Chanser, had been amenable to what she did.

"He might be referring to Lord Parshen's odd reactions, James," Flame muttered lowly. Several memories flashed through the dracheband, all of them instances in which the duke had seemed strangely unreadable.

"You think . . . ?"

Gemi had believed the mann was hiding something at the time. *Could he have been hiding an interest in his people? But then, why didn't he say anything when the king spoke of his desire to help his people?*

A squeeze to her shoulder brought her back to the present. Blinking, she looked around to find everyone watching her. When her gaze met Ferez's, he nodded.

Well, even if Lord Parshen wasn't completely amenable, he seemed much more willing to listen to his king than Lord Lefas did. Surely we could convince him to help, at the very least.

Satisfied, she turned back to her vater with a nod.

"Frenz is right: many of the herzöge seemed just as willing to accept my work as the king did. We might be able to convince Lord Parshen to help us find a way out of this katastrophe."

"You want to request an audience with the duke?" Isa asked. "With the trouble we're having, his wachen would most likely kill a nomade on sight. You wouldn't get past the front gate."

Gemi offered her tante a grin. "You're assuming we'd be using the front gate."

Isa stared at her for a moment before throwing her head back and laughing. "Ach—the benefits of having a dieb in the familie."

"James?" Ferez asked, catching Gemi's attention once more. "I'm no' sure I follow."

Gemi's grin softened. "Isa's right that attempting to enter Parshen Gut through the front gate would only get us killed before the duke ever realizes we're there. We'll need a way to gain an audience with Lord Parshen without meeting any of his wachen first."

"All right, tha' makes sense. But, uh, wha's a 'deeb'?"

Gemi chuckled. "A dieb is a thief. We'll need my training from Tarsur to avoid the front gate and the wachen."

Ferez nodded, frowning slightly. "Won' be too difficult to get in, will it?"

Gemi shook her head. What she had in mind was easy enough. Before she could say so, Isa and Zuk both spoke.

"What makes you think you're going with him?" Zuk growled, speaking over his tante.

Gemi glanced between her bruder and Ferez, who looked uncertain (they both knew he had to go to Parshen Gut with her). She frowned when her gaze landed on Zuk a second time. He had one hand pressed to his chest, and the pale lines around his mouth worried her.

"Maybe you should sit down, bruder," she said, ignoring his previous protest for the moment. "You look ready to collapse."

Zuk glared at her, but Mina stood and stepped forward before he could respond. Shooing away Ava, who still clung to Zuk's statusgürtel, she pulled her eldest toward his bedding.

"Mütter . . ." the twenty-one-year-old complained as she pushed him down onto his bedding. The fact that she could, Gemi knew, was sign enough of how he felt.

"James is right, Zuk." Mina's voice was quiet yet firm. "Mandel may have allowed you to leave his tent, but you obviously still need rest. Now lie down, or I will force you to."

The glare she leveled at him was proof that the threat was not an idle one. Zuk grumbled but swung his legs onto his bedding and lay down. Ava sat down next to him, and Lorenz scrambled to follow.

With her children settled, Mina turned back to the others, her hands on her hips and her face set in a frown. Gemi swallowed. Many underestimated the häuptling's lebenfrau, thinking her too emotional, but Gemi had had firsthand experience of her mütter's emotional strength when it came to the welfare of her familie.

"As for Frenz accompanying James to Parshen Gut," she said, her quiet voice steely, "he's really the only one who should."

Her words were met with gaping jaws, and she huffed.

"Honestly. If this is going to be a stealth operation, James should only take one person—someone whom he can trust to guard his back. And we don't know for sure how the duke will respond to nomaden. It would be best if only James and Frenz went."

She shrugged. "And it might even be best if they dress in plainclothes; less likely to get them killed, at the very least."

Hausef hooked his arm around her waist. "When did you become such a tactician, liebling?"

Mina huffed again but relaxed into his embrace. "I have attended your kriegrat, lebenmann," she murmured, naming the council the nomaden held to discuss battle tactics. "Even a pacifist like me can learn something from that."

"Ja, of course, liebling." He pressed a kiss to her temple, and she smiled contentedly.

Gemi glanced away from the couple. Even after all these jahre, such casual displays of affection made her feel as if she were intruding. As she turned away, her gaze met Ferez's, and she was startled to realize he had been watching her rather than her familie. Her cheeks warmed at the thought, but she held his gaze until someone asked for clarification on her plans for accessing Parshen Gut.

However, even as her geist moved on to the necessary techniques and information, she didn't miss the private smile Ferez offered her or the warmth that filled her when she saw it.

Six

6 Mid Autumn, 224
Parshen Gut
Zhulan, Evon

Kawn Parshen, Duke of Zhulan, sighed and dropped the reports onto his desk. With a groan, he leaned back in his chair and rolled his head back.

The reports from the städte had been coming more frequently for the past siebentäg—and with more urgency. The hauptmänner of Machtstadt and Wildestadt insisted on sending lists of captured nomaden and their conspirators, possible candidates for the new gouverneur positions, and questions and suggestions for how to deal with the current situation.

Gouverneur Othman had been sending similar reports, though his mentioned the hangings of two nomaden (for which Kawn very much wanted to yell at Othman) and hinted at an informant who had led his wachen to several nomaden safe häuser.

Kawn rubbed his hands over his face and groaned again. He was in desperate need of someone with whom he could talk about the situation. He was unwilling to trouble his familie with the matter, and the two männer outside his household who knew of his true views on the nomaden were now dead.

Kawn sighed mournfully as he thought of the two gouverneure. The two had shared his interest in the nomaden and, equally, his fears of the reactions of others should that interest be discovered by the wrong people. Unlike Kawn, they had been able to do something good with their desires to help the nomaden. He had encouraged, albeit quietly, the alliances that his two freunde had entered into with the clans.

Still, Kawn knew he had to do something about the reports. It had already been ten täge since Wilhelm was found in a pool of his own blood in his study, his hands tied together with a statusgürtel.

When Kawn had insisted on knowing the color of the statusgürtel, the answering report had sounded perplexed but certain.

The color was black.

The next täg, the people of Machtstadt had awakened to find Volker hanging from the window of his study, another statusgürtel tied around his neck.

Its color, too, had been black.

Kawn knew the colors of the belts were significant: They signified which clan claimed the wearer. And from his talks with Wilhelm and Volker, he knew the clan of the black statusgürtel had never been part of the alliance. It was for that reason alone that Kawn had done nothing yet. He had been hoping, with dwindling expectations, to be approached by two particular männer. After jahre of hiding his true feelings concerning his people, he feared to do what he wanted to without some support.

A sound from the corridor outside his study drew Kawn from his thoughts. It was nearly midnight, he knew, but the sound didn't worry him. Wachen, servants, and often his errant children roamed the corridors at nacht, and most nächte, someone would come to speak with him before he retired.

He was halfway out of his chair, curious who wished to speak with him tonight, when the door opened. He froze when it revealed not a member of his household but two männer whom he nevertheless recognized very well. As they entered and closed the door, he dropped back down into his chair. When they turned to him, one watching him warily, the other smiling warmly, Kawn tilted his head back and laughed.

~~*~*

Gemi frowned at the duke and glanced at Ferez. Thankfully, the king looked just as puzzled as she felt. While she had not known how the duke would greet them, she had certainly not been expecting laughter.

"Mylord?" Gemi asked. She was uncertain how to proceed since their plan had not accounted for the duke's amusement.

Thankfully, the duke quieted his laughter and waved them farther into the room, which Ferez insisted was Lord Parshen's study. "I may no' come here often, but I do remember tha' Kawn prefers to spend his time in there," the king had whispered as he'd led the way through the manse's corridors.

"Just the two männer I was hoping to see," the duke stated, pulling Gemi abruptly from her thoughts. She blinked.

"You were expecting us?" She wondered if they'd been seen and how they could have been so careless. She dismissed the thought when the duke shook his head.

"Nein, nein, I had simply hoped to speak with you two at some point soon. Although," he added with a wry smile, "I must admit I hadn't expected you to simply walk into my study."

There was a curious light in the mann's eyes that had Gemi chuckling. While she was hoping to find a new ally in the duke, she wasn't about to give away all her secrets. A glance at Ferez's grinning face assured her that, while the king might remember their journey into the haus favorably, he wouldn't give away her secrets either.

"What did you wish to speak with us about?" she asked, ignoring the implied question. The duke's responding chuckle and shrug proved he didn't resent her avoidance.

"Most likely the very situation you are here to discuss." He waved them closer, indicating the two chairs in front of his desk. "Kommt, sit. I do not bite."

That drew a chuckle from Ferez, who immediately took one of the seats. Gemi, though still wary, took the other. She wouldn't have been there if she didn't trust Ferez's judgment.

"You wished to speak with us about the situation between the städte and the nomaden?"

"Ja," the duke said, nodding. "Normally, I would speak with Wilhelm or Volker concerning anything related to the nomaden, but . . ."

He shrugged and sighed. "You can understand my predicament, ja?"

Gemi stared at the duke. After a moment, she snapped her jaw shut and shook her head. "Mylord, you—"

"Honestly, it's Kawn," the man interrupted with a frown.

"And ja, I have always considered the nomaden to be an important part of my people." He turned an apologetic smile to Ferez. "I am afraid I have simply never had the courage to share my views."

Ferez blinked. "I would've listened, yeh know. I listen to each o' yeh equally."

Pain underscored Ferez's words. Gemi reached over and squeezed his forearm in comfort.

Lord Kawn shook his head. "I'm afraid it was never that easy, Eure—"

He paused and glanced at the study door with a small frown. "Frenz," he amended, at which Gemi nodded. "Your vater was never one to show interest in the fringe groups of his people."

~~*~*

Ferez felt his throat tighten at the reminder of his father's reign. His father had been a good man—a kind man. Ferez would argue with anyone who said otherwise.

But Eden Katani's entire reign had been overshadowed by the war with Fayral. Ferez knew his father had believed winning the war and securing peace and stability for his kingdom outweighed any thoughts for the rights of his people.

Ferez remembered the arguments he'd often had with his father. Some had concerned Ferez's lack of interest in parts of his studies, aye, but the majority had involved Ferez attempting to change Eden's focus to his people rather than the war.

Ferez grimaced. His own interest in the welfare of all his peoples had been pushed aside with his father's death and his own crowning. Even with a peace treaty between Evon and

Fayral, it had taken him almost two years to rediscover that interest.

"I'm no' my father," he whispered, even as he reached up to rub his palm against his aching chest—an ache that had nothing to do with the scar that lay there.

"Nein, you are not," Kawn answered just as quietly. Ferez glanced up at the man, one of his closest advisors. The duke was watching him with a small, sad smile.

"But after so many jahre of holding my tongue around your vater and the others, I couldn't bring myself to mention my true views on the nomaden. I feared yours, and the others', reactions."

Ferez sighed. "Can yeh tell me now?" Anything to alleviate the regret dulling Kawn's eyes and filling his own heart.

Kawn smiled. "Ja, I can do that."

He waved a hand around the study, and Ferez's eyes followed its path, taking in the shelves that filled the study's walls. Honestly, Ferez had always considered the room more library than study. Shelves lined the entire length of the walls, running from floor to ceiling, and were filled with so many books and scrolls that Ferez couldn't imagine how one man could ever read them all.

"My familie has always been proud of Zhulan's history. Nearly two thousand jahre fill these shelves."

James gave a low whistle, and Ferez silently agreed. He often forgot that while Evon was only two and a quarter centuries old, the Zhulanese culture had been around for nearly ten times that—older, even, than Fayral.

James stood and wandered to the shelves, drawing his hand along the wood as he eyed the writings. "How can they be so well preserved if they're so old?"

Kawn chuckled. "The same way the städte and my own estate have been preserved: magie."

James turned from the shelves, a small frown forming on his lips. Ferez bit his lip to keep to himself the comments rising in his mind about how young and endearing the boy's obvious confusion made him look. Now was certainly not the time.

"What kinds of magier could possibly preserve animal hide and plant material for so long? I didn't think Tieremagier and Pflanzenmagier were capable of that."

Kawn shrugged and leaned farther back in his chair. "Perhaps not by themselves, but as I understand it, Schutzmagier—Protection Mages," he added when Ferez made a questioning sound, "were instrumental in the preservation of both these writings and the buildings along the river."

James nodded absently, a thoughtful expression chasing away the frown. "That would mean that most of these writings are over a thousand jahre old. That's when much of the old magie disappeared."

Kawn nodded. "That's also about the time when the nomaden began to lose their power."

Ferez stared at the duke. "The nomads?" This was history he didn't know.

Kawn smiled as James returned to his seat. "The nomaden were the original political power here in Zhulan. Almost two thousand jahre ago, the different clans were united under one mann, Walfred Kanten, the first erstchäuplting." He glanced at James. "He was also known as the Drache Krieger, as he was bonded to a wasserdrache, or water drake."

Ferez turned to James. The boy's face had reddened, and he was squirming in his seat.

"Flame's no' the only reason they call yehu the Drache Krieger, is she?"

And of course the boy wouldn't have told him the history behind the name. James had downplayed his importance to the rebellious groups since Ferez met him. That the nomads had named him after their first erstehäuptling, the very man who united them in the beginning of their near-millennium-long reign of power, had most likely horrified James.

James gave a small shake of his head, but it was Kawn who answered the question.

"Nein, the nomaden wouldn't hand out that title to just any mann bonded to a drache. After all, there are records of many nomaden bonded to drachen since Walfred Kanten, but James is the first since Walfred Kanten to be named Drache Krieger.

"As it is, when I first heard there was a new Drache Krieger, I thought it must be a witz. But then I heard it more and more, and Wilhelm and Volker began to hint that they had spoken with nomaden. Eventually, I realized that not only was there a new Drache Krieger but the clans were once again uniting and rebuilding the old alliances."

Kawn chuckled. "Of course, I had expected the Drache Krieger to be the erstehäuptling or, at the very least, someone from the original Kanten line. I never expected the name to be given to an outsider."

~~*~*

Gemi's cheeks burn. She had thought she'd been embarrassed when she was apologizing to Ulla, but that was nothing compared to how she felt hearing the duke's words.

She knew he meant them as praise—his smile and shining eyes made that clear—but she had always questioned Hausef's decision to name her Drache Krieger, especially once she had learned the full history behind the name.

"He's close enough to both," Ferez interjected fiercely. Gemi blinked, unsure what had warranted such a vehement response. Even she could tell the duke was only teasing. "He was adopted by Hausef Kanten, the current erstehäuptling."

Gemi reached out and squeezed Ferez's wrist. When he frowned at her, she patted his arm.

"I don't think he was disdaining the decision."

"Nein, of course not," Lord Kawn replied, shaking his head. "It is all the more impressive, really, that the nomaden would respect you enough to give you such a title when you were so young. And it is good to hear that the Kanten line is still so strong."

Gemi smiled, even as Flame gave a mental nudge to remind her just why they were there.

"I assume you know about the alliances Hausef built with Wilhelm and Volker?" When Lord Kawn nodded, she added, "Unfortunately, those alliances fell apart with their deaths. We only have the Kreis now, and even that is threatened by a traitor."

"A traitor?" Lord Kawn repeated softly before leaning forward and meeting Gemi's eyes. "What do you mean? What's the Kreis?"

Gemi grimaced. "The Kreis is made up of those river-dwellers willing to work with the nomaden. Unfortunately, someone in Schönestadt has been leading the wachen to members of the Kreis, even those who are only known to the Kreis and the nomaden."

"It is a good thing I had already planned to have words with Othman."

"Mylord?" Gemi asked, startled by the sudden heat behind the duke's words.

He shook his head. "Othman's reports have hinted at such an informant, but he's provided me with no details. If I can discover who has been passing him the Kreis's secrets . . ."

He held out one hand, palm up, as if he were giving Gemi a gift. She caught her breath, sharply aware of just what he was offering. Before she could respond, he bared his teeth in a fierce expression that reminded her sharply of Flame on the hunt.

"And once that matter has been resolved, I'll teach Othman that nomaden should be the least of his worries if he thinks public hangings are appropriate. If he's not careful, I'll be searching for three new gouverneure, not just two."

Gemi glanced at Ferez, who met her gaze with a grin. Her own smile grew as warmth filled her chest.

Maybe the Vereinte Clans can pull through this katastrophe stronger than they began.

"Then you will attempt to find new gouverneure who are not hostile toward nomaden?" she asked, attempting to ease the mann from his obvious anger and back toward their current goal.

The duke nodded, relaxing. "It might take some time. I'll need to speak with Othman, have the wachen called off the nomaden, and have those who have already been captured released. Only then will I be able to worry about new gouverneure."

Gemi sighed and felt herself relax back into her chair. "Danke."

Lord Kawn chuckled. "Don't thank me yet, Drache Krieger." Gemi made a face, and the mann laughed again. "I still have to find people who are willing to accept the nomaden. That is not going to be easy when such opinions are shunned."

"Couldn' yeh jus' look to the Kreis?"

Gemi blinked curiously at Ferez, who added, "Yeh implied tha' the Kreis was located in all three cities. Is tha' no' right?"

Gemi nodded slowly. "The Kreis does span the entire river in Zhulan."

"And if I knew who was part of the Kreis . . ." Lord Kawn chuckled. "That would certainly make things easier."

Gemi nodded and opened her mouth to ask for some writing materials (it would be easiest if she just wrote down the names), but a sound from the corridor made her stiffen and turn toward the now-opening door.

She relaxed just as quickly in surprise when she saw that the person on the other side of the door wasn't a threat.

Not a threat—just a tired little girl who looks to be younger than Lorenz.

"Vati?" the child mumbled, one hand on the door, the other rubbing at her eyes.

Lord Kawn was already on his feet and around the desk. As soon as he reached the door, he scooped up the child, tucked her in against his chest, and closed the door. As he returned to the desk, he ran a large hand over the back of her head.

"What is it, Gretchen?"

Gemi glanced at Ferez curiously when she noticed him twitch. "What is it?"

Ferez shook his head. "Nothin'. I jus' . . ." He shook his head again. "Haven' seen her since she was a babe, is all."

There was a sadness in his words that surprised Gemi, but Gretchen didn't give her a chance to ask about it.

"Der Geist won' leave me alone, Vati."

Her voice was small, barely reaching Gemi's ears, and Lord Kawn suddenly looked stricken.

"Geist?" Gemi whispered, uncertain what the girl meant. The traditional use of the word referred to the portion of a person's self that Geistmagier could manipulate, but the girl's use seemed to refer to something else.

"Ja," Lord Kawn replied, and the duke sounded as tired as his daughter did. "Last nacht, Gretchen came to me, unable to sleep. At first, she seemed unable to tell me why."

"Der Geist said I couldn' tell anyone yet," the little girl murmured. She looked half-asleep already, but she tilted her head as though listening to someone, and occasionally she would wince.

Lord Kawn swallowed and nodded, patting his youngest softly on the back. "It wasn't until morgen that she finally told us it was a geist. It—"

A tiny shake of the girl's head interrupted him, and he glanced down at her. "*Der* Geist, Vati." The girl looked as if she wanted to cry but couldn't. "'E said *Der* Geist."

The duke sighed and nodded. "Very well—*Der* Geist. It—he," he corrected himself as Gretchen gave another small shake of her head, "hasn't left her alone since last nacht, and she's been unable to sleep because of it."

Gemi nodded as he began stroking the girl's hair again. Standing up, she rounded the desk and knelt beside Lord Kawn. Glancing at him for permission, she waited for his nod before brushing a hand against Gretchen's cheek.

"Can you see Der Geist, Gretchen?" Gemi kept her voice soft, but a small twitch showed the girl had heard the question. "Or can you only hear him?"

Gretchen whimpered softly and shook her head. She raised a hand slightly, then dropped it. The girl was obviously exhausted.

"I canna see 'im," she whispered. "But 'is words . . ."

She bit her lip and then cried out, burying her head against her vater's chest. Gemi felt her own chest tighten as Lord Kawn stared down at his daughter, fear and helplessness evident in his eyes.

"Flame?" Gemi reached for her bondmate hopefully. *"Is there anything you can do?"*

Flame rumbled thoughtfully for a moment before answering in the negative.

"She is not a Mindspeaker with whom I can communicate. Even if she were, I would not be able to protect her. Whatever is afflicting her, I cannot sense it from here."

Gemi frowned. *"What could be causing this, then?"*

Flame hesitated. *"I cannot be certain, but I have learned over the years that young humans are more sensitive to powerful magic and spirits than older ones are."*

Gemi nodded. She could remember many times when children seemed to know or understand something their elders could not. Turning her attention back to the duke and his daughter, she realized with a start that Gretchen was staring at her.

"Gretchen?" she whispered.

The little girl's mouth worked silently for a moment before she blurted out, "Can you 'ear 'im, too?"

The next instant, she winced and pulled herself back into her vater's chest, though she still faced Gemi. Her eyes gained a faraway look that Gemi recognized from her tante and Ulla.

Placing a hand on the girl's knee, Gemi spoke calmly. "Nein, I can't hear him, Gretchen. What is he saying?"

For a moment, Gretchen simply shook her head. After a long stretch of silence, the girl whimpered. "'E says 'e won' leave me alone 'til I say 'allo."

Gemi felt a chill run through her. "Say hallo? To him?"

Gretchen shook her head. "Then who does he want you to say hallo to?"

Gretchen blinked and stared at Gemi. Then her eyes took on that faraway quality again, and Gemi wondered if the girl would be able to answer her question.

Suddenly, the girl's eyes focused and widened.

"You," she whispered. "'E—"

She squirmed in her vater's arms, and Lord Kawn tightened his grip on her. "'E . . . 'e . . ."

Suddenly, she whined and gasped out, "Markos says 'allo, Eirene."

~~*~*

War smirked as Peace stiffened. Satisfied, he pulled back from the girl, releasing the hold he'd had on her mind since the night before. Almost immediately, she collapsed in her father's arms.

War chuckled as the duke began to panic. Peace was soon able to assure the man that his daughter was simply sleeping, but it didn't matter—War had accomplished his goal.

"I'm not sure I see the point of that little exercise."

The smirk dropped from his face, and War snarled as he turned on the sudden intruder. *Or not so sudden.* The words and the way the pink spirit lounged in the middle of the room were proof enough she had seen more than he liked.

"Venita!" he spat. He paused as he realized he'd spoken the intruder's ancient name. Shaking his head, he growled "Love" in correction. "What are you doing here?"

It hadn't passed his notice that his pink-haired sister often trailed after Peace these days, even when Life and Hope were absent. He had hoped she would stay away from her for this, at least.

Unfortunately, Hope wasn't on his side, either.

"Don't you have your own twin to pester?"

The demigoddess waved a hand dismissively, causing him to scowl.

"Hate could use a little indulgence for a season or so." She smiled. "What I want to know is why you would bother to influence a five-year-old human for more than a day, only to drop her the moment she . . . what?"

Her expression twisted thoughtfully. "Gave your message to Peace? And using the ancient names, no less."

War's scowl deepened. "I don't have to explain myself to you, Love."

The demigoddess shrugged gracefully. "Nay, you don't, but I have to wonder: If you want Peace to decipher your meaning, why don't you just use your common names? Markos and Eirene haven't been used for millennia, dear Brother."

After a beat of silence, she added softly, "Neither has Venita, for that matter."

War frowned before forcing himself to relax and shrug. "She wouldn't make the connection if I used our common names. Besides," he added, his smirk returning, "I've always thought Markos sounded much more intimidating than War."

Love rolled her eyes, but she did chuckle at the joke.

"Very well, Brother. I just hope you know what you are doing."

The demigoddess turned her gaze back to their physically incarnated sister. War was thankful for that as he found himself staring at Love in surprise. Her voice had sounded so tired on those last words, and her eyes had seemed so old.

Love was always so carefree and loving that he often forgot she was part of the second-oldest pair of demigods. She had seen so much, and he now wondered if she knew something important, something he had felt he should know but could never quite recognize.

Scowling, he turned back to his twin, but the thought just wouldn't go away completely.

Even as they said farewell to the duke, with promises of future communications, Gemi couldn't put those four words out of her geist. The message seemed to confirm Ferez's theory that Markos was the name of the powerful force Mama Caler had warned them about. But Gemi couldn't understand the use of the name Eirene.

As Gemi and Ferez reached the San, they were joined by Flame and the pferde. The companions traveled north along the river toward Machtstadt, each keeping to his or her own thoughts. It was only as the lights of the stadt became visible in the distance that the silence was finally broken.

"Wha' do yeh suppose he meant?" Ferez asked calmly.

"What do you mean?"

Ferez shrugged. "Tha' name Eirene: I don' recognize it. But yeh were obviously the intended recipient o' the message."

"Obviously?" Gemi wondered if the king remembered something she had missed.

"Aye, obviously. E'en I can recognize tha' Der Geist mus' be a Zhulanese translation o' yer Baylinese title, The Ghost."

Gemi blinked. That was one translation of the word, though not one she had considered.

"Bu' still, why Eirene?" Ferez muttered.

Gemi shook her head and sighed. "I don't know. That's what I've been trying to understand. It must be important. Otherwise, why would he bother saying hallo?"

Ferez snorted. "Jus' to scare us, maybe?"

Gemi raised an eyebrow, amused. "You don't sound very scared."

Ferez shrugged. "No more than I already was." Gemi made a questioning sound. "We already knew somethin' powerful was threatenin' the peace we wan' for Evon. This jus' confirms that it does go by the name o' Markos."

Gemi nodded.

"An' givin' us a message in an attempt to scare us seems plausible for . . . him."

This time, Gemi chuckled. "Ja, but the name seems out of place." She sighed. "It doesn't seem as though we have enough information."

"Maybe we can mention it to Hausef." Gemi glanced at her freund in surprise. He shrugged. "It couldn' hurt, an' he migh' be able to help us understand."

Gemi blinked, then nodded slowly. "Ja, he might. I hadn't thought of that."

Ferez smiled kindly. "Yeh know, for a boy wit' two bondmates, yeh seem to spend a lot o' time thinkin' like a loner."

Gemi stared at the king. She was further surprised by her bondmates' murmured agreements.

"He's right," Shadow nickered. *"Outside of Flame and me, you never really consider asking others for help."*

"And even asking us for help is difficult," Flame reminded softly.

A hand on Gemi's shoulder drew her attention back to Ferez. "Yeh know yeh're not alone, right?" His silver-blue eyes were solemn, and his smile kind. "Yeh have so many people willin' to help yeh, it's amazin'." He shook his head. "Yeh don' have to depend solely on yerself, especially durin' this season wit' the threat Markos poses."

Gemi felt her eyes sting. Blinking, she glanced away, only to meet Flame's warm, red gaze.

"He is right," the drache murmured, echoing Shadow's earlier words. *"There are so many of us on whom you can depend."* Flame tilted her head thoughtfully, and her glance flicked past Gemi. *"Maybe Frenz can finally help you realize that."*

For some reason, Gemi felt her cheeks burn. The squeeze of the hand on her shoulder had her glancing back up at the king. He didn't say anything else; he simply smiled.

Slowly, Gemi let her own lips curl into a smile.

Maybe they're right.

She had spent so long thinking she alone had to take care of herself, as well as everyone else. Maybe she could start looking to others for help.

Reaching up, she laid a hand on Ferez's wrist and squeezed in return. His smile broadened.

Seven

As they approached Machtstadt, Ferez remembered a thought he'd had after riding all night from Helloase to the San. Turning to face his relaxed companion, he whispered the boy's name, not eager to break the easy silence.

"Hmm?"

James glanced at him, a small smile playing on his lips. Ferez felt his own smile grow.

"I was wonderin' if we migh' be able to spend the night . . . er, day in one o' the cities."

He almost wished he hadn't brought it up, as James's smile disappeared, a small frown replacing it.

"I mean, we're dressed in plainclothes, so no one'd be able to recognize us as nomads, right?"

This seemed to surprise James, and he glanced down at his own body, blinking. Then he chuckled, relaxing once more.

"Ja, that is true, isn't it? Honestly," he added, still chuckling, "I'm so used to wearing the clothes of the nomaden while in Zhulan that I forgot."

Ferez grinned. "So we can spend a day in the city afore returnin' to Helloase?"

James smiled at Ferez. "You really want to explore one of the städte, don't you?"

Ferez's cheeks heated. *Did I really sound so eager?*

Shaking off the thought, he nodded. "Aye, I do. When I was younger, one o' my favorite thin's was bein' able to explore Caypan under the guise o' Frenz Kanti. No one gave me a second glance; I was jus' another boy."

He shrugged. "It's been so long since I las' wandered the streets o' Caypan, an' I've never had the chance to explore one o' Zhulan's cities."

James chuckled. "We'll just have to remedy that, then. We'll spend the täg in Schönestadt."

Ferez frowned. He had assumed they would spend the day in Machtstadt since James hadn't led them from the road in order to circle the central city as they had on the way to Parshen Gut.

Before he could ask, James nodded toward the city ahead. "But first . . ."

Ferez turned and realized they were quickly approaching the city gate. James's nod had most likely been for the pair of guards who stood beside the gate, eyeing them as they approached. Ferez glanced past James and saw that Flame was nowhere in sight. When the dragon had disappeared, he couldn't say.

As they came level with the guards, the two men stepped forward, each holding out an arm to stop the horses. Shadow snorted and pawed the ground and Last Chance nickered unhappily, but both halted.

"Gute nacht, travelers." The guard who spoke smiled and nodded at James.

"Gute nacht to you as well, wachen," James replied. "Is there a problem?"

The second guard grunted and frowned up at the boy. "Little late fer travelin', don't ye think?"

Ferez frowned. From what James had told him, traveling at night was common enough in Zhulan not to be suspicious. James simply shrugged.

"My companion wanted to visit Schönestadt, and we thought we'd take advantage of the cool nacht to travel there."

The first guard hummed softly. "Ein bisschen of bad timin', then?"

Now James frowned as well. "What do you mean, bad timing?"

The second guard grunted again. "Don't tell me ye haven't heard about the deaths of the gouverneure. Gouverneur Wilhelm died first, after all."

Ferez bit his tongue to keep from responding. The men seemed to think they were from Wildestadt, a notion Ferez saw no reason to counter.

James nodded slowly. "Ja, we've heard, but what does that have to do with us?"

"Ach, don't mind Eward," the first guard replied, stepping aside to let them pass. "He's gained ein bisschen of paranoia since the gouverneur died."

Eward scowled and didn't move. "Not paranoia, Ottokar. I doubt the nomaden who killed the gouverneur entered the stadt dressed as nomaden. Or durin' the täg, fer that matter," he added, turning his scowl on James.

"Excuse me," Ferez interrupted then. As he spoke, he made sure his words were clear, rather than the softened speech he'd been using since he joined James. When the guards turned to him, both looked surprised. "I fear the night travel is my fault."

James glanced at him questioningly, but Ferez ignored the look.

"Oh? How so?" Ottokar asked, his lips twisting in a small smile.

"I'm from Caypan. I'd had enough of the desert heat when I first entered the province. I didn't really want to risk traveling the length of Zhulan in it."

Ferez wasn't sure if it was the lack of Zhulanese words in his speech or simply his accent, but Eward stepped back and nodded.

"Most likely not used to the odd hours, either, are ye?" he added gruffly.

Ferez chuckled and shook his head. "Nay, not yet."

Ottokar smiled more fully. "Ye can pass through the stadt." He glanced at James. "When ye leave, just let the wachen at the northeast gate, Irmigard an' Harvey, know that ye've already spoken wit' Eward an' Ottokar. They'll let ye through."

"Ach, an' if Wache Irmigard gives ye trouble," Eward added, "tell her that her lebenmann will explain in the morgen."

"Danke," James replied. Ferez echoed him with a quick "Thank you."

They rode into the city. Ferez was surprised to find the streets still thrumming with activity, despite the late hour. When he mentioned it to James, the boy chuckled.

"Remember how I'd said we would explore Schönestadt that first nacht?" Ferez nodded. "There's always something to do in the städte, and the same is true for the clans." James offered a smile. "You'll come to understand that once we can stay with the clan for more than a few hours."

Ferez hummed softly. "Yeh think they're questionin' all travelers?"

James shook his head. "Nein, only during the nacht, most likely. There would be too much traffic in and out during the täg to stop everyone. But there are probably wachen on the gates at all times now."

He sighed. "It's certainly enough to caution any nomaden still in the stadt against leaving."

Ferez nodded. "Tha' why we're here?"

"Nein." James shook his head and directed Ferez's attention farther down the road. One building was particularly well lit, and voices from within reached their ears, even at this distance.

"I thought we might take care of a little business while we're in the area."

As they approached the inn, Ferez spotted a sign hung above the door. In the lamplight that spilled through the inn's windows and from streetlamps on either side of the building, the words Rotvogel Gasthaus were visible below a red bird with wings spread.

"The Kreis?" Ferez whispered as the horses stopped in front of the inn's door.

"Ja." James swung down from Shadow's back and patted the stallion's neck. "Go ahead and get some water, Shadow. I don't know how long this will take."

Shadow dipped his head. Once Ferez had dismounted, the stallion nudged Last Chance, leading her down the street.

The purple-eyed youth led the king into the well-lit inn. As soon as they pushed open the door, their ears were assaulted with loud laughter and music. James stepped easily into the crowd, and Ferez stayed close, glancing around wide-eyed. It had been years, it seemed, since he was last in such a crowded place without being the center of attention. The thought made him grimace.

A cry of "James!" pulled Ferez's attention to the inn's bar, where a mountain of a man stood. As soon as James was close enough, the man pulled the boy into a bear hug, and the king wondered briefly if he should worry for his friend's well-being.

As he released James, the mountainous man held the boy out and looked him over.

"Been a while, James." The man's voice boomed easily over the ruckus of the crowd, yet no one nearby seemed to pay heed to his words. "Must admit, I'm surprised to see ye. I wouldn't've thought ye'd be stoppin' in now."

James grinned, his head tilted far back to stare up at the other man. "Believe me," he yelled, "I'm just as surprised as you, but I have business to discuss."

The large man nodded. "Well, komm, then. This is no place to be talkin' business."

He waved a hand at a petite woman behind the bar, yelling that he would be in a meeting. Then he gripped James's shoulder and steered him toward the back of the room. Ferez followed, winding his way through the crowd and wondering that others seemed to overlook him so easily these days.

Well, you wanted to blend in, he told himself as he caught the door the large man was beginning to close behind him and James. Ferez was glad to see that James was twisting in the man's grip, hopefully protesting that he wasn't alone, but Ferez couldn't hear him over the din. The large man turned and frowned at Ferez.

"Ach," the mountainous man practically growled. "Who're ye? Why're ye followin' us?"

~~*~*

Gemi huffed, finally managing to remove her shoulder from the large innkeeper's grasp. "*That's* what I've been trying to tell you, Berg: I didn't come alone."

Berg turned to frown at Gemi. "Ye didn't?" He peered back down at Ferez, his eyes narrowing as he took in the king's features. "He's not anybody I recognize."

Gemi heard Ferez sigh, despite the noise from the crowded common room, and she offered him a sympathetic smile. It was good that no one had recognized the king yet, but even she had caught the dismissive tone of Berg's last words.

"You wouldn't," she answered. "He's not exactly a local."

Berg's frown only seemed to intensify at that, but the large mann held the door open for Ferez. He didn't speak as he led them down the hallway and through another door. As soon as the second door closed, he returned his stare to Gemi.

"He have anythin' to do wit' the business ye wanna discuss, James?" His voice, which had easily been loud enough to be heard above the din of the inn's common room, was thankfully soft in the new room's near silence. "I doubt I'd have room for him if ye were hopin' to stash him away fer ein bisschen."

Gemi frowned, sidetracked by that piece of information. "How many nomaden are you currently hiding?"

Berg scratched his beard thoughtfully. "Eight at the moment." Gemi gaped. "From what I've heard, the others're all filled, as well."

Gemi's jaw worked for a moment before she finally

managed to speak. "There's that many nomaden in the stadt?"

Tante Isa had said that several nomaden had been caught in the stadt, but she hadn't hinted at such a large number. When Berg nodded, Gemi cursed, earning stares from both Ferez and Berg.

"This is worse than I thought."

"Even worse, actually," Berg replied.

Gemi pursed her lips. "How so?"

"From last report, seven nomaden have been imprisoned, as have Hariman, Millicent, an' Peppi."

"Peppi?" Gemi asked, shocked. "I can understand Hariman and Millicent; they're part of the public Kreis. But how did Peppi manage to get arrested?"

Berg grunted. "How do ye think? He tried to petition Hauptmann Herrick for the release o' the nomaden."

Gemi groaned. "And with everything going on, he would have been arrested on the spot." She rubbed her temples and shook her head. "Well, at least Herrick won't do anything without the duke's permission."

Berg growled. "Like that means anythin'. Everyone knows Lord Parshen don't care one wit about the nomaden."

Gemi saw Ferez wince, and she grimaced in turn. Lord Kawn's reputation, which he had cultivated to protect himself against those who shunned the nomaden, was only going to work against him now.

"Actually," Gemi replied, "that's the business I wish to discuss."

Berg frowned. "What?"

"I've spoken with the duke. It turns out that he is of the same mindset as Wilhelm and Volker."

~~*~*

For a moment, Berg simply stared at the Drache Krieger. He had first met the boy five jahre ago, and he had never heard anything so preposterous come from his mouth. He shook his head.

"Nein, I don't believe it. There's no way the duke could care fer the nomaden, not after all these jahre."

The Drache Krieger's companion winced, and Berg frowned at the mann. He didn't know this mann, and for that he didn't trust him. James's sigh pulled Berg's attention back to him.

"I understand how you feel, Berg, but Kawn Parshen spent his entire life as duke dealing with the king and the other dukes. Surely you remember what King Eden was like?"

Berg frowned. He did remember how the old king had been. The mann had been so intent on winning the Krieg mit Fayral that he had given not a single thought to the rest of his people. In fact, Berg thought the mann had often taken advantage of his people in that sense. He nodded to James.

"Then you surely you can see that if Kawn Parshen ever attempted to stand up for the nomaden under King Eden, he would have been laughed at, at best."

And imprisoned or killed, at worst, Berg finished the Drache Krieger's statement silently.

He growled. Ja, he did understand that. It was true that the herzöge were said to be the king's advisors, but that was the new king, Ferez. Under Eden's rule, the herzöge were more like the king's generals, leading his männer into battle and executing his orders.

However . . .

"King Eden died two jahre ago. What's the duke's excuse since King Ferez was crowned?"

Again, James's companion flinched, and again Berg

frowned at the mann. Before he could question the stranger, James shrugged, regaining Berg's attention.

"Until recently, no one knew the king's true views on the fringe groups of his people."

"True views?" Berg asked, suspicious.

James smiled. "It turns out he cares very much for all his people and is very interested in the united rebellious groups."

Berg silently mulled that news over. "He know ye're the Drache Krieger?"

James's smile widened, and he nodded. "Ja, he and the four herzöge do."

Berg blinked. "All of them?" When James nodded, Berg sighed. "All right, now I'm curious."

James laughed, and his companion chuckled softly. James proceeded to explain how he had met the king and his dukes in Port Calay, Cautzel. "When I spoke with them, only the duke of Baylin seemed averse to the king's interest in his peoples."

Berg shook his head. "An' ye've spoken wit' Lord Parshen since then?"

He found James's story difficult to believe, but Berg trusted the Drache Krieger. If the boy said it was true . . .

"Ja." James nodded. "He was quite eager to take up the alliance."

"So what's this mean fer the städte, exactly?"

"It means Lord Parshen is going to look to the Kreis for the new gouverneure, possibly all three."

For a moment, Berg simply stared at the boy. "Is this a witz?"

James shook his head, his smile softening. "Nein, it's not. That's the real reason for my visit. I wanted to let the Kreis know that the duke would be looking for the new gouverneure among their number."

Berg grunted but didn't answer. If what James said was true, then the ultimate goals of the Kreis could finally reach fruition: It would no longer be dangerous to accept and help the nomaden. He and the others who were private members of the Kreis could publicly show their support for the nomaden without fear of losing their businesses or the respekt of the other citizens.

Berg suddenly chuckled as another thought crossed his geist. "Ye do know who the best candidate fer gouverneur is here in Machtstadt, don't ye?"

James chuckled. "Ja, Peppi." He sighed and shook his head. "He's the most politically minded mann I have ever met. What possible reason could he have had for attempting to petition Hauptmann Herrick for the release of the nomaden? He should have known he would be arrested immediately."

Berg grinned. "Ye're assumin' the mann was thinkin' straight." James raised an eyebrow, and Berg chuckled again. "One o' the first nomaden arrested was Alys Reiter."

James groaned and dropped his head in his hands. His companion looked puzzled. "Who's Alys Reiter?"

Berg frowned at the mann. He didn't think the stranger had a right to be nosy about the nomaden if he was an outsider. However, James simply turned his head and answered the question.

"Alys is the eldest daughter of the häuptling of the Pferd Clan, and . . ." He chuckle softly. "Peppi has been verliebt with her for the past two jahre."

The mann frowned. "Vehr-leebt?"

Berg watched as James lifted his head and gave the mann an apologetic look. "Es tut mir leid. He's been in love with her for the past two jahre, er, years."

James's companion nodded. Berg growled and leaned

forward, slamming his hands on the table between them and causing James and his companion to jump.

"Why bother to teach Zhulanese to this . . . ausländer?" He spat the last word in contempt.

James went still. Berg suddenly wished he could retract the question. When James spoke next, his gaze was cool and his voice was slow and fierce.

"Frenz is a very close friend of mine, Berg. If I wish to help him understand those I consider my people, I will. Is that understood?"

Berg nodded frantically, pulling himself back off the table. He had never realized exactly how much of a Zhulanese accent James had managed to gain over the jahre or how scary it would be to hear it suddenly dropped. The boy had sounded completely foreign when he'd spoken those words.

The mann, Frenz, placed a hand on the Drache Krieger's shoulder. James shifted and glanced back, and Berg saw him relax as he met Frenz's eyes. That, more than the Drache Krieger's words, made Berg realize how much he'd misjudged the stranger. It was apparent that James trusted Frenz more than Berg had thought the boy could possibly trust anyone who wasn't familie.

Berg cleared his throat, catching the attention of the two companions. James opened his mouth to speak, but Berg kept his eyes on Frenz and spoke quickly and softly.

"Es tut mir leid. I didn't realize how important ye were to the Drache Krieger. Bitte, accept mein apologies."

The mann's cheeks reddened, but he smiled and nodded. "Not a problem. I understan' how hard it can be to accep' someone you jus' met an' have no reason to trust."

James looked ready to protest, but Frenz squeezed the

boy's shoulder and smiled at him. "An' nay, he has no real reason to trus' me." Frenz glanced back up at Berg. "Aye?"

Berg shrugged his massive shoulders. He was rather unwilling to upset James further, even if the stranger was providing a ready excuse. Instead, he cleared his throat rather uncomfortably and asked the Drache Krieger if the boy wanted him to spread the news among the Kreis. James frowned but nodded. When he spoke, his Zhulanese accent had returned, to Berg's relief.

"Ja, I was hoping you would." He paused a moment then smiled hesitantly. "If you would send a messenger to Wildestadt as well, I would appreciate it."

Berg sighed softly and nodded. "Ja, I will." After a moment's pause, he added, "Should I send someone to Schönestadt as well?"

James shook his head immediately. "Nein, don't bother. The messenger would only be risking his life since most of the Kreis are probably already imprisoned in Schönestadt."

"The rumors're true, then? Othman's been arrestin' the private Kreis as well as the public?"

James's eyes tightened in anger, and Berg was glad the look wasn't directed at him this time. "Ja. There is a traitor in Schönestadt. The duke has agreed to help us discover that information as well."

Berg wondered about trusting so many important tasks to their newest ally, but if James believed the duke capable and willing to fulfill his role, then Berg would trust the boy's judgment. No one had ever accused him of making the same mistake twice.

"Well . . ." James rubbed a hand over his face. "We should probably get going if we want to reach Schönestadt by morgen."

"James."

Frenz laid a hand on the Drache Krieger's shoulder as the boy turned to the door. When James had turned his attention to his companion, the mann added, "What abou' the nomaden still in hidin'?"

Both Berg and James stared blankly at the mann. "What about them?" James asked, and Berg silently agreed. The nomaden he was hiding had already settled in to wait until the situation calmed down. True, it would take a while, as far as they knew, but the nomaden had long accepted their position in the städte.

Frenz huffed. "Canna we help some of them out o' the city tonight?"

Berg shook his head. "Wit' all the wachen at the gates, I wouldn't recommend it. Ye'd all be arrested when they stop an' question ye."

James's companion shook his head. "Bu' the guards a' the southeas' gate gave us an easy way pas' the northeas' gate."

James frowned at his companion. After a moment, he nodded slowly. "Ja, they did." He seemed to ponder that for a moment before turning to Berg. "Who are you hiding?"

Berg listed the nomaden he was currently hiding. "Their pferde are in the stable." With the distances between Machtstadt and the oasen where the nomaden set up camp, the pferde were especially important.

James nodded. "They might all be willing to don plainclothes and leave the stadt with us. Then you might be able to take on some of those hiding with the public Kreis."

Berg shrugged. "If ye wish to try this, I won't argue."

He led them out of the meeting room and toward one of the large rooms in the back of the gasthaus.

As it turned out, all eight nomaden were quite willing. Several cited the possible worry of their clans and familien. Berg found plainclothes for them. Once they were changed, he led the ten to the stable, where Shadow waited with a pale-colored mare.

Berg watched silently as the ten mounted their respective pferde and they said their quiet farewells. He hoped James's trust in his companion was not misplaced. He wouldn't be able to sleep until he could confirm that the Drache Krieger had managed to leave the stadt safely.

~~*~*

Even as they approached the northeast gate, Gemi worried that Ferez's idea wouldn't work. Still, Gemi might know Zhulan better than Ferez did, but she knew the king was a better tactician. She'd had proof of that during the last few months of the Krieg mit Fayral and during the planning sessions in Kensy for the coordinated attacks on the rogue highwaymen. Despite her worry, she trusted Ferez to make this work, even if she wouldn't trust herself to.

"Halt!" called a frau as they came upon the gate.

Pulling Shadow to a halt, Gemi watched as two wachen approached, eyeing their group with narrowed eyes. She hoped none of the nomaden did anything to jeopardize their story.

"What reason ye have fer leavin' the stadt at this hour?" Again, the words came from the frau, whom Gemi assumed was Wache Irmigard.

Ferez huffed, and Gemi glanced at her freund in surprise. The king wore a put-upon look. He glanced at Gemi, who was amused to realize her freund was playing a part she hadn't expected.

119

"Is it customary for travelers to be stopped at every opportunity?"

Gemi pursed her lips to keep from smiling. Ferez had taken on a clear, haughty tone that reminded her strongly of Lord Lefas.

The second wachen, the mann, looked puzzled. "Ye've already been stopped?"

Ferez nodded. "I apologize."

Gemi restrained a snort. Ferez didn't sound at all apologetic.

"I left Caypan with the aim of traveling to Schönestadt. However, my friends in Wildestadt," Ferez motioned to Gemi and the surrounding nomaden, "would not let me continue my journey at first because of everything that has happened with the nomads and the governors."

Ferez's voice held just enough carelessness that Gemi winced for fear of the wachen's reactions. Wache Irmigard bristled, but Ferez continued before she could say anything.

"Even so, I was not about to let that stand in my way. I insisted on going to Schönestadt, and they insisted on coming with me. They say it is to protect me in case of nomads."

Gemi was shocked to see Ferez roll his eyes.

"Honestly, I do not know why. And now"— exasperation crept into his voice— "we have been stopped both entering and leaving Machtstadt." He turned to Gemi and made a beckoning motion with his hand. "What did those guards that stopped us earlier say?"

Gemi sighed, though she cut it short. She hoped Ferez knew what he was doing. All she could do now was play along.

"I apologize for my freund's attitude." Ferez frowned at her, but from a twitch of his hand, she knew it was for the part, not actual disapproval. "Wachen Ottokar and Eward told us to tell Wachen Harvey and Irmigard that we could pass through the stadt tonight."

Wache Irmigard pursed her lips and glared at Ferez. "Don't see why ye were even allowed into the stadt."

Gemi grimaced. "Es tut mir leid, but Wache Eward said your lebenmann would explain in the morgen?"

Wache Harvey chuckled, while Wache Irmigard grimaced. "Very well," she replied reluctantly. She stepped to the side and frowned at her fellow wache. "Ye may go."

"Danke," Gemi murmured, but Ferez's pretentious "Thank you" drowned her out. She sighed and threw him an exasperated look, but her freund didn't respond until the wachen were no longer visible.

When he did, he offered her an apologetic smile. "Thanks for followin' along."

Gemi sighed and shook her head. "You're just lucky that didn't get us arrested."

"James is right. Why act like that?" The question came from one of the Nomaden, a frau Gemi recognized from the Spinne Clan.

Ferez shrugged and smiled back at the frau. "I though' they migh' still be suspicious of our number if I used the same story we used to enter the city. I figured an arrogant outsider is more likely to have such a large entourage, so they wouldn' question the story too much.

"Besides, I though' they'd be more willin' to jus' kick me out o' the city than arrest me for my arrogance."

This earned chuckles from several of the nomaden. "Well, it certainly worked," answered a mann from the Falke Clan. "Where did you find this mann, James? Has he been traveling with you since Baylin?"

Gemi chuckled and shook her head. "Kensy, actually. Although," she added and smirked at the king, "he does play an arrogant Caypanbürger rather well, doesn't he?"

Ferez shrugged. "Who do yeh think directed the battles durin' the war?"

Gemi laughed, suddenly certain Ferez had based his attitude on the Baylinese duke.

With enough distance now between them and the stadt, the nomaden thanked Gemi and Ferez, said their farewells, and rode off in the directions of their respective clans. Not long after, Flame rejoined them, and the five companions continued toward Schönestadt.

Eight

7 Mid Autumn, 224
Parshen Gut
Zhulan, Evon

Ilse Parshen, Duchess of Zhulan and lebenfrau of Kawn Parshen, had been born to nobility, despite the relatively low rank of her familie of birth. However, unlike most noblewomen, Ilse had never been one for sitting idly by and depending solely on her lebenmann. Even before their lifebonding, Ilse had been interested in helping Kawn with any issues he had to deal with as duke.

It had been a shock, then, that Kawn had insisted on dealing with the recent katastrophe in the städte alone. It wasn't even that Ilse didn't know Kawn's true views on the nomaden; she had supported his views and his public silence for jahre.

But now he pushed her away, insisting he not bother her with the mess he was dealing with.

Ilse sighed sharply and shook her head. Her handmaid

paused in her attempts to tame the duchess's curls and glanced questioningly at Ilse in the mirror. Ilse smiled and shook her head again to indicate her previous actions weren't for the frau's work. The handmaid continued, leaving Ilse to her thoughts.

Her geist continued along the same line as she finished her morgen routine. It wasn't until she was checking her children's bedrooms, as she did every morgen before breakfast, that her thoughts moved on.

She paused outside her youngest's room, remembering what had occurred the nacht before last. Wondering if Gretchen had been able to sleep at all, she pushed the door open quietly.

Ilse smiled and sighed in relief when she saw the small lump under the covers on the bed. Stepping farther into the room, she noted the sound of steady breathing as her daughter slept peacefully. Grateful that her youngest had finally found sleep, she kissed the girl's forehead and opted to let her sleep longer instead of waking her for breakfast as she normally would have.

When Ilse entered the dining room several minutes later, she was startled by the sound of her lebenmann laughing heartily. Her other three children, her older two daughters and her only son, were grinning at their vater, though they seemed just as surprised as Ilse.

"And what is all this about?" she asked, approaching her lebenmann's side.

Kawn quieted to a soft chuckle and turned his gaze to her. She felt her breath hitch. There was a confidence in his gaze that she realized had been missing since they had learned of Wilhelm's death.

"I was simply telling the children I was planning to go

into Machtstadt this morgen, and they insisted rather emphatically that we make it a daytrip for the entire familie."

Ilse paused, surprised, before laying a light kiss on Kawn's lips. "You've made your decision, then."

It wasn't a question. Her lebenmann's steady gaze and voice were enough to answer any doubts. Somehow, Kawn had found the courage he needed to do what they both had always known was right.

His grin softened, and he nodded. "Ja, I have." He turned back to the children and rubbed his hands together. "And I believe a familie trip is in order. I don't think any of us have been to the stadt this season—not since I returned from Cautzel, at any rate."

All three children cheered and began talking among themselves about their plans for their daytrip. Ilse chuckled, kissed Kawn's temple, and took her seat at his side.

"So what brought about this sudden change?" Ilse asked once she had filled her plate. Taking a bite of a sweet roll, she hummed softly. Their cook, Weizen, always made the best breads.

Before Kawn could answer her question, the door to the dining room opened and a tall mann entered. He strode quickly toward Kawn, his movements seemingly unhindered by the large, dark falke that perched calmly on his shoulder.

"A message, Mylord." The Tieremagier stopped next to Kawn and offered him a scroll.

Kawn hummed and took the scroll, offering the mann a quick "Danke, Fohlen" as he opened it. A moment later, he chuckled. "Well, that was fast."

Ilse frowned, but Fohlen beat her to the next question.

"Fast, Mylord? I don't recall you sending a message yesterday or this morgen."

Kawn chuckled again as he laid the scroll open on the table and patted his pockets. "Nein, I didn't. This is from a freund I spoke with last nacht."

He huffed as the search of his pockets turned up nothing, and he turned to Fohlen. "Do you have any writing materials on you?"

"Of course, Mylord."

Fohlen reached into a bag at his belt and removed a piece of parchment, a quill, and a bottle of ink. As he arranged them on the table for Kawn, Ilse turned the scroll toward her and read it over.

A frown formed on her lips as she realized it was simply a list of names. Each one had something written beside it, and while the style seemed familiar, she didn't recognize any meaning in it. At the bottom of the page, the writer had simply signed *JC*, which did little to inform her of the writer's identity.

Turning her gaze to her lebenmann's parchment, she watched him write. At first, she was confused. Her lebenmann wrote in the same shorthand the sender had. As she watched, though, she began to realize why it looked familiar. It was the same used during the krieg in notices between the king and his herzöge.

Scanning what Kawn had written so far, she realized he was thanking the sender for the list and promising to consider his recommendations.

With that understanding, Ilse turned her attention back to the original scroll. *What could possibly be so important that Kawn has returned to using the Kriegschrift?*

A few scans of the scroll gave her a possible answer. Each name had the shorthand for a stadt, either Machtstadt or Schönestadt, written next to it, as well as at least two other identifiers. She thought one shorthand might refer to nomaden. It was the shorthand for *imprisoned, hiding, free*, and *unknown* that made her realize what this list might be.

"Who wrote this?" Ilse asked as Kawn finished his own letter.

He glanced at her and then at the scroll, where she was tapping the sender's initials. Instead of answering, he turned to the children.

"If you're done eating, why don't you three go get ready for our daytrip?" There was a flurry of movement as the three stood from the table, young Adal stuffing one last biscuit in his mouth before leaving. "Oh, and Didrika?"

Their eldest, a girl of fifteen, paused and glanced over her shoulder, even as she pushed Kuonrada, who had paused with her, toward the door.

"Ja, Vater?"

"Will you wake Gretchen so she can eat before we leave?"

Didrika nodded, replied with another "Ja, Vater," and left, steering Adal and Kuonrada away from the dining room as she went.

"Well?" Ilse asked once she was sure the children were out of earshot. The fact that her lebenmann didn't want the children to hear inflamed her curiosity. There wasn't much that would interest Kuonrada or Adal when it came to the political state of Zhulan: Kuonrada was only thirteen, and Adal wasn't even ten yet. Even Didrika, who had begun to show interest in her vater's work, shouldn't have worried Kawn enough for him to send her away.

Instead of answering Ilse's question, Kawn rolled up the letter he'd written and handed it to Fohlen.

"Have the falke take this back to the person who sent it."

The Tieremagier took the scroll but frowned. "How can

I be sure I'm sending the falke to the right person? I don't know who he came from."

Kawn chuckled. "I would think it would be difficult for the falke to forget that particular sender."

Ilse sighed and shook her head, laying a hand on Kawn's forearm.

"Honestly, liebling, stop being so secretive. You know as well as I do that everyone in Parshen Gut is trustworthy." She raised an eyebrow. "We've had to be sure of that with our opinions."

Kawn laid his hand on Ilse's and smiled at her. "You're right, I know." His voice dropped to a whisper as he added, as if to himself, "We do trust them with our secrets."

Ilse could imagine the question he wanted to add: *Can we trust them with another's?* She smiled and nodded. With a sigh, her lebenmann turned back to Fohlen.

"Let the falke know that he's to return that letter to the drache."

Ilse gasped, and Fohlen's eyes widened. *The drache?* Her hand tightened slightly on Kawn's forearm. *No wonder Kawn was hesitant to give a name.*

She watched as Fohlen nodded shakily and left, the falke on his shoulder ruffling its feathers in agitation. Once the magier was out of the room, she glanced back down at the scroll in her hands and traced the initials.

"JC," she whispered. "James Caffers?"

Kawn had told her about the boy after his return from Cautzel, but she'd nearly forgotten. She looked up and met her lebenmann's gaze. There was a calmness in his eyes that hadn't been there yesterday and had been missing for täge now, if not longer. In fact, a weight seemed to have lifted from her lebenmann, making him seem freer and lighter than ever.

A sudden thought distracted her from her lebenmann's new demeanor, and she frowned as she remembered something he'd said earlier.

"He was here last nacht and you didn't wake me?"

Kawn threw his head back and laughed. Ilse's lips twitched in response, and she pursed them to keep from smiling. Instead, she simply raised an eyebrow and waited for her lebenmann to calm down.

~~*~*

Kawn was content.

It seemed like an eternity since he'd last felt this way. Even before Wilhelm and Volker died, even before the Krieg mit Fayral ended, Kawn didn't think he had felt truly content. Since he could remember, he had watched as the nomaden suffered, unable to do anything for them for fear of the reactions of his peers.

Now, Kawn knew he had the support of his king. He could finally stand up for what he truly believed without fearing consequences that could not be reasonably resolved.

And to think, I have James Caffers, the Drache Krieger, to thank for this.

Kawn finally calmed his laughter and smiled back down at his lebenfrau. Ilse was trying hard not to smile, which only made Kawn's smile widen. Even after almost two decades, he didn't know how he had been lucky enough to find such a jewel of a lebenfrau among the noble familien.

"I am afraid I didn't think to wake you, liebling."

That wasn't completely true, of course. He had known then that she would have wanted him to wake her, but at the time, he had thought Ferez's secret was more important than Ilse's desire to help him.

Ilse eyed him for a moment and then turned her gaze to the scroll in her hands. Kawn chuckled softly, knowing that it might not matter that he hadn't wakened her. She was intelligent enough to figure out the truth eventually. It was one of the things that had drawn him to her when they first met.

Finally, she sighed and shook her head. "You are keeping something from me, lebenmann." Her voice was soft, but her gaze was steady as it met his. "However, I can't fault you for protecting another, especially if it's who I believe it is."

Kawn pressed a light kiss to her temple. "Danke, liebling."

Ilse finally let her lips spread in a smile, and Kawn was unsurprised when she once again tapped the parchment in her hands; however, before she could ask her next question, the dining room door opened again, and a small, tired voice caught their attention.

"Gut morgen, Vati, Mami."

~~*~*

Ilse quickly left the table and pulled Gretchen into her arms. As she returned to the table, her daughter wrapped one hand in Ilse's curls and smothered a yawn with the other. The girl's obvious tiredness would have worried the duchess if not for the bright smile that appeared after the yawn.

"And guten morgen to you, little perle," Kawn replied. Gretchen's smile widened at the use of her nickname, but she burrowed her face against her mütter's neck. "How are you feeling?"

"Ti—"

As if on cue, a yawn stretched her jaw once more. Afterward, she rubbed at her eye and smiled a little. "Tired."

"And Der Geist?" Ilse asked worriedly. She glanced at her lebenmann, but he shrugged and shook his head.

"Oh, 'e left," Gretchen murmured, burying her head against Ilse's neck once more. "'E jus' wanted to say 'allo to Eirene."

Ilse blinked. "Eirene?"

Kawn chuckled. "His name is James, liebling, not Eirene."

Gretchen lifted her head and frowned. "Bu' Markos insisted 'is name was Eirene."

Markos and Eirene? The names seemed familiar to Ilse, but she couldn't place them. She told Kawn as much.

Her lebenmann shrugged. "I think James recognized them, but he didn't tell me their significance. Otherwise, I've never heard of them myself."

Ilse nodded and promised herself she would try to remember why they sounded familiar. Watching another yawn plague her daughter, she lifted a sweet roll from her plate and offered it to Gretchen.

"Eat, perle. We're going to the stadt later todat, and you'll need your strength."

Gretchen gasped happily and took the roll, eating it quickly before grabbing another. As their daughter ate, Ilse and Kawn turned their attention back to the scroll.

~~*~*

Their pferde were approaching Machtstadt's southeast gate when a wache hailed them. Kawn pulled his pferd to a stop and frowned.

"Hauptmann Herrick?" The current military leader of Machtstadt smiled up at Kawn. "Why are you watching the gate?"

Herrick's smile turned slightly bitter. "I'm attempting to prevent a repeat of last nacht, unfortunately."

Kawn's frown deepened. Before he could reply, he felt a hand on his arm and looked up to find Ilse glancing between him and the hauptmann.

"If you don't mind, I believe the children and I should continue on into the stadt."

Kawn nodded and glanced at Herrick.

Herrick shrugged. "No reason you can't, Mylady. You have your knights with you, and this might take a while."

Ilse nodded. "Danke, Hauptmann."

Herrick gave her a small bow. "Mit vergnügen, Mylady. Guten täg!"

"And you," she replied before leading the children and five of the knights who had accompanied them through the gates. Sir Leal, Knight Captain of Parshen Gut, stayed behind, relaxing in his saddle.

Knowing Herrick was right, Kawn slid out of his saddle and handed the reins to a page, who had hurried forward to accept them.

"What happened last nacht?" he questioned, crossing his arms over his chest.

Herrick grimaced. "Two männer entered the stadt through this gate late last nacht. A while later, they left through the northeast gate, but they were accompanied by eight others."

Kawn raised his brows in surprise. Thinking about his late-nacht visitors, he asked, "And how did they manage to leave the stadt if you know this happened?"

Herrick sighed. "Unfortunately, the two männer managed to convince the two wachen at this gate that they were simply taking advantage of the cool nacht air to travel from Wildestadt to Schönestadt. So convinced, my männer gave them the names of the wachen at the northeast gate and a statement that would convince them that they weren't a threat so they wouldn't be too bothered."

Kawn nearly snickered. If the two männer of whom Herrick spoke were the Drache Krieger and the king like Kawn suspected . . .

Perhaps he should have been worried that the two might have managed to come and go without raising suspicions during a time like this and, at the same time, managed to sneak several nomaden out with them. It certainly didn't bode well for the security of the stadt, especially when the wachen were supposed to have been on high alert.

However, Kawn couldn't bring himself to care.

Trying not to laugh, Kawn asked, "Do you have descriptions of these two männer?"

Herrick, who didn't seem to notice Kawn's struggle, nodded. "Both were young, just barely Of Age. One spoke like an ausländer and had light-brown hair and pale-blue eyes. The other spoke like a Zhulanbürger, had long dark hair, and . . ."

Herrick hesitated. When Kawn encouraged him to continue, he added reluctantly, "All four wachen swear the second mann had purple eyes. I'm not quite sure if I believe such a report. It could have simply been a trick of the light."

Kawn finally chuckled, unable to help himself. "Believe me, the reports are correct."

"Mylord?"

Kawn grinned at the hauptmann. "There's no need to worry about them, Herrick. I doubt they would risk returning to Machtstadt for a while after pulling such a trick."

For a moment, Herrick simply stared at the duke, seemingly unable to speak. Finally, his eyes narrowed.

"Do you know of these männer, Mylord?"

Kawn nodded and patted Herrick's shoulder.

"The two are acquaintances of mine. While it might seem troublesome that they managed to pull such a trick, I wouldn't worry myself if I were you. There's no reason to believe they caused more harm than simply helping a few nomaden out of the stadt. And you can be sure that none of the nomaden they helped to escape were connected to Volker's death."

Instead of asking more questions or arguing, which Kawn nearly expected, Herrick searched Kawn's eyes. Kawn met the hauptmann's searching gaze evenly, knowing he needed his cooperation if he wanted to change the way things were.

Eventually, Herrick nodded, and Kawn released a small breath before glancing around.

"So, what exactly are you doing to prevent another such incident?" He turned a dubious look on the hauptmann. "I doubt increasing the number of wachen on the gates would help."

"Nein, increased numbers wouldn't help."

Herrick glanced across the heads of several travelers to the other side of the gate. One of the wachen on the other side noticed his gaze and nodded before turning his attention back to the incoming people. Herrick sighed and glanced back at Kawn.

"We're using Geistmagier."

Kawn straightened at the mention of the mental magier. "Geistmagier? Surely you aren't having them read everyone?"

Herrick shook his head before Kawn even finished speaking. "Nein, of course not, Mylord. But several wachen have agreed to allow the Geistmagier access."

"Ah," Kawn replied, realizing what Herrick was

implying. "The Geistmagier are reading those männer on the gates, then? Is that why you are here?"

When Herrick nodded, Kawn grinned. "Good, good. You've always been unwilling to ask your männer to do things you wouldn't do yourself. That's good."

Herrick lowered his head, his cheeks flushing lightly and a small smile curling his lips.

They fell into silence then. Kawn turned his attention to those entering the stadt. The flow wasn't as steady or as heavy as it normally would have been, but even the deaths of the gouverneure couldn't keep people from traveling to the städte when they needed to.

"Did you come to Machtstadt for business or pleasure, Mylord?" Herrick asked finally.

Kawn sighed and turned back to Herrick. "Business, I fear," he answered, knowing he'd been putting off what he'd decided to do. "The children decided we needed to make a familie trip of it, though."

Herrick nodded. "Ja, children have a way of taking over our decisions, don't they?" Kawn chuckled. "I take it you came to discuss Volker's death and the nomaden, Mylord?"

"Ja." Kawn contemplated how to begin revealing his decision to the hauptmann. As Herrick made a questioning sound, he sighed. "Could you take me to see those you've arrested in connection to this katastrophe?"

Herrick stiffened slightly. Before Kawn could question his reaction, the hauptmann beckoned forward a page and requested the boy bring their pferde to them. Once mounted, Herrick led Kawn through the streets to the stadt's prison.

Once inside, the hauptmann led Kawn down a hallway that, while well lit, seemed dusty and unused. Cobwebs hung from the corners of the ceiling, and the echoes of their footsteps preceded them.

"Because of the circumstances, I had the set of cells in this corridor opened. I thought it'd be best to keep the nomaden and their . . . conspirators separated from other prisoners."

As he finished saying this, they stepped up to a barred door. Kawn was surprised that no wachen guarded this door, but from what he could see once they'd stepped through, the prisoners seemed no worse for wear.

As Herrick closed the door behind them, Kawn took a moment to examine the prisoners. Eight wore the kopfabdeckungen and statusgürtel of nomaden. That was one more than James had claimed, which meant one had been captured sometime during the nacht or early morgen.

Several bore the green statusgürtel of the Pferd Clan, including one who bore the double green of the Pferd Clan's ruling familie. Two bore the pale yellow of the Spinne Clan, while the rest bore the red of the Wolf Clan.

Turning his gaze to the river-dwellers, he noted that the short, stocky frau must be Millicent Wäschemann, while the broad-shouldered mann must be Hariman Biermann.

The tall, slender mann, however, was someone Kawn recognized quite well: Peppi Kluger. Kawn had often seen the mann in Volker's court, petitioning the gouverneur for one consideration or another. Kawn remembered Volker often speaking fondly of the political mann.

To be honest, when James had labeled Peppi in his list as the best candidate for gouverneur of Machtstadt, Kawn couldn't have agreed more. When Kawn had read James's list, he realized he had been considering Peppi from the beginning. That he was a part of the Kreis was a pleasant affirmation.

Finally stepping away from the door, Kawn addressed Peppi first.

"I am surprised to see you here, Herr Kluger."

The mann, who hadn't reacted to his and Herrick's arrival like the others had, jerked his head up.

"M-mylord?" He shook his head, then peered back up at Kawn. "What are you doing here?"

Kawn sighed. "I am here on business, I fear." He raised an eyebrow and eyed the mann, despite his sudden desire to laugh. "You, though, Herr Kluger? I would have thought you of all people would have been clever enough to avoid detection as a member of the Kreis."

All eleven prisoners stiffened as they turned to stare at Kawn, horror dawning on each of their faces. Herrick made an odd sound, but Kawn ignored the hauptmann for the moment.

"Well?"

Peppi shook his head again and stood, the horror on his face slowly fading. By the time he spoke again, his voice was steady and smooth.

"I am afraid I forgot myself, Mylord. I was not considering consequences when I made my petition to Hauptmann Herrick." He glanced past Kawn, but Kawn didn't bother to look at Herrick.

"That doesn't seem like you, Herr Kluger," Kawn rejoined, tilting his head thoughtfully. "Volker always claimed you never did anything that would jeopardize your causes." The duke glanced at their surroundings and shook his head. "I wouldn't think you could do much good for the Kreis while imprisoned."

Peppi's cheeks reddened. Before he could reply, the nomade with the double-green statusgürtel stood and spoke sharply.

"Peppi was brave to stand up to Hauptmann Herrick when others simply hid themselves away." The strong voice was obviously female, and her features were set in determination.

Kawn turned and bowed to the nomade frau, which seemed to startle everyone.

"Of course, Adlige." The title was an old one, marking his respekt for her nomade nobility. "I never meant to impugn his honor or disdain his courage; I simply wondered why a politically minded mann like him would risk everything as he did." He turned his gaze back to Peppi.

He hesitated when he caught sight of the small smile that Peppi now wore. Glancing back to the adlige, the duke grinned at the sight of the frau's reddening cheeks.

"Well, then. Perhaps I do know why."

Peppi's eyes widened as he jerked his gaze back to Kawn, and he spluttered. "Mylord, I can—"

Kawn simply shook his head and waved his hand to dismiss the mann's protests. "Hardly necessary, Peppi. A passionate mann is exactly what we need in a gouverneur."

Silence followed, and Kawn chuckled at the shocked expressions on everyone's faces. He knew he could have gone about revealing his "change of heart" in a different manner, but really, he hadn't had this much fun in a while, and he doubted they would believe him otherwise.

The frau with the double-green statusgürtel was the first to recover. "You want Peppi . . . to become the next gouverneur, Mylord?"

Kawn smiled at her and nodded. "Ja, Adlige, I do. Especially in times like these, we need gouverneure who will stand for all of their people, not just the river-dwellers."

The frau eyed him thoughtfully, the distance in her eyes portraying her distrust. Finally, she glanced around at her fellow prisoners.

Most of the nomaden seemed to share her distrust, only the two Spinne and one of the Wölfe, an older frau by the looks of it, offering smiles of encouragement. Frau Wäschemann and Herr Biermann weren't watching her; instead, they continued to eye the duke. When she looked to Peppi, the politician shrugged but nodded encouragingly.

The small smile that formed on the Pferd's lips then encouraged Kawn's belief that this nomade frau was the reason Peppi had thrown caution to the wind as he had. The smile still in place, she turned back to Kawn and gave a small bow.

"I do not believe we have been properly introduced, Mylord. I am Alys Reiter, eldest daughter of Roswalt Reiter, häuptling of the Pferd Clan."

Kawn nodded. "Angenehm, Adlige!"

The greeting, like the title, was old and formal, but he thought it appropriate. Adlige Reiter's eyes widened slightly. Then her lips twitched, and the sudden crinkling around her eyes let him know she appreciated the greeting's significance, as well.

Herrick finally succeeded in catching Kawn's attention. "I don't wish to interrupt, Mylord, but may I presume you wish to continue the alliance Gouverneur Volker held with the nomaden?"

Kawn started. "You know about it?" The incredulous looks on most of the prisoners' faces showed that the others were having a hard time believing this.

Herrick had the grace to look ashamed. "I've known for several jahre, ja. I was the one who executed the gouverneur's orders with regard to the alliance."

"But you had us arrested!" accused a young Mann who wore the red statusgürtel of the Wolf Clan.

Herrick scowled. "Would you prefer I had left you to those river-dwellers who'd rather see you dead for a crime that wasn't yours?"

The Wolf gaped at him.

The hauptmann sighed and shook his head. "Believe me, I'm not proud to have gone against the alliance. But I'd rather see you imprisoned and alive than free and dead."

Kawn stared at Herrick, considering his words. The ease with which he'd dropped the issue of James and Ferez sneaking in and out of the stadt suddenly rose to the surface of his geist, as did his desire to separate the nomaden and their freunde from other prisoners. The latter could be interpreted as a desire to protect the falsely accused nomaden rather than to isolate them. Then . . .

Kawn shook his head and chuckled. "You even knew of the Kreis, didn't you?"

Herrick nodded sheepishly. "I hadn't realized you did, though. Volker implied several times that you wouldn't jeopardize the alliance but that you didn't wish to know the details, either."

"Nein," Kawn sighed. "At the time, I did not. I thought if I knew the details, I might become a risk the alliance could not afford. I was simply glad Volker and Wilhelm were willing to do what I believed I could not."

"But that opinion has changed, Mylord?" Adlige Reiter asked. When Kawn answered in the affirmative, she narrowed her eyes. "Why?"

Kawn chuckled. "James Caffers."

Herrick gasped. When Kawn turned to him with a questioning look, the hauptmann was gaping at him.

"You know the Drache Krieger?"

Kawn raised an eyebrow. "Do you?"

The hauptmann snapped his jaw shut and shook his head. "Nein, not personally, but Volker spoke well of the boy. I've heard he's the one who instigated the old alliance's renewal."

"In a way," Adlige Reiter said with a sniff. "However, I am surprised you would speak kindly of James, Mylord. I thought the King, his herzöge, and the other nobles considered him a fiend." The final word was spoken with disdain.

Kawn grinned, half at the Pferd's attitude. "We did. Right up until he sat us down and gave us a basic understanding of his history."

Herr Biermann snorted and leaned back against the wall behind him. "That sounds like James."

Adlige Reiter rolled her eyes. "If anyone can find a way to deal with a situation peacefully, James can. But I do not see how simply knowing his history would change how you deal with the nomaden, Mylord." She leveled her gaze at him, the doubt once again rising in her eyes. "I fear it is not very believable."

Kawn shrugged. "Perhaps not, but the king was very interested in James and the groups he represented. That gave me the courage to tell the king my own beliefs—beliefs he is very willing to support."

"So now you have decided to openly support and protect the nomaden?" Peppi asked. Kawn nodded. "And you wish to make me the new gouverneur?" Kawn nodded again and opened his mouth to reply, when a wache pushed open the door.

"Lord Kawn, komm, quickly. Your lebenfrau—"

Kawn turned sharply to the newcomer. "What?"

The wache blinked and glanced around before continuing. "Yer lebenfrau, M'lord! Several nomaden grabbed her an' are threatenin' harm to her if you don't come at once."

Several of the prisoners groaned, but Kawn was more focused on the messenger. "Where are they? And what of my children?"

"Your children're safe, M'lord. They're wit' their knights. But the nomaden have barricaded themselves wit'in the Tempel of Carith."

Kawn nodded and turned back to Herrick.

"I want you to release these prisoners as quickly as possible. Then, spread the word that no one is to harm the nomaden or any who act to protect them. I want this situation dealt with as quickly as possible."

After a quick pause, he added reluctantly, "Use the Geistmagier to spread the word among the wachen if you think it necessary. But join me when you can."

Kawn turned back to the messenger and nodded. "Take me there!"

Nine

Ilse walked with her children and their knights along Marktplatz, admiring the wares they found there. She had always enjoyed the road. The variety of colors found in the buildings and stalls was only matched by the variety of wares and people buying and selling them. Some might think the road was too loud, but the sounds of the merchants hawking their wares and haggling with would-be customers for the best prices combined with the common sounds of the stadt to bring a smile to the duchess's face.

The thing she enjoyed most about Marktplatz was the freedom she felt when she haggled with the merchants herself. Many might think she could get an unfairly good deal as a noblewoman, but as far as Ilse had been able to overhear over the jahre, the merchants of Zhulan were just as ruthless, and ingratiating, with her as they were with any other person. They had to be, or they risked being criticized for such unfairness.

Ilse was admiring a beautifully made silver-and-katzenauge necklace when Kuonrada tugged at her skirt. She smiled down at her second daughter. "Ja, liebling?"

Kuonrada simply pointed to a nearby building and pouted. "Bitte, Mütter?"

Ilse glanced at the building and chuckled. She hadn't realized they had already reached the Tempel of Carith, which stood about halfway down Marktplatz. The tempel fit into Marktplatz rather well, its multicolored façade blending with the colorful buildings and stalls of the market. As was usual, the tempel's doors stood open to accommodate any people who wished to enter, as well as any breeze that was willing to blow through.

Glancing back down at her daughter, Ilse smiled fondly and murmured her assent. As Kuonrada cheered happily and ran off to tell her siblings, her mütter chuckled. Ilse's second daughter had shown an interest in the old religion from a young age, and the girl never missed an opportunity to stop in at the tempel.

Turning back to the necklace she'd been admiring, Ilse sighed softly. Now that she had given her assent, Kuonrada would want to be going into the tempel immediately. Thanking the merchant for allowing her to look at the piece, she turned away and looked for her children.

Kuonrada was nearby, chattering happily, while her older schwester and younger bruder simply listened and nodded idly, their geister most likely still on the surrounding wares. Neither had ever been as interested in the tempel as Kuonrada had, but both knew by now not to protest.

Gretchen, tired as she was, didn't say a word, as she slept peacefully in the arms of her knight protector, Sir Ritter. The other knights stood around, their postures relaxed but their eyes scanning the crowd.

Catching Didrika's eye, Ilse nodded toward the tempel. Didrika nodded back, even as her lips parted slightly, no doubt emitting a soft sigh. Ilse simply smiled as her eldest then rolled her eyes and turned to Kuonrada rather deliberately.

Didrika might portray reluctance in her duties as the oldest sibling, but she understood how important this was. Such an extended interest in the old religion needed to be encouraged, as it meant Kuonrada might one day become a Handmaiden of Carith. Such an occupation was one of the few considered worthy of a noble-born frau.

As Ilse turned to the tempel, her children tarried, still perusing the selection of wares. Even Kuonrada, always eager to enter the tempel, seemed to have had her attention caught by something in particular. Knowing they would soon follow, Ilse approached the tempel alone.

~~*~*

"Go on, younglings," Hoffnung urged, waving a silver hand toward the distracting wares. They couldn't see or hear her, but the words and motion helped her focus her influence. "It's beautiful, ja? The tempel can wait a few minutes. It'll still be there. You just need to admire this for ein bisschen longer, ja?"

Even as Hoffnung spoke, she felt disgusted with herself. She was interfering more than she was comfortable doing.

True, it was not as bad as Krieg taking on physical form to speak directly with the mortals or Leben touching a geist directly to keep it from leaving its physical body. (Hoffnung doubted she was supposed to know about Leben's little indiscretions, but walls weren't always solid in the Spiritual Plane, and Leben was never very subtle in her desperation to save the geister under her protection.) It wasn't even that Hoffnung had never influenced a mortal before; she often did since it was part of The Game.

It was the current situation that made her so disgusted with her actions. Normally, she'd have no reason to make an item in a market stall seem more tempting than it actually was, especially to three younglings who lived rather happy lives. Hoffnung's specialty usually ran to the more subtle, like offering a small light to an otherwise dreary perspective. She provided silver linings, as the Fayralese liked to say.

"That's it," the silver halbgott encouraged once the younglings were thoroughly engrossed. Looking up from her current targets, Hoffnung gave an irritated huff as she watched Zhulan's duchess approach the tempel.

Of course, the duchess wasn't the one with whom Hoffnung was irritated—it was this verdammt situation or, rather, her younger bruder, Krieg. He was the one who set these events into motion. He, the one conscious halbgott not currently in Machtstadt, was the reason the Schicksale had gathered Hoffnung and her siblings to discuss things that could and needed to be changed without affecting the situation between Frieda and Krieg too much.

Apparently, though Hoffnung couldn't see how, the mess between Frieda and Krieg had to be settled between the two of them. It was something with which none of the older immortals could interfere.

Hoffnung was brought back to the present when the unwitting duchess was only a few steps from the tempel's open doors. Four nomaden suddenly appeared from within the tempel, one grabbing the duchess and putting a scharfmond to her throat. The others stepped around the frau, brandishing their own blades at the surrounding crowds.

Hoffnung winced as people began screaming and pulling back from the small group.

Remembering her mission, Hoffnung focused her influence onto the geister of the herzogin's two older daughters, making sure they didn't try to do something stupid.

Unfortunately, she should have been more worried about the boy.

~~*~*

Ilse hardly had time to blink at the sight of the nomaden before she was pulled tight against a mann's body and a scharfmond was laid against her throat. She swallowed her gasp and attempted to stay still, but the screams of the people around her had her craning her neck to make sure her children were safe.

"Mütter!" she heard Adal cry.

His older schwestern promptly followed suit. Through the crowd, which seemed to ebb away from her, Ilse managed to spy her two older daughters. Sir Waren and Sir Tabbert had grabbed the two, though both seemed too shocked to put up much of a fight. Sir Ritter appeared to tighten his hold on Gretchen, who was beginning to stir, while he grabbed for Adal with his free hand.

To her horror, Adal had already darted farther into the crowd.

He was just pushing past the edge of the crowd when Sir Neff, his knight protector, finally grabbed him around the waist and picked him up.

"Nein!" Adal yelled, gripping Sir Neff's arm with one hand while he beat at it with the other. "Lemme go!" Then, reaching out one hand toward Ilse, he screamed, "Mütter!"

Meanwhile, Sir Bren, Ilse's own knight protector, pushed past those people trying to get away from the nomaden. As he approached, the nomade who held Ilse tightened his hold and raised his blade higher. She winced as the blade pressed against her skin.

"Stay back!" the nomade who held her growled. As he shifted her, Ilse spotted the statusgürtel of the mann in front of her: a purple statusgürtel.

Katze? she thought, shocked. *But why?*

"Let her go and we won't hurt you," Sir Bren commanded, his own sword drawn but lowered to the side.

The nomade to her left struck out wildly with one scharfmond. To Ilse's dismay, that nomade wore the red of a Wolf.

"N-nein. W-we won't." The trembling voice was decidedly young, and Ilse realized the nomade was a girl. "N-not until . . ."

Ilse caught a glance of the girl's face as she looked to Ilse's captor. Her eyes were wide and wild, her chin trembling violently. The nomade looked as though she were about to cry.

"Send for her lebenmann," the nomade to Ilse's right, another Katze, finished. His voice was dark, but even it bore a slight tremble. "If you don't, we will harm her."

Abruptly, Ilse was wrenched backward toward the tempel's doors. She thought she heard Adal scream "Mütter!" one last time before the doors were pushed shut and barred from within.

Now, Ilse sat on some cushions in front of the altar, seemingly forgotten. A steaming mug had been pushed into her hands by the trembling girl before the nomaden gathered in a separate area of the tempel. Ilse noted idly that the area was usually occupied by those in need of healing.

"Es tut mir leid for this, Mylady."

The words pulled Ilse from her thoughts, and she glanced up at the fräulein who had addressed her. The fräulein was clothed in the simple dress of a Handmaiden of Carith.

"Do I know you?" she asked, realizing the Handmaiden looked familiar. She giggled and sat down beside the duchess.

"My name is Lise, Mylady. My bruder is Sir Ritter, young Gretchen's knight protector."

Ilse blinked. "I had thought his schwester was lifebonded to Lord Howe."

Lise bobbed her head. "Ja, Mylady. That would be our eldest schwester, Lind. But I did not wish to simply be a lebenfrau to some nobleman, and as you know, there are few other choices for those frau of our birth."

"Ach, ja! I understand how you feel. I am lucky that Kawn is willing to share his burdens with me, or simply being a lebenfrau is all I would have." Lise giggled, and Ilse nodded toward the nomaden. "Tell me, Fräulein Lise, what is happening?"

Lise's smile slipped as she, too, glanced toward the nomaden.

"We received news last nacht that room had opened up at one of the more private nomaden sanctuaries. As soon as we heard, the nomaden staying here decided to risk moving there."

The Handmaiden hesitated. "You see, everyone knows the tempel is always open to nomaden, so they were worried the wachen would soon come to search the tempel and arrest them."

She paused as a loud whimper reached them from the group of nomaden. "They didn't leave in time?" Ilse whispered in sudden comprehension.

Lise bit her lip and shook her head.

"Nein, they did leave. It's just—"

She paused and glanced again toward the nomaden. "Heilig Oswald tried to tell them he would never allow the wachen to break the sanctity of the tempel, but they wouldn't listen." She shook her head. "Even I hadn't realized the wachen were so strict about respecting the tempel as the Haus of Creation."

Ilse gripped the fräulein's hand. "What happened, exactly?"

Another pained whimper drew a wince from both of them. "The wachen captured one nomade, a young Wolf, almost as soon as he left the tempel. While the others began to come back, the Wolf's bruder attacked the wachen."

A sudden cry had Ilse climbing to her feet. "Is there no Heilemagier here to heal his wounds?"

Surely a Heilemagier could at least help with the pain.

Lise gripped Ilse's arm and tugged her gently back down onto the cushions.

"Nein, Mylady. The Heilemagier connected to the tempel had been called away on emergencies before this, and none has yet returned. The nonmagical healer has done all she can, but the Wolf's pain is too immense for the remedies we have available."

Ilse shook her head, worry for a young mann she didn't know filling her heart. "Is this why they abducted me? Did they think kidnapping me would help them get an Heilemagier?"

"Honestly, I don't know, Mylady." Lise glanced at the nomaden and lowered her voice. "I think they've simply become too desperate. When we saw you in Marktplatz, Jakob—he's the one who grabbed you—simply seemed to snap. The others followed his lead."

Lise turned imploring eyes to Ilse. "You see, the same messenger who brought news of open space also brought another message. He said that the duke would look to the K—er, the more nomade-accepting river-dwellers—"

"The Kreis," Ilse offered, understanding the fräulein didn't realize exactly how much Ilse knew. The widening of the fräulein's eyes confirmed Ilse's thought, and the Handmaiden nodded.

"Ja, the Kreis." After a quick pause, she added, "Then it is true? The duke is looking to the Kreis for the new gouverneure?"

Ilse smiled and nodded. "Ja, he is. He already knows who he wants here in Machtstadt." She glanced over at the nomaden and chuckled. "Assuming this incident didn't interrupt him too quickly, he should have already offered the position to the mann."

"Who?"

The breathy question drew Ilse's startled gaze. Desperate hope filled the Handmaiden's face, and an answering pang tightened Ilse's chest.

Is this what our people have come to? Is hope so rare, it hurts too much for them to even believe in it?

Ilse gripped Lise's hand once more. "He wants Peppi Kluger for gouverneur."

The painful desperation in Lise's face morphed into surprise. A moment later, she smiled widely and gave a soft, anxious laugh.

"Oh, bitte, tell me this is no witz."

"What witz?"

The rough voice spoke before Ilse could answer, and she looked up to find one of the nomaden standing in front of them. Unlike the others', his statusgürtel was blue, marking him as a Falke. He, the duchess remembered, was the one who had grabbed her outside the tempel.

"Oh!" Lise gasped, jerking her head up. "Jakob! You startled me." The mann glowered at the Handmaiden, and her cheeks reddened. "Uh, well, the duchess was just telling me that . . . her, er . . ."

Ilse squeezed the fräulein's hand as she trailed off, too flustered to continue. Glaring up at the intimidating mann, she said, "I was simply assuring Fräulein Lise that my lebenmann is now looking to the Kreis for the next gouverneur, as well as any other assistance they might be able to provide."

The mann, Jakob, snorted and shook his head.

"I find that hard to believe, Mylady." The last word left his lips with such disdain that Ilse raised her brows in surprise. "The duke has never shown any concern for us nomaden before now. Why should that change?"

Ilse pursed her lips, but Lise, who seemed to have recovered her tongue, spoke first. "But the duchess has already said that Peppi Kluger is to be the next gouverneur. Surely, you can believe that!"

Jakob laughed sharply, startling the other nomaden. "Can't you see it's a trick, Handmaiden? Surely you are not naïve enough to believe her lies!"

"Ruhe, young mann!"

Ilse jumped at the strong-voiced command, while Jakob only lifted his gaze past her head. Turning around, Ilse saw an older mann walking toward them from a doorway behind the altar. His bright, multicolored tunic marked him as a Heilig, or Holy Man, of Carith. His weathered face was set in a frown.

"Why should I?" Jakob sneered. "Do you, who have

always been open to the nomaden, now stand behind
this . . . lügnerin, as well?"

Ilse stiffened. It wasn't so much that he called her a liar.
Certainly, he was right that their decision seemed rather
sudden. But the way he sneered it made the word seem so
much . . . worse than it should.

"Ruhe!" the Heilig commanded again. While Jakob
simply sneered, Ilse knew that if the command had been
directed at her, she would have gone quiet immediately. "I
will not have such dreadful things spoken within these walls."

"Or what, old mann?" Jakob mocked. "You think you
can silence me?"

~~*~*

As a Geistmagier, Heilig Oswald had learned long ago to
keep himself from unconsciously touching the geister of
humans around him. However, he had also learned from a
young age that humans were not the only ones whom he
could hear, nor were other geister so easy to ignore.

Such geister could not be seen. Some, of course, were
the geister of the dead whom Adler, the Royal Eagle, had yet
to claim. This was most common in times when there were
many dead, such as after a battle or plague.

However, it was the immortals whom Oswald most
appreciated—and sometimes most dreaded—hearing. When
he was young, his mütter used to call Oswald's gift prophetic
and a gift of the götter. Oswald would always laugh at her for
such things.

Ja, he had learned many things from them over the jahre,
especially when he could get them to speak the truths of the
old religion, which most people had forgotten. He also had a
healthy respekt for them and the tasks with which each was

charged. But the immortals, especially the halbgötter, whom most people had forgotten, often spoke of mundane and repetitive things. Oswald had found that, because the immortals lived forever, so, too, did their arguments, interests, and sorrows.

Today was a täg in which he dreaded hearing the immortals. Early in the morgen, when the nomaden had attempted to leave and had been driven back with one injured, most of the halbgötter seemed to have settled themselves within the tempel.

It was the first time Oswald had heard so many of the siblings at one time. He was used to hearing only one pair at a time (usually Leben and Tod, as the tempel was often used as a place of healing, and not all who came for healing survived). The sudden presence of nearly all the halbgötter of which he knew was draining.

When he'd realized none of them would be leaving anytime soon, he had left the altar room to meditate. The activity had helped him relax and simply let the halbgötter's words drift over him.

Even so, he knew the moment the nomaden had abducted the duchess. The halbgötter persisted in conversing about the nomaden's activities, as well as teasing one of their own about the part she'd played in protecting the duchess's children. They didn't manage to drive him from his meditation, though, until a dark voice spoke from right next to him.

"You should not ignore us for too long, Heilig."

Oswald sighed and opened his eyes. He couldn't see the halbgott, but he had spent so much of his life listening to the siblings that he recognized Tod's dark amusement easily.

"And why shouldn't I?"

He didn't have to speak out loud for any of the

immortals to hear him, as they would respond just as easily to his projected thoughts as they would to his words. But it had become his preference over the years to use words as well as thoughts.

Tod hummed darkly. *"Because you know I do not relinquish geister easily, Heilig."*

Oswald straightened. He'd heard those words once before as a preface to a warning. Then, he'd been able to stop a massacre from occurring within the Tempel of Carith that would have allowed Tod to claim twelve geister. If Oswald had learned anything over the jahre, it was that even if Carith himself never set foot in those tempel claimed for him by his creations, the halbgötter, his children, did not take kindly to mortals destroying anything within a Haus of Creation.

"Who would dare?" He mindspoke the question, not wishing to be overheard.

"A mann who has not yet arrived is in danger."

Oswald frowned at the evasive answer. He knew the halbgötter, especially Tod, had good reason to be cryptic when speaking with mortals, but warning him before the would-be victim had even arrived was a bit odd.

Tod's dark huff quickly destroyed that thought.

"There will be little time between his arrival and his death, Heilig, so I suggest you remove yourself to the altar room. Besides, I know you are not fond of liars, and one of the nomaden is currently acting as such."

The halbgott fell silent. Knowing better than to ignore such a warning, Oswald picked himself up and left his small sanctuary.

That was how he found himself being insulted by an impertinent Falke. He scowled at the young nomade even as the halbgötter made several comments about the mann that made Oswald want to laugh. That was one thing about the halbgötter that Oswald had always enjoyed: they spent enough time around humans to not be completely indifferent to their personalities and attitudes.

"I do not hide my abilities, Falke," Oswald spoke once he felt they'd glared at each other enough. "I do not wish to incapacitate you, but I will if necessary."

For a moment, Jakob continued to glare at Oswald. Soon enough though, he huffed and turned away, grumbling under his breath. The other nomaden eyed him warily and didn't speak to him as he rejoined them. Oswald nodded, his lips lifting slightly in acknowledgment of the chuckles he'd earned from the halbgötter. Turning to the duchess, he gave a small bow.

"Es tut mir leid, Mylady. I'm afraid you haven't had the best reception this tempel can offer."

Lady Ilse shook her head and stood, offering a small curtsy. "No need to worry, Heilig Oswald. I understand these are stressful times, and the nomaden still have little reason to trust my word or that of my lebenmann."

Handmaiden Lise scrambled to her feet. "But, Mylady—"

Oswald laid a hand on her arm to quiet her and shook his head.

"The duchess understands the situation quite well, Lise." The fräulein opened her mouth to protest, but Oswald gave her a quelling look. "No matter how much we may not like it."

Lise flushed and nodded. "For what it's worth, Mylady," she mumbled softly, "I believe what you said about your lebenmann, the Kreis, and Herr Kluger." Before Lady Ilse could thank her, she quickly added, "I should continue with my duties," and hurried off to another room of the tempel.

Oswald chuckled. "Do not worry, Mylady." Lady Ilse turned to him with a lost expression. "She will be fine."

The duchess nodded, though the lost look didn't disappear completely. To distract the frau from her distressful musings, Oswald turned his attention to something Lise had said.

"So, Herr Kluger is to be the next gouverneur, then?" Lady Ilse stared at him in surprise, and he smiled. "That is good to hear."

Lady Ilse's lost look turned to confusion. "I didn't realize you had heard that part of the conversation, Heilig."

Oswald shook his head. "Nein, I didn't. But"—he glanced toward the murmuring halbgötter with a wry chuckle—"there are geister who are more than willing to share such news."

Giggles and some deeper chuckles were the halbgötter's response.

"Oh!" Lady Ilse blushed and smiled. "I'd forgotten you were a Geistmagier."

Oswald nodded and glanced toward the nomaden. "It seems many—"

His words were interrupted by a sudden pounding on the doors and a voice shouting from the other side.

"This is Kawn Parshen, Duke of Zhulan." There was what sounded like a momentary scuffle before the duke spoke clearly once more. "Nein. I go in alone. I will not risk unnecessary violence."

Oswald stiffened. *Surely Tod didn't mean—*

He was nearly overwhelmed by the fear and nervousness suddenly filling the room. Several nomaden moved toward the doors, and as the two Katzen lifted the plank from the doors, the Heilig moved forward. He couldn't knowingly let anything be destroyed, especially not in the Tempel of Carith.

As soon as one of the doors was opened, a nomade reached out, grabbed the duke, and pulled him through. The barest glint of a blade in the light coming through the closing door was the only warning Oswald had.

The next moment, just as the plank was dropped back into place across the doors, the sharp clang of metal against stone echoed through the tempel, quickly followed by a solid *whumpf.*

Ten

Oswald collapsed to his knees and gasped for breath, one hand on the back of the Falke's neck, the other braced against the stone of the tempel's floor. The sprint forward to grab the rogue nomade hadn't taken much effort, but the deep, focused, and instant penetration he'd made into the mann's geist had.

Soft, slow clapping caught his wavering attention. Casting his eyes in the direction of the sound, he realized he couldn't see the clapper, and he frowned.

"Gratuliere, Heilig," a voice seemed to whisper. It was barely audible, and it took a moment for Oswald to realize the halbgott wasn't whispering; his own magie was weakened. *"You protected the sanctity of our vater's tempel. You have our thanks."*

Those words seemed to drag Oswald back into awareness of the Physical Plane. The Heilig groaned as his ears were assaulted by noise and his vision went starry. He could feel his geist attempting to shut down as it screamed for rest, but he forced himself to focus on the physical. There was one more thing he had to do—a message he had to pass on.

Someone had to know what he had seen in the nomade's geist.

Oswald suddenly became aware of a hand squeezing his shoulder, and he focused on that to keep from blacking out. Raising half-closed eyes, he found the duke kneeling beside him and watching him with wide eyes.

"M-mylord." Oswald winced as his voice came out breathy.

"What happened, Heilig? Are you all right?"

The Heilig felt laughter bubble up in his chest, though all that emerged from his lips were weak groans as his vision swam. He closed his eyes and tried to take steadying breaths. His breathing wouldn't slow, and Oswald began to worry he wouldn't be able to pass on his message.

"You shouldn't . . . self. You . . . rest."

The voice was barely there, and Oswald knew if he was awake much longer, he would stop hearing the halbgötter altogether. Gathering what strength he could, the Heilig opened his eyes to look at the duke, who still watched him worriedly.

"He . . . tried to kill you, M'lord." Oswald's voice was still breathy, but he pushed on. "Would've—"

The noise level suddenly became unbearable, and Oswald lowered his head with a groan. The voices of those surrounding him overlapped and tangled together, but he managed to decipher some of what was said.

"How could . . ."

". . . he's a Falke . . ."

". . . allegiance to the duke . . ."

The Heilig shook his head without lifting it. That would

have taken too much effort—effort he couldn't afford to waste.

"Not . . . Falke."

Once again, the noise level soared, and Oswald swayed on all fours. He knew the only thing keeping him steady was the duke's hand on his shoulder, and he was thankful for that.

"If he is not a Falke, then what is he?"

The words pierced through the nonsensical noise filling Oswald's ears. The Heilig found himself thankful for the duchess's clear voice as well.

"Skor . . . pion."

He barely managed to whisper the final syllable before his starry vision went dark and the roaring in his ears melted into blessed silence.

~~*~*

Kawn caught the Heilig as he collapsed and slowly lowered him to the ground with the help of his lebenfrau and a familiar-looking fräulein in the plain dress of a Handmaiden. At the same time, an older frau bustled over, the large half-open bag in her hand marking her as a healer. Once the Heilig was settled enough for the frauen to fuss over him, the duke stood and turned his attention to the unconscious nomade.

Everything had moved too quickly for Kawn to be sure of what happened. In one moment, he was being pulled through the tempel door; in the next, the mann who had pulled him in was on the ground, the Heilig kneeling above him. There had been a few moments of shocked silence before everyone had reacted.

"What did he say?" The question pulled Kawn's attention back to the present.

Turning his gaze from the unconscious nomade, Kawn eyed the two male nomaden who were still standing. The two looked similar, and both wore the purple statusgürtel of the Katze Clan.

James's Clan.

"He said 'Skorpion.'" Even as he answered, he wondered if the unconscious nomade was the only one wearing a statusgürtel of the wrong color.

Both Katzen went still, and even the third nomade, who had been crying in another part of the tempel, lifted her head and went quiet. Then one Katze, the older of the two, shook his head violently and cursed.

"Nein! It can't be. It can't . . ."

He quieted as the second Katze laid a hand on his arm and gave him a quelling look.

"It makes sense, bruder," the second nomade replied. "It makes more sense than a Falke attempting to kill the duke."

The first shook his head again. "But to lie with one's statusgürtel? That's against nomade law. Surely even the Skorpione would not condone such a thing. It would only cause chaos."

"Isn't that what they want?" a young voice sniffled.

Kawn and the two Katzen turned to the young nomade girl, who now stood nearby. The Wolf glanced earnestly between the three männer, and Kawn had the impression that speaking up like she had had taken all her courage.

"What do you mean?"

The two Katzen simply stared at the girl in surprise, neither seeming to know what to say. The Wolf's eyes continued to dart back and forth. For a moment, Kawn was sure she was going to bolt. Instead, she took a deep breath, settled her gaze on Kawn, and steadied her trembling chin.

"Well . . . it's just that the Gift Clans aren't exactly fond of order. They refused the call of the erstehäuptling and continue to do so. They killed the gouverneure. What's to keep them from turning their backs on nomade law, especially if doing so helps them bring down an ally of the clans and makes life harder for the rest of us?"

Kawn just stared at the girl as she finished. She was not as young as he had originally thought. Without meaning to, he said as much, and the Wolf promptly blushed.

The younger Katze chuckled softly. "Ja, Viveka's Of Age, despite how young she looks." The Wolf's blush deepened. "And her tears only make her sound younger."

The fräulein's face paled, and her eyes welled with tears. "Aw, Viveka." The mann sighed, reached out, and patted her shoulder. She flinched under his touch, and he sighed again. "Harti will live. You'll see."

Instead of being comforted, the Wolf began to wail and hurried back over to a cot Kawn hadn't noticed before. She was soon joined by the healer.

"Harti?"

Kawn kept his eyes on the cot as he asked. There was a figure in the cot that lay still, and as soon as she knelt next to it, Viveka's keening grew louder. When the healer arrived, she leaned over the cot and touched the figure in a few places. She then reached back and patted Viveka on the shoulder, murmuring something that caused the fräulein to quiet. Next to Kawn, the older Katze nodded solemnly.

"Harti is Viveka's older bruder. He was badly wounded last nacht when we attempted to move to another safe haus and the wachen captured their younger bruder, Hewitt."

Kawn frowned. "Is there no Heilemagier here to heal such terrible wounds?"

"Nein," the younger Katze answered. "They've been gone since yesterday morgen, at the latest, and none are expected to return until tonight."

Kawn finally turned his focus to the two Katzen. Both brüder were young, but the shadows around their eyes and the lines of their faces proclaimed just how tired and strained they were.

It had been ten täge since Volker was found hanging from his study window. Ten täge that Kawn had spent mourning for his freunde and trying to decide what to do. Ten täge that the nomaden had spent running and hiding, fearing that they would be imprisoned or, worse, killed.

Kawn suddenly wished it hadn't taken him ten täge to make his decision.

Reaching out, Kawn laid a hand on the older Katze's shoulder. The mann blinked and then narrowed his eyes warily, but Kawn just smiled.

"We can get him help now instead of waiting for tonight." He glanced toward his lebenfrau, who stood nearby listening to their words. "Ilse can fetch a Heilemagier. The wachen should have some if the gouverneur's is not available."

Both Katzen gasped even as Ilse nodded and stepped forward. The younger bruder glanced between the duke and his lebenfrau, eyes wide.

"You would do that? Even though . . ."

He flushed as he trailed off, but Ilse nodded.

"From what Lise says, it seems you were simply following Jakob's lead, ja?"

Both Katzen nodded, the younger more emphatically than his bruder.

Kawn frowned. "Jakob?"

"The Skorpion," Ilse answered.

"Ah." Her lebenmann nodded in understanding.

"But why would a Heilemagier with the wachen be willing to Heal a nomade?" The older Katze sounded more skeptical than his bruder. "They have been hunting us for täge. What's to keep them from killing us the moment we open the tempel doors?"

Kawn began to shake his head before the question was even finished. "I won't allow any harm to come to my allies—not if I can help it."

The brüder traded a glance. They seemed to come to a decision together as they nodded to each other and turned toward the barred doors.

~~*~*

"They're all too trusting."

Hope shook her head as the two nomads unbarred the temple doors. A sudden hand on her shoulder startled her, and she glanced back to find her twin frowning at her.

"Too trusting, Hope? That doesn't sound like you."

The silver demigoddess offered her brother a humorless smile. Honestly, she hadn't felt like herself for a while. She had only noticed it in the past few days, but she was sure the effects had been there for years, maybe even the past two centuries.

"Would it be wrong of me to blame Peace?"

"Nay, it would not," Love said, surprising her silver sister. "We've all become more susceptible to each other's influence because of Peace's 'death.'"

Hope blinked. That hadn't exactly been her reasoning, but . . .

"What do you mean, Love?"

Love raised an eyebrow. "Haven't you noticed how War always has more influence on Peace whenever she's tired?"

Hope rolled her eyes. "Aye, I have. But that's understandable. War and Peace haven't been able to balance each other for the past two centuries. Of course they'd be more susceptible to each other, even if Peace seems to be affected more than War."

She shook her head. "I don't see what that has to do with the rest of us. We're still balanced." She glanced quickly at Fear, who nodded.

Hate chuckled even as his pink twin sighed. "Our pairs are not as independent as you seem to think. Surely after several millennia, you've realized that."

Hope frowned. Aye, she had wondered about it over the years, especially more recently, but it was not something she and her siblings often discussed. In fact, the discussion in Cautzel at the beginning of the season was possibly the only other time Hope could remember her siblings discussing the more serious aspects of their relationships.

"If one of our pairs is unbalanced," Love continued, dragging Hope's attention back to her, "then the rest of us become unbalanced. That's why you've become more pragmatic."

Hope made a face. Honestly, before Peace's "death," Hope was sure pragmatism hadn't been a possibility for her.

"That's also why I've become more serious," Love added. Hope chuckled. "And why Hate has become more willing to accept Soul Bonds."

Hope blinked. She didn't understand where that topic had come from or why Love was now eyeing her twin with a small smirk.

Hate rolled his eyes. "I've always accepted Soul Bonds,

Sister. There's nothing I can do against them. I've just become more willing not to interfere with potential ones."

Love laughed. While she might have become more serious because of Peace's "death," her laughter was still light-hearted and joyous.

"Oh, I know, dear Brother."

"It is also the reason," Death added, startling the four middle siblings, "that Leben has been having more difficulty keeping geister in their bodies." His voice was quiet and held a note of awe, as if he had just realized something important.

Hope turned her gaze to her eldest siblings. Life knelt next to the wounded nomad, her concentration evident in her steady gaze and lined face. Death stood about a foot away, his arms casually crossed in front of his chest, his face utterly relaxed.

Before Peace's "death," the stance would have meant that Death was giving up on claiming the soul.

Now, Hope realized, it simply meant he was giving his twin a fighting chance.

"Is that why . . . ?"

Hope trailed off. Discussing War taking physical form to interact with the humans was one thing. He was expected to go against the rules of The Game since he had been imbalanced for so long.

But should I even mention Life's indiscretions?

Then again, Life was part of the eldest pair of demigods. She and Death had been alive for several millennia before even Love and Hate were born. As far as Hope knew, they had invented The Game themselves. If one of them did something "improper," could it really be considered to stand against the mostly unspoken rules of The Game?

Death seemed to understand her sudden indecision and shook his head.

"Nein, that is not the reason. Ja, Leben has been having difficulties with the geister, but that is not the main reason she has been so . . . physical in how she deals with certain ones."

A small smile formed on his lips. "Unless, of course, you are thinking of something other than how Leben handles the king's geist?"

Before Hope or any of her other siblings could reply, a soft sigh drew their attention to Life.

"You know, just because I am concentrating on a geist, it does not mean I am not listening to your conversations."

Then, to Hope's surprise, she lifted her pale gaze from the wounded nomad. Wondering if the nomad had died when she wasn't looking, Hope focused on the Physical Plane. She blinked when she saw that another human knelt next to the injured man's cot. One glance at the newcomer's soul was all Hope needed to confirm that Life had relaxed because the nomad was now in the hands of a Mage Healer.

"Already?"

A soft, tired chuckle drew Hope's attention back to her eldest sister. "You need to learn to keep an awareness of the Physical Plane if you plan to have these kinds of discussions, Hoffnung." Life's white eyes blinked slowly, and she tiredly lifted a hand to point toward the temple doors.

Hope turned to find the duke standing in the doorway. In front of him, along Marktplatz, crowds of river-dwellers and guards murmured among themselves, their eyes mostly on the duke. Behind him, inside the temple, stood his family and several nomads, including the young Wolf who had been captured in the early morning. He was holding his sister, who sobbed against his shoulder. He, too, was watching the duke, as were the other nomads, their gazes holding more awe than those of the river-dwellers outside.

Confused, Hope turned back to Life, who chuckled again before she could ask what had happened.

"The duke just publicly accepted the nomaden as Zhulanbürger. He also said that all nomaden cannot be held accountable for the actions of a few and that while he and the wachen will continue to search for the gouverneure's mörder, the nomaden have just as much recht as any river-dweller to move freely around Zhulan."

Life sighed breathlessly as she finished, and Hope blinked. She wasn't really surprised by the duke's words. His lifemate had been insistent that he had decided just this and more. She was surprised by Life's continued use of Zhulanese when she was no longer influencing a Zhulanbürger. When she said so, Life just gave her a blank look.

Death laid a careful hand on his twin's shoulder, pulling her attention to him. As soon as their eyes met, Life leaned into the touch and sighed. Her face, which had relaxed some once she'd released her influence on the injured nomad, smoothed. Her shoulders dropped, and she settled her head against Death's arm.

"She is right, Sister. The influence of the nomad's soul should no longer be affecting you. You need to rest."

Life shook her head slightly, her eyes already half closed. "Nein, noch nicht, Tod. The Schicksale warned us—"

"That War was causing more trouble than we could allow him, aye."

He pulled Life to her feet, pulling a soft groan from her at the same time. Hugging her to his chest, he tipped her head back so he could look her in the eyes.

"But the others can take care of War's fallout as well as we can now that the Mage Healer is here. I won't let you push yourself like this, especially with the season less than half over."

Hope shivered. She watched as Life laid her head on Death's shoulder and the eldest demigods disappeared. No doubt Death had realm-jumped to a realm where they wouldn't be bothered by mortal affairs. A hand on Hope's shoulder pulled her attention back to her own twin, who was frowning thoughtfully.

"Do you think Death's right?"

Hope didn't need to ask what he meant. The way Death had spoken those final words sounded like a promise of worse to come.

Remembering Peace's last visit from Mama Caler, the Kensian Seer, Hope knew this trouble between Peace and War might be settled by the end of the season. But none of them, not even Life and Death, or even War himself, could imagine how that would happen or what the results might be. That Death was certain the season could only get worse made Hope feel heavy. Even if it did get better afterward, could that trouble really be worth it?

The hand on her shoulder squeezed, once again dragging her back to the present. Glancing up into Fear's face and seeing his earnest yellow gaze, Hope realized he wasn't just trying to get her attention. She placed her hand on his and squeezed it in return. Immediately, she felt herself relax and saw him do the same.

It was the same for each of their pairs. None of them could truly rest unless they were consensually touching their respective twin. Alone, each of them was constantly fighting the Chaos that the demigods had been born to balance.

Before Peace's "death," that had never seemed to be a problem for any of them. Now, with each of them more susceptible to the influences of the others, they seemed to be putting up twice the effort for the same situations.

"I don't know," Hope murmured, answering Fear's original question. "But I fear he might be."

"I hope not," Fear muttered.

Hope turned her attention back to the temple at large, keeping her hand entwined with Fear's. Catching sight of Love and Hate, she smiled when she realized that they, too, had decided to rest. As per usual with Love, their form of touching was a little more intimate: Love had her arms wrapped around Hate's neck, her ear pressed against his chest as she watched the mortals interact.

"However he does it, I hope War fixes this mess with Peace soon. I am tired of feeling so pessimistic."

Fear chuckled. "I agree, Sister. I'm supposed to be the pessimistic one, not you. I find it's a bit tiring being so hopeful all the time."

Hope snorted and slapped her yellow brother lightly on the chest. Silently, she acknowledged he was right.

They were each born to handle a specific emotion, range of emotions, or situation. It wasn't that they couldn't feel the other emotions or handle the other situations in their own lives, but they weren't meant to deal with them for long periods of time.

And even for immortals, two centuries was a long time.

~~*~*

Kawn was relieved by how easily the wachen seemed to trust his declaration of acceptance toward the nomaden. While they were trained to put aside personal feelings for the well-being of the stadt, Kawn had feared their reaction to such a drastic reform. Their obedience was gratifying.

To his surprise, Hauptmann Herrick and several of his higher-ranking officers took it even further and offered the nomaden a public apology. Adlige Reiter, as the highest-ranking nomade currently available, accepted the apology.

She did make one snide remark about the way the wachen had treated the nomaden, but Herrick simply bowed his head in acknowledgment. Behind him, a couple of his officers began to protest but were quickly hushed by their fellows with elbows to the ribs and sharp looks.

Unfortunately, the reaction of the onlookers wasn't as subdued. The crowd surged forward, their sudden shouts mingling unintelligibly. The wachen scrambled to hold them back from the tempel and the group that stood before it.

Kawn laid a hand on his sword when fighting broke out, but he hesitated to draw. These were his people as much as the nomaden, and he wished them no ill. Nearby, Adlige Reiter had one hand behind her back, no doubt reaching for a scharfmond, but her eyes were on Kawn, not on the unruly crowd.

Before Kawn could decide how to handle the sudden riot, a loud "Ruhe!" cut through the commotion.

Silence fell over Marktplatz with astounding speed, and Kawn turned to find a large mann towering over the crowd on the other side of the street. The people surrounding him cringed away, making his bulky presence appear even more conspicuous.

"The nomaden have every right to take the wachen to task fer their treatment," the giant mann growled. In the deathly silence, surely everyone in Marktplatz could hear him. "Their customs may differ from ours, but they're just like ye an' me." He glared around at the crowd. "They have familie an' freunde, they feel love an' pain, just like anyone here in this stadt."

The large mann glanced toward the tempel. "Even Gouverneur Volker believed that the nomaden were

Zhulanbürger, that they had the right to live in peace wit' us river-dwellers."

"Ja, an' look where it got him!"

The shout came from a single mann in the crowd. It wasn't difficult to spot him because, suddenly, no one was standing near him. The challenger looked wholly surprised to find himself so suddenly isolated.

"Dummkopf! Didn't the duke just finish sayin' that all nomaden shouldn't be held accountable fer the actions of a few?"

Kawn recognized the stocky figure of Millicent Wäschemann stepping toward the dissociated mann from the crowd surrounding him.

"That's not . . ." His confidence seemed to have disappeared with his anonymity. Murmurs filled Marktplatz as his silence lengthened.

"There's no need for name-calling, Millicent." Peppi Kluger stepped up beside the large mann and laid a hand on his forearm, securing his attention. "And I think you are scaring people, Berg."

Berg frowned and glanced around. To Kawn's surprise, a smile widened his lips, and he laughed loudly. "Es tut mir leid. I forget how easily intimidated ye lot can be."

"Don't know how!" shouted a mann nearby. "Yer size is half the reason ye're so well respected."

"The other half bein' the Rotvogel!" Kawn recognized the name of a popular gasthaus in Machtstadt. The words were quickly followed by laughter from most of the crowd.

"Didn't know ye were accepting of nomaden, Berg," a middle-aged frau spoke up as the crowd quieted.

"Weren't supposed to," Berg answered with a snort. "I find the volume of my guests cover the presence of any nomaden I hide quite well. 'Sides," he added with a grin, "I couldn't've found a better use fer the köter who fill my gasthaus."

The insult raised protests from several in the crowd, which prompted others to reprimand the protesters, but they all sounded good-natured. Kawn had never met Berg before, but he was infinitely grateful for the way the mann had turned the attitude of the crowd. If he was the owner of the Rotvogel Gasthaus, no doubt he had a lot of experience with rowdy groups.

Soon after, the crowd began to break up. From the way the people talked, the news of Kawn's announcement would reach the rest of the stadt by nacht and, quite possibly, the other städte by morgen. Kawn frowned. He had decided how he might approach Othman to find the traitor in Schönestadt, but if Othman heard about this before Kawn wanted him to, it could ruin his tentative plan.

"What is wrong, lebenmann?" Kawn turned to Ilse and gave a small, tight smile.

"I don't know if I'll be able to reach Schönestadt before the news of what has happened here does."

Ilse frowned thoughtfully. "I don't see why not. If you leave soon, you should have most of the nacht to speak to Othman without interference." After a moment of thought, she nodded sharply. "Ja, that would be best." She gave Kawn a significant look. "Just in case Othman decides he needs to make an example of anymore nomaden."

"But what about you and the children?"

Said children were standing around Ilse, the younger three holding onto her skirts while Didrika stood just to the side, one hand fingering her mütter's sleeve. "And the situation here in Machtstadt isn't completely settled."

Ilse shook her head and smiled fondly at her lebenmann. "The children and I will be fine, Kawn. We have our knight protectors with us. There is no reason we can't return to Parshen Gut safely."

She paused and glanced to the side, where Peppi now stood, watching them patiently. "I am certain, too, that Herr Kluger would be willing to help you settle the situation here in Machtstadt."

Taking that as his cue, Peppi stepped forward. "Ja, Mylord, I would. Assuming, of course, that your offer is still open?"

Kawn's lips spread wide. "Ja, it is." He offered his hand, which Peppi shook firmly. "I'm glad you've decided to accept, Peppi."

Peppi smiled. "Honestly, I would have accepted earlier, but you left too quickly."

Kawn chuckled. "Indeed."

"Mylord," someone spoke from farther into the tempel, and Kawn turned to find the older Katze standing nearby. He was watching those river-dwellers who still lingered near the tempel doors. "My bruder and I were wondering if we could speak with you about the Skorpion."

"Skorpion?" Peppi asked with a frown.

Kawn just nodded and led Peppi and his familie into the tempel. Both the Heilig and the Skorpion were still unconscious, but they had been moved to cots near the wounded Wolf. Two Pferde now stood guard over the Skorpion, along with the younger Katze.

"What about him did you wish to discuss?" Kawn asked.

Peppi made a noise of disgust then, no doubt realizing what was going on. It was the younger Katze who answered Kawn's question.

"I know he tried to kill you, Mylord—"

"He tried to kill you?"

Kawn nodded to Peppi, who looked shocked. "He did,

but after the announcement I just made, I would rather not punish him publicly. It'll give people the wrong idea, especially since he's not wearing the correct statusgürtel."

"But to not punish an attempted murderer would give people worse ideas."

Kawn nodded but was interrupted before he could reply.

"Excuse me, Mylord, but that's why we were hoping you'd let us take him."

The duke turned to the elder Katze in surprise. The mann looked frustrated, and Kawn smile apologetically.

"Es tut mir leid." He nodded to the younger Katze. "We didn't let you finish." Glancing between the two, he added, "Why do you think that would be best?"

The younger Katze's cheeks darkened, but he met Kawn's gaze. "If we took him to the erstehäuptling, he'd be punished for all his crimes, not just those that the river-dwellers consider crimes."

His eyes suddenly widened. "I mean . . . not that . . . "

Kawn chuckled and raised a hand. "Nein, I understand." He glanced at Peppi. "What do you think, Gouverneur?" Peppi looked at him in surprise. "Does that sound acceptable?"

Peppi thought for a moment before nodding. "I, too, would like to see him punished for wearing the wrong statusgürtel, though perhaps not quite for the same reasons as the nomaden. We river-dwellers, those who can recognize the meanings anyway, rely on those statusgürtel to know who is freund and who is feind."

He shook his head. "I never considered that anyone would wear the wrong color, let alone for these reasons." He smiled at Kawn. "I am certain that Hausef will provide a fitting punishment.

"Not to mention," he added in a lower tone, "the

nomaden will most likely find him ein bisschen useful before they punish him."

"Ach, we would." Adlige Reiter walked up, offered Peppi a small smile, and then gave a slight bow to the duke. "If you do not mind, Mylord, my männer and I would like to return home. I am sure my vater is worried about me."

Kawn nodded. "I'm sure he is. The wachen shouldn't give you any trouble. At the very least, the Geistmagier will have informed the wachen on the gates of the current situation."

"Danke, Mylord."

She made to turn away, but Kawn stopped her. "Do you need pferde, Adlige?"

She shook her head. "Nein, Mylord. We know the location of several others of our clan. They should have access to their own pferde."

Kawn nodded. "Very well. Guten täg, then, Adlige Reiter."

"And you, Mylord."

Adlige Reiter made to turn away again, hesitated, and then faced Peppi. "Gratuliere, Peppi, on becoming the new gouverneur. Perhaps, once you are settled in the position, you could . . . contact me." Her face tinted red, but her gaze never wavered. "I'm sure my vater would be interested in discussing the alliance further."

Peppi swallowed. "O-of course, Alys."

She smiled, nodded to Kawn, who smiled and nodded back, and called to her fellow Pferde. The two männer bid farewell to the Katzen brothers and followed the adlige away from the tempel. After a long moment of staring after her, Peppi shook his head, cleared his throat, and turned back to Kawn, his cheeks pink. Kawn held back a chuckle.

"I believe Hauptmann Herrick and I can take care of

anything else that comes up if you wish to leave for Schönestadt now, Mylord."

"Danke, Peppi." Kawn offered the new gouverneur his hand, and Peppi shook it before turning away to speak with Hauptmann Herrick.

Turning back to the Katzen, Kawn found them staring at him. "Is something wrong?"

Both shook their heads, even as the older replied. "Nein, Mylord. It's just that we, too, will be traveling toward Schönestadt, and we must leave soon if we hope to reach the oase before sunrise."

Kawn chuckled. "Then we can travel together, ja? Do you have pferde?"

Both nodded. "We stabled them with the Marktplatz stable master," the younger Katze answered. "He's always willing to care for any animal, no matter who the owner is."

"Good," Kawn said with a nod. "Why don't you fetch your pferde, then, and we'll prepare to leave."

The two Katzen left quickly, talking excitedly. A hand on his arm drew the duke's attention to his lebenfrau, though it was quickly drawn down to his children as his legs and waist were suddenly enveloped.

"Do you 'ave to go, Vati?" Gretchen whined.

She sounded more like herself, Kawn noted with relief. Chuckling, he lowered himself onto one knee so he could see her better.

"Ja, liebling, I do. I know it seems like I haven't been home that long, but there's something I need to take care of in Schönestadt as soon as possible."

"Bitte, can we come with you, Vater?" Adal begged.

A hand squeezed the boy's shoulder, and he turned his face up toward his mütter, a pout already pulling at his lips. The look had no effect on his mütter's stern expression.

"Schönestadt is too dangerous right now!"

Adal looked like he wanted to press the issue, but Kawn laid a hand on his other shoulder, pulling the boy's attention back to him. He gave Adal a warm smile.

"Your mütter is right, son. Besides, I have a task for you and your schwestern." Kawn glanced around at all his children. "I want you to cooperate with your mütter for the next few täge. She's going to need you to move quickly and stay out of trouble"—he emphasized the last four words with a stern look for all four children—"while she completes her own tasks."

Adal bowed his head, his cheeks turning pink. Kawn hooked a finger under his son's chin and raised it so he could meet the boy's eyes. "Can you do that for me, Adal?"

Adal nodded solemnly. "Ja, Vati."

Kawn looked around at his three daughters. "Girls?"

They all nodded and murmured their agreement, though Gretchen's was quickly followed by "I still wish you didn' 'ave to go, Vati."

Kawn chuckled and kissed her forehead. "I know, perle. But it should only take a couple of täge. Before you know it, we'll all be back at the estate, ja?"

Gretchen sighed but nodded reluctantly.

"Kawn?"

The duke looked up. Ilse looked just as confused as she sounded. Climbing to his feet, he pulled her into his arms and kissed her cheek.

"What tasks of mine do you mean?"

Kawn smiled. "Well, while Schönestadt is a higher priority for me, a gouverneur still needs to be chosen for Wildestadt."

Ilse blinked and narrowed her eyes, but Kawn rushed on before she could speak.

"I know it might sound like ein bisschen much since James didn't give us any recommendations and you'll still have to find out who is in the Kreis, but I am sure it is a task you can handle."

They stood for a moment in silence as Ilse studied Kawn's face. He simply smiled. He knew he had been pushing her away during this katastrophe, which had upset her. He wanted to make it up to her, and he knew how much she enjoyed helping him with his political burdens. Besides, Wildestadt did need a new gouverneur just as badly as Machtstadt had.

"You would trust me to make such a decision?"

Ilse sounded so unsure that Kawn kissed her lightly before nodding.

"Of course I do, liebling. You know our people just as well as I do, if not better. I trust your judgment more than I do James's, to be honest."

Ilse frowned and shook her head. "There is no need to demean young James, Kawn. I'm certain that, in matters concerning the Kreis and the nomaden, James knows better than anyone."

Kawn chuckled. "Perhaps, but he is only sixteen, liebling. He cannot possibly understand all of the political matters that need considering, not like you and I do."

Ilse smiled warmly, her cheeks tinting pink. "Very well, lebenmann. I will travel to Wildestadt and see if I can't find a proper gouverneur."

"Good!"

Kawn noticed the two Katzen returning then, both smiling widely. He leaned forward and kissed Ilse's cheek.

"Could you stop by the estate and send some of the knights to Schönestadt, just in case?"

Ilse chuckled and agreed.

~~*~*

Once Ilse and her lebenmann had said their farewells, the duchess took a moment to observe her familie.

While Kawn went to help the Katzen and Sir Leal with the Skorpion, Kuonrada wandered over to speak with Handmaiden Lise and Sir Ritter. Gretchen followed and immediately began babbling happily to her knight protector.

Meanwhile, Didrika and Adal approached the nomaden. The older struck up a conversation with the two Wölfe not mourning the wounded mann, while her bruder began talking with the Spinne männer.

Ilse smiled. They had grown up with their vater's love for the nomaden, and it showed in Didrika's lively expression and Adal's excited banter. Knowing they would be safe in the tempel, Ilse returned to the doors. She had seen some river-dwellers loitering around the entrance whom she thought might be part of the Kreis. Perhaps they could give her an idea of whom to approach in Zhulan's southern stadt.

Eleven

"*hadow, where are you?*"

The inquiry woke Flame from her light doze just as the sun sank below the horizon. Despite her nap, she knew exactly where Shadow was, even before he told Gemi that he and Last Chance had been at the river and were now heading back to the inn.

Flame uncurled her sinuous body, stretching out her wings and tail as she did so. Her jaw parted in a wide, toothy yawn, which ended with a loud snap, startling a flock of desert sparrows out of a nearby, barren-looking bush. The dragon hissed softly in amusement as the sparrows fluttered about before landing along the ground farther away.

Flicking out her long, snake-like tongue, Flame tested the evening air. She crooned softly.

Although the western sky was still painted with the warm colors of the desert sunset, the heat of the day had already begun to dissipate. In a couple of hours, the air would be quite chill. Such mattered little to her, but her bondmates always appreciated the cool night air after the long day of desert heat.

Knowing her bondmates and their companions were preparing to leave Schönestadt, Flame coiled her body and launched herself into the air. Taking advantage of the remaining heat, she quickly gained altitude with only a few flaps of her wings. Once high enough that no humans would notice her, Flame turned toward Schönestadt and sped toward the city.

Flame had purposefully hidden herself about an hour's trot west of Schönestadt. Not only had it assured she would not be seen, it now gave her the opportunity to really stretch her wings and fly at a speed she could not properly achieve while following a horse's steady pace. However, an hour's trot was not even a ten-minute flight, and she quickly found herself circling above Schönestadt, searching the streets for the two horses and their riders.

From this height, Flame had a perfect view of the entire city, as well as much of the desert that surrounded it. Even so, as a dragon, she could still see every detail of the city streets, which were quite lively at this hour. Along Marktplatz, children darted after each other, dodging browsing customers and vendors who were beginning to pack up or put out their wares. It was the time of day when the day vendors gave way to the night vendors.

In other parts of the city, things were not so much quieting down as shifting tone. The owners of daytime-only businesses were closing shop and heading home. At the same time, the nightlife for which the Zhulanese cities were famous was waking up. Inn and tavern owners lit torches outside their establishments, inviting in those who wanted a bed and food, or perhaps something a little stronger.

And among all the usual life of the city, the guards were out in full force, as they had been since Schönestadt had learned of the deaths of the two governors. Flame would have felt sorry for the guards if it had not been her friends they were hunting. Even for a dragon, ten days of constant awareness was exhausting.

Idly, Flame followed the path of one particular set of guards with her gaze. When she realized where they were going, she bared her teeth and growled.

"James," she hissed. Even so high above the city, she refused to use Gemi's real name, ever wary of Animal Mages and Mindspeakers. *"Guards are en route to arrest Heiss Schmied."*

Gemi groaned slightly, interrupting her conversation with Ferez. The dragon was distracted from the girl's response, though, as Flame's attention was suddenly drawn away from the city. Traveling north along the Evonese Highway at a quick yet steady pace were four horses. Flame recognized two of the horses as nomad trained. The other two held themselves like river-dweller horses, and they wore the saddles and tack of such.

Flame broke the circle she had been flying and drifted toward the four horses, idly wondering if some river-dwellers had managed to capture a couple of nomad horses. It was highly improbable with their training, but Flame could not think why a river-dweller would be traveling amicably with nomads.

In her mind, Gemi's and Shadow's curiosity echoed her own.

Once she was closer, she realized the riders of the two nomad horses did wear the kopfabdekung and statusgürtel of nomads; their statusgürtel were even purple.

"Katzen."

She circled lower to get a better look at the river-dwellers. Surprise flitted through her mind as she recognized one. *"Lord Kawn is approaching Schönestadt."*

"Already?" Even as Shadow nickered the question, he turned south, following Gemi's prodding.

Flame hissed in agreement. None of them had expected the duke to deal with Zhulan's northernmost city so soon. With her bondmates' questions echoing in her mind, Flame pulled her wings close to her sides and dropped into a dive.

Flame landed as silently as she could and padded up to the road. She stepped up onto it just as the four horses approached. All four slowed to a stop and nickered at her curiously, though the two river-dweller horses shifted and whinnied uncertainly. However, it was the horses' riders who caught Flame's attention, as all four shouted her name.

Flame recognized the two nomads as Katze brothers who often traveled between the oases and the cities to trade goods with the Clans' allies. They greeted her with friendly shouts of her nickname, the younger brother raising a hand to wave at her. The duke greeted her similarly with her full name, though his tone was tinged with surprise. He obviously had not expected the Drache Krieger to still be in Schönestadt.

The fourth voice, however, was unexpected. The river-dweller, whom Flame had not recognized on first glance, wore the armor of a knight. The colors decorating the leather proclaimed his own house and that of his Knight Master, Lord Kawn. Even so, he addressed Flame with the same familiarity the nomads had, his voice filled with a shocked recognition that caught the attention of the other humans as much as hers.

Flame narrowed her eyes and observed the knight more closely. As far as she was concerned, there was no reason for a knight of Zhulan to recognize her, as she had always made certain none saw her. But he did indeed look vaguely familiar, yet Flame could not place his face. That, alone, was disconcerting.

Suddenly, the wind shifted, and Flame found herself downwind of the horses and their riders. Inhaling the scent of both horses and humans, she sifted through them, hoping the knight's scent would trigger her memory.

When she found the scent she sought, she jerked her head back.

At the same time, the knight bowed his head. As he gave it a small shake, she heard him mutter, "James Caffers. I should have known."

Baring her teeth, Flame hissed.

~~*~*

Sir Leal Highknoll hadn't felt this shocked in years. Not since he, Paeter, and the other survivors from Cosley Estate had returned from the Battle of Farvis only to find that the estate had been attacked in their absence. Leal remembered wandering through the ashes of the manor, hoping to find some sign that someone had survived.

But there had been no sign of life. The massacre had been complete and utterly devastating. Even the horses and livestock had been butchered, the crops burned, and as they later discovered, the fields strewn with salt. That had convinced them, more than the words burned into the manor's lone brick wall, that the land had been damned.

The manor fire had burned so hotly that no identifiable human remains were distinguishable among the ashes. Only some items had been recovered, including Lord Jem's sword and Lady Kit's favorite jewels, neither of which would have been left behind willingly. Both had been found among the remains of the Lord's Chambers, and Leal and the others had known it could only mean that both had been caught and killed during Lady Kit's afternoon rest.

The one hope that had sustained them all was of the lack of evidence concerning young Gemini and her bondmates. Gemini's sword, a strong blade of simple design, had not been among the ashes, Shadow's corpse had not been among the dead animals, and Flame, who as a fire dragon would not have burned in the fires, had been nowhere to be found.

It was a small hope, of course, but they had held onto it fiercely.

As the years had passed, that hope had faded. The longer they went without news of Lord Jem's only child, the more they had wondered if she still lived. None of them doubted she had survived the attack, but Leal wasn't the only one who had wondered if something else had claimed her life since.

Now he had proof she still lived. As a dragon, Flame had no reason to interact with humans on her own. Leal knew that from personal experience; he had trained the three to cooperate in fighting, with James both on the ground and on the backs of her bondmates. While Leal had learned to interpret many of the dragon's sounds and expressions, he had also learned she wouldn't seek out humans unless Gemi needed her to.

"James Caffers," he whispered with a shake of his head and a soft laugh. "I should have known."

When Lord Kawn had mentioned that the Drache Krieger was a boy named James Caffers, Leal had recognized the family name. He remembered young Jake Caffers's constant teasing of the duke's daughter. He was certain the boy's family had been killed in the attack, but he had wondered if this James was a surviving relation he hadn't known about.

That the Drache Krieger might have an actual dragon . . .
Should have been my first thought.

Leal was pulled from his thoughts by a hand on his arm. Lifting his head to look at his Knight Master, Leal took in the man's concerned frown and gave a slight smile.

"Are you all right, Leal?"

Lord Kawn was studying him. Lifting a hand to his face, Leal found wetness on his cheeks. Scrubbing both cheeks dry with his hands, Leal sighed and nodded.

"Just memories, is all."

"Memories?" A sharp growl interrupted Lord Kawn's curiosity. Flame bared her teeth and glared at Leal.

The knight sighed again. Even after all these years, he could still interpret that. It was a warning, most likely to keep James's secret. But the warning was unnecessary. Lord Kawn may be his current Knight Master, but Kensy was where Leal had been born, and the Duke, or Duchess, of Kensy deserved his loyalty first and foremost.

Leal nodded, both in acceptance of Flame's warning and in answer to Lord Kawn's question. "Aye, memories. I haven't seen Flame in seven years."

The dragon's growl pitched higher, but Leal ignored her. He wasn't planning on giving anything away. Nothing important, anyway.

The significance of the number of years was apparently not lost on Lord Kawn, who raised his eyebrows and glanced at Flame.

"You knew Flame Tongue in Kensy?" Leal nodded. "Why didn't you ever mention her?"

Leal chuckled, even as Flame's growl rose in volume. "She was a bit of a regional secret, you could say."

The growl suddenly dropped to a more threatening octave, and Leal grimaced.

"By the gods, Flame, I know you're protective of young James, but no one here wants to harm him, do they?"

The growling came to a sharp end, and Leal almost chuckled when a confused whine replaced it. With a soft sigh—Leal hadn't fancied being attacked by a dragon, especially one he'd known several years ago—he turned back to Lord Kawn. In the dim light of the stars and moons, the duke looked decidedly bemused as he glanced between Leal and Flame. On his other side, the two Katzen snickered softly.

Lord Kawn's gaze finally settled on Leal. "I take it you know James, then."

The knight nodded. "I used to, at least. Like I said before, it's been seven years." His voice dropped to a whisper. "I wasn't even certain the boy had survived the attack."

He remained silent for a moment before shaking his head and speaking more loudly. "That he has become the Drache Krieger, let alone everything else, is not something I would have imagined." He chuckled. "When you told us who the Drache Krieger was, I didn't even make the connection."

A soft croon eased through the air, and Leal glanced back at Flame. Smiling at the red and purple creature, Leal swung off his horse, who shifted nervously. Leal wasn't surprised. The animal was his second mount since Kensy.

Leal rubbed his mount's nose soothingly before approaching Flame. Once close enough, he lifted a hand toward the dragon's snout but stopped just shy of touching her. He knew better than to presume such familiarity after all these years.

They stood like that for a full minute, Flame watching him warily. Leal simply waited. He wouldn't rush this, not when the trust of his old Knight Master's heir would be his reward.

Finally, with a soft snort, Flame pushed her face against his hand. Leal smiled and smoothed his palm up the dragon's nose, between her eyes, and back to the base of her horns, where he remembered she enjoyed the attention. She closed her eyes, and a deep rumble started in her chest, reminiscent of the purr of a large cat.

Leal chuckled softly. "How are you, Flame?"

There was a slight pause in the dragon's rumble before it continued smoothly. Flame's blood-red eyes opened to a thin slit and seemed to pierce him in their intensity. Leal sighed. He still recognized that look, too. Something was going on, something Gemi needed help with, which she would never willingly admit.

The knight would have responded to the look, but a steady beating sound, which had quickly been gaining volume, suddenly became recognizable as hoofbeats. Looking toward Schönestadt, Leal saw two horses galloping toward him and Flame.

"Sir Leal!" one of the riders cried as the two horses slowed to a halt.

Suddenly, a pair of arms wrapped around his neck, and his arms were filled with the slim body of a child he had feared he would never see again.

~~*~*

Ferez didn't know why they were traveling south out of Schönestadt. They had originally planned to leave through the same hole in the wall they'd used several days before. But James had urged Shadow south instead, and Ferez simply thought the boy had decided the gates would be an easier exit. Ferez was surprised, then, to find four horses and their riders standing in the middle of the Evonese Highway with Flame.

He certainly wasn't prepared for the sight of James throwing himself into the arms of the man standing next to Flame. Nor for the fire that seemed to ignite in his gut at the sight.

Ferez pursed his lips and glanced away. For the first time since the season began, he found himself wishing he hadn't asked to travel with James. If he hadn't, he wouldn't be afflicted with this churning pain or the confusion that seemed to have grown within him as the day wore on.

Today, he and James had simply been commoners. They hadn't had to worry about fighting or planning attacks. They hadn't had to worry about the political consequences of their actions. They had simply relaxed and explored the city, and Ferez had seen a new, relaxed side of James, one he found he liked just as much as he did any of the others. One he wished James could show more often.

That liking and wishing had grown and, with it, the confusion.

"You survived."

The words were whispered, but the voice was so choked with sorrow and relief that Ferez was jerked from his thoughts. The words were James's, and Ferez suddenly realized he recognized the name the boy had called out.

Sir Leal?

He peered through the soft light of the desert night at the man who hugged James. Sure enough, the man was none other than Sir Leal Highknoll, current Knight Captain of Parshen Gut and previous Second Captain of Cosley Estate.

Suddenly, Ferez remembered his assumption that James

was from Cosley Ruins. *If he lived on Cosley Estate before the massacre . . . if he didn't think anyone else had survived . . .*

Ferez grimaced. If that was true, he couldn't fault the boy's reaction.

"Aye, I did, James," the knight replied, pulling back enough to look the boy in the face.

Ferez couldn't see the knight's expression very well in the dim light. Instead, his own mind provided him with an image of hunger-filled eyes that Ferez quickly banished, alarmed.

"We were certain you had survived the attack. But when we received no news of you, many of us feared you had fallen to something else."

Ferez couldn't see James's expression, but the choked, teasing tone of his response hinted at a small smile on the boy's face. "I don't know why, when you and Paeter trained me personally."

Ferez blinked, surprised. Apparently, a smile wasn't the only thing James's response implied.

The next moment, James started and glanced around. Ferez's stomach clenched as he realized that Flame or Shadow must have reminded James that they weren't alone. No matter how close he felt to James, it seemed there were still some things about himself that the boy was unwilling to share. He supposed he shouldn't blame the boy; they'd only known each other for little more than a month.

And what does that say about me, then?

The harsh sound of a throat being cleared dragged Ferez from his thoughts and his attention to one of the other riders who had been waiting for them. The kopfabdeckungen declared him and the rider next to him as nomads. The third mounted man, Ferez realized with little surprise, was none other than Kawn.

"I do not mean to interrupt your reunion, Drache Krieger," spoke one of the nomads, "but we should leave for the oase as soon as possible." He patted something large that lay across the saddle in front of him. "We won't be traveling as quickly as we normally would."

Ferez still couldn't see James's face, as Last Chance stood behind the boy, but Ferez couldn't miss the sudden tensing of his shoulders or the way he shifted slightly from side to side. Ferez thought he could even guess the conflicting sides of the boy's sudden internal struggle.

On the one hand, they had intended to return to Helloase tonight and the nomad's words would have piqued James's curiosity, if nothing else. On the other, James had suddenly been presented with a chance to catch up with an old friend and mentor, someone he had once thought dead.

Ferez didn't like to see James so distressed, especially since he had been so relaxed not that long ago. The sight only added an ache in his chest to the other emotional pains he'd been feeling.

"James."

Dark eyes turned to Ferez. For a second, he was struck by how lost James looked. It was something the king had never fancied seeing before, and he realized he would do anything to dispel that look.

"One more day in Schönestadt wouldn' hurt, would it? I'm sure the duke an' his knight have news to share, an' they could prolly use any help they can get, aye?"

James relaxed as Ferez finished. His face softened into a small smile, his eyes shining in a way that made Ferez shift in his saddle. Then Flame crooned softly, and James huffed softly, his smile widening.

"Ja, and I don't relish introducing you to an unwetter while traveling."

Ferez blinked. Before he could ask what an "oon-veh-tehr" was, the nomad who had spoken before groaned and guided his horse off the road.

"Komme, bruder. Let's water the pferde and be off. If a storm is coming and James insists on not riding with us, then we must leave immediately."

The second nomad quickly followed the first off the road. The others remained quiet as the nomads led their horses to the river to drink and returned.

"Is there any message you wish us to take to your vater, Drache Krieger?"

The nomad's voice was tight, his disappointment obvious. It seemed that, like so many others Ferez had met, the nomad had looked forward to traveling with the Drache Krieger, if only briefly.

James reached up and patted the man's leg. "Just let him know that we should return tomorrow nacht. He'll understand." The nomad nodded stiffly, and with several wishes of "Gute nacht"—and a quick "Danke" to Kawn— the two nomads rode west for Helloase.

~~*~*

Gemi turned to introduce Sir Leal to Ferez as soon as the nomaden were out of sight. No sooner was the king's pseudonym out of her mouth than the knight turned to stare up at her companion.

"Frenz?"

The word was sharp with recognition. Gemi frowned as she peered between her old mentor and her newer freund.

"You know him?"

She wouldn't have been surprised to learn that Ferez

knew the knight, but she had been sure Ferez's alter ego had been more of a secret than that.

"Aye, he knows who I am," Ferez answered. While Gemi frowned, he leaned over Last Chance's neck and offered his hand to Sir Leal. "Good to see yeh again, Sir Leal."

"And you, Frenz." The old knight took the mann's hand and shook his head slowly. "I must admit, I never expected to run into you here in Zhulan."

A chuckle came from behind them, reminding Gemi that Lord Kawn was still with them. "He has been riding with young James almost since the beginning of the season, Leal." The knight nodded, and Lord Kawn turned his attention to Gemi. "And Leal knows Frenz so well because he trained him as well for several jahre."

He glanced between Gemi and her old mentor. "Maybe longer than he trained you?"

Gemi sighed. She didn't know how she was going to explain her previous slip. She had never been able to think of a probable explanation for her young sword training that wouldn't give away her true identity. Thankfully, she'd never had to explain her childhood to any who didn't already know who she was—before now.

"Nay." Sir Leal's denial startled her from her considerations. "I trained them both for about the same amount of time."

Gemi stared at her old mentor in the ensuing silence. *Is he mad?* He had sounded more than willing to help her keep her secret, but now he edged dangerously close to giving her away.

"Yeh were only four when yeh began to train?"

Ferez's voice was heavy with disbelief, and Gemi closed her eyes as that heaviness sank into her. *Stop it! I have no right to be hurt by that! Today has been great, but if I can't even—*

Panic joined the heaviness in her chest and clawed up her throat. She clenched her fists, but that couldn't prevent the answering thoughts from filling her mind.

Not yet. I don't—I can't—

"Aye, he was," Sir Leal answered Ferez. Gemi snapped her eyes open and glared weakly at the knight. He simply ignored her. "Being the best friend of the very stubborn daughter of a duke will do that."

"Sir Leal!"

"What?" the knight asked, amusement clear in his words. "Was that supposed to be a secret?"

Gemi gaped at her old mentor, her mind as silent as her tongue. And it wasn't necessarily his words that had shocked her into silence as much as the fact that he had managed in a few minutes what she had been unable to do in six jahre. With one sentence, he had provided a plausible explanation for her entire childhood that still hid her true identity.

When Gemi finally found her voice, she scowled at the knight. That no one would see it in the darkness didn't matter.

"It wasn't exactly something I wanted to advertise."

Sir Leal sighed. "Gemini can't stay hidden forever, James."

Gemi felt her scowl deepen. "I know that." After a moment, she quickly added, "We both know that."

She shook her head. It felt odd referring to herself as two different people. "But you know what's likely to happen the moment she comes forward as heir to the duchy. You can't blame her for being a little wary."

"You might be surprised, James," the knight responded. "I'm sure her political pull as future duchess combined with your own influence would lessen any negative reactions her return might cause."

Gemi stared at her old mentor as she processed his words. With a huff, she tossed up her hands in frustration.

"And what influence could I possibly have that would affect the way her future peers treat her?" After a beat, she added, "No offense, Mylord," with a quick glance at the duke.

Lord Kawn chuckled lowly. "None taken, my freund. However, as interesting as this conversation is, we really must head into Schönestadt. I have a gouverneur to speak with before anyone else from Machtstadt can come and spread rumors of what has happened. I am sure you can finish this while we travel or even once we reach the stadt, ja?"

The words piqued Gemi's interest, but they also made her wary. "Surely you aren't suggesting Frenz and I travel with you to the Regierhaus," she cautioned, naming the home of the gouverneur and the political center of the stadt.

"Ach, nein, nein," the duke assured with a quick shake of his head. "That would hardly help my plans. Nein, I simply meant that Sir Leal should travel with the two of you. It would give you a chance to catch up. After all, a few minutes of reunion can hardly make up for the last seven jahre."

"But, Lord Kawn," Sir Leal quickly protested, "I'm here as your knight protector. I should—"

The duke cut him off with a raised hand. "I'll only be going to the Regierhaus, Sir Leal. I doubt there will be anything there you need to protect me from that I cannot handle myself."

Sir Leal remained silent, but Gemi was certain he still wanted to protest. After a quick thought to her bondmates and an affirmative response from Shadow, Gemi broke the growing silence.

"In that case, Mylord, may I send Shadow with you?"

Ferez and Sir Leal spoke out in surprise, but Lord Kawn's "Why?" only sounded curious.

Gemi shrugged. "I would feel more comfortable if you had someone to watch your back, Mylord. Also," she added before anyone could question that, "if Shadow goes with you, we can keep in contact. Shadow will let us know if you need any help."

There was a moment of silence while the duke seemed to consider her offer. Hesitantly, he asked, "Do you wish to switch mounts?"

Immediately, Shadow and, to Gemi's surprise, Last Chance both snorted loudly and tossed their heads. Flame hissed in amusement, letting Gemi know that both pferde had expressed the same thought. With a chuckle of her own and a shake of her head, Gemi answered the duke.

"Nein, that wouldn't be a good idea. Shadow does not take kindly to anyone but myself riding him unless absolutely necessary. And it seems that both he and Last Chance are in agreement that I should ride no pferd but them."

Glancing at Ferez, she added, "If you don't mind."

The king chuckled. "Course not. Didn' mind the las' time. Why would I now?"

Gemi considered mentioning that last time was a necessity born of the approaching threat of wachen, but the touch of relief in the mann's voice gave her pause. Before she could think too long on it, Lord Kawn spoke up.

"Very well. I don't see any harm in having Shadow follow me to the Regierhaus. But we should head into Schönestadt now."

Nodding in agreement, Gemi and Sir Leal mounted their respective pferde. As Flame took wing once more, the small group turned their mounts north and continued riding toward the stadt.

Twelve

Kawn arrived at the Regierhaus with little incident. The wachen on the gate had recognized him, and after James had changed mounts, they escorted Kawn farther into the stadt. They had eyed his pferd shadow curiously, but they seemed to know better than to ask about the stallion.

As they entered the Hauptplatz, which the Regierhaus bordered on one edge, the stench of death nearly overwhelmed Kawn's senses. Taking in the horrible sight of two corpses hanging from the gallows, he covered his nose and mouth with one hand to block out the putrid scent of rotting flesh, with little success.

A tap on his arm drew his attention to the wache next to him, who offered him a bundle of cloth. Taking it from the mann, Kawn noticed that he and the other wachen had pulled scarves up over the lower portions of their faces.

"Es tut mir leid about the smell, Mylord," the wache said as Kawn wrapped the cloth around his head in imitation of the other männer. "Gouverneur Othman insists the bodies be left up as an example to any nomaden who might still be free in the stadt."

Kawn paused in tucking the cloth in place. The wache's voice had grown bitter toward the end. Looking around, the duke noticed the other wachen watching him with weary eyes. He hoped it boded well for the transition he had planned for Schönestadt.

"Then we shall simply endeavor to end this quickly," Kawn replied, but the wachen didn't look impressed.

They led Kawn past the gallows, which thankfully stood at the end of the Hauptplatz opposite from the Regierhaus. The distance seemed to lessen the stench somewhat, but Kawn still found himself thankful he had seen worse during the krieg. His stomach would have rebelled otherwise.

Word of his arrival must have preceded him, as Gouverneur Othman was standing by the doors to the Regierhaus when Kawn pulled his pferd to a halt. Swinging off his mount, Kawn greeted the portly mann with a stiff handshake and small nod.

"Mylord, I'm glad you were finally able to come deal with our situation."

The words would have made Kawn suspicious of the mann's attitude, but his smile looked sincere. That Kawn could see his smile at all startled the duke. The gouverneur didn't appear to be bothered by the stench.

Othman gave the duke little time to respond as he gestured across the Hauptplatz in the direction from which Kawn had arrived.

"You had a chance to take a look at our precautions, ja, Mylord?"

Kawn frowned and glanced back across the Hauptplatz. As before, all he could see were the gallows and the two rotting corpses that hung from them.

"You mean the dead nomaden."

He tried his best to keep his voice neutral. He had hoped to cajole the gouverneur with an agreeable attitude of his own, but the sight of the executed männer, paired with Othman's cavalier attitude, left him scrambling for his wits.

The stout mann nodded energetically. "Ach, ja. An example had to be made, Mylord. Two nomaden for two gouverneure, and those were the first two young männer that we captured. Of course, we had captured several nomaden before them, but I couldn't very well execute a mütter and her children or any elderly. The people would have rebelled."

Kawn's gut twisted in a way it hadn't at the stench of death. *Why have I never noticed that Othman is capable of this . . . this . . . horrifying disdain for human life?*

Hoping the horror didn't yet show in his eyes, Kawn asked, "And how long have they been hanging there?"

Othman paused and seemed to consider. "Almost a full siebentäg, I think." He shrugged and smiled once more. "A fine warning it is, too, since I am still alive and well."

Kawn doubted the dead nomaden had as much to do with Othman's continued survival as the wachen's vigilance and willingness to protect their gouverneur. And even that he questioned as he glanced at the surrounding männer. With their faces partially covered, several of them seemed unwilling to hide their disgust at their gouverneur's words.

Soon, they'll be able to do more than simply stand by while Othman speaks so casually of the death of other human beings.

Hoping to move the corpulent mann away from the subject of the dead nomaden, Kawn murmured, "You mentioned other nomaden, my freund." He grimaced as he used the word and hoped it didn't show in his eyes. "How many others have you captured?"

Othman hummed softly, his head tilting to the side as he thought. "Well, not sure exactly. Maybe thirty. Possibly forty. I can't be sure."

"Forty-three, Gouverneur, not including the executed."

Kawn looked sharply to the wache who had answered and recognized the stony-faced mann as Schönestadt's hauptmann, Waller.

Othman blinked and turned to Hauptmann Waller. "Really?" When the hauptmann nodded, Othman hummed and turned back to Kawn. "Well, what do you know? The wachen are more efficient than I thought."

Kawn wasn't sure if the snort following the statement came from a mann or a pferd. Othman didn't seem to notice, and Kawn attempted to move the conversation further.

"Is that just nomaden?"

Thankfully, Waller took up the question without waiting for Othman to try to answer it. "Ja, Mylord. We also have twelve freunde of the nomaden in custody. In fact," he added, directing a glance of something other than his previous stoniness at Othman, "my männer just arrested Heiss Shmied."

Othman nodded. "Ach, a shame that. He was my favorite blacksmith." The gouverneur shrugged. "Ach, well. He is a conspirator against the stadt. It cannot be helped."

The duke's anger finally piqued, but he reined it in as he recognized the opening Othman had provided.

"Ach, ja, the conspirators. In your letter, you mentioned an informant who was willingly giving up these conspirators, Othman. Could you tell me about him?"

The stout mann shrugged. "Can't tell you much, I'm afraid."

Kawn frowned. "What do you mean?"

The mann shrugged again. "Simple, Mylord. The letters we received were anonymous and delivered by . . ." Othman snapped his fingers at Hauptman Waller. "What did Hunder call that verdammt bird?

"I believe the phrase you're looking for is 'silent falke,' Gouverneur."

The answer was not provided by Waller but by another mann approaching the group. None of Kawn's current companions seemed surprised by the mann's appearance, though Othman appeared annoyed.

"I apologize for interrupting, Mylord," the new arrival added, turning to Kawn, "but I couldn't help overhearing and thought I might be of some assistance."

Kawn nodded. "And you—"

"Hunder, we hardly need your assistance," Othman interjected.

Hunder ignored Othman and offered Kawn his hand. "Hunder Wolfmann, Tieremagier for Regierhaus, Mylord."

Kawn took the mann's hand, surprised and impressed. He had heard of the Wolfmanns. They were a well-known familie of Tieremagier that had run the Regierhaus's kennel since its founding.

"Can you tell me anything more about Othman's mystery informant?"

"Only that the falke who delivered the letters was always the same and would never speak, no matter how I asked it to."

A sudden snort and nicker drew Kawn's attention to Shadow, who suddenly hovered at Kawn's back. Hunder frowned at the pferd.

"I don't think I understand the question, Herr . . ."

Shadow snorted and tossed his head, then pawed at the ground. His agitation was obvious, and Kawn wondered just how important this information could be. Hunder shook his head.

"Nein, it wasn't a falke I recognized, but I don't see how that's significant. I can hardly be expected to know every bird in the stadt."

Instead of increasing Shadow's agitation, the words appeared to calm him. The stallion gave Kawn a single nudge with his muzzle before backing away and lowering his head to the grass of the Hauptplatz.

"What was that about?" Othman asked, indignant.

Kawn sighed but turned his attention to placating the gouverneur. He hoped James could make sense of whatever information he had just gained, because Kawn certainly couldn't.

~~*~*

As soon as they parted ways with Kawn, James directed their small group to a nearby tavern. On the way, Sir Leal told them about the events that had unfolded in Machtstadt, especially those surrounding the city's temple.

Well, that explains the nomads' extra bundle, at least, Ferez thought as they entered the tavern.

Now, Ferez found himself settled at a small table in a quiet corner of the tavern, cradling a pint of ale as James and Sir Leal traded stories. He listened, fascinated, as they seemed to alternate between catching up on the last seven years and reminiscing over their shared time at Cosley Estate. He would have felt forgotten, as he often had this season, if not for the many looks and stories that were directed at him as much as each other.

So it was that Ferez learned not only that James was the childhood friend of Gemini Cosley, only child and heir of the late duke of Kensy, but that the two had been nigh inseparable until about a year after the attack. According to James, it was then that he had discovered the spy responsible for the massacre and had taken revenge. Not long after, he'd been taken in by Kephin and had not seen Gemini since.

"Can you be sure Gemini's still well, then?" Ferez had asked uncertainly. To his confusion, his two companions had smiled amusedly in response.

"I haven't seen her," James had answered, "but she's familie, so Flame has kept tabs on her over the jahre, you can be sure." Sir Leal had simply chuckled in response.

When Sir Leal began telling about his time in Caypan after the attack, Ferez offered his own tidbits. The three were sharing anecdotes about Sir Paeter when Ferez noticed James's eyes grow distant. Pausing midsentence, he laid a hand gently on the boy's forearm.

"James?"

He kept his voice calm, despite his worry over his friend's sudden distraction. He idly wondered if Kawn needed their assistance but thought James might move more quickly if that were the case.

It seemed like a full minute had passed before James's purple eyes grew focused once more and settled on Ferez. Immediately, the boy smiled and laid a hand on Ferez's own, squeezing.

"It's good news," he finally murmured, before quickly draining what little remained of his drink and standing. Ferez and Sir Leal followed suit, Sir Leal dropping a few gold onto the table before the younger men could.

"How so?" Ferez asked, even as he squeezed Sir Leal's shoulder in gratitude. He didn't miss the smile James offered the knight.

"I think I know who's been giving away the secrets of the Kreis."

With that, James led the two men out the door and into the streets.

~~*~*

Gemi couldn't help the smile that stretched her lips as Ferez and Sir Leal bombarded her with questions about her sudden pronouncement. She knew she should give her companions more information as she led them through the alleys of Schönestadt. However, Flame had been the one to make the realization, and Gemi hadn't yet caught all the drache's reasoning. Flame might still be learning about humans, but she knew magie and animals well and Gemi trusted her judgment.

"Will yeh a' leas' tell us where we're goin'?" Ferez finally asked, exasperated.

Gemi chuckled and glanced over her shoulder at her freund. "The haus of one of the three members of the Kreis who has yet to be arrested."

Ferez rolled his eyes, a twitch of his lips indicating he knew he'd walked right into that one. Sir Leal beat him to the next obvious question.

"Is there a name to go with this house, so we at least have an idea of who we're dealing with?"

Gemi sighed and ducked under a clothesline strung across the alley. "Rune Handelmann, but he's not the one responsible for this mess."

"James."

A sudden hand on her shoulder pulled Gemi up short, and she turned to find the king watching her with a steady gaze.

"Who's responsible, then? We need to know what we're gettin' into."

Gemi nodded, knowing Ferez was right. She may not be able to explain the reasoning well enough, but she could give them this.

"Poison Clan nomaden," she said, then turned to continue down the alley.

Ferez's hand slid down her arm as she did so, and she ignored the shiver that trailed down her spine in response. Now was not the time to consider the meaning of *that*.

"We can't be sure which clan," she added, sidestepping a drowsing animal, which simply raised its head to eye them as they passed. "But we can be sure there's a Tieremagier, at least."

There was a moment of silence before Ferez muttered hesitantly, "Animal Mage, then."

Gemi smiled over her shoulder at her freund and nodded. "Ja, Animal Mage."

Her smile slipped as she added, "But that's all we can be sure of. Flame hasn't seen any movement from the haus all täg. There's no telling how many nomaden are hiding there, Poison Clan or otherwise."

"Which means we'll be attempting to take them by surprise, but at the same time, we have to be careful who we attack." Sir Leal's voice was calm as he described the dilemma Gemi had been considering.

She nodded. "We'll take a back entrance, similar to the one in Dame Clarimonde's haus." Ferez nodded. "We can work our way through the haus from there. Most likely, those being held captive will be kept farther inside the haus, away from any possible exits."

"Yeh know a general layout o' the house, aye?"

Gemi nodded, not bothering to look at Ferez. She

doubted he would mind. His own voice had been thoughtful. His geist was no doubt focused on the strategy they were forming.

"We'll follow yer lead, then, an' watch yer back. If the layout is anythin' like Dame Clarimonde's, we'll need to be wary of attackers from behind as much as from the front."

Gemi agreed, and they fell into silence. Now that her two companions weren't pestering her for information, Gemi was able to turn her geist back to Flame and request a more thorough explanation. Through the bond, Flame replayed Shadow's conversation with Herr Wolfmann. The drache then proceeded to point out that a "silent falke" meant Tieremagier, and Flame knew that none of the three remaining Kreis members employed one. And since Herr Wolfmann hadn't recognized the bird, it was more likely to belong to the Tieremagier that had sent it, despite Wolfmann's insistence that he couldn't possibly know all the birds in the stadt.

Most Animal Mages do not realize the animals they regularly use for messages and such are part of a select group. Hunder Wolfmann would probably recognize the bird if it had been called from the city rather than brought into it.

"*As for the specific house,*" Flame added, her voice dropping to a hiss, "*once I knew the Poison Clans were involved, I realized there had been very limited movement around the Handelmann house, and quite a bit around the other two.*"

Her hiss turned angry. "*I should have realized it sooner.*"

Gemi sighed and imagined smoothing her hand down Flame's neck. As she hoped, the mental touch soothed the drache's anger somewhat.

"*You couldn't have, Flame,*" she mindspoke softly. "*You didn't know the Poison Clans were involved, so you didn't know a lack of activity was noteworthy. Besides,*" she added with a touch of amusement, *"you haven't exactly been watching the häuser consistently today. You only knew which haus it was through a process of elimination from pure glück, ja?"*

Flame grumbled softly and reluctantly agreed. Leaving her bondmate to her musings, Gemi realized she had found the alley they needed. Motioning for the two männer to stop, she peered at the door that led into the haus of Rune Handelmann.

"Is tha' the door we want, then?" Ferez murmured, softly enough that his voice barely reached her ear. Gemi nodded, even as she imagined the question hovering on his tongue.

And who is that guarding the door?

Through the semi-darkness of the desert nacht, Gemi could see a figure leaning against the alley wall beside the door. Because of the incoming unwetter, the darkness was growing and she couldn't see the person very well.

"Flame?" she asked, knowing the drache had already circled lower in anticipation of their need.

"He is dressed in plainclothes," Flame rumbled. *"I do not see any weapons, but . . ."*

"But if he carries scharfmonde, you wouldn't be able to see them." Gemi sighed, thinking of her own curved blades that lay sheathed at her lower back. If the figure was a nomade in disguise, then like her, he would have his scharfmonde hidden under his tunic.

Without taking her eyes off the sentinel, Gemi turned her head slightly and passed the information on to her companions in a voice just as quiet as the one Ferez had used. A light pressure on her shoulder let her know that Ferez, at least, had heard and understood.

"Then he may or may no' be an enemy," Ferez rejoined.

"Yeh think we could sneak up on him? Knock him out afore he warns anyone we're here?"

Gemi was silent as she considered their options. It was possible they could incapacitate him from a distance, but that would require hurting him, possibly mortally.

And Ferez was correct. They couldn't yet be sure the mann was a nomade, so for now, that was out of the question. Gemi was considering some form of distraction so they could get close, when Flame informed her that Sir Leal was no longer behind her and Ferez. She could do little more than glance over her shoulder and hiss a soft *"What?"* to her bondmate before a long, low whistle pierced the air from the other end of the alley.

Turning her eyes back to the door, she noticed movement from the sentinel's position, but by now, it was too dark to see what he was doing. Thankfully, Flame's vision was unimpaired.

"His hand is at his lower back!"

The drache's words were all Gemi needed to hear. Instead of reaching for her sword or her own scharfmonde as she had originally planned, she dropped her hand down to her right thigh. Quickly slipping a small blade from the leather band she wore around her thigh and depending solely on Flame's sight (a disconcerting task), Gemi threw the knife at the nomade.

A soft grunt, followed by a heavy thump, was the only sound the mann made when her blade hit. Approaching the nomade and kneeling next to him, Gemi retrieved the throwing knife from the mann's neck, verifying Flame's claim that it had landed where Gemi had hoped it would. The soft whistle sounded again, much closer this time, and Gemi lifted her gaze to find her two freunde standing over her.

"Impressive," Sir Leal muttered. "I see you weren't happy with just knowing standard blades, then."

Gemi shrugged and stood, though not before verifying the mann did carry a pair of scharfmonde under his tunic. "I learned what those who took me in were willing to teach."

She frowned at her old tutor then. "And what was that?" she hissed, gesturing down the alley where he had surely stood when he whistled.

"A distraction," Sir Leal answered with a shrug. "I figured we would need one." Gemi gaped at her old mentor. Sir Leal chuckled. "Don't think you're the only one with an idea of the layout of the city, James."

Gemi snapped her mouth shut and frowned.

"Who'd yeh learn tha' from, then?" Ferez whispered, finally drawing her attention away from the knight. The king squatted next to the dead nomade and appeared to be feeling for the wound.

Gemi sheathed the small knife. "The thieves in Tarsur." Trusting Ferez to hold the rest of his curiosity for after the coming fight, she unsheathed a scharfmond and opened the door their fallen feind had been guarding.

~~*~*

Ferez followed James through the door, Sir Leal close behind. He paused to look around as the knight closed the door softly behind them.

Unlike Dame Clarimonde's house, this alley door opened directly onto a corridor. The hallway was softly lit by shaded oil lamps set every couple of body lengths. Across from and underneath several of the lamps, items stood on display, and even some tapestries hung on the walls.

Ferez stepped toward a pedestal to take a closer look at what looked like a piece of tack.

"The Handelmann familie has invested in various businesses and artisans for generations," James explained softly when Ferez asked about the displays. "Each display represents one of their interests, as I understand it."

Ferez hummed in response and turned his attention back to the corridor. Unsheathing their swords, he and Sir Leal followed James down the hallway. Surprisingly, their journey through the corridor was unimpeded. It wasn't until they reached an open doorway that spilled out both firelight and the low tone of soft voices that Ferez remembered these nomads would have been there for almost ten days. They would be comfortable enough not to be monitoring the halls at all times.

When they reached the door, they fell to either side of it, pressing their backs against the wall. From these positions, the words of the room's occupants easily reached them.

"Verdammte magier!" one male voice suddenly spat.

"Halt die klappe!" a female voice hissed sharply. There was a slight pause before she hissed softly, "Those are the häuptling's children you speak of."

The first voice snorted. "I wouldn't care if they were the häuptling himself," he sneered. "If they had done their job correctly from the beginning, we wouldn't still be here."

"And what exactly do you think they could have done more quickly, Trennen?" a second male voice drawled.

"Wolfrik is a powerful Geistmagier," Trennen sneered. "He could have gotten the names we wanted in a single session." The man made a noise of disgust. "Instead, he keeps going back into the mann's geist, and he only brings out a name or two at a time." There was another noise of disgust. "Sometimes, not even that."

There were a few moments of silence. They were broken suddenly by the dull sound of flesh hitting flesh, the sharp scrape of wood on stone, and a soft grunt.

"Dummkopf!" snarled a male voice that hadn't spoken before. "You obviously know nothing of magie. If Wolfrik had attempted to gain all the names at once, he would have destroyed the mann's geist."

"So?" Trennen sneered, his voice sounding thicker than it had earlier. "What care should we have for our feinde's freunde? I still think we should kill them all."

"Of course you do," the woman huffed. "But we want the Kreis to turn on itself. They won't do so if they know the traitor was coerced."

"This verdammt plan depends too much on the reactions of others. I say we—"

Trennen's words were suddenly interrupted by the sound of wood scraping against stone and muffled grunts.

For the first time since they'd taken up their positions around the door, Ferez risked a quick glance around James and into the room. Two men grappled with each other, one standing above the other, who appeared to be attempting to rise from the chair he sat in.

The scuffle didn't last long. It ended with a sharp wheeze as the standing man punched the seated man in the stomach. Ferez quickly pulled himself back against the wall as the victor jerked the other man to his feet.

"You are too hotheaded, Trennen," someone—Ferez assumed it was the victor—growled. "It would be best if you went to your room to cool off."

James suddenly motioned sharply with one scharfmond, though Ferez didn't need the warning. Two sets of footsteps, one strong and steady, the other stumbling, approached the door they were flanking. Ferez brought his sword up across his body and tightened his grip on the hilt.

The stumbling nomad was first through the door. Ferez caught a glimpse of a purpling jaw and widening eyes before James's scharfmond sliced him across the back of his shoulder. As the man cried out and stumbled forward, James stepped away from the wall to follow. The movement turned James's back to the doorway and the second nomad.

Surprise flitted across the second nomad's face, but the man didn't hesitate to pull his left scharfmond. Even as the man swung at James's back, Ferez stepped in behind the boy, raising his sword to block the attack.

When the scharfmond met his sword, however, it didn't stop. Instead, his own blade slid along the curve of the nomad's, leaving Ferez's chest vulnerable. Cursing, he attempted to twist his body away from the nomad's strike. His voice dropped to a hiss as sharp steel bit into his left shoulder.

The nomad smirked as his blow landed, and he twisted the blade and pushed, knocking Ferez back against the wall and driving the blade deeper into his shoulder. The next moment he was gone, and Ferez groaned. The pain had flared brighter as the weapon was ripped from the wound.

"Frenz!" someone called urgently.

A pair of hands gripped Ferez's face, pulling his attention from the pain. He blinked open his eyes, surprised to realize he had closed them. James held him and searched his face, the worry in his eyes more powerful than Ferez had expected.

"Are you all right? Can you stand?"

The king frowned. The whispered words were concerned and urgent, but they didn't make any sense. It was just a shoulder wound, but James made it sound like he'd been incapacitated. Yet . . .

He pushed past the pain so he could take in his surroundings. To his surprise, he was on the floor, slumped against the wall. His sword lay nearby, and while he couldn't remember doing so, he had the impression he'd dropped it before he'd slid down the wall, rather than afterward.

I shouldn't have released it at all, he thought, confused. *It wasn't my sword arm that was injured.* He groaned. *And I'm usually much better at handling pain from this kind of wound.*

The pain in his shoulder suddenly flared, and he hissed. *All right, so it's been a while since I've been injured this badly.*

He stiffened. "Frenz?" he heard someone whisper again, but that last thought had shocked him.

That isn't true. Images of large cats passed through his mind, and he shivered.

Maybe not. The thought slid through his mind smoothly. *But it's been a while since I've been this badly injured and remained conscious.*

Ferez might have accepted the thought as his own if it hadn't been for the previous one. Now, as his mind grew hazier with increasing pain, he remembered that the nomads had mentioned a Geistmagier: a Mindspeaker.

"James."

The word came out as barely a whisper, and he had to open his eyes again—they weren't going to stay open for long. James eyed him worriedly and nodded when Ferez met his gaze.

"The nomads . . . they mentioned a . . ." He paused and took a deep breath. He tried to push past the pain, which seemed to have radiated to other parts of his body. "A Min'speaker?"

A sigh slid through his mind as his eyes once again closed against his will. This time, he had no trouble differentiating the other's words from his own.

"Es tut mir leid, freund, but you will feel better with sleep."

A sharp burst of pain engulfed his mind, dropping him into oblivion.

Thirteen

Ferenz?" Gemi cried out as Ferez's head lolled to one side. His body collapsed back against the wall. Even as she tried to get him to open his eyes and look at her again, she knew he wouldn't be able to.

"James." Sir Leal gripped her shoulder.

She looked back at him. She knew her eyes were wide, but so much had happened recently. She couldn't stand to see Ferez like this again.

"We should bind his wound. Then we need to decide if we want to retreat or continue on."

Gemi frowned and turned back to Ferez. Pulling his tunic to the side, she grimaced as she examined the wound. It wasn't life threatening yet, but the nomade had managed to part the flesh more than a simple cut would have and she could see bone. He would need to see a Heilemagier as soon as possible. Briefly wishing she had her pack with her, she began to tear strips of fabric from Ferez's tunic.

As she worked on her freund's shoulder, Sir Leal stood over them, keeping watch on the door they'd previously fought around and the hallway through which they'd come. They had managed to dispatch the five nomaden quickly. After taking out Trennen, which had not taken long since he had still been recovering from his scuffle with the other nomade, Gemi had gutted the mann who had been holding Ferez.

She hadn't been able to focus on the king until the kitchen, the room on which they'd been eavesdropping, had been emptied. However, the fact that a great swordsman like him could be injured so quickly had reminded Gemi that she hadn't had time to train him in fighting against nomaden. Using a straight blade against scharfmonde required certain techniques that were only taught in Zhulan. As she knelt in front of her freund, she cursed their busy schedule and swore to find time to teach him the necessary techniques.

"James." Gemi paused only briefly to let Flame know she was listening. *"Frenz was right; there is a Mindspeaker there. I can feel him attempting to access your mind."*

Gemi smiled grimly, even as she finished wrapping Ferez's wound to her satisfaction. *"Any chance you can take advantage of that?"*

She knew drachen were capable Geistmagier, but Flame hadn't fully grown into her magie yet. Even so, it had been a while since Flame had attempted to defeat an unknown Geistmagier on the battleground of his own geist.

"I do not know." Gemi felt Flame grow distant and knew she was attempting to breach the magier's geist.

Standing, Gemi informed Sir Leal of the situation. The knight grimaced. "You'd have a better protection against him than I would, I think."

Gemi nodded. Ever since they had first met Tante Isa, Flame had had mental barriers set up around all three of their geister. She had set them up as a precaution against Gemi's true identity being discovered, but they doubled as protections against this kind of attack, as well.

Glancing back down at Ferez, Gemi sighed. "I would prefer to move forward since we're already here, but we can't just leave Frenz alone like this."

She turned back to her old mentor. "And if we leave now, the Poison Clans will know we're onto them and we may not get another chance."

For the second time that evening, Gemi felt torn about what to do. *And the person I've come to depend on in such times of indecision is now wounded and unconscious.*

A hand on her shoulder drew Gemi's attention back to Sir Leal. The knight looked worried but determined.

"If you think it's necessary to finish this now, you should continue on." He grimaced. "As much as I hate the idea of you going in by yourself, your skill far exceeds my own and you're better protected from the Mindspeaker. You know the layout of the house, aye?"

Gemi nodded and knelt next to Ferez once more. She lightly brushed the impromptu bandage with her fingers and then her freund's face. "And you'll stay and watch over Frenz?"

"Of course." Sir Leal's voice was soft yet determined.

Gemi nodded again, more sharply this time, and stood. With a quick wave to the knight, Gemi unsheathed her scharfmonde and headed back down the corridor in the direction from which they'd come.

She took the first side hallway, knowing it would lead her deeper into the haus and closer to more Poison Clan nomaden and those they held hostage.

~~*~*

When Flame agreed to try to do something about the
Mindspeaker, she had not expected to make much progress.
The last time she had attempted to enter a Mindspeaker's
mind unwelcome, she had barely grazed the surface.

Of course, that had been six years ago, when she and her
bondmates had first arrived in Zhulan. After that incident,
Flame had decided to remain on the defensive when it came
to mind magic. As a result, her defensive mental magic was
more powerful than any human Mindspeaker could break.

Now, however, defense only was not an option. While
the Mindspeaker in the Handelmann haus could not harm
Gemi with his magic, Flame's bondmate was not the only
human at risk. The Mindspeaker had already incapacitated
Ferez, something for which Flame would gladly repay him.

Ignoring the questions that cropped up with that
thought—she still wondered at how quickly she herself had
come to consider the king family—Flame felt along the
barriers of Gemi's mind. The Mindspeaker was subtle, and it
took the dragon a couple minutes before she found his
presence.

Instead of assaulting the barrier like Flame would have
expected, he lightly tested it here and there, feeling it out for
any cracks or weaknesses, and he was thorough. Flame
realized, with a jolt of surprise and respect, that if any
Mindspeaker could break through the barriers she had set up
around Gemi's mind, this man could.

Wolfrik, she thought, tasting the name that Gemi had
overheard.

The other nomads had mentioned he was the son of a
häuptling, though Flame could not tell which one since all the
nomads so far had been dressed in plainclothes. She
wondered idly if he was the eldest of his siblings. Despite his

current activities, Flame thought he was a man she could respect in a position of power.

A sharp hiss suddenly drew Flame's attention. *"As much as I appreciate the compliment, Dame Flammezunge,"* a voice growled lowly in her mind, *"you could have offered it a little more gently."*

Panicking, Flame struck out wildly with her mind as she searched for the Mindspeaker's presence. The more she searched for it, the more she realized she did not recognize the mental landscape through which she moved.

"Gratuliere, Dame Flammezunge," the Mindspeaker grunted testily. *"Somehow, you managed to bypass my barriers without even noticing."*

The thought *And with so little effort at that* sardonically trailed the direct words.

Flame stilled. She had latched onto the Mindspeaker's magic where it had touched her bondmate's mind. She had hoped to follow the magic back to the man's mind since she had doubted her ability to seek out and penetrate his mind otherwise. She had not expected the process to work so well.

"I suspect that has to do with the knowledge of mental defenses you must have if your own are anything to go by." The mind she occupied shifted uncomfortably. *"Interesting technique, I must admit."*

With her mind still, Flame recognized mental pain behind the man's words and radiating from the surrounding mind. She had not caused pain in another mind since the early days of her bond with Gemi and Shadow. She hesitated when she sensed it. She did not like causing such pain to her bondmates nor, it seemed, even to her enemies.

Thoughts tumbled through the Mindspeaker's mind, surprise coloring them. *"Even though I caused such pain to your freund?"* The voice held a note of curiosity. *"Just a moment ago, you wished to repay me for that."*

Startled, Flame realized the voice held no trace of hostility toward her, despite her invasion of his mind and the mental anguish she caused him. The thought *I have felt worse* slipped along her mind, and she twisted her head, curious. The thought had held more than a touch of bitterness.

"Who are you?"

She could not prevent incredulity from seeping into her tone. This human was nothing like what she had expected from a Poison Clan Mindspeaker.

There was a pause, the "silence" broken only by the considering thoughts that filled the man's mind. Hesitantly, the Mindspeaker answered. *"My name is Wolfrik Giftschwanz."* The words held a touch of subdued pride, as if the man was proud of his identity but had learned that others would not be.

"Skorpion," Flame muttered, immediately recognizing the last name. The Skorpion Clan's häuptling had borne the name Giftschwanz—literally "venom tail" in their tongue—since the clan had first formed.

"Of course," Wolfrik replied, the pride in his voice stronger.

The sudden suspicion filled Flame that it was his own clan who had taught Wolfrik that others would not appreciate his true self. A mental snort echoed through the man's mind, but he otherwise ignored the thought he surely must have heard.

"And to address one of your previous questions," the Mindspeaker added, drawing Flame from her contemplations, *"I am the youngest of my brüder. Only my schwester, Käfe, is younger than I am."*

Wolfrik must have heard Flame's thought on his sister's name because he huffed quietly. *"Ja, her name is derived from our word that would translate into 'beetle' in your tongue."* Flame had the sudden sense that the man was rolling his eyes as his voice turned bitter. *"It refers to her Kräftetier, but she was also given the name in derision."*

The man's obvious bitterness increased Flame's curiosity. Distinctly aware of the pain she had caused him before, Flame attempted to lighten her presence in his mind, hoping the techniques she used in dealing with her bondmates would translate into the minds of strangers.

Once satisfied she would cause him minimal pain, Flame began to explore the surrounding mental terrain. A soft growl filled her mental ears as she lightly touched on various thoughts and memories. As it seemed to be fueled more by anger and less by pain, Flame ignored it.

The deeper into the memories she went, the more resistance she met. It was not until she found herself faced with a form of resistance mentally resembling a securely locked box guarded by a snarling animal that Flame paused in her exploration.

As Flame eyed the image of the snarling beast, she found herself oddly disappointed. She had thought the Mindspeaker subtle, but the use of this kind of creature to guard one's most precious secrets drew the attention of an invader all too well.

She was gathering her magic to begin dissecting this piece of resistance when the irony of the thought occurred to her. Releasing the gathered magic, the dragon turned from the image of the now-snapping animal. Casting her mind about the nearby terrain, she sought something less obvious, something that would not draw the mental eye quite so well.

As she did, she could feel panic rising around her, and she allowed herself a small baring of her teeth. She had turned her attention to a portion of the mental terrain that resembled an open field when she felt the protective beast from before lunge for her presence. However, the Mindspeaker had complimented her knowledge of mental defense earlier and rightly so. Her own defenses were still in place, so the lunging beast simply met her barriers and bounced off them ineffectually.

"You are slipping, Wolfrik Giftschwanz." Flame immediately regretted the taunt. The man may be a Skorpion, but there was no reason for her to add insult to injury.

Softening her tone, she added, *"Panic does not help your defense. It only leads your enemy where you do not want her to go."*

Then, to prove her point, the dragon snapped up the single beetle she had spotted hiding in the field.

Immediately, images tumbled through her mind, and she quickly realized the significance of the beetle guarding the Mindspeaker's most guarded secrets. As he had mentioned before, his sister's Power Animal was the beetle, and while she might have been female and younger than he was, she was apparently the only person he trusted.

After only a minute of viewing the onslaught of memories, that singular trust was more than understandable. When the dragon first came upon the more distressing memories, she did not want to believe what she was seeing. When Wolfrik's mind began to snarl and thrash around her presence, she knew she was interpreting the images correctly.

Along with the realization came horror.

Image after image filled her mind, seeming to span many years and various instances. In all the images, it was obvious that, out of all their siblings, the brother and sister were inseparable.

However, that was not what shook Flame. What did was the way the two were treated by the people they should have been able to consider family. Flame watched, disturbed, as the two children were belittled and pushed aside. She saw memories, too many for her taste, of times when both had been beaten by their older brothers.

However, despite these horrors, none of it compared to the treatment they received at the hands of the man who had sired them.

Never had Flame met a creature, human or magical, who was willing to use mind magic on their offspring for reasons other than communication and dire emergencies. That the man who had sired them had continually torn through their minds with his magic from such a young age made Flame see red, and she pulled back from the memories roughly. She idly noted that when she mentally dropped the beetle she had grabbed, it scurried away, shaking.

"That is how the Skorpion Clan treats their children?" Flame was too shocked to mind the strength of her presence, and Wolfrik's mind shuddered around her.

He answered hesitantly. *"Nein."*

He seemed ready to leave it at that, but Flame mentally prodded him. He winced. *"That is how our häuptling treats his children if they don't do as he says or live up to his expectations."* His voice held no resistance now, only a tired resignation. *"He considered us weak, and as we are the youngest and his expectations of us were therefore higher, we could never satisfy him."*

Flame growled. This man had endured immeasurable mental anguish at the hands of someone he should have been able to trust, and he was still sane. Considering some of the memories she had seen, he had even learned to protect his sister from an early age and eventually build his own defenses such that their sire had not even realized his mental attacks were, by this age, ineffectual. That anyone would consider this man weak . . .

"I would never consider a Mindspeaker and man of your abilities weak, Wolfrik Giftschwanz."

The thought-filled silence from before returned, and Flame could feel the heavy touch of his regard. Suddenly, part of his mind gave before her. *"Danke. You might be surprised by how gratifying it is to hear such praise from a drache like yourself, Dame Flammezunge."*

Flame paused. The name he had used was a literal translation of her name into Zhulanese. She had not heard it since the first seasons she and her bondmates had lived with the nomads. It had taken several months of determined insistence on her part to get the nomads to call her Flame instead.

However, this was not the first time he had called her this, and to her surprise, she recognized a deep respect in his use of it.

For a moment, Flame considered him. Now that she had seen his most sordid secrets, he seemed to relax under her presence. The dragon wondered briefly if the man had expected her to react to the memories with disgust for him rather than respect. Putting the thought aside for now, Flame turned to find that the snarling beast from before was gone. She knew that might have been attributed to the man's relaxed state, but she doubted he could relax his defenses that much.

Turning her attention to the chest the beast had been guarding, she found it now resembled a simple box, unlocked and easily opened.

"You wanted me to open this?" Shock froze her briefly: The man had used the beast to draw her attention on purpose. He had wanted her to bypass these defenses. *"But why?"*

Wolfrik did not answer. Instead, the box slid open, and memories poured over her—more quickly than any others had before. The speed did not hinder her understanding; the Mindspeaker simply seemed to be in a hurry.

"Your bondmate is getting closer."

The memories flowing through her mind were much more recent than the others had been. Wolfrik's sire had assigned this task to both him and his sister, not realizing his attempt at imposing his will on his youngest children had failed.

Instead of immediately seeking out the information he had been tasked to, Wolfrik had spent much of his "sessions" with Rune Handelmann conversing with the investor and learning about him and the work he did.

Occasionally, Wolfrik would pull a name or two from the man's mind to keep his sire's men happy, but he proclaimed that the process was slow because they did not want to draw the suspicions of anyone, now or once they had left. When Käfe sent the names off to the governor, she purposefully silenced the bird, hoping to draw suspicions from that side.

Throughout it all, Wolfrik had worked his magic into the minds of his sire's men, preparing his magic to drop them into sleep the moment someone came to rescue the Handelmann family.

Flame pulled herself from the memories as she recognized the significance of that last information.

"You have already dropped the other Skorpione into sleep?" At the Mindspeaker's affirmation, she narrowed her eyes. *"Then why did you incapacitate Frenz?"*

A tired sigh brushed against Flame's mind.

"Es tut mir leid. I had not expected to, but the wound he received was a terrible one. I did not wish for him to suffer needlessly, not when the fighting was already over."

Flame considered his words. *"And if you had not incapacitated him?"*

"If he had attempted to fight with such a wound, which I am sure he would have, it most likely would have resulted in permanent damage."

Flame winced. That was something for which Flame was sure Gemi would not have forgiven herself. Flame was suddenly grateful to the Mindspeaker.

"Perhaps you could pass that gratitude on, dame." Wolfrik's words were rushed, and Flame eyed him curiously as he attempted to push her from his mind. *"Your bondmate is almost upon us!"*

Startled, Flame slipped out of Wolfrik's mind. Once fully in her own, Flame turned to Gemi's and was shocked to find rage overwhelming the girl's thoughts.

Cursing, Flame plunged herself into her bondmate's mind.

~~*~*

When Gemi came across the first body, she knelt beside it and placed her fingers at its throat. The pulse she found there was strong and steady, but the mann didn't react to her touch. Frowning, she hauled the mann onto his back, noting, as she did, the bulge under his plainclothes where his scharfmonde lay.

Despite bearing no visible signs of damage, the nomade still didn't move. Deciding he would pose no threat to her, Gemi left his side and continued down the corridor.

Farther down that hallway, she found two more unconscious bodies. One lay sprawled across the corridor, while the other sat propped up against the wall. Together, they flanked a door that was closed and barred. This door, Gemi knew, led to a room most often used to house visiting

nomaden. Gemi suspected, and thought the unconscious
wachen confirmed, that it still housed those nomaden who
had been there when the Poison Clan nomaden arrived. It
was the reason she had headed in this specific direction.

Checking the two unconscious nomaden, Gemi found
them in a similar state as the first. She eyed the sprawling
nomade—the position had to be painful—but left both as
they had landed, turning her attention instead to the door.
Knowing the Poison Clans would not guard a room for no
reason, Gemi gave the door a light rap with her knuckles.
Almost immediately, a stifled gasp filtered through the door,
confirming there was indeed someone trapped within.

Making short work of the bar that crossed it, Gemi
quickly opened the door. As soon as it was open wide enough
for her to pass through, a pair of hands roughly grabbed her
shoulders and propelled her backward. Not to be surprised
again after Raymond's assault only a few nächte before, Gemi
planted one foot and allowed her attacker's momentum to
carry him past her and into the wall opposite the door.

As footsteps sounded behind her, Gemi gripped the
mann's shoulders and forced him back against the wall as he
would have done to her. She allowed herself only a few
seconds to note that he still wore his kopfabdeckung and
statusgürtel—the bright blue of which declared him a Falke—
before she murmured a low, forceful "Ruhe, bruder!"

The words had the effect she desired. The footsteps
behind her faded, and the Falke she held against the wall
jerked his head to one side and eyed her warily. That wariness
faded as recognition widened his eyes.

"Drache Krieger?" His voice was sharp with confusion.

Gemi nodded and released her grip on the mann's tunic.
"Ja, I am."

She glanced away from the Falke then, taking in the faces

and statusgürtel of the surrounding nomaden. There were seven in all: an elderly frau, a young child, and the rest were young männer.

"Are you all well?"

The seven nodded, though the frau muttered, "As much as can be expected when we've been locked in here for täge."

A tug on her statusgürtel called Gemi's attention down to the child, a young girl who looked to be no older than Ava. "Ja?"

"Why did you take so long to open the door, Drache Krieger?" Gemi furrowed her brow in confusion. Before she could ask for clarification, the girl pointed to the fallen männer. "We heard the Skorpione drop several minutes ago. Why did you wait so long before opening the door?"

Gemi frowned. She hadn't considered the implications of the unconscious nomaden before since she had been intent on seeking out the nomade hostages. Now, her thoughts turned to the Geistmagier that both Ferez and Flame had mentioned.

She knew only a Geistmagier or a Heilemagier would be able to make a person unconscious with no physical trace of the cause, but it didn't make sense. According to the nomaden they'd overheard before, the Geistmagier was the son of a häuptling. He would have no reason to help them.

Unless this is a trap. She glanced sharply at the two fallen nomaden. *If the Geistmagier can bring them to consciousness as quickly and easily as he knocked them unconscious . . .*

"Drache Krieger?" The girl's voice brought Gemi back to the situation at hand, and she shook her head.

"I'm not the one who knocked out the Skorpione, young one."

"You mean," a Wolf spoke up, "you have an ally here?"

Gemi shook her head again and glanced up and down

the hallway. "I'm afraid it's not that simple, freund. It could be a trap."

"How so?" asked the old frau.

Gemi focused on the frau. She, too, wore the blue statusgürtel of the Falke Clan, as did the child, but for the first time, Gemi noticed their statusgürtel were dyed at both ends. She gasped suddenly.

"You—"

The frau smiled fiercely and repeated, "How might it be a trap, child?"

Gemi grimaced at the implied rebuke but understood. Whether the other nomaden, those not from the same clan, had recognized who the frau and girl were, they didn't need Gemi drawing their attention to the fact.

Even so, she had finally recognized who the two were. The frau was Valborga, former häuptling of the Falke Clan and mütter of the current one. The girl had to be Lakritze, youngest daughter of the Falke Clan's häuptling and a Heilemagier. The last thought reminded Gemi sharply of Ferez's wound.

"The Skorpione have no visible injuries," Gemi finally said, answering Valborga's question. "It's most likely the work of the Geistmagier."

The frau nodded. "Wolfrik Giftschwanz." She must have noticed Gemi's surprise because she added, "He was insistent on introducing himself to us."

"Mentally?" Gemi asked, horrified. Her horror faded as all seven shook their heads.

"Nein," the frau answered. "It seemed he only wished to let us know who he was."

Gemi frowned and gestured to the männer on the floor. "We should probably stay wary of the unconscious Skorpione. We don't know what Giftschwanz has planned."

The others nodded, though Valborga continued to look thoughtful.

"Now, I came from the alley door and the kitchens, so we should probably head toward the main living quarters next. That's most likely where they're keeping Herr Handelmann and his familie."

The five männer agreed, and showing that they all still carried their scharfmonde—and why the Skorpione hadn't confiscated them, Gemi couldn't fathom—they quickly continued down the corridor. When Valborga and Lakritze made to follow, Gemi gripped the frau's arm. Valborga turned narrowed eyes on Gemi, but Gemi hurried to speak before she could follow the glare with a reprimand.

"I didn't come here alone, dame." Gemi kept her voice low, not wanting the other nomaden to overhear. "But one of my freunde was wounded and I was forced to leave them behind at the kitchens." Gemi glanced down at the girl, then back up at her grossmütter. "If you don't mind, I would appreciate it if the young one could do something for him."

Valborga harrumphed softly and laid a hand on Lakritze's shoulder, but her eyes had softened. Before she could answer, the girl nodded enthusiastically.

"Anything for a freund of the Drache Krieger."

"Lakritze!" the frau hissed sharply, confirming Gemi's assumptions.

The young Heilemagier turned a glare of her own up at her grossmütter and crossed her arms over her chest.

"I want to help, Oma, and I certainly can't fight. After the Drache Krieger saved us, the least I can do is Heal his freund."

For a moment, the two glared at each other, which Gemi would have found amusing if the situation hadn't been so dire. Thankfully, Valborga seemed to remember their situation, too.

With a sigh, she directed her gaze back to Gemi. "The kitchens, you said?"

Gemi nodded and watched as the elder frau led her charge back in the direction from which Gemi had come. As they disappeared around a corner, Gemi turned around and ran to catch up with the other nomaden.

They passed several more fallen Skorpione before they reached the main living quarters of the haus. They were closer to the front now, though there were still entertaining- and business-related rooms farther toward the front. Those, Gemi knew, wouldn't have seen activity since the katastrophe began.

She led the way toward Rune Handelmann's bedroom. Most might find her intimate knowledge of the haus uncomfortable, but she and several others had investigated the haus of each member of the Kreis before they'd been allowed to use them as safe häuser.

To her surprise, the bedroom door was open. Gemi warily stepped through and hesitated when she found six people unconscious around the room. Only two, a frau and a mann, still stood, and burning anger flooded Gemi as she realized that the mann must be the Geistmagier who had incapacitated Ferez. She growled as her vision narrowed to the single mann and red seemed to color everything.

"You!" she snarled lowly.

She was vaguely aware of unsheathing her scharfmonde as she rushed the Geistmagier, but no other thoughts filled her geist beyond repaying this mann for his treatment of her freund. He deserved nothing less.

She was only a couple steps away from him when her vision suddenly tilted and her geist became overfull with a presence she recognized all too well. Stumbling to a halt, she slammed her eyes shut against the sudden oddness of her vision.

"Flame!" She wasn't sure if the cry had been verbal as the drache had forced her to suddenly focus solely on the mental.

"He is not the enemy, James!" Flame's hiss filled Gemi's geist, and she winced at the mental fullness she felt.

"How can you say that, Flame? After what he did to Frenz—"

Flame sighed, and the fullness shifted. *"Do you not trust me?"* Gemi winced at the sadness in her bondmate's voice, and her anger eased.

"Of course I trust you."

"Then believe me when I say he is not the enemy, but a potential ally." Gemi frowned. *"Just let him explain. Please!"*

She added the last with a force that surprised Gemi and leeched the remaining anger from her geist.

"All right," she offered softly. *"I'll listen."*

Flame nodded and finally eased the fullness of her presence from Gemi's geist. Gemi winced as she did and wondered idly if Flame's magie had increased during her encounter with the Geistmagier.

Once she could see again, Gemi stared at the conscious mann and forced herself to really see him. Unlike his fellow Skorpione, he still wore his kopfabdeckung and statusgürtel, which bore the double brown of a noble Skorpion. The frau beside him wore the same.

Also, while she and the nomaden who had entered with her all had their scharfmonde unsheathed, neither Skorpione had reached for a blade. Instead, the mann had one arm raised in surrender, the other holding his schwester partially behind him for protection. Gemi was sharply reminded of her own familie and the love and loyalty she held for them. With a sharp slash through the air with one scharfmond, she silenced the shouting, of which she had only been half aware, and brought the mann's attention fully to her.

"You would turn against your own familie?"

Her words might have been harsher than necessary, but she could not imagine turning her back on those she loved.

The mann—*Wolfrik,* Flame sharply reminded her—took a small step forward, raising his second hand to show he would not go for his scharfmonde. He shook his head as he did, the glance he offered her both tired and bitter.

"Käfe is the only one of them I have ever considered my familie, Drache Krieger." Gemi quirked an eyebrow at the use of her title. The Poison Clans usually insisted on not using it, believing her unworthy.

"And the trust they've placed in you?"

Her words were softer than before. The mann's willingness to consider her a nomade despite her birth set him apart from any other Poison Clan nomaden she had ever met.

Wolfrik snorted and shook his head again. "They do not trust us, Drache Krieger. They never have."

He met Gemi's gaze, and she was caught by the sadness that lay in the back of his eyes. It looked like it had settled there permanently.

"The six warriors you see here were simply meant to keep us in line, not to protect us. And that was only after our häuptling thought he had imposed his wille over ours."

Gemi jerked back a step. She wouldn't have thought much of those last words if she hadn't remembered that Häuptling Giftschwanz was also a Geistmagier. A shudder ran through her as she considered the implications.

"Your own vater—"

"He is *not* my vater!" Wolfrik nearly shouted, his eyes wild.

The next moment, he jerked his head back and his eyes widened. His startled expression mirrored what Gemi herself felt.

After a moment of heavy silence, the mann grimaced and cast his gaze to the side. "He is my häuptling," he muttered. "That is all."

"Bruder." Käfe laid a hand on Wolfrik's arm and stepped up to his side. To Gemi's surprise, the fräulein hardly looked older than her. "Don't exert yourself."

Wolfrik snorted, but he laid a hand over hers and offered her a small smile.

Gemi watched the two with interest. Wolfrik seemed to relax under Käfe's hand, and the fräulein returned his smile with a larger one of her own. For that moment, the two seemed to forget they weren't alone.

"All right," Gemi finally spoke, startling the pair and bringing their attention back to her. "I believe I understand."

Wolfrik's gaze turned wary, but Gemi offered him a small smile, hoping to express that he could trust her, if no one else.

After a moment, Wolfrik nodded, and his gaze relaxed.

"You do, don't you, Drache Krieger? You, who have chosen your own familie these past several jahre, would understand if anyone could."

Gemi chuckled quietly. She hadn't considered that, yet she couldn't help but agree. Except . . .

"It's James." The Geistmagier blinked and frowned, and she chuckled again. "Call me James," she insisted. "I imagine, since you are turning your back on your häuptling, that you will come with me to see the erstehäuptling?" Wolfrik nodded slowly. "I'm sure we'll get to know each other ein bisschen better, then, ja?"

Thinking of travel, Gemi once again remembered Ferez. "Although, I do have one more question."

"About your freund." Wolfrik made it a statement, and Gemi frowned. The Geistmagier sighed. "I did not mean to cause him so much pain."

"So you did increase his pain levels?" Wolfrik raised his eyebrows, looking surprised. "I mean, I thought you must have since Frenz recognized your presence. He shouldn't have been able to with how subtle Flame says your magie is."

Wolfrik chuckled, but the sound was sad and tired.

"It was a bad wound. You saw it. You must understand what I mean."

Gemi nodded. The way the attacking nomade had managed to part Ferez's flesh had looked extremely painful.

"I was only attempting to knock him unconscious so he wouldn't have to suffer through it, or worse, force himself to fight with it."

Gemi winced. If Ferez had fought with such a wound, she knew it could have caused much worse damage than just torn flesh.

"But you caused him a lot of pain," she insisted. "I watched him suffer through that."

Wolfrik sighed. "Es tut mir leid. I had started at a surface level of his geist only, where the senses are the easiest to manipulate. It takes more effort and some time to subtly and safely dig deeper to the level on which I can easily drop a mann into sleep."

He shook his head. "I had hoped to overwhelm him with the pain and cause him to black out, but . . ."

He shrugged helplessly.

Gemi sighed in turn. "You didn't expect Frenz to be able to fight through that level of pain."

He nodded. "It did almost work, actually, but he came

back from the brink of unconsciousness, which I hadn't expected." He smiled then. "He is an amazing mann, your freund, truly worthy of his place."

The final words made Gemi frown. They didn't make sense until Gemi caught the pointed look Wolfrik offered her. She stiffened.

"You dug further down into his geist." The Skorpion's nod was simple confirmation.

"It was the only way I could make him sleep, of which he was in desperate need by then." His lips twitched into a small smile. "But you don't need to worry about any knowledge I might have gained in doing so. I swear on my life as a Skorpion that I will pose no threat to your freund."

It was Gemi's turn to eye Wolfrik warily, but the Geistmagier met her gaze steadily. After a moment, she nodded. She didn't need Flame's confirmation of his sincerity to realize he was speaking the truth.

"Very well," she said, finally turning away from the Skorpion. The five other männer were ranged out behind her and still had their scharfmonde unsheathed. She waved at them to put the blades away.

"We're safe here. Of that, I believe we can be sure."

"But what about Herr Handelmann and his familie, Drache Krieger?" a Spinne asked. "We haven't found them yet."

Gemi glanced at Wolfrik, who answered easily. "The familie is in the children's rooms. They are safe, I swear."

"And we still have an unknown number of unconscious Skorpione to worry about, Drache Krieger." Even as the Falke spoke, he and the others reluctantly sheathed their blades. "Surely you don't expect them to stay unconscious for the entire time we will be here. We still don't know when we will be allowed to leave the stadt."

Gemi chuckled. "Soon, I imagine." Not giving the others a chance to respond, she turned back to Wolfrik. "Are there any among the unconscious who might be persuaded to become loyal to you rather than the current häuptling?"

The Skorpion shook his head. "The häuptling only sent those with us that would do as he said. He didn't want to take any chances."

Gemi grinned. "Apparently, he's been underestimating your power for some time." She chuckled and shook her head. "Very well, I'll have no qualms, then, with turning all of the unconscious Skorpione over to the wachen."

Gasps came from every side of her, even the Skorpione, and the Spinne who'd spoken before even gripped her arm.

"You are working with the wachen, Drache Krieger?"

Gemi thought her grin might split her face. "Rather they are working with us, freund. Even now—"

She was interrupted by a series of amused snorts filling her head, and she turned her attention to her pferd bondmate.

"Shadow, what is it?"

Shadow continued to snort and even gave a loud whinny, his version of a full-bellied laugh. Once the laughter had began to calm, he finally managed to answer.

"Lord Kawn just ordered the city guards to arrest Othman. The pompous beast actually had the audacity to act confused!"

Gemi sighed as he dissolved into snickering snorts once more.

"Has Lord Kawn decided on a new gouverneur, then?"

Shadow sighed, letting the laughter dissipate finally. *"Aye, he has."* He offered Gemi an image of Lord Kawn talking seriously with Dame Clarimonde of all people.

Gemi blinked. *"Really? This is no witz?"*

Shadow tossed his head in denial. *"Oh, it's true, all right. I'm not really surprised, either. We all know how stern and political Dame Clarimonde can be. I can't think of anyone better, myself."*

Gemi nodded. She was a bit surprised Lord Kawn would choose a frau, but she really shouldn't have been. In Zhulan, frauen had always been seen as having the potential for leadership that they hadn't been allowed in other regions.

The light touch of a hand on her arm drew her attention back to the room in which she stood. "Drache Krieger?"

Gemi turned her gaze on the fräulein who now stood beside her. Käfe blinked up at her with large eyes, and Gemi couldn't help the smile that spread her lips.

"James," she insisted. Like Wolfrik, Käfe would be returning to Helloase with them, and Gemi didn't relish being addressed by her formal title for that length of time. However, she was surprised when the fräulein dropped her chin, allowing the edge of her kopfabdeckung to droop over her eyes. When she lifted her eyes to stare up at Gemi through her lashes, Gemi groaned inwardly.

Verdammte frauen, she cursed in her thoughts.

This wasn't the first time she had garnered such attention from other fräulein, but she generally tried to avoid giving the impression that she was returning the attention. She thought she might have just made a mistake.

"Females," Shadow nickered, amused. *"Such tricky creatures."*

Gemi rolled her eyes and gave a mental swat to the stallion's rump, but her freund only snorted in response.

Tentatively, she patted Käfe's hand and prayed to the götter that she would not make the sudden situation with the fräulein worse. Turning her attention to the other nomaden, she began to explain the new alliance with Lord Kawn and the changes he would be making in the städte. As she did, she focused part of her geist on Shadow once more.

"Can you ask Lord Kawn and Gouverneur Clarimonde to send us some wachen, Shadow?" She paused a moment to consider and added, *"And a Heilemagier if one is available. I don't wish Lakritze to exhaust herself in an attempt to fully Heal Frenz."*

Shadow agreed, and Gemi turned to Flame.

"Can you send a message to Helloase requesting they postpone the Skorpion's interrogation? I want to give Wolfrik the chance to speak for the mann before Tante Isa causes any permanent damage."

Flame murmured her own agreement before drifting off in search of a willing falke. With her messages sent, Gemi turned her full attention to the nomaden surrounding her. Their shocked questions, she knew, would require it.

Fourteen

"**W**ake up, *freund.*"

Ferez became aware of the darkness gradually, as if it formed around him, yet he couldn't think what had been there before. He felt like he was floating, and he found the sensation disconcerting.

"The sleep accomplished its purpose, freund. It's time to wake."

Ferez grunted. The voice sounded familiar. Before he could think why, a sharp pain filled his head, and he groaned.

"Es tut mir leid." The pain in his head eased until it was no more than a dull ache. *"I hadn't realized I still caused you that much pain."*

Suddenly, the pain increased again, but it was no longer focused in his head. Instead, it throbbed sharply in his left shoulder and radiated from there. The presence in his mind shrugged.

"I said the sleep accomplished its purpose—to keep you from suffering through the wound and making it worse. Your freund, though, insisted I wake you sooner rather than later. But don't worry—someone is working to Heal your shoulder."

Who . . . ?

Ferez couldn't complete the thought before the voice was chuckling quietly. *"Once you wake, I am certain your freund will properly introduce us. But you must wake first."*

Ferez was suddenly aware of voices and the press of hands on his body and people around him. Releasing a soft breath, Ferez opened his eyes slowly, blinking when he found himself face to face with a young girl.

The girl giggled when he met her gaze, and she turned to look over her shoulder. "He's awake!" Then she turned back to him and smoothed her hands over his right arm, which was closest to her.

"Your shoulder's doing better, Herr Kanti, but you shouldn't move too much yet. If you're not careful, you could still wrench it and cause permanent damage."

"You are correct, Fräulein Lakritze."

The girl ducked her head, her face flushing. Ferez turned his head to find a man to his left. His hands were pressed gently against Ferez's shoulder. When Ferez caught the man's eyes, the man smiled.

"For a mann with your history of battle wounds, you are amazingly healthy, Herr Kanti. You seem to have been extremely lucky in your access to Heilemagier."

Before Ferez could reply to the man, whom he assumed was a Mage Healer himself, a cry of "Frenz!" reached him. He turned to find James pushing past several people. The boy dropped to his knees in the place where Fräulein Lakritze had been just moments before.

"How are you feeling?"

James's violet eyes were wide, and he reached a hand up to lightly touch Ferez's cheek. The king blinked at the gentle touch but offered a small smile.

"Better, I think." Suddenly loath to break eye contact with James, Ferez nodded vaguely to his left. "The Healers seem to think it reparable as long as I don' move."

"Not much, anyway," the Mage Healer added. James's eyes darted to the other man, and Ferez sighed, reluctantly following his gaze.

"How long before he can risk standing up?" James asked.

The Healer chuckled. "Not too long before then, but if you're hoping to get him on a pferd any time soon, you're better off letting me Heal the shoulder completely."

James's breathing hitched. Surprised, Ferez glanced at the boy, barely catching the soft smile the Healer offered.

"Whatever your attacker did with his scharfmond, he managed to separate the flesh from the bone. It's not a wound I would recommend attempting to recover from slowly. At least, not with your schedule as I understand it, hm?"

James nodded and turned his gaze back to Ferez. His brow was tightly knit and his purple eyes were dark with turmoil. The king felt his own breath catch.

"I swear," James whispered, "as soon as we return to Helloase, I'll show you how to protect yourself against scharfmonde." The boy squeezed his eyes shut and shook his head. "It was dumm of me not to do it sooner."

Ferez's chest tightened as he took in the boy's pursed lips, clenched jaw, and furrowed brow. Reaching up with his right hand, Ferez wrapped it around the back of James's neck. Those purple eyes flew open once more. When James began to speak, Ferez shook his head.

"Don' blame yerself, James." He held the boy's gaze as he spoke. "We haven' had the time. After all"—he offered a small smirk—"when would yeh have taugh' me, hm? While

we crossed the desert? When we wen' to see Lord Kawn?"
He chuckled. "Maybe while we slept?"

James snorted, and he finally relaxed under Ferez's
touch. "All right, all right. I get your point. We haven't exactly
had the chance to train." James finally allowed a small smile
of his own to stretch his lips. "What do you think about just
staying with the clan for the rest of our time in Zhulan? I
think we've both had enough of politik for a while."

Ferez nodded. Before he could verbally agree, an oddly
familiar voice spoke up.

"You still have ein bisschen of politik to play yet, ja,
Drache Krieger?"

Ferez lifted his head as James leaned to one side. He
found himself staring at two nomads: a woman and a man.
Despite having never met either before, Ferez instantly knew
who they were.

"You . . ."

He should have felt angry—he was pretty sure the man
had caused him excess pain and put him to sleep—but the
words that had awakened him ran through his head.

James glanced back at him warily. Ferez simply
continued to stare, and after a moment, the boy seemed to
relax once more.

"Frenz." The king finally turned his gaze back to James,
drawn by his soft tone. "These are Wolfrik Giftschwanz and
his schwester, Käfe." Ferez nodded. "They've turned their
backs on their häuptling and agreed to meet with my vater."

Ferez turned his head and met Wolfrik's gaze. Perhaps
James's words should have surprised him, but it didn't.
Instead, the Mindspeaker's words continued to run through
his mind.

"How long was I out?"

Beside him, James started, but Wolfrik simply smiled. "About three hours."

Ferez winced. Even if the pain hadn't been as bad as he remembered it being before he'd lost consciousness, three hours straight of it would have been a nightmare. And he would have attempted to fight with it, not knowing the severity of the wound until it was too late.

And I can't even protect myself against armed nomads.

Holding the Mindspeaker's gaze, Ferez replied, "I understan' yeh saved my shoulder."

Wolfrik dipped his head—not in agreement, Ferez recognized, but in acknowledgment.

"Many in my clan love that maneuver. I have seen too many good people suffer from such wounds. It is not a fate I would wish on anyone, even those I consider my feinde.

"Which I don't consider you," he added hastily, lifting his gaze back to Ferez's.

Ferez chuckled. "Nay, yeh've called me freund too many times for me to misunderstand." He sobered and offered a small smile. "Thank you."

Wolfrik actually gave a half-bow then, which his sister imitated, causing Ferez to blink. "Mit vergnügen, mein freund."

He placed such a heavy emphasis on the final word that Ferez wondered if he meant something more than just friend. When he glanced at James curiously, the boy met his gaze and mouthed *He knows.* Ferez nodded, understanding. Wolfrik was recognizing him as king. Maybe that should have shocked (and even worried) him, but Ferez doubted anything could at the moment. He turned to the Mage Healer with a small frown.

"Am I in shock?"

During the war, he remembered seeing so many of his men acting calmer than happy babes, when they normally would have been screaming in pain or distress. He couldn't imagine any other reason that he would be taking these revelations so easily.

Wolfrik snorted. "I think you underestimate your own geist, freund."

Meanwhile, the Healer offered a small, almost guilty smile. "I had your body release some naturally calming chemicals into your bloodstream. I didn't want you getting upset before you were fully healed."

Ferez blinked but nodded. He remembered seeing that trick, too. Some Mage Healers had been able to calm hysterical patients with a single touch, allowing the Healers to treat them without the risk of more damage.

"Es tut mir leid, freund." Ferez glanced up at the Mindspeaker, wondering why the man had decided to keep these words between the two of them. Wolfrik offered a sad smile. *"It seems I stirred up some nasty memories."*

Ferez shook his head. While James glanced at him curiously, the king kept the next thought to himself and the Mindspeaker.

Not nasty—just old.

Forcing his thoughts back to the present, he asked James what else had been happening.

~~*~*

Wolfrik listened idly as the Drache Krieger described recent events to the king. His geist, on the other hand, was focused solely on the king's. The mann didn't know it, but the memories from the krieg flitting through his geist were signs of a much larger problem—a problem Wolfrik was determined to fix.

He had told the Drache Krieger he had delved deeper into the king's geist, but the only significance the boy had recognized from that was the fact that Wolfrik now knew the king's true identity. The boy didn't understand the force necessary for Wolfrik to reach that deeply as quickly as he had. Wolfrik had been forced to abandon the subtlety he usually depended on to quickly drop the mann into sleep.

The result was that Wolfrik's magie had torn through the king's geist, destroying any natural mental defenses he might have had. It was something Wolfrik had immediately regretted. He had promised himself from an early age that he would never turn the full force of his Geistmagie on another human being.

Even more devastating was the realization that this mann was not only the king of Evon but also a kind and compassionate mann who actively sought to learn more about his people. It hurt to know he had harmed a Mann who would most likely forgive him with an ease Wolfrik had never known possible.

With the king's thanks ringing in his ears, Wolfrik eased his magie through the mann's geist. With his natural defenses torn away, the king's geist was not only open to any Geistmagier willing to invade it, it practically shouted his thoughts and would, in a way, actively attract even the weakest magier.

Already, Wolfrik had begun work on rebuilding the king's defenses. He had dulled the mental pain as much as he could, but it was currently only hidden. It would remain until the king had recovered fully from Wolfrik's attack. With the pain dulled, Wolfrik began to build a barrier around the mann's geist. In Schönestadt alone, there were tens of Geistmagier, so repelling possible intruders was of highest priority. Even so, it would take several hours to build a barrier strong and complex enough to protect the king's weakened geist to Wolfrik's satisfaction.

He thanked me for saving his shoulder. The least I can do is save his geist, as well.

~~*~*

Despite her curiosity over Ferez's thoughts, Gemi told Ferez everything that had happened since he'd fallen asleep. She even included Shadow's thoughts on Othman, knowing he would find them amusing.

Ferez didn't disappoint as he smirked and chuckled— and looked queasy—in the appropriate places. However, only half his geist seemed to be on the conversation, and she was less than halfway through the story before she thought she knew why. Although he'd slept, the wound, or the fact that the sleep had been magie-induced, had kept him from properly resting.

With that thought at the front of her geist, Gemi managed to quickly finish the story by the time the Heilemagier proclaimed Ferez satisfactorily healed for the nacht.

"Mind you," the Heilemagier had conditioned, "I will be back after midday to make sure you're completely healed." He had let his smile soften, even as his eyes had remained stern.

"But we all need sleep, you more than the rest of us. I expect you will still be abed when I return." He'd left then, as had the remaining wachen. On the way out, one paused to remind Gemi that Lord Kawn and Gouverneur Clarimonde would also be stopping by the next täg.

Gemi and Sir Leal, who had insisted on remaining with them for the nacht, helped a half-asleep Ferez to a bedroom. Rune Handelmann had offered several for those nomaden electing to spend one more nacht—an option most opted for with the unwetter still drenching the stadt.

Once they got Ferez into bed, Gemi insisted on taking the room's second. Sir Leal didn't argue. He simply smiled and left to find his own bed for the nacht.

Now, Gemi fiddled with Ferez's blankets, telling herself she was just making sure he'd be comfortable for the nacht. She knew she was stalling, unwilling to leave his side, but she didn't care. Ferez had been badly injured tonight. It was the second time this season.

Almost the third, she thought, thinking of the incident with the katzen.

She had panicked and almost lost herself when Ferez lost consciousness. If it hadn't been for Sir Leal's insistence, she might have broken down right then.

Even now, with Ferez alive and well and right in front of her, Gemi could feel a prickling at the back of her eyes. Closing them, she took a deep breath.

There's no reason to break down now; we're all safe.

A hand closing on hers had her opening her eyes and blinking down into sleepy silvery-blue orbs. When Ferez rubbed his thumb against the backs of her fingers, she numbly realized she had fisted her hands in the blankets. Relaxing her grip, she turned her hand over and gripped his. Ferez squeezed in return.

"James?" The word was soft and half slurred. Gemi thought he must be on the edge of sleep. "Yeh remember the war?"

Gemi blinked. After everything that had happened recently, the Krieg mit Fayral was the last thing on her geist, but . . .

"Of course I do," she whispered back. "I probably fought in it as long as you did."

Longer, actually. But she didn't say it, not when she was two jahre younger than Ferez.

Those silvery eyes blinked slowly, and Gemi found herself mesmerized by the colors. She'd never noticed before, but there were separate patches of blue and silver, as if the two colors mingled but refused to become one color. It was oddly calming, the idea that one could mix with another without completely losing itself.

"Yeh shouldna had to," Ferez murmured suddenly, breaking the silence. Gemi blinked, but those blue-and-silver orbs were still locked on hers. "Yeh were so young . . . we were so young."

Gemi swallowed against the lump that suddenly appeared in her throat. Leaning over the bed, she laid her other hand along Ferez's cheek. It was only slightly rough, and Gemi felt the prickling in her eyes return.

So young.

"We did what we had to, Ferez."

She knew she probably shouldn't risk using his real name, but she couldn't bring herself to speak his alias just then; it didn't feel right.

If only he knew my *real name.*

Gemi felt Flame press against her geist, but Gemi pushed her away. She didn't need the drache insisting again that she tell him who she was. Ja, the desire for him to know was there, but the fear was still stronger.

And I don't want to jeopardize this . . . whatever it is.

"We shouldna had to," Ferez muttered again. His eyes fell closed, and Gemi felt her stomach clench when they didn't open immediately. "So . . . much . . . death."

Gemi's breathing sped up. Images began to fill her. Battlefields strewn with the dead and dying. Walking past dead mann after dead mann in the hopes of finding one or two who still breathed. Watching from the deck of the *Pretty Pauper* as other ships sank, hoping and praying to the götter that their ship would not meet the same fate.

Nein!

Gemi shoved the memories away. If she was good at anything, it was burying the truth in her geist, along with whatever images accompanied it. Unfortunately, she couldn't prevent the tears that leaked from her prickling eyes as she focused on Ferez once more.

Squeezing his hand, she rubbed her thumb under his eye. "But that death was not in vain, Ferez. Those männer gave their lives for our current peace. Isn't that worth it, Ferez?

"I believe *they* thought so. I *know* many of them fought in the hope that one täg we would have peace—that we would have the freedom to live without fighting."

Gemi hadn't been sure if Ferez was still awake; he certainly looked asleep. So she startled when he chuckled dryly.

"Still no' free from fightin'," he muttered lowly.

Gemi huffed a soft laugh, though amusement wasn't what drove the sound.

"Nein, not yet." She sighed. "But soon, Ferez. Remember Mama Caler's words?"

She almost choked as she said it. She remembered the Seer's words all too well, and she knew they'd overwhelm her if she thought on them too hard. But there had been hope in those words.

"It's almost over. If we can survive this season, we can have peace."

"One las' obs'acle." Ferez breathed the words and blinked open his eyes once more. "One las' season," he muttered. "D'yeh really think . . . it'll be that easy?"

Gemi bit her lip. She didn't think it would be easy at all. They hadn't even reached Mitte Jahreszeit, yet so much had happened. And if Mama Caler was right—and Gemi had never known her to be wrong—then there was still so much that could go wrong.

But Gemi had been reaching for the hope in the Seer's words, and that's what she would give her freund.

"Ja, Ferez. One last season."

Ferez closed his eyes and sighed. He turned his face into her hand, and Gemi's breath hitched as his lips moved against her palm.

"One more season. Will I still see yeh . . . af'erward, James?"

Gemi felt like her breath had frozen in her lungs. Pressure built in her throat and behind her eyes, and that desire to tell Ferez who she really was swelled until she could feel her real name burning on the tip of her tongue.

That, too, froze as Flame brushed across her geist once more. Gemi closed her eyes against the pressure there and swallowed against the lump in her throat.

Nein, not yet, not yet.

"James?"

Ferez's voice was louder now and tinged with panic. Startled, Gemi opened her eyes and stared back down into those blue-and-silver orbs that held more than a little fear.

"Will yeh leave afterward?"

And no matter that the fear of her true identity was still strong or that she wished, more than anything, to give it to him, she knew one thing she wanted without a doubt. Not caring how it might seem to the half-asleep mann, she leaned over him and placed a light kiss to his forehead.

"Nein, Ferez. I won't leave." Praying to the götter that she was not proven wrong, she added, "No matter how this ends, I will never leave you."

~~*~*

When Ferez woke, he kept his body still and his eyes shut as he took stock of himself and his surroundings. He lay on bedding comfortable enough to suggest a bed, yet not one belonging to an inn. It was too comfortable for that; it didn't have the overly slept-in feeling that Ferez was accustomed to finding at inns. And while parts of his body ached, but he was certain it had nothing to do with the bedding.

In fact, as memories from the night before slowly rose in his mind, Ferez realized the aches had more to do with the mostly healed shoulder wound and not a little bit from the way he was sure he'd been lying half against a wall for several hours.

Sighing softly, Ferez shifted under his covers and opened his eyes. The room he'd slept in was dark, but he could make out the outline of the door that must have led to the hallway and a second bed standing in the other half of the room. Frowning at the tidy bed, he wondered if anyone had claimed it for the night.

Suddenly, the murmur of voices from the hallway made themselves known, and Ferez became aware of other, more muffled sounds that indicated that the day had begun long ago. Ferez nodded to himself as he realized whoever might have slept in the room as well was already awake.

A memory formed in his mind, an image of wide purple

eyes. The memory, oddly, seemed to mix with scattered images from the war and the words that Ferez could remember Mama Caler speaking before he and James had left Kensy. There were other words attached to the image, but they were vaguer and too indistinct to recall.

One set of words stood out in his mind against all others, words that he must have repeated to himself again and again as he'd drifted into sleep for them to be so sharp in his mind.

No matter how this ends, I will never leave you.

It was a promise, Ferez realized, one that James had not made lightly. The thought fueled a warmth in his chest.

He was drawn from his contemplation when the door to the hallway swung open and warm lamplight spilled across the floor and his bed. Squinting against the sudden brightness, Ferez saw a figure standing in the doorway, an unknown silhouette against the bright light. Before his eyes could adjust, a familiar voice reached his ears.

"Ach, so you are awake, Herr Kanti." Ferez recognized the voice from the night before as the Mage Healer stepped closer to his bed. "Your freund had feared you would sleep straight through the täg."

Ferez blinked up at the Healer, frowning. "How late is it?"

"A couple hours before sunset, I'm afraid." The Healer leaned down and laid a hand on Ferez's temple. "It seems Herr Giftschwanz did ein bisschen more damage than I first suspected."

He shook his head and stood. "But it seems the sleep has helped you recover from that, at least. Now then, let me take a look at your shoulder."

It was almost an hour later by the time the Healer led Ferez to a parlor toward the front of the house. There, James was speaking with Kawn and a tall woman Ferez recognized as the moneylender whose hospitality they had sampled when they'd first arrived in Schönestadt. James had his back to Ferez when he entered, but he quickly turned when Kawn nodded to him in greeting.

"Frenz!" Suddenly, James was in front of Ferez and looking him over, a hand on each of his shoulders—the grip on his left noticeably lighter than the right. "How do you feel?"

Ferez chuckled as he vaguely recalled the boy asking him the same question the night before. Reaching up and squeezing the hand on his left shoulder, he offered a smile.

"Fully healed, for the mos' part."

James frowned. "For the most part?"

Ferez shrugged and glanced uncertainly at the Healer, who still stood nearby. The man seemed to understand the look. Instead of acting insulted as Ferez had feared, he chuckled.

"It seems," the Healer said, addressing James, "your freund has become rather verwöhnt where Heilemagier are concerned."

Ferez didn't know what "verwöhnt" meant, but he thought he understood the gist of the man's words. He shrugged again and added, "He's not as good as Lakina."

For a moment, James simply blinked at him. Then a grin spread across his face, and he snickered.

"Frenz, I don't think anyone is as good as Lakina." He glanced quickly at the Healer. "No offense, Heilemagier."

The Healer smiled warmly and shook his head. "None taken, Drache Krieger." James grimaced, and Ferez wondered if anyone else noticed or realized it was the boy's reaction to the constant use of his title.

"If this Lakina was the last Heilemagier to Heal Herr

Kanti, then I can agree that her magie far exceeds my own. She is certainly a master magier."

Ferez nodded in agreement. However, the reference to his last Healing brought to mind images of large cats attacking him, images he had been attempting to avoid. His thoughts must have shown on his face because James squeezed his shoulder and turned Ferez's attention to the people with whom he had previously been conversing.

"Frenz, I want to reintroduce you to Dame Clarimonde. I know you met her several nächte ago, but we didn't exactly spend much time in Schönestadt during our last visit."

Ferez nodded. As he made to offer the stern woman a small bow, James added, "Lord Kawn has named her the new gouverneur of Schönestadt."

Ferez pulled himself up straight in surprise. In the next moment, he realized he vaguely recalled hearing something similar the night before. Hoping the dame didn't feel slighted by his startled reaction, he lowered himself into a bow once more.

"A pleasure to meet yeh again, Dame Clarimonde, An' congratulations, as well. I'm sure yeh'll make a fine governor."

The stern-looking woman dipped her chin and offered a small smile. "Danke, Herr Kanti. I fear it is an idea to which I am still accustoming myself." She glanced at James, then back to Ferez, her smile twitching into a small smirk. "And I am glad you are healed. Herr Caffers has been worrying himself fiercely over your health."

James ducked his head, but not before Ferez saw red infusing his cheeks. "You were asleep for an awfully long time."

Ferez's smile softened, and he laid a hand on James's shoulder. The boy lifted his gaze to Ferez's and smiled shyly.

"I told you it was only natural that our freund slept so long, Drache Krieger."

Ferez blinked as the voice broke whatever had passed between him and James. Turning his gaze from the boy, Ferez realized that Wolfrik and Käfe Giftschwanz also stood nearby, though he hadn't noticed them before.

"After all," Wolfrik added, "his geist had to recover as much as his body. That form of exhaustion is not easily shaken."

James nodded. Turning back to Ferez, he gripped the king's good shoulder once more.

"Since you're feeling better and there's less than an hour of sunlight left, we might as well leave for Helloase now." James looked to the Mage Healer but didn't release his hold on Ferez. "And you are certain he is healed enough to ride through the nacht?"

The Healer chuckled. "Do not worry, Drache Krieger. There is no risk of the wound reopening. It might ache for ein bisschen, and he might grow tired more quickly, but riding a pferd through the nacht will cause no problems, I can assure you."

James nodded again, but his frown told Ferez he wasn't completely satisfied with the Healer's assessment. Patting James's hand, Ferez smiled.

"I think I could use a nightlong ride after spending all day in bed."

James chuckled.

~~*~*

In the alleys of Schönestadt, not far from the Handelmann haus, a nomade hissed like the schlange for which his clan was named. Adalwolf pulled his magie back from the geist he had just attempted to infiltrate.

Impossible.

"Not a very accurate assessment, since he seems to have achieved it," a voice drily added.

Adalwolf scowled but didn't reply. He had first heard the voice two siebentäge ago. Although it delighted in taunting him, it had also provided invaluable advice. Many in his clan might doubt his plans if he told them the ideas had come from a disembodied geist, but this particular geist had spoken too many truths to Adalwolf for him not to accept the voice's advice.

That advice had led to the death of the two gouverneure known to be friendly with the Vereinte Clans, as well as the ten täge of chaos that had followed. If only the verdammt Caffers boy had kept himself out of the way, then the Vereinte Clans would have lost all their river-dwelling allies.

"I did warn that you needed to prepare for his interference," The voice, as usual, sounded amused. *"I warned you he would strike hard and fast."*

Adalwolf hissed again, but his annoyance was directed at his own arrogance. He had believed himself prepared, despite the voice's amused warnings that Caffers would break down his plans.

Now he had even lost his chance to work his way into the geist of Caffers's new human freund. Indeed, that chance had been lost the moment Wolfrik worked his way into the mann's geist and set up a complex barrier that, after some exploring, Adalwolf knew he would be unable to bypass undetected.

It irked Adalwolf beyond measure. He *knew* Wolfrik. The other Geistmagier was weak, was abschaum. Yet the boy was obviously clever enough to create a barrier that Adalwolf would not be able to overcome so easily.

I knew I should have insisted on overseeing this part.

Even as he thought it, he knew he had had little choice in the matter. While he had offered the plan originally, Häuptling Giftschwanz had claimed the idea as his own, and Adalwolf's häuptling had forbidden him from interfering.

Dark laughter, hinting at violence, filled Adalwolf's geist.

"Are you angry because your plans are falling apart or because the Giftschwanz children knowingly gave up the chance to prove themselves worthy as children of the häuptling? A chance you'll never receive."

Adalwolf ignored the voice's taunts. He had learned quickly that the voice was harsh, but so were his clan and his life. That was the fate of an unclaimed son of his häuptling.

For jahre, he hadn't known for certain if it was true. His mütter had always claimed it was so, but the rest of the clan called her schlampe and hexe as she seduced even the most faithful of männer into her tent. It had been the violent voice that had assured him of the truth. It had claimed that the strength of his Geistmagie, magie he had inherited from his mütter, could only come from the line of the häuptling. It was a line Adalwolf should have been heir to since he was several jahre older than the eldest son of the häuptling's lebenfrau.

"So easily distracted," muttered the voice.

Adalwolf sneered. *"I am easily distracted? The plans fall apart before us, and you spend your efforts baiting me."*

"Be patient, Geistmagier." Amusement filled the voice more than ever. *"I have a plan to bring down Caffers himself—a plan I believe you will take great pleasure in carrying out."*

Fifteen

It was about an hour after midnight when Wolfrik and the others approached Helloase. Despite the late hour, campfires burned throughout the camp, and perhaps half the tents glowed with lamplight. Not unusual, given the oft-nocturnal lifestyle of most Zhulanbürger, but Wolfrik hadn't expected a group of six people to be waiting for them on the edge of the camp.

One nomade, a mann by the tone of his voice, stepped forward to greet them as the pferde slowed to a halt. He laid a hand on the nose of Herr Schattenrenner, the Drache Krieger's mount. The nicker that emerged from his mouth immediately marked him as a Tieremagier.

Once Herr Schattenrenner had responded, the Tieremagier turned his face up. "James, it is good you have returned." He hesitated a moment. "You are well?"

"Ja, Vater, of course." There was a note of curiosity in the Drache Krieger's voice, as though he wondered why the mann would think otherwise.

Suddenly, Wolfrik stiffened and ducked his head as the

boy's words sank in. If this mann was vater to the Drache Krieger, then this was Häuptling Hausef Kanten, erstehäuptling of the Vereinte Clans.

Wolfrik's gut twisted. *What if he doesn't see me as worthy?* The thought slipped through his geist before he could control it. He grimaced as a familiar bitterness settled through him. *He would not be the first.*

A hand on his arm brought him back to the present, and he glanced to his right, where Käfe rode beside him. Even in the moons-light, he could see the comforting smile she offered him. He allowed a small smile to lift his lips in return, but he knew she couldn't understand—not completely.

Though their häuptling had started in on her geist when she was a toddler, Wolfrik had managed to draw the mann's magie onto his own little more than a jahr later. Any memories she might have of that jahr were buried in the past and Wolfrik's magie. She was his little schwester, and he wouldn't let anything happen to her if he could help it. But that meant she had never felt the full extent of the pain he had. While he was usually happy to know that, there were times, like now, when it simply made him feel alone.

"His shoulder is fine, except for some possible soreness." A different voice brought Wolfrik's attention back to the group in front of them. He frowned, wondering if the mann who'd spoken was an Heilemagier. "But it is not his shoulder for which I fear."

Wolfrik raised his eyebrows. The Heilemagier must be powerful if he could sense the remaining effects of his Geistmagie on the king.

"His geist is healing."

He winced as everyone turned to look at him. He knew better than to speak so defensively when no one had even addressed him. Such action had only ever brought suspicion and anger from his häuptling, something he had learned to avoid jahre ago. The hand on his arm tightened its grip, showing that even Käfe was surprised by his outburst.

"Bruder—"

"You think that, do you?" The Heilemagier stepped closer, not even glancing at Käfe. "And did you realize there was physical damage as well as the damage to his geist?"

Wolfrik inhaled sharply and finally looked at the king. Only then did he realize why they were speaking of him in the first place. The mann was slumped in his saddle, only the Drache Krieger's hand on his shoulder keeping him at all upright.

How long has he been flagging?

He couldn't remember feeling the king's exhaustion creep up on him. Instead, it seemed to have come upon him suddenly.

"Wolfrik?" The Drache Krieger's voice was sharp, and the Geistmagier turned his gaze to the boy, who had twisted in his saddle to look at him. The Drache Krieger pursed his lips. "You didn't tell us there was lingering damage. Why?"

Wolfrik scrambled for a response, suddenly feeling lost. He didn't know these people, didn't know how to respond to them or how to act to get the responses he wanted. And he knew his magie would do him no good at this point, not when he had only worked it into the geist of one mann and at least one of these people was a Geistmagier as well.

"James." The king's gentle sigh stilled Wolfrik's geist.

The Drache Krieger gripped the mann with his second hand as he swayed, and the boy murmured an affirmation of his presence.

"Maybe we shoul' ge' more comfortable afore we have this conversation."

"Right."

With the help of the nomaden on the ground, the Drache Krieger managed to get the king safely dismounted, then swung off Herr Schattenrenner. Käfe quickly dismounted as well, and after a moment's hesitation, Wolfrik followed suit. To his surprise, as soon as he was firmly on his own feet, his pferd followed Herr Schattenrenner and the others toward the waterhole.

"This way." The erstehäuptling led them to a tent embroidered with a pair of circles intertwined. The symbol represented the Gemini moons at their fullest, marking the tent as a Heilemagier's. Once they were inside, the king was lowered onto a cot, and the Heilemagier turned his full attention to the injured mann.

"Well, Wolfrik?" The Drache Krieger crossed his arms over his chest and ignored the flask offered by a fräulein. "Why didn't you tell us about the lingering damage?"

Wolfrik sighed. He was tempted to glance around at the other nomaden, but he kept his gaze solely on the Drache Krieger. They knew him even less than Caffers did, so he would get no help from them.

"Es tut mir leid, Drache Krieger. I—"

He hesitated. How was he supposed to explain the guilt that racked him and his desire to heal the damage himself? How could he explain his pride in his magie and the fear he felt when faced with its full power?

"James, please."

Wolfrik started. He had been sure the king was already asleep. But when he focused on his geist, the Skorpion found only determination. Both guilt and gratitude bombarded Wolfrik as he realized Ferez had spoken up not because of his own discomfort but rather to stop the Drache Krieger's impromptu interrogation.

"You need to rest, Herr Kanti," the Heilemagier scolded.

The king attempted to raise a hand, no doubt to wave the Heilemagier away. The hand barely made it a few inches above the surface of the cot before he dropped it back down. He did manage to shake his head, though.

"Yer're bein' an idiot, James."

The muttered declaration was met with gasps, though Wolfrik noted with some amusement that two männer, both of whom looked to be about his own age, snorted instead. The Drache Krieger stiffened.

"Wolfrik may not've explicitly told us how bad the damage was, but he did mention it." The king yawned hugely. When he continued, his voice drifted a bit. "Yeh may not've realized it, but I knew the damage was still affectin' me."

It was Wolfrik's turn to stiffen, and the king's lips twitched.

"Yeh didn' think I'd noticed, did yeh, Wolfrik?" Ferez slowly shook his head again. "I know my body. I've been injured an' Healed too many times over the pas' few years no' to recognize my body's reactions to such things."

He paused. Though he didn't yawn, it seemed the exhaustion was slowly shutting him down. Wolfrik winced. He wished the mann would let himself rest so the Heilemagier could Heal him, but the determination he had noticed earlier was still strong.

"This exhaustion has nothin' to do wit' my shoulder." Ferez's words renewed suddenly. Wolfrik frowned when he brushed his mind and found that the king didn't even realize he'd paused. "I've known tha' since the firs' time I woke."

A snort drew everyone's attention to the tent's entrance, where Dame Flammezunge had stuck her head through. She glared at the Drache Krieger, but her words seemed to address everybody who could understand her.

"Would you leave Wolfrik alone, James? Frenz obviously will not let himself sleep until you do."

The boy opened his mouth, most likely to protest, but Dame Flammezunge didn't give him the chance. *"Nay, James!"*

The boy sullenly closed his mouth and pursed his lips. Drache and Drache Krieger glared silently at each other for a full minute before Caffers's expression relaxed and he looked away.

Dame Flammezunge dipped her snout toward the ground. *"Besides,"* she added so Wolfrik and the others could understand, *"Wolfrik has been actively healing and protecting Frenz's mind almost since the damage was done."*

Wolfrik frowned. He had thought the drache too young to touch other geister unless they could actively accept her, as he had after she'd accepted him as an ally. The drache turned to him and hissed softly, sounding amused.

"I may be young, but I understand what happens to a creature's mind when the natural barriers are destroyed. Even I should have been able to hear Frenz's thoughts when he woke that first time, but they were noticeably silent."

Silence filled the tent. To Wolfrik's surprise, only two people appeared to have missed Dame Flammezunge's words: the Heilemagier, who smoothed his hands over the king's head, and one of the two young männer Wolfrik had noticed earlier. The rest of the tent's occupants, Wolfrik realized, must have been either Geistmagier or Tieremagier.

One nomade, whose scarred face spoke of tragedy, knelt beside the Heilemagier, focusing on, but not touching, the king. With a jolt, Wolfrik realized he knew who this frau was. Even among the Gift Clans, the name Isana Kanten was well known.

Acknowledged as the strongest Geistmagier throughout

the Vereinte Clans—and Wolfrik had always secretly wondered if she was the strongest in all the clans—Isana Kanten had once been considered the most beautiful frau, as well. As firstborn, she had been in line to be häuptling of the Katze Clan, and even long before Unification, männer throughout the clans had been eager to claim her as their lebenfrau.

But her scarred face was how Isana Kanten was now recognized, and her younger bruder had become häuptling instead of her. The right half of her face might still shine with the beauty for which she had once been known, but the left was scarred and saggy. Even jahre after the fire that had stolen her beauty and fertility, her flesh looked ready to melt right off her bones.

"Flame is right." Isana's words startled Wolfrik from his contemplations. "Frenz's geist is well protected now." She tilted her head. "A powerful barrier, at that."

She lifted her eyes from the king's form to Wolfrik. Those dark eyes studied him. "This is yours?"

Wolfrik ducked his head, uncertain how to respond to the curiosity and awe in the frau's voice. "Ja, dame."

There was a soft rustle, like cloth moving, but the Skorpion didn't move until a pair of boots stopped in front of him. Lifting his head, he found Isana Kanten standing before him, her black eyes intent on him.

"James, you haven't introduced your new freunde yet." Isana's tone was lightly admonishing, though her gaze never left Wolfrik.

"Es tut mir leid, Tante."

Though the Drache Krieger's words addressed Isana Kanten, Wolfrik found with a glance that the boy's shy, apologetic smile was directed at him.

"Vater, Tante, these are Wolfrik and Käfe Giftschwanz."

Wolfrik expected shock or indignation. Instead, the introduction was met with surprised smiles. "Giftschwanz?" the erstehäuptling asked. "As in Häuptling Giftschwanz?"

Wolfrik nodded numbly. Their unexpected reactions made him falter, and even Käfe's hand gripping his wasn't the comfort it usually was.

When Isana Kanten held her hand out to him, palm up like she was offering a gift, Wolfrik stared at it. Why would she offer him, son of her feind, such a sign of friendship?

"If you are here as you are, then you have proven yourself to my nephew and his drache." Isana offered a lopsided smile that softened her scarred face. "Neither trust easily, so their judgment is well respected."

Wolfrik swallowed against the sudden dryness of his mouth. With a small nod, he released Käfe's hand and took the offered one.

"Danke."

He didn't think the one word was enough to fully express his gratitude for their acceptance, but he didn't trust his voice to carry any other words. He met her gaze and hoped she'd understand. If she did, she didn't dwell on it.

Instead, she gripped his shoulder with her free hand. "Perhaps, when we are all rested, you would be interested in joining the geisternetz of the Vereinte Clans, hm?"

Wolfrik spluttered. To be accepted as an ally whose physical presence was trustworthy was something for which Wolfrik had thought he could only hope. But to be allowed to join the geisternetz, which connected all the Geistmagier throughout the Vereinte Clans, was unthinkable.

"Why?"

Isana snorted and her smile turned playful. "Don't

misunderstand me, Wolfrik Giftschwanz. I am sure you can understand that it is easier to keep an eye on a new ally when his geist is easily available, ja?"

But not necessarily easily accessible.

That was the mistake his häuptling had made again and again. Through the geisternetz of the Skorpion Clan, the mann had preyed on the geist of any Geistmagier who opposed his will. But he had never understood that just because he could reach a geist did not mean he was able to reach inside it. The misconception had saved Wolfrik's life many times. His häuptling never realized that the pain he inflicted on his youngest two had been ineffective for jahre.

Isana's sudden laughter startled Wolfrik from his thoughts, and he stared at the scarred frau. Once she had calmed, she smirked.

"Your geist may be well protected against intrusion, freund"—Wolfrik felt his throat tighten at her easy use of the word—"but your face is surprisingly open."

Wolfrik ducked his head again. This time, he could feel his embarrassment burning his cheeks. He lifted his head, though, when Käfe stepped forward.

"If you are going to insult us," she spoke fiercely, "then perhaps we shouldn't have come."

Wolfrik blinked. His schwester was usually rather mild-mannered. Her current stance was anything but, and the stiffness of her shoulders suggested she was glaring at Isana Kanten. Dropping the Geistmagier's hand, Wolfrik laid a hand on Käfe's shoulder, hoping to calm her.

Isana, for her part, raised her hands, her eyes turning serious. "I meant no harm, fräulein. The words were meant only as a witz to ease your bruder's worries." She turned her dark eyes to Wolfrik and offered a small nod. "I realize now that was not the best tactic."

The small, lopsided smile returned. "You needn't be ashamed of having such an open expression, though. It speaks highly of you."

Käfe relaxed under Wolfrik's palm, but she glanced back at him, her mouth turned down in obvious confusion. Wolfrik couldn't fault her. Normally, he could keep from showing his emotions so freely, or he could at least control which emotions he did show. He never would have survived life with his brüder and häuptling otherwise.

Here, he had been caught flatfooted at every turn, and hiding his tumultuous emotions hadn't been a priority.

"James." Everyone turned to the erstehäuptling. "I assume our new freunde are the reason you asked us to postpone the Skorpion's questioning?"

Wolfrik started and glanced sharply at the Drache Krieger. The boy hadn't mentioned another Skorpion.

"Ja, Vater. I wanted to give Wolfrik the chance to speak for him, if he so wished."

"Speak for whom, exactly?"

The boy turned to Wolfrik and nodded. "Before we met, earlier that täg, there was an incident in Machtstadt involving a Skorpion by the name of Jakob."

Käfe gasped and Wolfrik grimaced. Jakob was known to them, and he was disliked even by those of his own clan. The mann had lost his place in the clan several siebentäge ago and had been stripped of his statusgürtel. Whatever he had done to get himself captured by the Vereinte Clans would most likely have resulted from an attempt to regain favor with their häuptling.

"You know him, then?" Isana Kanten asked.

Wolfrik nodded. "What are the accusations against him?"

Käfe glanced sharply at him. No doubt she thought they

should denounce him without question. After all, if he was loyal to anyone, it would be to their häuptling.

But Wolfrik understood something he thought she might not. The Vereinte Clans had accepted them as allies, but they might also consider Wolfrik as a potential häuptling for a clan they had previously considered lost. If Wolfrik was to salvage any of his clan once the Vereinte Clans defeated his häuptling and brüder, then he had to begin acting and thinking like a future häuptling now.

As if to confirm his thoughts, the erstehäuptling, his schwester, and the Drache Krieger all nodded approvingly. It was the Drache Krieger who answered his question.

"He was found wearing the statusgürtel of the Falke Clan, and he attempted to kill Lord Parshen."

Wolfrik nodded. "A triple transgression, then." The others made questioning sounds. Even Käfe didn't seem to understand. "The first accusation," he clarified, "would be doubly wrong on his part, as he had been stripped of his statusgürtel nearly a month ago. For him to wear any, even one from the Skorpion Clan, would be punishable."

"Had he been exiled?" the erstehäuptling asked warily.

Wolfrik shook his head, understanding the worry. If Jakob had been exiled, then another clan even taking him into custody as a prisoner would have violated his punishment. Centuries ago, when all the clans had been united under the erstehäuptling, a clan could be punished for doing so.

"Nein, he had simply been stripped of his status within the clan. As it is, though, he was on the verge of being denounced as a nomade."

Shaking his head again, Wolfrik added, "I believe he deserves whatever punishment you deem just." He nodded to Isana. "And whatever method of questioning you deem necessary."

The frau's lopsided smile widened, and she chuckled darkly. "Would you like to be involved in his interrogation?"

Wolfrik considered her offer. Though they seemed to have accepted him easily enough, he realized that assisting in Jakob's questioning could help him prove himself further to Isana, at the very least. Plus, if he wanted to take responsibility for the future of his clan, then he might as well begin with this.

When he offered his assent, Isana nodded and gripped his shoulder once more.

"Ulla," the erstehäuptling said after a few moments of silence.

"Ja, Vater?" responded a fräulein Wolfrik had noticed earlier.

"Now that everything has been settled, why don't you show Käfe around the oase? And I'm sure she would appreciate an introduction to your freunde."

Wolfrik felt his schwester stiffen, and he brushed his geist against hers.

We are safe here, schwester. Already, they are treating us like guests and equals.

Käfe slowly relaxed. It was treatment they were unused to from their own clan, but the old ways, which Wolfrik was beginning to think the Vereinte Clans still followed, held a spirit of open heart and open geist. It was a mindset to which Wolfrik thought he could accustom himself.

"Ulla Kanten," the fräulein introduced herself. She had stepped forward and was offering her hand to Käfe.

Hesitantly, Käfe took Ulla's hand and muttered her own name. When the Kanten fräulein simply beamed in response, Wolfrik could feel his schwester's geist stir with excitement. The sudden realization that she might find freunde filled her geist as she followed Ulla from the tent, offering Wolfrik no more than a single backward glance.

~~*~*

As the tent was slowly vacated, the pink Liebe took a moment to revel in the alliances and friendships she had just helped begin. In all honesty, this was her favorite part of guiding mortals through their relationships. Of course, she loved to see relationships continue and thrive, but there was nothing more enjoyable than that first blush of a relationship, whether it was a full-blown romance or a simple alliance.

Once the tent was mostly empty and she had enjoyed the bliss of the new relationships long enough, she turned her gaze to her red twin. Idly noting that she was still affecting some nomaden—most likely young Käfe and those fräulein to whom she was being introduced—Liebe let her gaze settle into a glare.

"You weren't even trying."

She ignored the fact that her words sounded more pouty than angry. Even with her twin's influence, Liebe did not do anger well.

"You just let me have that one."

Hass, who had stood at the edge of the tent for the entire exchange, smiled at Liebe. "That's not completely true." Though his words were the denial she expected, the mild tone made Liebe frown.

"Frieda nearly turned on the Giftschwanz Geistmagier, and you let the opportunity pass."

Hass shrugged. "I tried to affect Peace in Schönestadt."

Liebe started. Her twin wasn't attempting to affect the nomaden at all. Knowing that, she stopped actively influencing the surrounding nomaden. It wasn't fair if her bruder wasn't even trying.

Hate chuckled as Love pulled in her influence. "I decided that actively affecting Peace takes too much effort." Love frowned. "It's difficult enough influencing her alone, but she's tempered by her bondmates, and that pretty much makes it impossible."

Love hummed. She knew Hate was right. But Love had also noticed it seemed easier for one bondmate to influence the others toward a positive emotion than toward a negative one. She wondered idly if it was because Peace herself influenced a positive state.

"You've noticed it, too, haven't you?" Love glanced at her twin, wondering what he could possibly mean. "The flip side of what we discussed at the temple in Machtstadt?"

Love raised an eyebrow. It was rare that Hate offered his own thoughts on this kind of subject without her pressing him for them. He huffed and rolled his eyes as he heard her thoughts.

"I just find it unsettling, that's all."

"What exactly do you find unsettling, Brother?"

As she spoke, Love moved closer to Hate. When he automatically opened his arms to her, she snuggled against his chest. There were no relationships they needed to fight over now, and she figured they could use as much rest as they could get. After all, Death had been right before. The season wasn't even half over.

"We all may be more susceptible to each other's influence, but actively influencing each other is more draining than ever."

Love lifted her head to look at Hate. The red demigod was staring past her, his mouth set in a frown. She reached up and smoothed her fingers over his lips to ease the tension. Hate quirked a brow, but she simply smiled softly as her mind considered his words.

It had been a long while since she had last considered the drain that actively influencing another demigod produced. They had all played with influencing each other, of course— not to mention the other immortals—when they were younger. It was part of learning the limits of their own abilities. As they did, they had all quickly learned that attempting to influence another immortal was the fastest way into the arms of their twin and a significant stint of rest.

However, Love had learned early on that she had a bit of an advantage over her siblings. As she influenced the emotion love, an emotion that was considered just as sacred to immortals as it was to mortals, Love had found certain pairs of immortals somewhat receptive to her influence. These, however, had mainly been limited to their parents and, surprisingly, Life and Death.

When Peace and War had been born, she had found that Peace was just as receptive to her influence as any mortal would be. She hadn't understood why at the time, since War was as resistant to love as Hate was.

It hadn't been until their mother was thrown into the Cycle of Incarnation that she'd considered the Mortal Realm as the source of Peace's receptiveness. Love suddenly blinked as thoughts of her youngest siblings filled her mind. Focusing once more on her red brother, she found he was watching her calmly.

"Well?" he asked as she shifted in his arms.

Love shook her head. "You may be right: not even War tries to influence Peace."

When Hate raised an eyebrow, she rolled her eyes. "Not

since that year after her parents died. And I'm not even sure
he was actually attempting anything then. Her parents had
just died; it's only human nature to want revenge for that."

Hate's brow wrinkled. "But Peace is not a mortal soul,
Love."

Love chuckled. "Maybe not, but I think the only
difference between us and the mortals is the strength of our
spirits and our specializations. Otherwise, Peace is human."
Her tone turned dry. "And if you haven't noticed, she plays
human rather well."

Hate snorted and lifted his gaze. Love turned her head to
see what he was looking at, and she found it easily enough.
Peace was the only person still in the tent besides the
unconscious king and the Mage Healer. Her expression, easily
visible to both demigods, was twisted in guilt and worry. But
that wasn't what caught Love's eye.

Peace had her hands wrapped tightly around the king's.
While her expression spoke of sorrow for the man's wounds,
the glint in her eye told of a determination to protect what
was most precious to her.

"Oh, aye," Hate answered with a chuckle. "Peace plays
human very well."

~~*~*

Unbekanntoase, Zhulan

Several hours' ride southeast of Schönestadt

Adalwolf's lips twitched. He had just relayed the
information he had learned in Schönestadt to the Gift Clan
häuptlinge. The thunderous expression on Häuptling
Giftschwanz's face was enough to fill the Schlange with
satisfaction, but it was the sneer his own häuptling aimed at

the Skorpion that threatened to bring a smirk to Adalwolf's lips.

"Can't you even control your own children, Giftschwanz?" Adalwolf allowed the smirk to stretch his lips when he heard the disgust that colored his häuptling's words. "You assured me there would be no problems."

Giftschwanz glared at Adalwolf's häuptling. "And there shouldn't have been any." The Skorpion, a large, thickset mann, growled. "I made sure my own magie was thick in their geister before I sent them to Schönestadt."

Adalwolf felt his lip rise in a sneer, unintentionally mimicking his häuptling, who then echoed his thoughts.

"Why send someone in need of such effort? I know Wolfrik is not the only Geistmagier among your children."

Giftschwanz snorted. "And risk my heirs? Nein! I would rather lose those two than risk my eldest being imprisoned by that verdammt gouverneur, Othman."

"And that is the very reason he lost two children." Adalwolf didn't bother glancing toward the voice. Its violence was all too recognizable. *"If he had sent his eldest son, the mann most likely would have completed the task and been back several täge ago."*

Adalwolf nodded absently, knowing the geist was correct. He had even mentioned it when Giftschwanz had decided to send his youngest, but Adalwolf's häuplting had reprimanded him for interfering with a plan that did not belong to the Schlange Clan.

"You do realize our clans will have to migrate sooner than expected because of this." Adalwolf's häuptling snarled and slammed his fist down on the ground beside him. "This mistake could very well cost us, Giftschwanz!"

The Skorpion häuptling growled again. "Don't worry. I'll make Wolfrik pay for his betrayal."

"Make sure you do," Adalwolf's häuptling snapped. "Or I'll send Adalwolf to do the job you should have done from the beginning."

Adalwolf's smirk slid back into place, even as warmth filled his chest. It wasn't often his häuptling praised him, but it was such offhanded comments that showed exactly how highly the mann thought of him.

Even the geist's amused *'It's a wonder your two clans can do anything at all'* didn't faze Adalwolf.

~~*~*

Gemi was awakened from a light doze when the flap of Mandel's tent dropped shut. Glancing over her shoulder, she realized she must have slept longer than she had thought if Wolfrik had already returned from Jakob's questioning. She nodded to the Geistmagier before turning back to watch Ferez sleep.

The king hadn't stirred, and his face was smooth and relaxed. Before Mandel had left for his living tent—unlike Lakina, Mandel refused to sleep in the same tent as his patients unless it was an emergency—the Heilemagier had assured Gemi that all the physical wounds had healed. The only thing left to heal fully was his geist, but Mandel had believed it wouldn't take much longer.

Then again, Mandel's expertise on weakened geister was rather limited.

"I truly am sorry."

The words startled Gemi from her observation of her freund, and she glanced over her shoulder once more.

"For what? You have done nothing to me, and Frenz—"

She paused and glanced around, even though she knew the three of them were the tent's only occupants.

"Ferez has already forgiven you," she murmured. When Wolfrik nodded slowly, she added lightly, "Besides, Flame is right: I overreacted."

The Skorpion snorted, and Gemi frowned at him. Though she had been the one to say it, it hurt that he would agree so quickly and casually.

"You agree."

"Nein." Wolfrik took a couple steps closer. "I wouldn't call it overreacting." Gemi raised an eyebrow, and he shrugged.

"I've seen what you two have been through together. You may not have known each other for long, but you two are close. And you've nearly lost him several times already." He shook his head. "I think it's only natural you'd be so protective of him."

Despite the burn in her cheeks, Gemi continued to stare at him for a moment, studying his face. Finally, she nodded and glanced away. "Danke."

Gemi turned back to watch Ferez, listening to Wolfrik's footsteps as he approached. He was nearly to the bench where she was seated when she heard him gasp and stumble. Turning, she caught his arm just as his hands hit the bench and he fell to his knees.

"Scheisse!" he cursed through gritted teeth. One hand lifted, settling over his eyes, and he groaned.

"Wolfrik? What is it?" Gemi was up and beside the Geistmagier before she could think about it. Laying a hand on his back, she asked, more quietly, "What happened?"

There was a moment of silence, only broken by the Skorpion's heavy breathing. Shaking his head, he finally hissed out, "Nothing. It's nothing."

Gemi snorted. "This is hardly nothing, Wolfrik."

Even as she said it, she watched the lines of pain in his face smooth out.

He chuckled dryly, lifting his gaze to her face. "You're right." He hauled himself to his feet, and Gemi helped him onto the bench. He settled with his head in his hands. "But it's nothing I can't handle."

She sighed as she sat beside him. "Are you even going to tell me what just happened?"

Wolfrik shook his head but answered anyway. "It seems my häuptling has discovered my betrayal."

Gemi inhaled sharply. "Already?" Before he could answer, another question occurred to her. "But how was he able to affect you? He can't possibly be anywhere nearby."

Wolfrik didn't look up, and Gemi thought he must still be in pain. "I'm still connected to the Skorpion Clan's geisternetz."

Gemi frowned. The geisternetze were practical for communication over the long distances of the desert, but . . .

"Is that going to be a problem? Can you protect yourself from him?" She hesitated. "Can you break away from the geisternetz?"

She wasn't sure if the last would be preferable or not. While it might be useful to have an ally connected to the geisternetz of one of the Poison Clans, the connection might also be a liability if Wolfrik couldn't stop another geist from invading his own.

Wolfrik shook his head again and finally sat up. He looked comfortable, much to Gemi's surprise and relief.

"No need. I'm accustomed to protecting myself against the power of my häuptling's geist. I'm simply used to having some kind of warning and was caught off guard."

He rubbed gently as his temple, though Gemi doubted

he was still in pain. "I've managed to fortify my barriers, but . . ." He offered Gemi a wry smile. "I've had to pull some of my magie from the barriers around our freund's geist."

Gemi blinked, then laughed and shook her head. "I doubt he'll mind. Mandel's already healed all the physical damage, and he thinks his geist should fully recover by morgen."

Wolfrik nodded. "I believe he is correct. Our freund has a surprisingly resilient geist for a mann who bears no magie." When Gemi frowned, he shrugged. "Most non-magier would take far longer to recover from such an attack, even with the kind of help he's received. Even most non-Geistmagier would suffer longer."

Gemi's frown deepened as she turned to gaze at Ferez once more. "He doesn't deserve this."

She grimaced. Her voice sounded small to her own ears. She flinched as Wolfrik laid a hand on her shoulder, though he didn't comment on it.

"Few victims of such attacks ever do."

Gemi glanced sadly at Wolfrik. She remembered his words and what Flame had told her about his and Käfe's experiences.

"Nein. I don't suppose they do."

They fell into silence, both watching the sleeping king. Gemi knew she should find a bed soon as morgen would be arriving quickly, but she was loath to leave Ferez alone after the last couple of täge.

She was startled from her thoughts as a hand landed on her knee. She glanced sharply at Wolfrik, but the mann still had his eyes on the king. She frowned but waited for him to speak.

"I meant what I said before, you know." Gemi's frown

deepened. When Wolfrik finally glanced at her, his lips twitched.

"He is a good mann, one I am very proud to call king." He kept his voice low, for which Gemi was thankful, even if they were alone. "To be honest, I never expected a mann in such a position of power to be so . . . homely and down to earth."

Gemi chuckled. "I know what you mean." She shook her head. "It was a complete surprise to me when he asked me to allow him to travel the Ghost Trail with me. And when he finally managed to get it through my head that he was serious about knowing his people . . ."

Gemi shrugged, a small smile tugging at her lips. "He's unexpected, but I think that's what makes him such a great king."

"The others will think so, too, I believe." Gemi looked at the mann, wide-eyed. Wolfrik shook his head.

"I don't mean that I will tell them, Drache Krieger. I simply meant that when they do find out he is king, despite the deceptions, they will be happy it is he who sits on the throne. He is a good mann, one worthy of his title."

Gemi felt a smile slowly stretch her lips as she realized what Wolfrik was saying. She knew Ferez worried about what the people he met would think when they learned that this supposed farmer who had befriended them was actually the king of Evon.

It was a worry she knew all too well. After all, she had befriended them under a false name as well, and one täg, she would have to step forward as Duchess of Kensy. But Wolfrik was assuring her that the pretenses didn't matter. The name may be false, but the friendships and the feelings were not.

Gemi leaned forward and picked up Ferez's hand, squeezing it as she did. She knew Wolfrik had only been speaking about Ferez, but she felt lighter.

If what he says is true, then perhaps, one täg, the same will be true for me.

Sixteen

12 Mid Autumn, 224
Helloase, Zhulan

For Ferez, the next three days passed in a blur.

Not because of mental injuries. Thanks to Wolfrik and Mandel, those had fully healed. It was simply that James had managed to pack so much activity into those three days that Ferez was reminded of the first few days they had spent together at Main Highwayman Camp back in Kensy.

Then, he had introduced Ferez to every person they met, overwhelming the king to the point of pained frustration. Now, James insisted on introducing him to life as a nomad. Which, for their purposes, included long training sessions covering every technique Ferez might need to protect himself from the scharfmonde of nomad warriors.

At least he's engaging my instincts this time and not just my memory.

Ferez chuckled as James offered him a flask of water

after their most recent bout. The boy paused in using his kopfabdeckung to dry his face and smiled.

"What's so funny?"

Ferez shrugged. "Jus' thinkin' how much has changed, an' yet how little." When James frowned in obvious confusion, Ferez chuckled again. "A month ago, the firs' three days in camp wit' yeh led me to Lakina's healin' touch. Now—"

"I really am bad about overwhelming you, aren't I?" James's eyes darkened.

Ferez shook his head and clapped a hand to James's shoulder. "Yeh're a better teacher than yeh think. Like I was sayin', this time yeh've managed to make the information stick.

"Course, trainin' me to fight helps."

James snickered, his purple eyes flashing with amusement. He met Ferez's smile with one of his own, which only made Ferez grin. James's smile was infectious and warm, and Ferez tilted his head closer, curious how the boy would respond.

"James!"

Cold cut sharply through the warmth in Ferez's chest, and his hand spasmed on James's shoulder. The boy's infectious smile disappeared in a blink as he turned toward the voice, offering the speaker a small imitation of the expression. Reluctantly, Ferez turned and followed his gaze.

Käfe Giftschwanz sauntered toward them, one hand gripping a flask like the one James still held for Ferez. The king narrowed his eyes as she paused briefly, but the bright smile on her face never faltered. When she continued walking, she seemed to almost bounce in her enthusiasm.

"More water?"

She barely glanced at Ferez. Instead, her wide eyes focused solely on James. The king had to bite his tongue to keep from snapping at her. Pointing out how much of a fool she was making of herself would only make him look the same.

The reasoning did little to ease the anger burning within his chest.

Upon waking in Helloase that first day back, Ferez had discovered an instant dislike for the Skorpion girl. It was odd since he'd found himself in friendly discussions with her brother, but then, Wolfrik still addressed James by his title. Käfe, on the other hand, had shown no compunction about freely using the boy's given name.

"Er, well . . . extra water's always a good thing."

Ferez turned just in time to see James glance away from him. Frowning, the king turned back to Käfe. Wanting to save James any further awkwardness—*and, really, that's the only reason*—he took the proffered flask.

"Thank yeh."

He tried to keep his voice gracious, but a growl tinged the edges. The girl turned and gaped at him for the briefest moment before she snapped her jaw shut and pursed her lips. Ferez would have smirked if the growl hadn't felt like it still lingered in his throat.

"Ja, well . . ."

Käfe hesitated. Then, suddenly, her confidence seemed to return, and she turned back to James, smiling brightly once more. Ferez's frown deepened, and he took a drink from the flask, hoping to keep his displeasure from becoming obvious.

"You're such a wunderbar teacher, James!" Käfe clasped her hands behind her back and lowered her chin, allowing the edge of her kopfabdeckung to sweep over her eyes. "Maybe you could teach me?" She had lowered her voice, but her tone was still bright. "I've never been very good at fighting. I received most of my training from my vat—"

Her smile disappeared instantly, and her skin paled dramatically. Despite the dislike that had burned in Ferez's chest a moment before, he reached out, worried she was about to faint.

Instead, she glanced around, her eyes wide and face stricken. Ferez thought he knew what she was searching for even before Wolfrik appeared behind the group of young women who had accompanied Käfe. The moment Wolfrik appeared, Käfe's expression eased, but it wasn't until he'd wrapped an arm around her and pulled her close that she relaxed and the color began returning to her cheeks.

"Dummkopf." The older Skorpion's tone was affectionate, and a sad smile tugged at his lips.

Ferez suddenly felt uncomfortable. The siblings were obviously close—a result, no doubt, of their troubled upbringing. Käfe, however, suddenly seemed dependent on her brother in a way that made the confidence she'd shown since Ferez had awakened ring false.

Glancing toward James, he noticed the boy shifting his weight from foot to foot—a sure sign he was just as uncomfortable.

"Should we go help the others pull down tents?"

The clan would be leaving Helloase once the sun set, and preparations for the Wanderung, as they called the journey, had already begun. Ferez knew James had offered this last training session as an excuse to keep Ferez from being roped into helping with the preparations. The king thought the preparations now provided an excellent reason to leave the siblings alone while Käfe recovered from her slip.

James nodded. Then, to Ferez's surprise, the boy gripped his hand and fled.

~~*~*

Wolfrik was grateful to the king and Drache Krieger for giving them space, but at the same time, amusement filled him as he watched the Drache Krieger's hasty retreat.

The emotion disappeared quickly when Käfe stirred against his chest. Tightening his grip on her, Wolfrik brushed his geist against that of Ulla Kanten, who stood nearby. She responded immediately with agreement and ushered the other fräulein away.

Cupping Käfe's cheek, Wolfrik tilted her chin up. At first, she resisted, her hands tightening in his tunic.

"Käfe."

She relented, lifting her gaze to his with a sigh. Her face was serious and her eyes sad, but there was no trace of the panic he had felt in her geist before.

"Better?"

She closed her eyes and nodded. "Es tut mir leid."

Wolfrik sighed and shook his head.

"Don't apologize, schwester." He tapped her cheek with his thumb, and she opened her eyes again. "It's *his* fault and no one else's."

"Do we—do we truly not have to go back?"

The timid question startled Wolfrik, and he brushed his geist against hers once more. He cursed himself mentally as he realized the confidence she had shown since they arrived in Helloase had been a brittle mask. He was surprised it had lasted the three täge it had.

He lifted his hand from her back and laid it against her other cheek, holding her so she couldn't look away from his gaze. He didn't want to give her any reason to doubt his words.

"Never! I swore when we were younger that I would protect you from him, Käfe. Now that we're away, we are never going back."

Her eyes widened, and Wolfrik nearly growled at the anxiety he could see building in them.

"But . . ."

She hesitated. Wolfrik listened as her breathing increased, but he knew there was nothing he could do about it. She had to get this out on her own. He could easily pull the thought from her geist, but if Käfe was to find a place for herself away from their häuptling's influence, Wolfrik had to let her do some things herself.

"What if the Vereinte Clans decide we're too much trouble?" Her voice was nearly too soft for him to hear.

"Then we'll become river-dwellers!"

He didn't think the Vereinte Clans would turn them away now that they had accepted them, but even if they did, Wolfrik would never go back to their häuptling. He might still consider himself a Skorpion, but he would give up his life as a nomade if it meant protecting his little schwester.

For a moment, Käfe simply stared at him with a brittle expression he recognized all too well. After everything they had been through, Wolfrik was the only person his schwester trusted, but there were still times when she seemed hesitant to believe even him. She may never have felt the amount of mental pain he had, but as the only daughter of their häuptling, she had been subjected to pain and humiliation of a different kind.

Finally, the tension around her eyes eased, and she offered him a tiny smile. He let his own grow in response.

This was the girl he knew and loved. Although the confidence she had shown recently had made him hope the new environment and greunde were helping her come out of her shell, he knew the bold attitude was just not her.

Abruptly, he chuckled.

When she frowned curiously at him, he dropped his hands to her shoulders and kissed the top of her head. "You do realize you don't have a chance with the Drache Krieger, ja?"

Käfe sighed. "I know. The other fräulein said he'd never shown interest in anyone before." She shrugged and glanced in the direction the boy had run. "I thought maybe . . ."

She trailed off, her eyes distant. Wolfrik cupped her chin again, bringing her gaze back to his.

"That's not exactly what I meant." He chuckled when she frowned again. "I believe someone's already caught his eye."

Her frown deepened. "Who? Ulla's his schwester. Surely she would have known and said something to me." She squirmed slightly. "Then I wouldn't have made such a dummkopf of myself."

Her final words were soft and embarrassed, but Wolfrik simply kissed her forehead.

"I doubt their interest in each other is obvious to most people. I only figured it out myself because I've touched one of their geister."

Käfe's brow furrowed, and Wolfrik chuckled again. "Do you remember Hamlin?"

Wolfrik's apparent tangent confused Käfe even more. "Ja, of course I do. But what does he have to do with . . . ?"

Understanding suddenly lit her face, and she blinked rapidly. Wolfrik smiled. Hamlin was a Skorpion whom many in the clan had looked down on for his feminine features and ways. For jahre, he had appeared romantically apathetic, deftly ignoring the fräulein who attempted to flirt with him.

That had changed when a mann from the Schlange Clan began to court him. The two were lifebonded a jahr later.

Käfe's voice was a whisper when she finally spoke again. "You think James and . . ." She glanced back toward the oase. "That might explain why he doesn't seem to like me much."

Wolfrik was suddenly glad he had decided not to tell his schwester the true identity of the Drache Krieger's companion. The thought might have terrified her.

Käfe sighed and pouted. "And here I was hoping I could attract the son of the erstehäuptling."

Wolfrik stared at her, surprised, until he noticed the amusement in her eyes. He rolled his own.

"You do realize he's not the erstehäuptling's only son, ja?"

Suddenly, all amusement left Käfe's eyes as she once again lowered them, her cheeks pinking. Wolfrik blinked at the sudden change. He sighed as he considered the possible reason.

"Käfe." He hooked a finger under her chin. She didn't resist this time, but her gaze was hesitant as it met his. "Talk to me."

She took a deep breath. Letting it out, she glanced away from him. "Do you think Zuk would even be interested in someone like me?"

Ah.

"Is that who you're truly interested in, schwester?"

Käfe pulled her lower lip between her teeth. Wolfrik nodded.

When Käfe had first shown interest in the Drache Krieger, she must have been more attracted to the idea of the boy than to the boy himself. After all, while the two of them were considered weak among their clan, they were still the children of a häuptling. They had been trained from an early age to seek partners worthy of their status.

However, her current reaction, as well as her refusal to turn her confident attentions onto the erstehäuptling's heir, told Wolfrik that her interest in the eldest Kanten sibling had more to do with the actual mann than what he was.

"Would you like for me to speak to him for you?"

Ja, there were some things Käfe had to do for herself, but Wolfrik knew his schwester well enough to know that this was not one of them. When she nodded hesitantly, a faint smile touching her lips, he pulled her into a hug.

"If it will make you happy, I would be glad to."

They stayed there for a while longer, her face buried against his chest, his lips pressed against her kopfabdeckung.

~~*~*

Gemi probably shouldn't have run. She had heard the giggles issuing from the fräulein as she pulled Ferez away, but Käfe had been making her uncomfortable for täge. Ulla even knew how Gemi felt about other fräulein flirting with her, but her schwester had simply watched and smirked.

So she'd been all too eager to take the excuse Ferez had offered. When she ran, though, she didn't aim for any place in particular. So when Ferez finally pulled her to a stop, she was surprised to see that they were near the spring. Flame lay nearby and lifted her head, cooing curiously.

"Are yeh all right?"

Gemi was glad to hear only a touch of amusement in Ferez's voice. Offering him a small smile, she lifted a hand to tug at her kopfabdeckung and nodded.

"Ja," she muttered, glancing to the side.

Her cheeks heated as she debated whether she should play off her hasty retreat as a discomfort around hysterical women or simply leave it at that. Either way seemed too dishonest, and she'd found herself wanting to share more and more with the king since that conversation at the Handelmann haus.

Hesitantly, she added, "I've never been comfortable with the flirting of fräulein."

Ferez squeezed her shoulder, and she lifter her gaze back up to his face. He offered her a bright grin, his eyes shining warmly.

"Nothin' wrong wit' that."

He fell silent, and Gemi stared into his eyes. Those mingling patches of blue and silver drew her in, and she found herself wanting to get lost in them.

"Oy, James!"

The voice made them both jump, and Gemi took a step back as she realized she'd only been a few inches away from Ferez. Swallowing down a sudden disappointment, she turned toward the voice.

Zuk was waving at them from a nearby tent that was in the process of being dismantled. "If the two of you have time to stand around, why don't you help with the preparations?"

A sharp, angry whistle had Gemi turning to gape at Flame. Zuk only responded to the insult with a short bark of laughter and his own whistle, which Gemi couldn't understand. Whatever it was, it didn't calm Flame, who rose to all fours and began to burble angrily.

As drache and Tieremagier continued to trade insults, Gemi felt the hand on her shoulder squeeze, and she turned back to Ferez. His grin had softened.

"Why don' we lend a hand, James? I'm sure they could use as much help as they can get, aye?" He leaned forward and smiled conspiratorially. "Besides, I still wanna learn as much abou' my people's lives as I can."

Gemi nodded, though mentally she snorted. She didn't think he understood exactly what he was asking to do.

But then, who am I to deny the king?

~~*~*

Ferez groaned as he settled himself into Last Chance's saddle. The pale mare twisted her neck to look back at him, the look in her dark eye one of concern. Patting her withers lightly, he offered her a small smile. He'd be all right; he was just incredibly sore.

He didn't know how the nomads managed to do this so often, but it was their way of life, according to James. They were constantly migrating. They may not have moved as often as James did, since James said they only migrated between three different oases over one season. However, all of James's belongings fit on his person or within Shadow's saddlebags.

To pack up your entire home that often . . . ?

Ferez shook his head. He couldn't imagine it.

"Are you all right?"

Ferez turned to find James and Shadow sidling up next to them. To his amusement, Shadow shifted his weight so his shoulder brushed Last Chance's. Last Chance twisted her neck, in turn, and lipped his neck affectionately.

"Is it jus' me," Ferez asked with a nod toward the horses, "or are Last Chance an' Shadow growin' closer?"

Shadow shifted his weight away from Last Chance and turned to eye Ferez with a snort. James laughed.

"I'd say Shadow's offended by the suggestion, but in all honestly, that would be a lie."

Shadow twisted his neck more to give his bondmate the horse's equivalent of a glare. He relaxed with a soft nicker, though, when Last Chance lipped him once more.

Ferez chuckled. "So I'm not imaginin' it."

James shook his head with his own chuckle. As he sobered, the boy reached up and squeezed Ferez's shoulder.

"How do you feel?"

The question was serious, but the tone wasn't as worried as Ferez remembered from several nights ago. The king smiled and shrugged, though he immediately winced as his left shoulder twinged.

"Jus' a little sore." He rubbed his hand over the back of his left shoulder. He had backed into the end of a tent pole at one point, and his shoulder apparently hadn't forgiven him yet.

"I guess I asked for it, though."

Another chuckle brought his gaze back to James. He was pleasantly surprised to find a distinct lack of the guilt that had appeared earlier in the day. Instead, the boy's purple eyes danced in amusement.

"You were rather insistent."

Ferez couldn't stop the grin that spread his lips, and he chuckled in turn. Their conversation continued, only pausing briefly when Hausef gave the signal for the clan to begin the nightlong Wanderung to Friedlichoase.

~~*~*

Ferez slowly opened his eyes.

For the second time this season, he found himself

waking to the view of softly glowing pale fabric with no memory of how he had gotten there.

He could remember the journey from the night before. They'd left Helloase just before sunset. The journey had lasted so long he had apparently been out of it when they finally arrived. He vaguely recalled seeing pink in the sky, being coaxed to drink something refreshing, and then being maneuvered a couple of times.

What really puzzled Ferez was the fact that he was obviously once again in a tent. How the nomads had managed to put up a tent after a full night of travel and a few hours spent dismantling the entire camp was beyond him. The very fact that he could barely remember their arrival told Ferez he himself had certainly not been up to the task.

A sudden rustling caught Ferez's attention. He might have thought it was the sound of cloth moving against cloth except the sound, though soft, was too solid. Turning his head away from the wall of fabric, he looked over the tent's interior. Unsurprisingly, the room was laid out exactly as it had been in Helloase.

It took a moment of squinting through the low lamplight before Ferez pinpointed the source of the rustling sound. As his eyes landed on the sleeping area of James's two youngest siblings, a quiet chittering joined the rustling.

He chuckled. The two young mages were speaking to each other, though he doubted they understood what the other was saying. It was more likely that the two wished to let the other know they were awake without waking anyone else.

The thought drew Ferez's attention back to the other beds. To his surprise, other than the two children, he was the first to wake. It was unprecedented. Ferez had never been one for waking early, and the schedule he and James had been pulling had found him sleeping in whenever possible.

Shaking his head in wonder, Ferez shifted his blankets to the side and carefully climbed to his feet. He tried to be quiet, but he must have made enough noise to catch the attention of the children. The tent suddenly went silent save for the even breaths and soft snores of the still-sleeping nomads.

Offering a quiet chuckle to the silence, Ferez stretched his arms above his head, relieved to note his shoulder, as well as the rest of his body, seemed to have mostly recovered overnight. The rustle of cloth caught his attention as he dropped his arms, and he turned back toward Hausef's youngest.

The two had already climbed from their bedding. Ava was helping Lorenz situate his kopfabdeckung, hers already settled atop her head. When Ava finished, she turned to Ferez, smiled, and motioned him toward the tent's entrance. Grabbing his own kopfabdeckung, he followed the children outside.

He had ducked through the entrance, his kopfabdeckung half settled on his head and the fabric of the entrance catching on his shoulder, when he stopped and gaped. A giggle reached his ears, and a tug on his statusgürtel propelled him forward enough to get him out of the entrance.

"Wha' . . . ?"

He was surrounded by tents—the very ones he'd seen around the häuptling's tent at the other oasis. He couldn't understand how the nomads had managed to raise every tent they had before they went to sleep. It seemed impossible for them to have managed it with how exhausted they must have been.

Another giggle caught his attention, and he dropped his

eyes down to Ava, who still stood next to him, grinning. In the next second, he found something else to gape at.

The ground was green.

Grass had been sparse at Helloase, and what had been available was tough and reserved for certain food animals. While he wasn't an Animal Mage, he knew Last Chance had despaired that she had to depend on the shrub plants and the rationed grains the nomads carried for their horses.

Here, the ground was covered in greenery that spread farther than Ferez would have ever expected in the desert. There were trees, too, and not the sparse, small ones that stood about the height of a man. These trees towered in comparison to the ones at Helloase, though they couldn't compare in size to those of the northern forest.

The tugging at his statusgürtel brought his attention back to Ava once more.

"How . . . ?"

She twittered.

"It's part of the Wanderung for the adults to raise the tents once we reach a new oasen." Her grin widened, and she pointed toward his head. "You might want to fix your kopfabdeckung. Bruder won't be happy if you get senf seeds in your hair."

At the mention of the desert seeds that seemed to prefer living hosts, Ferez reached up and straightened his kopfabdeckung, which had hung half off his head. Once he'd settled the corded circlet around his head, securing the cloth in place, Ava took his hand and led him through the camp.

"The adults do all the work with pulling down the tents and putting them back up, so it's ein bisschen of a tradition that the adults sleep late after the Wanderung. We children always entertain ourselves while they sleep."

As they moved through the camp, more children wandered out of the surrounding tents. Ferez noticed one adult attempting to stifle a yawn as she pushed past her tent's entrance, but the lump in the middle of her tunic told Ferez she was a young mother awakened by her hungry infant.

"So wha' do the children do while the adults sleep?"

And is it safe?

He tried to ignore the images of giant desert cats filling his head. Still, he couldn't imagine allowing the clan's children such unobstructed freedom, no matter how involuntary it might be.

Ava flashed him a smile over her shoulder. "We nomaden learn from an early age the dangers of the desert. We generally stay gathered together near the springs and play while we wait for the adults to finally wake."

Glancing around, Ferez noticed the other children were all heading in the same direction Ava was pulling him. At the same time, he noticed they were leaving behind familiar tents.

"Where're we—?"

"Ava!"

The voice was young and female. The speaker was easy to spot, as the girl was waving at them with one hand, her other gripped in the hands of a smaller child. The smaller child turned out to be Lorenz, who had left them behind when Ferez was staring around the camp in wonder.

Once they were closer, Ferez recognized the girl as well.

"Yeh're the young Mage Healer who helped Heal my shoulder."

The girl nodded, offering him a smile. Ava tugged her hand free of Ferez's and stood between him and the girl. "Frenz, this is Lakritze Flügelschutz, daughter of the Falke Clan häuptling. Lakritze, this is Frenz Kanti, freund of the Drache Krieger."

Lakritze gave a small bow, her smile widening. "Angenehm, Herr Kanti! Though I'm afraid I wasn't actually much help for your shoulder. I'm still in training."

Ferez offered a smile of his own. "Well, yeh migh' still be learnin' to control yer magic, but I'd say yeh've already perfected yer bedside manner."

The girl's smile turned shy. She ducked her head as pink tinged her cheeks. "Danke."

"Well, this is a surprise."

A man walked up behind Lakritze and laid a hand on her shoulder. A glance at his statusgürtel told Ferez this man was quite possibly the häuptling of the Falke Clan.

"I wasn't expecting any Katzen adults to be awake for several hours yet."

Lakritze tilted her head back to smile at the man. "Vati, this is Herr Kanti. He's the mann whose shoulder was injured while rescuing us from the Handelmann haus."

"Ach." The Häuptling lifted his gaze back to Ferez, who could feel his cheeks heating at the girl's words. "You are the Drache Krieger's companion, then."

"Aye, sir." Ferez bowed his head to the man. "An' yeh're the häuptling o' the Falke Clan?"

The man grinned and offered his hand. "Meinhard Flügelschutz, häuptling of the Falke Clan, ja." Ferez shook the offered hand. "Komme!" Meinhard dropped Ferez's hand and motioned toward the spring. "I'll introduce you to the Spinne häuptling."

Ferez hesitated. "I don' wish to be a bother."

Meinhard shook his head. "Nein, of course you're not. Ever since we learned the Drache Krieger had taken on a human companion, we've wanted to get to know the mann who could convince James to let someone travel with him."

The häuptling's grin softened. "The götter know the boy needs as many freunde as he can get."

Ferez nodded. The boy was well known and well liked, but Ferez had learned there were few people he actually let close. Murmuring his agreement, Ferez followed him farther into the oasis.

~~*~*

Gemi woke with a sigh, though she kept her eyes shut at first. The Wanderung was the only time she let herself sleep for as long as she could. When she did finally wake, she always lingered in the dark and comfort of her bedding for several minutes.

As the soft rustle of cloth began to fill the tent, Gemi finally opened her eyes. Smiling at the familiar fabric of her familie's tent, she rolled over and pulled herself from her nigh-irresistible bedding. She stretched her body, happy to find a distinct lack of kinks. Her next task was to straighten her statusgürtel and situate her kopfabdeckung upon her head. It wasn't until her clothing was settled that she finally allowed herself to glance around the tent at her stirring familie.

Ulla, who had joined the tradition of the Wanderung at the same time Gemi had, was still sound asleep. Even Zuk, who had been a part of the tradition for jahre longer, was still abed, though Gemi could see him shifting restlessly beneath his blanket. The others—Mütter, Vater, Tante Isa, and even the Giftschwanz siblings—were already out of bed, all in various stages of preparing for the täg.

With a sense of her familie in her geist, Gemi glanced at Ava and Lorenz's beds. Empty, as expected. They always were when she woke from the first sleep after the Wanderung.

Nodding at the familiarity, she finally turned to Ferez's bed. She had learned over the past few siebentäge that the mann would sleep in whenever he could. No doubt she'd have to wake him, much like someone would for Ulla.

Except Ferez's bed was empty. Her throat closed up. She must have cried out, though, because suddenly hands were on her arms and voices sounded in her ears. Not that she could understand them. Her geist sought Ferez's presence despite his empty bedding.

"James!" Flame's shout filled Gemi's geist.

"Flame! Where's Ferez? Where—"

Pain bloomed across her cheek, and she caught her breath. Gemi blinked a few times and focused on Wolfrik. He stood in front of her, one hand gripping her upper arm, the other flexing.

"Get hold of yourself, Drache Krieger! *Frenz* is safe and well."

Gemi inhaled sharply. She'd nearly given away the king's true identity! Flame protected their geister from Geistmagier, but their mindspeech could not always be so easily hidden.

Taking a deep breath to calm the panic clawing up her throat, Gemi nodded and refocused on Flame. *"Where is Frenz, Flame?"*

Flame considered her for a moment. *"He is with the children."*

Nodding again, Gemi excused herself from the tent. Questions followed her, but she barely heard them. She could think of nothing but finding Ferez and making sure he was safe.

She managed to keep from running farther into the oase,

but panic still twisted her gut and tightened her chest. When she reached the closest spring, she found the Katze children playing as they always did after the Wanderung.

Ferez was not among them.

She couldn't breathe. She gasped Ferez's name, but she couldn't hear it above the throbbing in her ears. Warmth filled her geist, but even Flame's presence couldn't distract her from Ferez's absence.

Where is he? Where's Ferez? Where—

"Bruder!"

Gemi spun toward the voice. Ava ran toward her, a grin decorating her lips. Gemi's geist rebelled against such happiness. She would have snarled if her gaze hadn't moved past her schwester and fastened on a sight that hit her like a torrential unwetter.

Ferez sat with several others around a fire pit closer to one of the other two springs. He offered her a small smile and a wave, but his attention was already being drawn back to the people around him. Gemi stared, pain digging into her palms. *Ferez is safe. There's nothing to fear.*

"Really, your trust in us is gratifying."

Shadow's words were heavy with sarcasm, and Gemi snapped her gaze from Ferez. Behind him, grazing on the lush green grass of the oase, stood Shadow and Last Chance. The stallion didn't even bother to lift his head, but Last Chance did, turning toward Gemi.

When Shadow answered whatever question the mare had asked, Gemi's cheeks burned, and she glanced away from the pferde. Why did they have to become so close? She didn't need any others knowing of her unreasonable panic.

"Hardly unreasonable after everything." Flame caressed Gemi's geist with her own. Gemi nodded tightly but

otherwise didn't reply. Unreasonable or not, her reaction had been entirely unnecessary.

"Bruder?"

Gemi looked down. Ava stared up at her, a small frown replacing the grin from before.

"Are you all right?"

Gemi nodded and forced a small smile to her lips. "I'm well, Ava." The young Tieremagier continued to eye her for a moment but finally nodded. Grabbing Gemi's wrist, Ava pulled Gemi toward the firepit.

As soon as she could, Gemi seated herself on the log beside Ferez. He flashed her an easy smile, though it dimmed as he focused on her. Worry darkened his eyes, but Gemi shook her head before he could speak. All she wanted was to know he was there. She couldn't . . . accept acknowledgment of it.

Ferez nodded and touched Gemi's wrist. She took a deep, shaky breath and let her shoulder relax into his. *He's safe. He's all right.*

Only then did she realize the pain in her palms came from the bite of her nails. As Ferez's fingers settled more firmly against her wrist, her hands relaxed.

"I see the Katzen have finally decided to rise."

The words came across the fire, and Gemi reluctantly allowed her attention to move from Ferez. To her surprise, Häuptling Meinhard Flügelschutz of the Falke Clan sat across from her.

"Ja, we have." She nodded to the häuptling, but her eyes scanned the circle of nomaden.

She quickly recognized everyone. Seated next to Meinhard were his lebenfrau and his mütter, Valborga. Gemi suspected his daughter, Lakritze, had been around as well, since Ava had been, but the girls had already left to play with the other children. On another log sat Häuptling Genevieve Seidenstrang of the Spinne Clan, her lebenmann and her eldest son seated beside her.

Gemi shot Ferez a smirk. "You certainly know how to make freunde, don't you?"

Ferez raised his free hand, his renewed smile betraying the witz of it. "They found me."

"He is right," Genevieve added, her voice melodic. Gemi glanced at the Heilemagier. "We've wanted to meet him since we learned you had taken on a human companion, James." She offered Ferez an apologetic smile. "Es tut mir leid if you have felt harassed, Herr Kanti."

"Course not," Ferez answered with a wide smile. "Though I do wish yeh'd call me Frenz; Herr Kanti seems so formal."

The Spinne häuptling's response was a ringing laugh.

Gemi glanced around the group once more and frowned as she realized why the group seemed odd. "Where is Wüstenwolf?"

Wüstenwolf Seelenesser was häuptling of the Wolf Clan, which was usually the first clan to arrive at the seasonal gathering oase. Their previous oase was east of the San, farther away than any others. The Pferd Clan, whose previous oase was also east of the San, was usually the last to arrive, so Gemi didn't expect them until the following morgen.

Both häuptlinge shook their heads. "The Wölfe have yet to arrive," Meinhard answered.

Gemi's hands tightened into fists once more. "Have you heard from them?"

When both Meinhard and Genevieve nodded, she relaxed. Flame made an offhand comment about her constant state of worry not being healthy, but Gemi pushed the thought aside and focused on the conversation with the nomaden.

"With all the trouble in the städte," Genevieve elaborated, "Wüstenwolf decided to stay at Schattigoase until their missing clan members returned. I believe the last message said they'd joined the Pferd Clan at the River San." The Heilemagier glanced at Meinhard, who nodded in confirmation.

"They should arrive in the morgen with the Pferde, then?" Gemi asked.

The others nodded in agreement. The group fell into silence. For her part, Gemi wondered if the katastrophe was finally coming to an end.

Meinhard was the one who broke the silence. "I do have one question I wasn't sure Frenz was up to answering." Gemi tilted her head and waved for the häuptling to continue. "Is it true there are those among the Skorpion Clan who are willing to join the Vereinte Clans?"

A grin stretched Gemi's lips, and Ferez gave a barking laugh. When she glanced at the king, he offered a grin that reflected her own, and she turned her gaze back to the other nomaden.

"Better than that," she answered. "A son and a daughter of the häuptling have offered their allegiances to my vater, and they wish to save those in their clan who would willingly follow the erstehäuptling."

"And you trust this?" Genevieve sounded both hopeful and wary.

It had saddened all five häuptlinge of the Vereinte Clans when both the Skorpion and the Schlange Clans had not only rejected Hausef as erstehäuptling but had actively worked against the Vereinte Clans. That a step was being taken toward total unification was exactly what the clans had been wanting for jahre. That nothing had moved forward for so long meant any new steps could only be taken with caution.

Gemi nodded. "Flame and I have spoken with the Skorpione enough to know they are sincere in their desire to join the Vereinte Clans. Also . . ."

She trailed off and glanced at Ferez. The king's grin softened, and he lifted a hand to squeeze her shoulder. Taking a deep breath, she turned back to the häuptlinge, who watched them with raised brows.

"Wolfrik saved Frenz, both in body and in geist. He has my dankpflicht, if nothing else."

All six nomaden inhaled sharply and glanced at each other. Gemi nodded. Dankpflicht was more than just gratitude—it was a formal obligation born of that gratitude. Gemi had learned the importance of this nomade tradition early on when she earned Hausef's dankpflicht by saving Zuk's life. His offer to adopt Gemi as one of his own and officially accept her as a nomade had been his way of repaying the dankpflicht.

Both häuptlinge bowed their heads. Genevieve was the one to speak the words of acceptance that Gemi hadn't expected to hear until much later.

"We would gladly accept into the Vereinte Clans him who has the Drache Krieger's dankpflicht."

Gemi bowed her head in return. In most situations, the use of her nomade title annoyed her. However, these words were formal, so the formal title was necessary.

"Danke, Häuptling Seidenstrang, Häuptling Flügelschutz. Your acceptance is appreciated."

With the formalities completed, Gemi lifted her head and met the smiles both Meinhard and Genevieve offered with her own. A motion to her left quickly caught her attention, and she turned to find Ferez shaking his head.

"I still have a lo' to learn, don' I?"

Gemi laughed. Ignoring the curious looks from the others, she patted the king's knee.

"Frenz, two siebentäge is nowhere near long enough to learn everything you would want to know about the nomaden."

Ferez chuckled. To Gemi's bemusement, the conversation quickly turned to educating him about nomade tradition.

Seventeen

14 Mid Autumn, 224
Friedlichoase, Zhulan

Flame viewed the fire-lit area with growing exasperation. It always amazed her how long it took the nomads to begin these interclan meetings.

It did not help, either, that two clans of nomads had just arrived this morning and had awoken only hours beforehand.

They really should put these meetings off an extra day, even if tomorrow they will be preparing for the festival.

A chuckle echoed through her mind. She swung her head toward Gemi, who was currently conversing with Alys Reiter about Peppi Kluger's new position as governor of Machtstadt. When she realized her bondmate was not even paying her any attention and had simply been amused by Flame's annoyance, the dragon felt her irritation grow.

A steadily growing rumble began to drown out the surrounding conversations. As the nomads began to quiet and look around, Flame realized the sound was coming from her. She tried to quell it but was unsuccessful, even once all the nomads had stopped talking.

Hausef stepped up to her and laid a hand on her nose, trilling comfortingly. Gemi brushed against her mind, murmuring contritely. Flame finally stopped growling and huffed.

"Just start the meeting already, will you?" She swung her head out from under the Animal Mage's hand and curled up tightly along the edge of the surrounding crowd. Even the warmth of the fire dancing along her scales couldn't fully soothe her.

~~*~*

Hausef sighed. *How did we manage to irritate Flame so thoroughly?* Turning back to the gathered nomaden, he made sure he had everyone's attention.

"It seems we have taken ein bisschen too long in starting the Gleichrat." He motioned toward the log benches surrounding the fire. "Shall we?" There were murmurs from the others, but the benches were quickly occupied by the appropriate people.

The Gleichrat was a tradition Hausef had eagerly renewed once the clans were united once more. Though held outside where anyone could attend and learn of the current events each clan was dealing with, the Gleichrat was essentially a seasonal discussion between the erstehäuptling, the häuptlinge, and the Drache Krieger.

While the other four häuptlinge took their usual places, Gemi hesitated near the Katze bench. When she glanced at him, he smiled and nodded.

There were only five benches, one for each häuptling and any of his, or her, familie who wished to take part in the discussion. Hausef and Gemi were often joined by Isa and

Mina, but the bench was not nearly long enough to accommodate all four of them plus the two Skorpione.

And Frenz? His daughter continued to hesitate, casting her eyes toward the farmer. Hausef frowned. *She wishes him to be involved in the discussion?*

He knew they were close—very close if the looks they'd been exchanging for the past few täge were any indication. That she would want to involve him in the politik of the nomaden, though . . .

That spoke of a position of importance Hausef had not yet considered.

But why would a farmer register such importance to Gemi?

They had hesitated long enough for everyone else to notice, and the standing nomaden began to mutter curiously.

"Erstehäuptling?"

Genevieve of the Spinne Clan was the häuptling who finally spoke up, breaking him from his thoughts. He nodded to her and turned back to his daughter.

"James." He motioned to their bench. When she opened her mouth, he simply raised an eyebrow and she snapped it shut, her cheeks darkening. He had called her by name, not by title, and she would have recognized it for the order it was.

Apparently, she'd also fully understood his message. She beckoned Frenz and the Giftschwanz siblings to sit beside her, her companion to her left and the Geistmagier to her right. She glanced at Hausef for confirmation, which he gave with a small nod.

To his surprise, the rest of his familie settled into guarded stances behind the four, even young Ava and Lorenz looking serious. Hausef checked a sigh. It had been jahre since his familie had felt the need to stand together like this when facing the other clans.

"What is going on, Hausef?"

He did sigh then. He wasn't surprised Roswalt Reiter, häuptling of the Pferd Clan, was the first to speak up. Hausef walked around his familie, approaching the fire, as Roswalt continued.

"Who are these . . . ?"

A sharp inhale seemed to echo through the crowd. Hausef pursed his lips, knowing Roswalt wasn't the only one to have suddenly noticed the brown of the newcomers' statusgürtel. Would chaos interrupt this meeting like it hadn't since that first jahr? Genevieve and Meinhard might have formally accepted the Skorpione, but neither had met them either.

"Skorpione!" Roswalt's hiss was closer to wind rushing over a blade of grass than to a snake's. "What are these köter doing here?"

Hausef stiffened at the use of the slur. Before he could respond, Meinhard leaned forward.

"Ruhe, Roswalt! Is this how you would treat those who would willingly join the Vereinte Clans?"

"Do not scold me, Meinhard!" Roswalt snapped. "How can we possibly trust any Skorpione when they were behind the katastrophe with the städte?"

Meinhard looked ready to respond, but a quiet voice beat him to it.

"I can promise you, Häuptling Reiter, that we have no intention of betraying your clans or hurting them in any way."

All eyes turned to Wolfrik, who sat up straight and held his head high. "Already, we have turned our backs on our häuptling. Would you judge us by the color of our statusgürtel as the river-dwellers judge us by our dress?"

Roswalt opened his mouth and then hesitated. The

comparison, if nothing else, would have caught the mann off guard. His eldest daughter, Alys, sitting to his right, laid a hand on his knee.

"Vater." Roswalt turned to meet her stern gaze warily. "Even the river-dwellers are learning to hold their judgment. Shall we do any less?"

Roswalt firmed his chin but glanced around the fire. Hausef looked with him. Genevieve nodded calmly while Meinhard simply glared at the Pferd häuptling. Even Wüstenwolf of the Wolf Clan, who had arrived that morgen with the Pferde, met Roswalt's stubborn glance with a grin. Of course, Wüstenwolf was a Geistmagier, so Hausef suspected he had at least had the benefit of a mental introduction to Wolfrik.

Roswalt finally huffed and turned a glare on Wolfrik. "What possible reason could you have for joining the Vereinte Clans and turning your backs on your own clan?"

Silence followed, long enough that Hausef began to doubt the Skorpion would even answer.

"Wolfrik."

As Gemi spoke, she and Käfe each touched one of his knees while Frenz laid a hand on his shoulder. Hausef thought the show of support might be more convincing than whatever words the Skorpion might use.

"You misunderstand me, Häuptling Reiter," Wolfrik finally whispered.

"How so?" Roswalt sneered. Beside him, Alys rolled her eyes

"We have not betrayed our clan—simply our häuptling."

Murmurs ran through the crowd, and Roswalt's sneer changed to a confused frown. "How are those not the same thing?"

Hausef cleared his throat, thinking a formal introduction

would be best. The four häuptlinge turned to him. Roswalt still frowned, but the other three offered him attentive, if slightly knowing, smiles.

"Häuptlinge, may I present Wolfrik and Käfe Giftschwanz, youngest children of the häuptling of the Skorpion Clan."

The final words were unnecessary, he knew. The name Giftschwanz was as old and as well known as any of the häuptlinge's names. Indeed, gasps and whispers broke out among the crowd the moment he spoke it. Roswalt looked like the pferd he had been riding had come to a sudden halt.

"You are . . ."

When Roswalt seemed unable to finish the thought, Wüstenwolf hummed and nodded.

"You would take up the mantle of häuptling once those in your familie who follow your v—er, the current häuptling are defeated?"

Hausef raised an eyebrow. Now he was certain Wüstenwolf had spoken mentally with Wolfrik. He had apparently already had a taste of the Skorpion's temper when it came to referring to his vater as such.

Curious, Hausef glanced toward his own familie and caught Isa's eye. He felt the familiar brush of her geist against his as she gleaned the question he wanted to ask.

"Remember, bruder," she answered with a touch of amusement, *"I did invite him to join the geisternetz."*

Hausef nodded and turned back to the discussion.

"I would," Wolfrik answered, sounding more confident, "as long as the erstchäuptling agrees."

"And I already have," Hausef answered. "Although it could be a while." He smiled apologetically. "We haven't been able to find the Gift Clans in jahre."

Wolfrik smirked. "It doesn't have to be."

Hausef frowned at the Skorpion, confused.

"You had said your häuptling already knew of your betrayal." When Wolfrik nodded, Hausef shook his head. "He would not have allowed the clan to remain at the same oase, would he?"

Wolfrik shook his head. "Nein, he wouldn't have, but that matters little."

He paused, and Hausef wondered if he would explain. Only Gemi, Frenz, and Käfe seemed to understand what he meant, though the twist of Isa's lips proved she might already be privy to the knowledge as well.

"As I said," the Skorpion finally continued, "our häuptling knows of our betrayal. I know this because my geist is still merged with our clan's geisternetz."

Shocked murmurs broke out among the nomaden. Wolfrik was quick to add, "I have protected and hidden my geist from others in the geisternetz."

Hausef sighed, even as the crowd quieted. Wolfrik was subtle in his magie; Flame and Isa had both spoken highly of his skill in that matter.

But is it wise to have our geisternetz connected to theirs, even with such skill?

"Our häuptling doesn't even know I still live, let alone that I've salvaged the connection."

"And you can learn of the clan's location through it."

That was Wüstenwolf. Throughout the crowd, other Geistmagier nodded and murmured their agreement. Only then did Hausef realize their own geisternetz must have been opened to another level of discussion.

"Enough!" Silence followed Isa's sharp command. "This is not a kriegrat. This is Gleichrat."

"Agreed." Hausef let his gaze skim over the crowd. "The

next few täge are for celebration and the Adlerfest. Only afterward should we let ourselves consider krieg."

Reluctant agreement spread through the crowd.

"Well then, Erstehäuptling," Genevieve said, "shall we return to the topic at hand?"

Hausef nodded to the Heilemagier. She was the gentlest of the häuptlinge, but she was also the most formal in this type of setting.

Hausef watched her trade looks with Meinhard. "The Spinne and Falke Clans have already accepted these Skorpione into the Vereinte Clans."

After a short pause, she nodded toward the Katzen. "If the Drache Krieger will be our witness?"

"I will," Gemi answered with a bright smile.

"Very well, then," Wüstenwolf muttered.

Hausef frowned at the Wolf, who had sounded serious. At the age of twenty-six, Wüstenwolf was the youngest of the häuptlinge. His vater had died unexpectedly only a jahre after Unification, and the young Geistmagier had become häuptling at the age Zuk was now—the same age Hausef had been when he had taken up the mantle. While Hausef had found the sudden responsibility difficult and heavy, Wüstenwolf had managed to keep a boyish, mischievous charm that endeared him to his people.

Hausef watched the Wolf sat up straighter, his eyes and lips firm as he met each of the häuptlinge's gazes. "As the häuptling of the Wolf Clan, I, Wüstenwolf Seelenesser, accept Wolfrik and Käfe Giftschwanz as representatives of the Skorpion Clan within the Vereinte Clans."

The moment he finished citing the acceptance, Wüstenwolf broke into a grin. "Now I'll have another häuptling my age with whom I can mindspeak!"

Hausef snorted, as did several others, and even Genevieve rolled her eyes and shook her head.

"You would accept him so easily because of that, Wüstenwolf?" Roswalt snapped.

The Wolf shrugged. "My personal reasons have nothing to do with my acceptance of them as häuptling. I've heard enough to deem them acceptable for the Vereinte Clans. That he will be a Geistmagier häuptling is simply an extra prize."

Roswalt made a series of rustling sounds that Hausef suspected were curses in the plant tongue, especially when Lorenz made a shushing sound and buried his head against Ava's arm. Hausef glared at the Pferd, but it was Alys who elbowed and scolded the Pflanzenmagier.

"Vater! There are children present who can understand you."

Roswalt quieted and pursed his lips, still looking upset. Alys huffed and shifted away from him.

"Very well. If you are going to be like that, then I, as the future häuptling, will speak for the Pferd Clan and accept them."

Roswalt gaped at his daughter, and Hausef raised his brows in surprise. Alys was proud enough to take such decisions from her vater, but that she would accept the Skorpione when her vater would not was unexpected.

"Why . . . ?" Roswalt asked.

Alys glared at Roswalt. "They have proven themselves to the Drache Krieger and his drache." When the words appeared to have no effect on him, she added, "And if that is not enough for you, then know that the Drache Krieger owes them dankpflicht."

Roswalt's face contorted. Hausef could see the conflict in his eyes and nodded. A dankpflicht was important enough to outweigh whatever personal vendetta he might hold against the Skorpion Clan.

Eventually, Roswalt sighed, and his shoulders slumped.

"Very well," he muttered. "The Pferd Clan will accept those who hold the Drache Krieger's dankpflicht."

"Such enthusiasm."

The soft hiss came from behind Hausef, and he turned to Flame. The drache had barely moved, but she seemed more relaxed now. He wondered if this was the reason she'd been so anxious before the meeting began. She was the one who had originally spoken for the Skorpione. She must have understood there might be some who would be reluctant to accept them.

Hausef caught the her eye and offered a small smile. Flame lifted her head from the ground and nodded, crooning softly. As reluctant as the acceptance was, they both knew it was the best they could hope for at this point. After all, Roswalt was a Pflanzenmagier. Considering some of the plants that managed to survive Zhulan's harsh desert climate, it only made sense he would be the most stubborn of the häuptlinge.

The meeting turned to other topics then. Each häuptling shared their clan's experience during the ten täge of chaos. Gemi spoke about the renewed alliance with the river-dwellers, including the duke's apparent long-time interest in the nomaden and the newly chosen gouverneure.

To the surprise of most of the nomaden, Wolfrik even spoke of the tentative agreement between the two Gift Clans.

"They do not get along?" Surprised colored Genevieve's tone. Wolfrik shook his head. "Then how did they manage to agree to an alliance?"

"Why did they even want one?" Roswalt put in.

Wolfrik eyed the Pferd. "You underestimate the incentive of a common feind, Häuptling Reiter. Both our häuptling and that of the Schlange Clan see the Drache Krieger as a powerful enough threat to our clans to necessitate an alliance."

Gemi jerked and turned to stare at the Skorpion. "Me?" She shook her head. "I may be Drache Krieger, but I'm still just a child. Surely, they can't feel that threatened by me."

Hausef snorted. His daughter often underestimated the importance of her position.

"You forget, James. To the Gift Clans, you are the one who instigated the Unification. They would feel more threatened by the idea of you, at the very least, than they would by anyone else, even me."

"The erstehäuptling's correct, Drache Krieger," Wolfrik confirmed. "According to our häuptlinge, you are the greatest threat to our clans' ways of life. Whether or not it is true, there are those in our clans who believe that if you were removed, the Vereinte Clans would fall apart."

All of a sudden, Frenz Kanti straightened. "Speaking of . . ." the farmer muttered.

Hausef frowned at the mann. He had remained quiet so far, and the erstehäuptling had begun to think Gemi had simply wished to keep the mann by her side rather than having any intention of getting him involved in the meeting.

However, the farmer turned purposefully toward Hausef. "May I speak?"

Complete silence fell over the crowd. Most likely, those nomaden who had not already met the mann had thought him a companion of the Skorpione. His accent, however, would have made it clear he was not even a Zhulanbürger, let alone a nomade.

As quickly as the silence fell, it was broken just as quickly by murmurs spreading through the crowd. Confusion, and even anger, filled the voices, and Hausef stifled a groan. Perhaps it had been a mistake to allow Kanti a seat at the Katze bench.

No matter how important the mann might be to Gemi, the tradition of the Gleichrat was a trading of information between those of highest rank within the clans. As such, even the Giftschwanz siblings had the right to speak since they were the children of a häuptling and one was to be the future häuptling of his clan.

Kanti, on the other hand, was a simple farmer and, worse, an ausländer. That Hausef had let him have a place in the Gleichrat implied that he acknowledged the stranger as higher than most nomaden.

Even considering his friendship with Gemi, Hausef did not believe the farmer had earned such a rank. And many would resent such a position being held by an ausländer, regardless of whether the position was real.

Despite his sudden misgivings, Hausef would have to acknowledge him and let him speak. If he denied him a chance to speak when he had allowed him a place in the Gleichrat, the trouble Hausef faced would only worsen.

"You may." He ignored the cries of outrage from the surrounding crowd. They might wish to protest, but they weren't allowed to speak formally in the Gleichrat unless called to by someone seated at a bench.

Kanti dipped his head. Hausef glanced briefly at Gemi; she, too, watched Kanti curiously. His previous thought must have been correct, then. His daughter had not expected her companion to speak, and she was just as clueless as he was about what the farmer wished to discuss.

When Kanti turned to face the fire, Hausef twitched his gaze back to him. He blinked and stared. The mann had shifted his posture, and he now sat straight, tall, and . . . proud?

Hausef blinked again and shook his head.

The farmer suddenly radiated an aura of power that Hausef hadn't sensed before. It wasn't the power he associated with a magier, either, but that of a leader who respected his people. And his words, as he began to speak, were much clearer than Hausef had become accustomed to hearing from the mann.

Hausef abruptly remembered his earlier question of the mann's importance in Gemi's eyes. Was it possible Gemi had been mindful of the Gleichrat's tradition? Whoever Frenz Kanti was, Hausef was now certain he wasn't just a simple farmer. He was also certain Gemi knew the mann's true identity. It would explain why she insisted he be involved in everything she did.

An intense curiosity burned through Hausef, but he quickly squashed it. He knew his daughter well enough to know she wouldn't have kept this secret from him without good reason. Keeping that in his geist, he turned his attention to the mann's words.

Kanti offered an introduction of himself to the clans first. Hausef hadn't expected that, but it only solidified his suspicions of the mann's true position, whatever it was. He specifically called himself a farmer, and Hausef suspected a real farmer wouldn't have made the distinction.

A glance at the four häuptlinge revealed looks of surprise and possibly suspicion.

As Kanti paused to scan the crowds, Hausef noticed Wüstenwolf glance sharply at Wolfrik. The Skorpion jerked his head to one side, as unobtrusive a denial as one could give in this setting.

Hausef raised his brows again. If Wolfrik was protecting

Kanti's geist from even his new allies, perhaps even he thought the mann's true identity safe and important enough to keep secret. Wolfrik may have been a Skorpion, but that any nomade would go to such lengths for an ausländer reassured Hausef.

"I would place before the erstehäuptling," Kanti began, and Hausef snapped his gaze back to him, "the häuptlinge, and all the nomaden of the clans,"—Hausef raised a brow at that address—"a request for information. Not just for myself, but for the Drache Krieger, as well."

"Frenz!" Gemi muttered sharply.

By then, silence had fallen over the crowd, and her complaint was loud enough for everyone to hear. Kanti simply turned toward her and caught the wrist of the hand she'd raised in protest.

"You are not alone, James. Remember? You can depend on others. You don't have to do everything by yourself."

Gemi's mouth opened, and Hausef knew she would argue. If the Drache Krieger was known for one thing throughout the clans, it was his insistence that others depend on him, not the other way around.

It came as a shock, then, when Gemi closed her mouth instead, a thoughtful frown marring her features. To Hausef's surprise, she nodded and offered Kanti a small smile.

"You're right."

That was it. No further protest, no arguments—just a soft, simple agreement.

Hausef stared as Kanti turned back to the fire. He had known Gemini Cosley for five and a half jahre. Getting her to accept help from others was a battle. She simply couldn't allow herself to depend on others. Hausef knew even her bondmates struggled with it.

Yet this mann, Kanti, had known her for less than half a

season, and he had managed to get her to accept help with four sentences.

Hausef shook his head. Whoever he was, Frenz Kanti was important to Gemi in a way that had nothing to do with his mysterious position.

~~*~*

Gemi might have surprised many nomaden with her seemingly easy acquiescence, but it had been far from easy. Both Flame and Shadow had had to remind her of the conversation she'd shared with Ferez as they traveled along the San just a siebentäg ago.

Even then, it had taken a lot to overcome the pride and fear the thought of asking for help evoked. Through it all, Ferez had held her gaze. The look in his eyes, or possibly the way he held himself, had told her that while he respected her and her opinion, he would not back down from this.

Is that how I need to be handled, then? she thought snidely. *With a firm grip and unyielding stubbornness?*

"It is not that simple."

Flame was right. Gemi was simply mocking her own responses. They seemed to imply she trusted Ferez at a level she had trusted almost no one at, and that terrified her.

"Settle, James," Flame soothed. *"Listen."*

Gemi acknowledged the drache and focused on Ferez's words. He was describing the situation they'd discovered at Parshen Gut with young Gretchen Parshen and Der Geist. She had forgotten about his recommendation that they ask others for information.

Bringing it up now, in front of a large representation of the Vereinte Clans, was a smart move.

She was shocked, though, to realize his description—in

fact, his entire speech—was littered with Zhulanese words. Despite his accent, he spoke like a Zhulanbürger, mingling the Fayralese and Zhulanese in a way that had been perfected by the Zhulanese over the jahre.

Gemi shook her head. Once again, she had underestimated the king. He recognized the formality of the Gleichrat through his words just as much as through his speech and his actions.

"My request," Ferez finished, after telling of the message that Gretchen had passed on, "is for any information that might reveal to whom the names Markos and Eirene refer."

Whispers passed through the crowd, their tone different from those that had preceded Ferez's speech. Gemi felt her lips twitch as she realized the nomaden were taking the king seriously despite whatever anger or resentment they might have felt toward him as an ausländer.

That is a good omen.

The more they could accept him now, the more likely they would accept him as king when the revelation occurred.

"Häuptling."

The voice was soft but it carried, and the crowd fell silent once more. Gemi turned toward the Spinnen. Genevieve waved forward the mann who had appeared behind her, turning to Hausef as she did so.

"May my mann speak, Erstehäuptling?"

"He may."

As the mann stepped closer to the fire, Gemi realized he was old. Although she couldn't see his hair for his kopfabdeckung, his face was thick with wrinkles and his eyebrows were bushy and white.

"May I present Altmann Seeleweber, Heilig of the Spinne Clan."

Gemi started. She hadn't realized the Spinne Clan had its own Heilig. How hadn't she after five jahre with the clans? Then again, since her parents' deaths, she had avoided as much mention of religion as she could. She briefly recalled the strange tapestries she had seen in Tearmann before forcing her attention to the present.

"Markos and Eirene are ancient names," the Heilig began. "They come from the ancient culture and ancient language that ruled this land before Zhulanese and Fayralese replaced it.

"Even so, they are relatively young names. They were not used for long before they were replaced with the names we use today, so I doubt many would recognize them."

"And the names we use today?" Gemi asked.

She twitched as Ferez's hand landed on her knee and squeezed, but she couldn't remove her gaze from the Heilig. He claimed to recognize the two names. She and Ferez might be on the verge of learning exactly who stood against them.

She wasn't sure if the sudden churning in her stomach came from anticipation or dread.

Heilig Altmann gave a small shake of his head. "Markos is known to us as Krieg, and Eirene as Frieda."

Her stomach dropped. *Krieg? War? Why would—*

She couldn't breathe, couldn't see, couldn't focus beyond the implication of the holy man's words.

Nay, nay, nay! Oh, gods, please, nay! Please! I can't—

~~*~*

Ferez cursed and grabbed James's shoulder as the boy suddenly slumped. On his other side, Wolfrik did the same, his own face pale in the firelight.

Gasps rang through the crowd, but Ferez ignored them.

He couldn't focus on anything but James. He murmured lowly, hoping to rouse the boy from his sudden stupor. As he did, the holy man's words echoed in his ears—words Ferez had understood well enough despite the language barrier.

War and Peace.

The implication was frightening, but Ferez could understand the use of the latter, at least. James had been working for peace for about six years now. After that long, it only made sense that he be called Peace.

Forcing aside the revelation, Ferez cupped James's cheek and turned his face toward him. The boy's breathing was quick and shallow, his eyes stared sightlessly, and his skin held a pallor Ferez had never seen on him.

"James." He kept his voice low, ignoring Wolfrik and Käfe, the Kantens who stood over them, and even Flame, who crooned from beyond the crowd. "Snap out of it. You can't let him have this power over you. It's what he wants."

A hand on his shoulder drew Ferez's attention up to Mandel, but he shook his head and turned back to James, focusing on those dark purple eyes. He didn't think a Healer was what James really needed right now.

"Focus on me," he murmured. The crowd went silent, and even the crackling of the fire and the whisper of the wind seemed to quiet.

"Listen to my voice and focus on me. You are safe here. You are among friends. You have your clan. You have your family. You have your bondmates." He paused and let his voice soften. "You have me."

As Ferez murmured rhythmically, James's breathing began to slow and deepen. When Ferez paused, James began to blink again, those amethyst orbs shifting to focus on Ferez.

When Ferez whispered the last, James's lips twitched. He

lifted a hand and wrapped it around the wrist of the hand Ferez had at his cheek and squeezed firmly.

"Thank you."

Ferez nodded and squeezed his shoulder in turn but didn't remove his hand from James's face. Even if the boy hadn't held him so tightly, Ferez wasn't willing to let go.

When James's gaze finally darted from Ferez's face, red bloomed across his cheeks. Ferez glanced around. Everyone was watching them, concern, awe, and surprise filling their faces.

James pulled Ferez's hand from his face but didn't release it. Instead, he lowered it to his lap, locking the fingers of one hand with Ferez's and squeezing the other around Ferez's wrist. Ferez rubbed his free hand across the boy's back, offering as much comfort as he could.

"Do you really think the very essence of war is against us?"

Ferez eyed James worriedly. His voice was soft and hesitant. But more than that, he'd lost his Zhulanese accent. He sounded like a shadow of the boy Ferez had first met in Cautzel.

"Ach, I doubt the actual halbgott Krieg is the one responsible for Fräulein Parshen's distress."

Ferez glanced up at the holy man, surprised. He sounded very confident in that.

"Even if that is the third time we've heard the name this season?"

The holy man shook his head. "The halbgötter simply do not involve themselves so personally with specific humans. Nein, it is most likely some vengeful geist trying to scare you with such references."

Ferez pursed his lips, displeased with the old man's unconcerned tone. However, James relaxed, his eyes wide and desperately hopeful. Ferez's heart clenched. It hadn't passed his notice that James had been a bit desperate to keep Ferez with him ever since the Handelmann haus. He feared James was teetering on the edge of a full breakdown, of which this latest shock was just a glimpse.

Unwilling to let that happen, Ferez nodded to James when the boy turned to him. He would agree with the holy man's words for now.

No matter that I don't believe them.

Seyan had told him it was a young man who had called himself Markos in Cautzel. Charlen, the Animal Mage in Kensy, had called Markos "more than man" and "more powerful than any mage."

Ferez doubted either of those descriptions could match a simple ghost or spirit, even a vengeful one. But the demigods . . .

With the little he knew of them, he wouldn't be surprised to learn they had the ability to take physical form or to express their power and desires to a human.

Yet he didn't fully disbelieve the holy man, either. He couldn't imagine that a god of any kind would involve themselves personally with a specific mortal. That Markos had addressed James as Eirene—as Peace . . .

If Markos really is the demigod War, is it possible that James could actually be his counterpart, Peace?

"Strange, but not wholly impossible, I think."

The familiar voice whispered through Ferez's mind, and he glanced at Wolfrik. Still pale, the Mindspeaker switched his concerned gaze from James to the king.

"Whether or not the Drache Krieger is somehow a halbgott, I do agree with you about Krieg."

Ferez blinked. Wolfrik must have heard his questioning thought because he quickly continued.

"I do. I did not wish to alarm the others, but there is a voice that has been encouraging the recent violence of the Gift Clans. The voice has been speaking to one Geistmagier in particular, but I have heard him myself on occasion. I would not be surprised if that voice belonged to Krieg."

Ferez shuddered. *Thank you,* he thought, hoping Wolfrik would hear. *I don't think James would have been able to handle that information right now.*

"I believe you are right."

Ferez soon felt the mage's presence in his mind lessen, but he didn't think it left completely. It seemed the Mindspeaker was still protecting his mind, even after he'd been declared fully healed.

Someone has to make sure your secret is safe.

The lingering thought was barely noticeable, and Ferez smiled.

~~*~*

War cursed and kicked the ground, growling loudly when the surface didn't provide the resistance he desired. He had provided Peace a perfectly simple message, one that had been relatively easy to decipher if they could just find someone who knew the ancient names.

Even that had been ruined. The holy man had deciphered the message in one moment and given a perfect reason why it couldn't be accurate in the next.

He cursed again.

"It didn't go as planned, did it?"

War snarled at the soft words and lashed out at the speaker, but Love was farther away than he'd thought. She shook her head.

"I'd ask you to control your temper, but I think you lost your control jahre ago."

War snarled again and turned away from his pink sister. She was right. He had lost control of himself, and he felt like he was quickly losing his sanity, as well.

Sometimes, he wanted to simply scream at Peace, beg her to remember who she was. There were times when he wanted her to feel the torture he did, to know what it felt like to lose the one person that understood you better than anyone else did.

And there were times, more recently, when he simply wanted to watch her die.

That, more than anything, scared him. He had already been without her for two centuries. Logically, to watch her die would only bring him more pain, but that urge to have her killed was only growing stronger.

War released a frustrated scream and swiped at the air again, but there was nothing on which he could take out his sudden rage. Nothing except . . .

He swung around and stalked toward Love. He barely noticed the sigh she gave and didn't care that she just stood there, waiting for him. Once he was close enough, he raised his fist, intent on taking out his anger on something, anything.

A hand grabbed his fist, stilling him midswing. Red filled his vision, and he snarled at the brother who had stopped him.

"Release me!"

"Nein," Hate said. His voice was calm and low, but it only served to make War angrier. He brought his other fist around, and Hate caught that one, too. "We're not the ones with whom you're angry, bruder."

War snarled and stepped back, attempting to pull his

hands from Hate's, but his older brother wouldn't let go. Shaking his head and giving a short yell, he lifted a leg and aimed it at his brother.

He fell backward, his hands no longer clamped in Hate's grip. The moment he hit the ground, War snapped his eyes shut and Transported himself elsewhere. He couldn't stand the looks he knew his siblings would give him. He couldn't stand the Chaos that filled him. He couldn't stand it; he just couldn't.

I have to do something! he thought savagely, snapping his eyes open to view the camp of the Poison Clans.

The plan that had been forming in his head lately, the one he'd mentioned to Adalwolf, swiftly filled his mind. It calmed the rage and Chaos and all the other unwelcome emotions that had plagued him a moment ago.

Aye, I have to do something.

Eighteen

16 Mid Autumn, 224
Friedlichoase, Zhulan

On the afternoon of Mid-Season, Ferez was rousted from his bed not by any humans but by the thick scent of roasting meat. In fact, Ferez was once again the first awake in the Kanten tent. With a quiet laugh and his kopfabdeckung in hand, Ferez eagerly pushed his way through the tent's entrance.

Mid-Season was Ferez's favorite day of the season. Every season without fail, Ferez made time to celebrate the holy days. Most seasons, he managed to celebrate them in Caypan—the one day each season when he could wander the streets as himself without worrying about reverence or fear from the citizens. The two seasons after he'd been crowned, he had convinced Fayral to agree to a ceasefire on the holy days so they could all celebrate in peace.

His father, Eden Katani, instilled in him an appreciation for the holy days' importance, but the anticipation he felt every Mid-Season was all his own. Every Mid-Season, since he could remember, he would wake at the earliest possible time, eager to enjoy the festivities of the day.

This season was no different. In fact, Ferez thought the prospect of experiencing the holy day through the perspective of another culture made it even more exciting. Once outside the Kanten tent, he spun in a circle as he secured his kopfabdeckung. He was grinning like a fool, but he simply couldn't wait to experience this Adlerfest, as the nomads called the festival.

Already, the camp was decked out in all its glory. Lamps, yet unlit, were hung in every spot imaginable, and brightly colored cloth hung over all the tents and trees in a brilliant spray of color.

What intrigued Ferez most were the small statuettes of eagles that now perched at the top of every tent. The day before, when all the preparations had been completed, Ferez had learned that Adlerfest meant "Eagle Festival" in Zhulanese.

To his amusement, even James hadn't known why. The Skorpion siblings, who had accompanied them in their work, had teased James for not knowing after being a nomad for five years. When Ferez had pursued an explanation, they told him he would learn the reason during the festival.

Putting the thought from his mind, Ferez turned his attention back to the scents that had originally drawn him from his slumber. He followed his nose to one of the cooking fires burning throughout the oasis.

As he approached, the sweltering heat of the fire combined with that of the desert sun, and he grimaced, stopping several feet away. How could the nomads tend these cooking fires for so many hours during the hottest part of the desert day? The task was surely torturous, but if the food was to be ready a couple of hours before sunset, it was also necessary.

Ferez's mouth began to water from the tantalizing scents of roasting meat, underscored with a spiced scent, most likely from a mulled cider or ale. As he glanced around the fire, the king found not only various meats roasting over the fire but also bowls of berries, roots, and other foods he couldn't even name, tempting him with their plumpness and bright colors.

A sharp sting on the back of his hand suddenly had Ferez wincing. Pulling the hand back to his chest from where he'd unconsciously reached for the nearest bowl of berries, he glanced up at the woman who'd slapped his hand. She glared at him, her arms akimbo and her lips pressed together sternly.

"Nein! Not until the fest begins, young mann."

The woman sounded as stern as she looked. Ferez was sharply reminded of the head cook at the palace, who had always been quick to scold him whenever she caught him attempting to sneak snacks between meals.

He smiled apologetically. "Sorry, Ma'am. I wasn' tryin' to cause trouble."

To his surprise, the woman's expression softened, and she offered a small smile. "Ach, Herr Kanti." She shook her head. "As bad as a child, you are."

Ferez raised his brows, but she made a shooing motion with her hands. "Away with you now. I'm sure the Drache Krieger will make sure you get a little of everything later, but no food until the fest begins."

Ferez chuckled as he left the cooking fire behind. He hadn't meant to reach for the berries. Even in Caypan, people really didn't eat much before the festival began. The food had just looked so tempting, he hadn't been able to resist.

He stopped by the spring that bordered the Katze Clan's camp, one of three large springs making up the lush oasis.

Once he'd drunk his fill, he wandered around the spring's edge toward the open field between the three.

When he'd first noticed the large, open area, which had been unoccupied at the time, he'd asked James why none of the clans set up camp there. Ferez thought it might be large enough to fit nearly an entire clan.

James had answered that the middle ground of the oasis was an interclan area. It was reserved for those activities in which all the clans participated. Indeed, the meeting two nights before had been held within the central area.

Now, it was solely dedicated to the festival.

The night before, the middle ground had appeared to be filled with chaos, but as Ferez surveyed it now, he found his anticipation steadily climbing. There were still several open areas, including one especially large area nearby, where Flame currently lounged, her long tail sweeping idly across the grass. On the other side of the field, another open area stood adjacent to one of the openings between two of the springs.

There, outside the ring of water, no clan had camped. Instead, herds of horses, goats, and other animals the clans kept stood or lay about, lazing in the heat of the desert sun.

Turning his gaze back to the middle space, Ferez eyed the stages that ranged throughout it. One, which stood farthest to his right, past the open area where Flame lounged, was crowded with objects. He couldn't see what they were from this distance, but he made a note to find out later.

Meanwhile, he was more interested in one of the other stages, around which several people were crowded. The stage stood at waist height. As he approached, he realized it held two people. They appeared to be sparring, their scharfmonde flashing in the bright sunlight as they swung at each other. The murmurs of the watching nomads rose and fell as the two fighters lunged back and forth, dancing around each other even as they engaged in a fight.

Just as Ferez joined the group, a sharp whistle split the air, and the two fighters immediately broke apart and sheathed their weapons. Slapping each other on the back, they jumped down from the stage and joined the others, who quickly congratulated them on a good practice.

"Oi, Katze!"

Ferez blinked when he realized the speaker was addressing him. The man who'd spoken jerked his head toward the stage.

"Are you participating in the boxkämpfe, then?"

"Don't be dumm," said another man, who bore the purple statusgürtel of a Katze. "That's the Drache Krieger's companion, Herr Kanti. He doesn't know how to use scharfmonde."

"That doesn't mean he can't box," said the first man, a Pferd. He was wiping his face with his kopfabdeckung, and Ferez realized he was one of the two who had been sparring previously. "What say you, farmer? Can you box?"

"You think an ausländer would know how to box?" sneered a Spinne, the Pferd's sparring partner.

The Pferd shrugged, his eyes not leaving Ferez. "Well, farmer? Can you?"

Ferez glanced around at the young men around him. Many of them regarded him with nearly hostile expressions. Only the Pferd and the Katze seemed open to his presence, despite the anxious glances the Katze was shooting him and the Pferd.

Unsure if he should attempt to spar with people who didn't want him around, he turned his gaze back to the Pferd.

"I've ne'er participated in the sport."

Another young man, one of two Falken in the group, snorted.

"Of course you haven't, ausländer."

Several of the others chuckled, but the Pferd continued to hold Ferez's gaze.

"Even if you haven't participated in a boxkampf before, surely you have fought with your fists, ja?"

The others quieted and frowned as Ferez considered the Pferd's words.

He had been in fistfights before. It was not uncommon for noble children to ignore their parents' preferences for the fine art of dueling with swords and simply attack each other with flying fists when they disagreed.

He had also learned during the war that, when necessary, one's fists were just as powerful a weapon as one's blade. He'd learned the lesson rather well from one particular Fayralman. The swordsman had disarmed Ferez, but he fell to Ferez's fists because he couldn't adapt to the close range that Ferez had then demanded.

Shaking his head to rid himself of the war memories, the king eyed the Pferd once more.

"Aye, but surely boxin' isn' as simple as that?"

Several of the nomads sneered, but the Pferd simply smirked. "There is nothing simple about depending solely on your fists, freund." He jerked his head toward the stage once more. "Care to give it a try?"

Protests erupted from each of the surrounding nomads. The Pferd mostly ignored them, pausing only when the Katze grabbed his arm.

"Are you sure you want to do that, Eloy? The Drache Krieger's rather fond of him. If you hurt him too much, you'll have to deal with both the Drache Krieger and the erstehäuptling."

Eloy offered a small shrug. "I am hardly going to use my full power against a beginner, Reiner. And I have heard that the Drache Krieger has involved Herr Kanti in every aspect of clan life possible, ja?"

The Pferd glanced inquiringly at Ferez, who nodded.

"Then he should get a chance to experience a boxkampf since he cannot handle the scharfmonde."

The explanation only seemed to upset most of the others, even as Reiner nodded reluctantly and released Eloy's arm. The Pferd waved Ferez toward the stage.

Once they stood next to the platform, Eloy paused and unsheathed his scharfmonde. Ferez frowned, but the Pferd simply chuckled as he passed the blades off to one of the other young men.

"It's customary to remove all weapons from your person before beginning a bladeless boxkampf. Pulling blades can be instinctual, especially for those who are not accustomed to depending solely on themselves."

Ferez nodded and bent down to retrieve the knives he kept in his boots. When he straightened and offered them to the nomad who had taken Eloy's scharfmonde, he was met with surprised stares.

"What?"

Eloy hesitated before shaking his head. "I had not even noticed you were armed, freund. I never expected a farmer to carry hidden blades."

Ferez shrugged. "When yeh've spent years fightin' a war, e'en we farmers learn to ne'er be unarmed."

The others hesitated, and Reiner attempted to catch Eloy's arm again, but the Pferd shook him off and waved for someone to take Ferez's blades. Once Ferez was disarmed, the sport's few rules were explained: fists only, no blows below the statusgürtel, and crossing the bound line resulted in an automatic loss.

Ferez frowned at the last one and glanced at the stage. There, a couple feet from the edge of the platform, was a chalk line he hadn't noticed before.

He remembered the one boxing match he had seen with his father several years before in Wildestadt. Then, they had had rope surrounding the platform to keep the boxers from falling off. Apparently, the nomads hadn't adapted that variation.

Ferez's hands were wrapped in what looked like undyed statusgürtel before he was helped onto the stage. As they faced each other several feet apart, Eloy nodded to one of the nearby young men.

"Two minutes, since he's a beginner." He turned back to Ferez, and a sharp whistle pierced the air.

To Ferez, the following bout seemed to last much longer than the two minutes for which the Pferd called. Even so, Ferez wasn't exactly sure just what they had done.

He remembered ducking and sidestepping to avoid blows, as well as a particularly strong blow that connected with his left shoulder, reminding him it was freshly healed only a sevenday beforehand. He didn't remember landing any blows himself, despite being assured later that he had landed several good ones, including a spectacular uppercut to the Pferd's midsection.

What Ferez did remember clearly about the fight was how it ended. James's voice cut through the fight-induced fog in his mind. He pivoted, both to avoid the coming blow from Eloy and to glimpse James, whose voice had come from behind him beyond the growing crowd.

The next moment, Eloy stumbled past Ferez and nearly slipped right off the edge of the platform.

~~*~*

Gemi paused at the edge of the crowd as Eloy barely managed to keep from stumbling off the platform. The surrounding crowd pressed against him, keeping him upright, but an uneasy silence fell over the nomaden as it became obvious the Pferd had lost the match.

No one would have expected Eloy, one of the best boxer in the Vereinte Clans, to lose to a stranger.

What none of them realized was the very reason Gemi had broken into a run when both Flame and Wolfrik told her that Ferez was being coaxed into a boxkampf.

She pushed through the crowd until she reached the Pferd, who was now seated on the edge of the platform. He was hunched over with one arm wrapped around his midsection. Once close enough, she cuffed his ear. He cried out and covered his ear, but Gemi doubted it was as much from pain as from surprise. When he met her glare, he gaped.

"Drache Krieger?"

Gemi huffed. "Dummkopf."

Looking past the boxer, she beckoned Ferez down from the platform. He winced as he lowered himself to the ground, and she frowned worriedly. He shook his head.

"Gave me a good knock to my lef' shoulder, I think."

Gemi nodded. "We'll have Mandel look at it later." Certain her freund would be all right, Gemi turned back to the still-seated Pferd.

"Dummkopf." She spoke the insult louder this time so most of the crowd could hear her. "What did you think you were doing?"

Eloy hunched his shoulders more. "It was just a friendly boxkampf, Drache Krieger. No harm meant."

Gemi snorted. "Maybe not, but you could have gotten yourself killed."

Silence answered her. While the Pferd and his freunde frowned at her, Ferez touched her shoulder.

"James?"

His voice reflected the confusion on the nomaden's faces, and Gemi offered Ferez a sad smile.

"Es tut mir leid, Frenz, but boxing has certain customs and rules for a reason, some of which these boxers have blatantly ignored."

She eyed the young männer distastefully. They obviously still didn't understand, so she changed tactics and focused on the Pferd.

"Would you have challenged me to a bladeless boxkampf, Eloy?"

The boxer paled and shook his head vigorously.

"And why not?"

Eloy glanced around, but even his freunde had backed away from him. Gemi sighed. She hadn't meant to be mean, especially since Flame insisted he'd only attempted to include Ferez as Gemi had. But the mann was a dedicated boxer and knew all the rules and customs surrounding boxing. He had risked his life because he underestimated Ferez, something everybody seemed to be doing lately, even Gemi.

And for once, Ferez himself hadn't realized the danger surrounding him. Gemi had to make sure everyone was aware of it so it wouldn't happen again.

When nobody seemed willing to help Eloy, he met Gemi's gaze once more. "I wouldn't challenge you because your instincts are attuned to krieg, not to boxing."

Gemi nodded. "Exactly."

The Pferd frowned. "But he's a farmer. I should have been able to treat him as a beginner."

Gemi sighed. "Ja, he's a farmer, but he's also from Kensy, the center of the Krieg mit Fayral. He's been fighting for . . ."

She paused and glanced at the king, who still frowned at her. "How old were you when you first fought in the krieg?"

She asked to prove her point, but she was also curious about the answer. She didn't remember hearing anything about Ferez before he was crowned king, though she knew he had fought before then.

Ferez tilted his head to the side. "Jus' pas' my fourteenth year." He paused and met Gemi's gaze. "About four an' a half years ago."

Murmurs spread through the crowd, and all the boxers paled at the implication.

"Fourteen." Eloy shook his head and then stared at Ferez with a look of respekt Gemi hadn't expected. "So young?"

Ferez shifted uncomfortably and shrugged. "The land is our livelihood. We couldn' le' the Fayralese take it from us."

Gemi smiled bemusedly. The king had become very dedicated to the story of Frenz Kanti.

The Pferd bowed his head. "Es tut mir leid, my freund, for endangering us both."

Ferez shifted again. "Turned out all right; no real harm done." After a brief pause, he quickly added, "I didn' hurt yeh too badly, did I?"

The worry in his voice made Gemi smile, and the Pferd shook his head, chuckling.

"Nein, freund, no more than I can handle. Besides, I've had much worse. I will admit, though, I was surprised and impressed by your power." He chuckled again, "I guess that's what I get for inviting a raw warrior to box."

Gemi nodded, satisfied she had gotten her point across.

Turning back to Ferez, she laid a hand on his right shoulder. "Shall we find Mandel, then, and have him look at your shoulder?"

"No need to go looking for him, Drache Krieger."

Häuptling Seidenstrang's sudden words startled Gemi. She turned to find the frau eying Ferez with a small frown, though it soon morphed into a soft smile.

"If you'll let me Heal your freund, that is."

Gemi nodded and dropped her hand from Ferez's shoulder. She took a small, hopefully inconspicuous, step away from the king as Genevieve approached. The frau was considered the most powerful Heilemagier in the Vereinte Clans. She had never indicated recognition of Gemi's true gender, and Gemi was always reluctant to give her the chance. Lakina had discovered Gemi's secret through her magie, and Genevieve was possibly more powerful than the Kensian Heilemagier.

The Spinne laid her hands on Ferez's shoulder. "I agree with you, Drache Krieger, that Eloy should not have challenged Herr Kanti to a boxkampf, but I now find myself curious about his skill and power."

Gemi frowned. "What do you mean?"

Genevieve flashed Gemi a smile.

"I wonder if the two of you might provide us with a demonstration to start off the boxkämpfe. After all, I'm sure I'm not the only one curious to see the two of you cross swords after that."

Many in the crowd, which had grown during Ferez's bout, raised their voices in agreement.

Gemi hesitated. It wouldn't have been the first time she had participated in such a demonstration, especially for Mitte Jahreszeit, but it had been jahre since she had done so with a sword. Not that she doubted her ability to do so, but . . .

She glanced at Ferez, unsure how to respond to the
häuptling's request. To her surprise, Ferez was grinning, his
eyes shining. When she met his gaze, his grin widened.

"Can we, James?" Gemi blinked at the childlike tone his
voice had taken. "We haven' exactly had a chance to spar wit'
swords since we met."

Despite her uncertainty, a smile spread her lips. Ferez
was right. She hadn't unsheathed her sword since they
crossed into the desert. And when they'd practiced in Kensy,
it was always with other people who needed the extra
training. She had believed there was no reason for them to
practice together, not when she had witnessed his skill
firsthand in the first battle on the highway and again in
Puretha.

However, Ferez's excitement hinted at a reason for them
to spar that had less to do with practicing and more to do
with the simple enjoyment of the challenge. When Gemi
nodded, Ferez let out a soft whoop, earning chuckles from
the surrounding nomaden.

"We'll need to get our swords," Gemi added.

"No need," a voice called from the edge of the crowd.

The crowd parted, and the Kanten familie filed through
the gap, Hausef in front, two swords in his hands.

"I believe these are yours."

Gemi gaped at her vater. "How . . . ?"

He chuckled and nodded to the Skorpione, who had
accompanied them. "Wolfrik said you might want them. It
seems he was right."

Gemi shook her head and took the offered swords.
"Danke." She offered Ferez his as Genevieve proclaimed him
fit to spar.

Despite being ready then, they waited until Adlerfest
officially began a half hour later to spar. Hausef climbed up

onto the platform, as he did at the beginning of every fest, to introduce Gemi and Ferez to the crowd as the first demonstration. The continuation of tradition made Gemi smile.

She and Ferez took the stage to cheers. As they settled across from each other, their swords unsheathed, Gemi took in Ferez's stance. He held himself lightly on his feet, the heels of his boots just touching the platform. He stood with his right foot forward, the stance wider than necessary.

Gemi frowned.

Then she noticed he held his sword more vertically than was practical for a normal swordfight.

Recognition snapped through her. The stance was one Sir Paeter had taught her when she was much younger: the offensive beginning stance for the Sword Dance of Carith.

Lifting her gaze to Ferez's, she found him eying her with raised brows and a wide grin. She chuckled softly. Well, it had been a while, but Gemi was sure she remembered the Sword Dance well enough.

She answered his challenge by shifting her weight to her back leg and lifting and turning her sword so she held it parallel to the ground in front of her.

When the sharp whistle sounded, there was a beat of stillness before Ferez moved. He flowed forward, in a rhythm faster than Gemi had expected, but she easily matched the speed and met his first blow. She quickly responded with her own blow, which he easily deflected.

They moved through the first steps of the Sword Dance in that way, faster than Gemi remembered from her childhood, but at a speed she knew matched their abilities. And that was the true purpose behind the Sword Dance: to demonstrate the participants' abilities to their fullest. In the beginning, the abilities were displayed in the speed of the well-rehearsed motions. Later, the dance became unscripted, allowing the participants to battle for dominance.

As the swordsman who began in the offensive position, Ferez began with a slight advantage, but Gemi doubted it would make a difference. She hadn't lost a one-on-one swordfight since her days under Sir Paeter and Sir Leal.

When they reached the more creative part of the dance, though, she found herself still on the defensive.

Her grin widened and she laughed, even as she scrambled to block Ferez's next blow. She had known Ferez was a powerful swordsman, had learned recently that he had been trained by her childhood mentors, but until now, she hadn't considered he might actually be her equal.

Gemi finally managed to counter one of Ferez's blows, knocking him back several steps. Taking advantage of his stumble, she aimed a blow toward his neck and shoulder.

As expected, he lifted his sword to catch the blow, but he lifted it higher than necessary. For the split second before the blow landed, she feared she would catch his wrist instead of his blade, and she attempted to lighten the blow.

Metal clashed against metal as her blade struck the shoulder of Ferez's, just above the guard, and Ferez slid his blade down hers and twisted.

Before Gemi could process what he had done, she found herself facing the crowd, her back to Ferez, and he had both of their swords crossed in front of her chest. Stunned, she idly mused that the move must have been an adaptation of a maneuver she'd taught him to disarm nomaden.

Cheering quickly petered out into silence. Grinning breathlessly, Gemi tapped Ferez's arm to offer her surrender, and he quickly released her. Once she'd turned around, he offered a half-bow and her sword. She grasped the outstretched hand with both of hers and laughed.

As if that had been their cue, the crowd of nomaden surrounding the stage broke into cheers and whooping calls, and Ferez lifted his head and grinned widely at her. Taking her sword back, Gemi gripped his hand and led him off the stage as a pair of boxers prepared for the next spar.

As they moved through the crowd, they received hearty claps on the back and shouts of compliments and congratulations. They were met at the edge of the crowd, which had begun to disperse for the various other activities of the fest, by Zuk, Ulla, Wolfrik, and Käfe. The four complimented them on their bout and then insisted on helping Gemi introduce Ferez to a nomade fest.

~~*~*

Wolfrik might have known the king's geist, but not even that had prepared him for the duel the king and Drache Krieger had shared. It wasn't just their obvious skill that had made the duel an amazing spectacle; it was their obvious enjoyment, as well. Wolfrik thought their laughter, when they'd had breath for it, had been heard even at the edges of the crowd.

When they joined Wolfrik and the others, they were both grinning and unarmed, their hands clasped tight. Wolfrik knew they would have left their blades by the platform; there was no chance of them being stolen and no point to carrying them around during the fest.

Everyone insisted on food first—Wolfrik was sure most nomaden did—and they made their way to one of the cooking fires distributed around the oase. To everyone's amusement, Ferez tried a bit of everything, even a couple of fire-cracked insects, which Wolfrik hadn't expected from someone unused to their culture.

With their appetites settled for the moment, they returned to the central area to continue watching the spars and other displays the various stages offered. When Ferez asked again about the reason for the fest's name, Zuk answered with a chuckle.

"Patience, Frenz. That doesn't come until sunset."

The words didn't settle any of the king's confusion, but he didn't ask again.

Less than an hour into the festivities, they were joined by Zuk's freund, Raymond, who greeted them all gruffly before leaning in and whispering something to Zuk. Almost immediately, Zuk shoved the other mann away and shook his head.

"Who do you think I am, Raymond?" He jerked his head toward the rest of them. "Ask her yourself."

Raymond's face burned red as he turned to Ulla. Wolfrik raised his brows. The few times he'd seen the two interact, the barbs they traded always seemed to leave the air blistering. He couldn't imagine what the mann wanted to ask her.

There was a minute of silence as everyone waited for Raymond to speak, but the mann was apparently unwilling to open his mouth. Finally, Ulla huffed and grabbed Raymond by the arm.

"Dummkopf," she muttered before dragging him away from their group.

Zuk started laughing as soon as the two disappeared, and even the Drache Krieger chuckled. Wolfrik eyed them curiously, uncertain he would be welcomed in asking about what had just happened. Ferez apparently didn't have any such misgivings.

"Wha' was that about?" The king's grin was tempered but still wide.

The Drache Krieger smiled as Zuk answered the question.

"Raymond was asking for my permission to court Ulla, which is ridiculous because you just don't tell Kanten frauen what to do." He shook his head. "Especially when they're Geistmagier."

Wolfrik frowned. "I didn't think they got along that well."

The Drache Krieger chuckled. "Oh, they get along well enough. They've just danced around each other for a while, is all."

The next moment, he frowned toward the large, open space where Wolfrik knew Dame Flammezunge still lounged.

"Well," Zuk added, turning toward Käfe and offering his hand, "since this is a nacht for pairing off, would you do me the honor of accompanying me around the clans to admire the decorations, Fräulein Käfe?"

Wolfrik stifled the chuckle that wanted to make itself known. He'd spoken to Zuk not long after their arrival in Friedlichoase, and the Kanten Tieremagier had appeared both surprised by and curious about Wolfrik's request. He'd agreed to at least get to know Käfe better, but this was the first time Wolfrik had seen the mann request his schwester's presence alone.

Käfe dropped her chin, her cheeks tinting. Wolfrik didn't miss the small smile that played on her lips. She twittered softly, a sure sign of her nervousness.

To their surprise, Zuk made a chittering sound in response. Käfe's head shot up, her eyes wide and her mouth slightly ajar as she met his gaze.

When she finally gained control of herself, she swallowed and darted a glance at Wolfrik. He smiled and nodded, waving for her to accept the Tieremagier's invitation. This was what she wanted, and he wasn't about to interfere.

Käfe turned back to Zuk, the small smile once again playing at her lips. She took his hand and practically whistled her response.

Wolfrik did chuckle then as Zuk led her away. *"Viel glück, Schwester,"* he murmured against her geist. Happiness flooded through her.

Wolfrik accompanied the Drache Krieger and the king for a while longer, his thoughts distant. He was glad Käfe had found someone among the Vereinte Clans so easily, but he doubted he'd find anyone for himself. To most of these people, he was just a Skorpion, a mann whose trustworthiness was still uncertain.

As the sun began to set, Wolfrik directed his two companions toward the stage closest to Dame Flammezunge, which had yet to be used. Zuk had told him that was where they held the Geisterstücke, which would answer the king's questions about the reason behind the name Adlerfest.

As soon as they were settled near the stage, Wolfrik excused himself. He wasn't keen to watch the Geisterstücke himself. Every nomade grew up learning about the immortals, including the four Guardians of the Cycle of Incarnation: Adler, the Royal Eagle; Wolf, the Hungry Wolf; Schlange, the Great Serpent; and Phönix, the Splendid Phoenix.

Adlerfest recognized Adler's role in the Cycle of Incarnation. It celebrated his great flights between Carith's Realm or the Mortal Realm and the Cycle of Incarnation as he carried newly created—or newly dead—souls.

And it was the same for every fest. Wölfefest in Winter celebrated Wolf's eternal hunger for the memories of the newly dead. Schlangenfest in Spring celebrated Schlange's fierce protection of the souls within the Cycle. Phönixfest in Summer celebrated the rebirth of souls as Phönix placed them from the Cycle into fertile wombs.

Someone calling his name jarred Wolfrik from his contemplations. Turning, he found Wüstenwolf Seelenesser, häuptling of the Wolf Clan, approaching him, a fräulein striding along beside him. Smiling, Wolfrik offered his hand in greeting.

"Wüstenwolf, it is good to see you again."

"Ja, and you." The young häuptling clasped his hand. "I had hoped to speak to you sooner, but we haven't had much chance since the Gleichrat."

Wolfrik resisted the urge to roll his eyes. That wasn't exactly true, since they had spoken several times since Wolfrik joined the Vereinte Clans' geisternetz. However, he understood the words might be more for Wüstenwolf's companion than Wolfrik, so he nodded.

"What did you wish to speak about?"

Wüstenwolf offered a sly smile, more than worthy of a wolf, and indicated the fräulein.

"I wished to introduce you to my schwester, Eule Seelenesser."

Wolfrik raised his brows. "You are a Tieremagier?" Eulen, for which the fräulein had been named, were birds of the nacht, fierce predators, and often considered wise.

The fräulein nodded and smiled softly. Her silence and soft expression might have reminded Wolfrik of his own schwester, but the way she held herself was more reminiscent of Zuk's schwester, Ulla.

"Eule was curious about your plans for your clan once you become häuptling."

Wolfrik glanced at the other Geistmagier in surprise, and Wüstenwolf shrugged.

"I thought it might be easier for you to tell her yourself. Besides," he added with a grin, "Eule was of great help to me when I first became häuptling. I thought you might enjoy some proven assistance."

He clapped Wolfrik on the shoulder and bid the two of them a "Gute nacht."

After watching the other Geistmagier walk away, Wolfrik shook his head and turned back to Eule. She was a very pretty fräulein, and he was sharply reminded that the feste represented fertility, among other things.

He quickly pushed the thought aside. He doubted she was interested in more than discussing his plans for his clan.

"Did you have anything in particular you wished to discuss, or did you just wish to hear what I was considering for my clan at the moment?"

Eule's smile sharpened and she stepped closer. To Wolfrik's surprise, she was nearly the same height as he was, and the edges of her kopfabdeckung just brushed the edges of his.

"Well," she said, her voice dark and low, "there is that."

Her eyes shifted down and then back to his face, and Wolfrik felt his breath catch. Her eyes had sharpened, as well, giving her the look of the bird for which she was named or even the wolf that her clan represented.

"But there are other things we could . . . discuss, as well."

Wolfrik hesitated. He was not used to bold frauen. Such an attitude would not have been tolerated by his häuptling and the männer who supported him. Since he'd joined the Vereinte Clans, he'd met many strong-willed frauen, like Ulla and Isana, but he hadn't actually believed any of them would be interested in a Skorpion.

When Wolfrik didn't answer, amusement softened the angle of Eule's smile.

"If you're not comfortable with anything else, we could just stick to your plans. I helped my bruder learn to sharpen his teeth and claws," she added, referring to the main weapons of a wolf. "I'm sure I can help you sharpen your stinger and strengthen your pincers, as well."

She laid a firm hand against his elbow and stroked her thumb once along the inside of his arm. He jerked and swallowed.

"I . . . think I would appreciate that," he finally managed.

The sharpness returned to her smile, and Wolfrik felt his own lips curving in response. His häuptling might have disparaged him for falling to the klauen of such a bold frau, but Wolfrik could imagine the truth of her words.

Perhaps I can match her, predator for predator, instead of falling as her prey.

Nineteen

The Geisterstücke, as Wolfrik had called them, ended just as the last traces of light disappeared from the sky. Ferez turned to James to ask what they should do next, when a loud explosion behind them made him jump. Another explosion sounded above them, and Ferez spun around, dropping into a crouch. His heart raced as he looked up, his mind already calculating the distance to his sword.

His thoughts faltered against the sight that met him. He straightened slowly and stared at the brilliant red showering across the sky.

Mid-Season in Caypan had always included watching the sky fires. Ferez had spent many a Mid-Season marveling at the displays put on by the Royal Fire Masters. He had studied them until he thought himself versed in their beauty.

But these . . .

Further explosions preceded the addition of more colors to the canvas of the sky. There were yellows that shone like the sun, reds as deep as the richest rubies, and greens that looked so alive, the sky could have been an entire living world of its own.

"Is it always like this?"

James chuckled. "Why do you think I'm so insistent on staying with the nomaden during Mitte Jahreszeit?"

He tilted his head back as Flame took wing, steadily burning sky fires hanging off her body and dangling from her tail, talons, and wingtips.

"Nomaden hold the best feste," James whispered. "And Flame always enjoys taking part when she can."

Ferez watched the dragon fly among the sky fires the nomads sent up. She appeared to dance in the fires, reveling in the festival as much as any of the humans did. The sky fires hanging from her body reflected off her red and purple scales, outlining her in the dark night.

When one of the more temporary sky fires exploded against her side, Ferez leaned closer to James. "Aren' the sky fires dangerous at such a close range?"

James laughed. Ferez snapped his gaze down to the boy's, and his breath caught at how his face shone. A light that seemed to rival the sky fires above them danced in his purple eyes, and Ferez was suddenly struck by just how beautiful he was.

The king blinked and pulled back, both physically and mentally. He'd never looked at another man that way before.

Then again, he reckoned, *I've never seriously considered anyone else before, have I?*

"Flame is a feuerdrache, a fire dragon. She was literally born to bathe in fire." James chuckled more softly. "At least, that's what Flame tells me."

Ferez nodded and looked back up at the sky. He hoped there was little enough light that the blush he could now feel heating his cheeks wouldn't be noticed. He tried to convince himself it was the beauty of the lights and the joyous atmosphere of the festival that formed such thoughts in his head.

But memories of James's grace in battle and his kindness, patience, and fairness in his dealings with different peoples stirred in his mind. Ferez had noticed the boy's beauty before; he simply hadn't let himself acknowledge it.

My throne and duty demand I court a woman. He pursed his lips. *Am I willing to forsake both because I find a man beautiful?*

A sudden strain of drifting notes cut through Ferez's increasingly disturbing thoughts. Turning his gaze toward the sound, he sought the source.

He briefly noted the soft whistle of bone flutes and the deep vibration of hide drums. It was in recognition of the bright strumming of the strings of the saitens, though, that his heart leapt and his fingers twitched. Abandoning his distress, Ferez crowed joyously and grabbed James's hand, pulling him toward the sounds.

~~*~*

Gemi laughed as Ferez began pulling her toward the open area the musicians occupied, adjacent to where the animals were kept. The king was acting like a child at his first fest.

He had been so excited during the boxkämpfe, and he seemed to have utterly enjoyed tasting the different foods the nomaden had to offer. Even the himmelfeuer, the sky fires, which Gemi knew he had seen before, left him gaping in awe.

Now he led her through the crowds, his excitement showing through in his grin and the clutch of his hand around hers. Her heart ached that this side of him had to be buried beneath the kingly façade. Everyone deserved a nacht like this, when they could simply enjoy themselves without worrying about consequences.

Especially Ferez.

"And you."

Gemi pushed Flame's words aside. *This is not a nacht for introspection.*

She was startled from her thoughts when one of the musicians, with whom Ferez had bent to speak, suddenly grinned and handed him his instrument—a saiten. Gemi watched, open-mouthed, as the king seated himself cross-legged on the ground and cradled the saiten against his chest.

He ran one hand lovingly over the edge of the saiten's wooden belly and the other over the long neck. Then he curled his fingers in against the spidersilk strings and plucked some chords, drawing an appreciative murmur from the saiten's owner.

"Do you know any fest songs?"

Ferez grinned up at the mann and began to play in earnest. The musician gave a loud whoop. The tune was easily recognizable as one of the more traditional fest dance songs. The other musicians quickly took up the song as well, adding the beats and tunes of their own instruments to Ferez's.

As many of the nomaden around her began to dance to the music filling the air, Gemi found she could only stare at her freund, stunned. Never once, in all the time they'd traveled together, had she thought the king might play an instrument. It just hadn't crossed her geist. For that matter, it didn't really make sense except for the passion Gemi could see shining in Ferez's eyes.

Nobles simply didn't encourage their sons to take up music. To them, it was a skill for their daughters and lebenfrauen. Gemi herself would have been encouraged to take up music in some form if her lady-training had ever actually begun.

"Stop thinking so hard."

The sharp nicker drew Gemi's attention away from Ferez. She glanced out to the adjacent area outside the ring of water, where only a large herd of pferde now milled.

"You're ruining the mood for the rest of us." Shadow nudged Last Chance and nickered calmingly.

Gemi grinned at the sight of the pferde gathering. Turning back to the musicians as the first song wound down, she laid a hand on Ferez's shoulder. He looked up at her, his body relaxed and his smile still firmly in place. Unwilling to disturb his peace, Gemi kept her voice at a whisper.

"I don't suppose you know the *Pferdetanz?*"

Ferez's smile grew to a grin. "Aye, I know the *Pferdetanz:* the Horse Dance." And he launched himself into the song, the other musicians quickly joining him.

Gemi knew, as she had learned from the first time she'd heard it, that the *Pferdetanz* was not a song meant for dancing. Not human dancing, at any rate. According to Shadow, the song had the power to make a pferd move. Some even said the song had been created by Tieremagier.

Now, as Gemi wondered at the king's skill, a sharp whinny filled the air. Turning back to the pferde, Gemi watched, awed as she always was, as the largest stallion, a chestnut beauty that stood eighteen hands at the withers, dropped back down to all fours.

Then, as the music filled Gemi with a sense of the wild, the entire herd began to move.

~~*~*

When Ferez had first learned the *Pferdetanz*, he had believed the name came from the wildness of the music. Now, as he drove his fingers into the silk strings, he found himself learning the truth of the song.

It left him breathless.

He'd been so startled by that first whinny, as the large stallion raised himself up on his hind legs and pawed at the air, that he'd nearly stopped playing. The shouts of the nomads and the screams of the horses were all that drove his fingers through his shock.

His fingers moved over the strings automatically as he played a song he'd learned as a boy—at his own insistence. His mind, on the other hand, was completely focused on the horses flowing together, the movements distinct to each horse, but the overall effect striking.

The horses moved together: running, kicking up their heels, rising up on their hind legs, bowing, leaping, and some moves that Ferez thought must have been trained into them. The sounds that rose from the herd—nickers, whinnies, outright screams of excitement—filled the air and mingled with the music, complementing it in a way that made Ferez marvel.

About a minute into the song, Ferez finally spotted Last Chance and Shadow. His mare seemed to be following Shadow, her movements only slightly off beat from the stallion's.

The king smiled sadly as he watched her dance. This was as new to her as it was to him. Although she mimicked the black stallion's movements, Ferez could tell by the arch of her neck that she wasn't as relaxed as he might wish her to be.

~~*~*

Shadow could still remember his first Mid-Season Festival with the nomads. He had unsuspectingly succumbed to the magic of the *Pferdetanz*. He'd been so upset by the loss of control that he'd run off into the desert the moment the music ended. Flame and Gemi had flown after him to comfort him, effectively ruining the festival for all three of them.

It had been Gemi who helped him recognize the pleasure he'd felt beneath the panic at losing control. He'd eventually found himself looking forward to the next Mid-Season and its *Pferdetanz*, to which he gave himself up completely. Ever since, he always looked forward to giving himself up to the wildness of the *Tanz*, a feeling that was unavailable in the day-to-day life of a domesticated horse.

When he and Last Chance began their friendship anew on their way from Schönestadt, Shadow had begun to anticipate introducing the mare to the magic of the *Pferdetanz*. As the herd gathered for the *Tanz*, he had tried to explain that the *Tanz* was a dance that encouraged horses to let themselves go to the wild nature of their ancestors. When Last Chance hadn't relaxed, Shadow had nickered soothingly.

Now, even a minute into the *Tanz*, Last Chance still wasn't letting herself go. Shadow could sense edginess radiating from her in waves. It increased the wildness of the other horses, which only seemed to increase her panic.

Giving a mental sigh that pricked his bondmates' attention, Shadow suddenly stopped. His muscles strained against the abrupt change, and the wild music made them twitch, but there was a different kind of wilderness to be had here.

It took Last Chance a bare moment to follow his lead. Instead of stopping beside him though, the mare executed a perfect about-turn maneuver, landing only steps before him.

For a couple beats, they simply stared at each other, their sides heaving. Once Shadow was sure Last Chance wouldn't move either, he dropped into a half-bow.

"You're not relaxing!"

He didn't mean for it to sound like an accusation, but he was frustrated. Why couldn't she just let the music take over?

"It's Animal Magic!"

Shadow tilted his head, his ears flicking forward. *"Aye, and?"*

Last Chance snorted and pawed at the ground nervously. *"I was trained to resist Animal Magic."*

I'm an idiot.

Shadow had known that: He distinctly remembered Ferez sharing the information along with Last Chance's history. He should have realized how that would affect the mare in this.

Sadness swept through Shadow, adding weight to his twitching limbs. He had wanted her to enjoy the wildness of the *Tanz*. Not for his own sake, as might have been the case with any other mare. Shadow was a flirt, but he had never felt the respect for other mares that he felt for Last Chance.

Suddenly, Shadow lifted his head and shifted his ears forward. *"Just because you can resist doesn't mean you have to, does it?"*

Last Chance shifted her weight from one side to the other. That, to Shadow, was answer enough.

He dropped into a full bow. The music demanded he move in some way, and he wasn't sure he could look at Last Chance while saying the words that filled his mind. When they spilled forth, it was as a gentle nicker.

"This isn't Animal Magic that's trying to harm you or use you to harm others. How can it, when your own master is leading the song?"

Shadow could practically feel Last Chance's surprise. He had no doubt her gaze had shifted toward the musicians.

"The only thing standing between you and enjoying the wildness of the Tanz *is your pride. Believe me; I know how hard it can be to get over that."*

Memory after memory threatened to distract him, but he pushed them away. Gemi was right: this was not a night for introspection, but for enjoyment.

"Just relax for tonight. Drop your training. You can always regain it tomorrow."

Shadow let silence fall between them. Not that there was actual silence, with the music of the *Tanz* filling the air and the hoofbeats and screams of the herd flowing around them. Shadow gave a single curious thought to what they must look like: two still horses, one bowing, one standing, surrounded by the constant flow of the herd as their bodies responded to the pure wildness of the *Pferdetanz*.

The longer the silence stretched, the more worried Shadow became that he would be forced to move without Last Chance's answer. The instincts inspired by the *Tanz* had begun to scream that the courtship of this one mare could not be as important as the wildness of the dance. And despite the number of mares Shadow had flirted with over the years, Last Chance was . . . beyond them.

In every way.

He was shaking and struggling not to rise when the shock of pain pierced the edge of his ear. He snorted and jerked up out of the bow, his eyes wide as he stared at Last Chance.

Last Chance, whose muscles had stopped twitching and who now eyed him with amusement.

"I'll give myself over to the Tanz," she nickered, *"as long as*

we're agreed that we're both equals in this relationship—that neither of us will submit to the other."

Shadow would have flushed if he had been human. Aye, the bow had been a sign of submission, that he would follow her decision, no matter what it was. But Shadow knew, and it seemed Last Chance might too, that there was a meaning behind the bow that had nothing to do with Shadow attempting to persuade the mare to dance with him. It had a more primal meaning, one that Shadow didn't wish to contemplate right now.

"Agreed."

As though his response had been her cue, Last Chance raised herself onto her hind legs and released a scream of pleasure so pure Shadow found himself responding in kind.

As both horses landed on all fours once more, they turned as one and began to dance with the rest of the herd, lending themselves to a dance as old as horsekind.

But even as they danced with the herd, they might as well have been dancing alone, just the two of them.

~~*~*

Ferez handed the saiten back to its owner after several more songs. He still contemplated the scene he'd watched play out between Last Chance and Shadow. He didn't know what Shadow had done, but Ferez had never seen his mare as relaxed as she was afterward. He promised himself that he would thank the stallion later.

As the saiten player thumbed a few chords, Ferez took the hand James offered and climbed to his feet. When he found himself nearly nose to nose with the boy, his breath caught and his earlier thoughts returned with renewed force.

"That was amazing." James's eyes were bright and his grin wide. "How long have you been playing?"

Ferez blinked and took a step back to gain some distance and clear his head. "Since I was seven. I asked a travelin' musician to show me how to play."

James chuckled and shook his head. "Did your vater know you were taking up the saiten?" His grin turned playful.

Ferez stared at James in wonder. He didn't get to see this side of James very often, not with how much time they seemed to spend working on political issues and training with weapons. He wondered if James was like Last Chance: he had to force himself to relax.

"Actually," Ferez said, returning to James's question with a smile. "My father was shocked to learn that afternoon when he found me learnin' the chords."

He joined James in chuckling. Leaning forward and lowering his voice, he added, "But he was the one who offered to have a saiten made for me an' to hire a Zhulanese musician to teach me when he found out how much I wanted to play."

As soon as he finished speaking, Ferez wondered if James would understand the significance of his father's support. Ferez didn't think most people realized how much the noble class disapproved of boys learning music when they could be learning something of more importance.

The soft smile James offered and the gentle look in his eyes told Ferez he understood exactly how much the old king's acceptance had meant to him.

More than his beauty, it was that understanding that had the king leaning closer to the purple-eyed young man. Despite his earlier conflict, Ferez didn't hesitate to lightly grip the boy's shoulder in one hand and lay his lips gently against James's.

~~*~*

Gemi stilled when Ferez kissed her. It wasn't so much from surprise—*"I should hope not,"* Flame rumbled; *"you two have been dancing around each other for most of the season"*—as much as from wariness.

"Relax," Shadow nickered calmly. *"Enjoy yourself."*

"Easy for you to say," Gemi replied mentally as she slowly pulled back from the kiss. *"You're not hiding your true identity from a potential lover."*

"Not that he could," Flame added dryly.

Shadow blithely ignored Flame. *"Well, it's not like you'll be doing much more than kissing tonight. Let's face it: neither of you is the sort to begin mating on the first night."*

Gemi gave a short bark of laughter. Immediately, she threw a hand over her mouth, her gaze snapping up to Ferez's tightening expression.

"Es tut mir leid," she whispered quickly as she shoved her bondmates' presences away. "Unrelated comment from Shadow." She reached for Ferez's hand and gripped it.

"Not entirely," Shadow muttered before Gemi managed to shove her awareness of her freunde to the back of her geist. It settled there as a quiet buzz.

To Gemi's relief, Ferez began to relax again. Despite the red decorating his cheekbones, there was a determined set to his jaw, as if he had decided how he felt and wasn't changing his geist no matter how Gemi reacted.

Good. Leaning forward, she proceeded to kiss him right back.

She was able to enjoy the kiss for all of two seconds— long enough for Ferez's grip on her to tighten approvingly— before whistles and clapping had her pulling back and looking around her in surprise.

Big grins decorated the faces of the surrounding nomaden. Even the musicians, who hadn't played anything since Ferez gave up the saiten, were clapping and otherwise showing their approval.

Gemi's face burned. She had lived through a lot in the last seven jahre, but this had to be one of the most embarrassing. She glanced at Ferez. While his face was flushed, his mouth still curved in a small smile and his eyes focused solely on her.

That warmed her and brought her own smile back.

"Come on! Give it a rest!"

Pulling her gaze from Ferez again, Gemi was surprised to see Zuk and Käfe making their way toward them.

"Leave them be, you köter!" Zuk shouted at the crowd as he reached Gemi. Laughter answered his insult. Zuk turned to the muskier. "This is a fest, isn't it? Music!"

As the musicians picked up their instruments once more and struck up a lively dance tune, the laughter subsided and the dancing began again. Once the other nomaden were sufficiently distracted, Zuk turned back to Gemi and slapped her on the back.

"That should get you some peace for now. But, you know . . ." He smirked. "Everyone's going to want to congratulate you on your first kiss."

Gemi ducked her head as the fire in her cheeks reignited. When Zuk laughed, she reached out and shoved him. If he was going to tease her, she saw no reason not to be childish, too.

"Excuse me for being too busy to care."

Zuk's laughter subsided, and his grin softened. "You know I'm just teasing, bruder." He squeezed Gemi's shoulder. "Everyone's just happy you've finally found someone you find interesting enough to kiss.

"And Frenz?" He turned to the king.

Ferez tore his gaze from Gemi. "Aye?"

Zuk leaned forward menacingly. "If you hurt my little bruder . . ." He let the threat hang in the air between them.

Ferez nodded solemnly. "I wouldn' dream of it."

Zuk and Ferez continued to stare at each other, until Zuk finally nodded, satisfied. Grinning once more, he clapped them both on the shoulders. "Enjoy the rest of the fest, you two."

Gemi grimaced as her bruder gripped Käfe's hand and walked away. "Es tut mir leid about that," she said to Ferez. "Unfortunately, you'll probably be getting a lot of . . . that . . ."

She trailed off and looked up as Ferez gripped her arm. He stared at her, his eyes still solemn.

"I mean it, James." His voice was just loud enough for her to hear over the music. "I won't hurt you. I promise."

Gemi swallowed as she stared into his silver-and-blue eyes. Thoughts of the secret she still kept from him surfaced in her geist.

I have to tell him.

"Not tonight." Flame's words startled Gemi. *"Just enjoy tonight. You can worry about the secret tomorrow."*

"You want me to put it off?" Flame had been pestering her to tell Ferez the truth almost since she first accepted him as a companion.

The drache sighed. *"You deserve the chance to enjoy tonight without worrying about consequences."*

Gemi relaxed and smiled softly. Flame was right: She could worry about it tomorrow. She wanted to enjoy tonight with Ferez. She wanted to just be herself with him before the pressures and expectations of the truth clouded their relationship.

"I know," Gemi answered Ferez's proclamation, smiling. "Danke."

Turning to glance at the dancing nomaden, Gemi added jovially, "Now, I've been waiting to dance since you started playing." She grinned at Ferez and held out a hand. "Care to join me?"

Ferez's smile returned full force, and he grasped her hand. "Of course."

Together, they joined the other nomaden in dance.

The remainder of the evening sped by in a blur for Gemi. There was dancing and laughter, food and conversation. At one point, Ulla and Raymond found them and congratulated them on the new dimension of their relationship.

While Raymond shook Ferez's hand and pounded him on the shoulder, Ulla leaned into Gemi. "You couldn't have found a better one, Gemi. I'm so proud of you."

Gemi's grin widened at her schwester's words, which Gemi would have thought impossible. She was grinning like a dummkopf the entire evening, but she couldn't bring herself to care. Somehow, being with Ferez made the whole fest, something she had always found enjoyable, more wunderbar.

Once Gemi and Ferez decided they'd had enough dancing, Gemi led Ferez farther out into the desert, away from the oase. She had not had a reason to leave the camp during the fest since her first season with the nomaden, though she knew many took advantage of the privacy the desert provided. She felt an extra thrill run through her, among all the other emotions she felt, that for once she was doing something others her age normally would.

They settled on the ground, nothing but their kopfabdeckungen and each other to keep them warm in the chill desert nacht. They spoke softly and watched Flame's continued flight, trading kisses occasionally. As Gemi drifted into sleep, curled happily against Ferez, she knew, for the first time in jahre, she was truly happy.

~~*~*

Adalwolf watched the bright colors of the himmelfeuer light up the sky, a sneer pulling at his lips. Ja, the himmelfeuer were beautiful, but the Vereinte Clans didn't seem to care that they also gave away their position to any who cared to look.

"Yet I sense you wish you could celebrate Adlerfest with such carelessness." The taunt came from the bodiless voice that had guided him these past few siebentäge.

Adalwolf sneered. *"To drop one's guard so completely is more than dumm; it's insane."*

The voice chuckled darkly. *"Then there is a great deal of insanity in that oase."*

"Oi, Schlange!"

The Geistmagier growled as a hand landed on his arm. He turned and shook it off, glaring at the Skorpion who had dared to touch him.

"What?"

The Skorpion sneered. "You were muttering to yourself, Schlange. I thought you Geistmagier were supposed to keep everything in your head."

"Stein," muttered a second Skorpion, who didn't move from the edge of the tiny spring by which they'd stopped. "Stop baiting him."

Stein frowned at his fellow Skorpion, and Adalwolf's lip twitched. He turned back toward Friedlichoase so neither Skorpion could see the smirk that wanted to form. He was not amicable with Skorpion as a principle, but he was always amused when his feinde were chastised by their fellows.

Not long, he thought, eyeing the eastern sky. Soon, the sky would begin to lighten, and the drache, whom he could see outlined against the sky with the himmelfeuer hanging from her body, would return to the camp and find her rest.

Then, we can destroy Caffers.

"I thought you might enjoy this task."

Adalwolf only nodded. The geist had mentioned the plan when he was still in Schönestadt, but he hadn't detailed it until two täge ago. The only reason that had been enough time to put the plan in motion was that both häuptlinge agreed it was a very good idea. Thankfully, Häuptling Giftschwanz still refused to risk his heirs, so Adalwolf hadn't had to argue to oversee the task.

The three nomaden silently watched the sky as it turned predawn gray and continued to lighten. The only sounds were the soft nickers of their pferde. As predicted, the drache soon returned to the ground, but they waited still, until the sun had pulled itself fully over the Tarsur Mountains in the east. By then, they were sure the drache would be asleep, along with the rest of the camp.

Knowing they had to move quickly lest they risk being caught, the three Gift Clan nomaden walked toward Friedlichoase, leaving their pferde at the small spring. The two Skorpione carried a litter between them; Adalwolf led them, his eyes half closed as he sought the geist of the Caffers boy.

Adalwolf smirked when he found him. They had expected the possibility of having to move through the camp and risk exposure that way. However, the Schicksale seemed to be on their side; the Caffers boy and his human companion had decided to leave the safety of the camp for the supposed privacy of the desert.

The two slept on the ground, the long black hair of the Caffers boy spread out underneath them. Their heads were tilted together, as though they shared secrets only they knew. Sneering in disgust at the display, he kicked the brown-haired mann away from their prey.

"Oi!" Stein hissed, grabbing Adalwolf's arm once more. "Careful, Schlange! You could wake them."

The Geistmagier turned a glare on the Skorpion and shrugged his hand off once again. The mann was really beginning to annoy him. Before he could spit out the insult that sat on his tongue, the second Skorpion pulled Stein back.

"Easy, Stein." His eyes met and held Adalwolf's. "Don't you know how easily Geistmagier can suppress your geist?"

Stein stiffened. Adalwolf allowed his glare to ease into a smirk as he turned his attention to the second Skorpion. He, at least, spoke sense, more than most Skopione with whom Adalwolf was acquainted.

It's a shame, really. He dropped his gaze to the mann's brown statusgürtel. *He would make a good Schlange, and his Tieremagie would be useful, as well.*

"So how are we doing this, Stach?"

Adalwolf gave a mental snort as Stein turned fully to the Tieremagier, apparently deciding to ignore Adalwolf.

"We," muttered Stach, indicating Stein and himself, "are doing nothing more than transporting the Ausländisch Krieger." He motioned to the black-haired boy.

A soft snort sounded behind Adalwolf. *"You Gift Clan nomaden are amusing, aren't you?"* Adalwolf fought to keep his expression neutral despite the sudden annoyance thrumming through him. *"Ausländisch Krieger, indeed. You deny him the ancient title, yet you still acknowledge him as a warrior in his own right."* The dark chuckle that followed seemed to echo through the

Geistmagier's bones. *"You allow him a respekt you do not even allow each other."*

Adalwolf turned back to his prey, even though the taunting geist called from the same direction. He couldn't prevent his mouth from opening in a silent snarl, and he was unwilling to let the Skorpione see it. Allies they might be, but he refused to show them such weakness.

Dropping into a crouch beside his prey, Adalwolf examined the Caffers boy. His face was relaxed, a smile curving his lips. Yet the lines of his face spoke of stress and hardship.

Good! Adalwolf's snarl relaxed into a smirk. *If he has found a happiness to which he is unaccustomed, it will be that much more satisfying to bring him down from it.*

Adalwolf laid a hand on the boy's forehead. Though physical contact was unnecessary for his magie to work, it would speed up the process and increase his hold on his prey's geist. Diving past the first layer, which he had already claimed to keep the boy from waking, he found the barrier the drache had placed around his geist.

Under normal circumstances, the barrier would have been successful at keeping Adalwolf from his goal. Even among the Gift Clans, the defensive Geistmagie of the drache was legendary. Even with the drache's concentration weakened by her nacht-long flight and her current deep sleep, bypassing the barrier was no small challenge.

Once past the barrier, Adalwolf stilled and nearly removed himself from the geist in disgust. Sharp, thick anger thrummed through his veins.

This is the Drache Krieger? This is the . . . creature we all fear? A verdammt girl?

He had thought it preposterous that they considered a

mere boy such a threat to their clans' ways of life. But a mere girl . . . ?

Adalwolf snarled silently as the bodiless geist chuckled darkly. More determined than ever for this plan to succeed, he worked his magie through the dracheband that connected the verdammt girl to her drache and stallion.

Once satisfied with his work on the two animals, he pulled back into his prey's geist. With another silent snarl, he built up a barrier between her and her bondmates so thick, nothing would leak through and no one but he would be able to break it.

Certain that neither pferd nor drache would prove a threat to them, Adalwolf secured the prey's unconsciousness for the next few hours, pulled out of the prey's geist, and nodded stiffly to the Skorpione. The two männer moved forward and lifted their prey onto the litter.

"What about him?" Stein nodded toward their prey's companion. "We can't just leave him here alive."

Adalwolf frowned down at the sleeping stranger. *"Kill him!"* hissed the geist. Adalwolf shook his head. He didn't think it was worth the blood on his scharfmond to kill the ausländer.

"He is of little consequence."

"You must kill him," the voice hissed again.

Adalwolf's frown deepened. It was true that the geist had yet to lead him wrong, but Adalwolf saw no reason to shed this mann's blood when they had completed their task and could return to their camp triumphantly.

"He is dangerous," the Geist hissed. *"He will lead an army to hunt you down if you leave him alive."*

An image filled Adalwolf's head, not of an army but of this seemingly unremarkable mann seated upon a throne, a simple gold crown decorated with a handful of gems resting upon his brow.

Adalwolf smiled grimly. Such knowledge had been available in the . . . girl's geist, but he hadn't made the connection.

The smile disappeared with a sharp hiss as he refocused on the newly revealed king. A small, brown skorpion, all the deadlier for its dull color and small size, was crawling steadily across the king's tunic toward his bare throat.

With the speed and precision of a schlange, Adalwolf drew his right scharfmond and struck the skorpion, knocking it off the mann's chest. It landed on the ground several feet away and skittered a few steps before Stein snatched it by the tail and dropped it in a bag at his hip.

"Why did you do that?" Stein asked indignantly. "You said he didn't matter."

Adalwolf glared at him. "I meant to leave him be," he growled. "Even if we were to kill him, I would not let you use your skorpion. Such a death would lead the Vereinte Clans straight to yours. While I may not care about your clan, my own clan is allied to yours in this, and I will not have you creating such a risk."

Stein narrowed his eyes and opened his mouth, but Stach laid a hand on his shoulder. Adalwolf turned his glare on the Tieremagier, wondering why the mann had let his fellow clansmann place the skorpion on the still-sleeping king.

"Your argument makes no sense, Adalwolf." Stach's gaze was steady as he met the Schlange's glare. Adalwolf frowned, unaccustomed to others returning his looks with such calm.

"The Vereinte Clans will suspect our clans either way. They would still have to find our camp in order to save the Ausländisch Krieger and exact revenge. That is something they haven't managed to do in the five jahre since they unified."

Adalwolf growled. He knew Stach had a point. After all, if they had not felt secure in safety of their clans' location, they would simply have killed their prey rather than attempt to kidnap her as they were. Still, Adalwolf did not wish to kill the brown-haired mann, especially now that he knew who he was. There was something he could do to the mann that was much worse than death.

"This discussion is moot. We will not kill him." When Stach raised an eyebrow, Adalwolf added, "I have my own plans for his geist."

The Tieremagier continued to gaze at him steadily for a moment before eventually nodding. Gripping Stein's shoulder, he turned back to their prey. "Stein and I will head back to the pferde then. We'll wait for you there."

Adalwolf nodded and turned back to his new prey, not bothering to watch the Skorpione leave with their first. Kneeling beside the young king, he held one hand above the mann's head and paused, listening.

The bodiless geist remained surprisingly quiet. It hadn't left—he could still sense it—but it seemed unwilling to speak, even to taunt him as it often did.

Adalwolf shrugged and laid his hand on the king's forehead. Smiling grimly, he began to work his magie into the king's geist. He eased past barriers similar to, yet nowhere near as strong as, those he'd found in his first prey's geist.

"I am afraid you will not be returning to Caypan, Eure Majestät." Adalwolf dug deeper and deeper into the king's geist. "No need to worry, though. You will not remember enough to care."

To Be
Continued
in
Lost King

Language Glossary

Zhulanese Glossary

abschaum (*ahb-showm*) – scum

Adlerfest (*ahd-lehr-fehst*) – Mid-Autumn Festival; literally "Eagle Festival"; represents the Royal Eagle, first guardian of the Cycle of Incarnation

adlige (*ahd-lee-ghuh*) – noblewoman, lady; old term; generally used more for nomad ruling families, while Mylady is used for nobles recognized by the Evonese monarchy

Angenehm! (*ahn-gheh-nem*) – old, formal greeting used more among nomads than river-dwellers

ausländer (*ouse-land-uh*) – foreigner

Ausländisch Krieger (*ouse-land-ish kree-ghehr*) – Foreign Warrior; one of the names the Gift Clans use for James Caffers

bitte (*biht-uh*) – please

boxkampf (*bohks-kahmpf*) [-kämpfe (*bohks-kaymp-fuh*)] – boxing match

bruder (*broo-dehr*) [brüder (*brew-dehr*)] – brother

Caypanbürger (*kay-pahn-bewr-ghehr*) – citizen of Caypan

clansmann (*klahns-mahn*) [-männer (*klahns-may-nehr*)] – clansman

dame (*dah-muh*) – madam

danke (*dahn-kuh*) – thank you

dankpflicht (*dahnk-flickt*) – formal thanks; obligation born of gratitude; held in high regard by the nomads

dieb (*deeb*) [-e (*dee-buh*)] – thief

drache (*druh-kuh*) [-n (*druh-kin*)] – dragon

Drache Krieger (*drah-kuh kree-ghehr*) – James Caffers's title in Zhulan; literally means "dragon warrior"; title originally belonged to first erstehäuptling of the clans

Dorothy Tinker

dracheband (*drah-kuh-bahnd*) – dragonbond

dumm (*doom*) – stupid; dumb

dummkopf (*doom-kohpf*) – idiot

ein bisschen (*ine bees-shin*) – a bit

erstehäuptling (*ehr-stuh-hoypt-ling*) – leader of Vereinte Clans

es tut mir leid (*ehs toot meer lyde*) – I'm sorry; literally "it gives
    me sorrow"

eule (*oy-luh*) [-n (*oy-lin*)] – desert owl

falke (*fahl-kuh*) [-n (*fahl-kin*)] – falcon

familie (*fah-mih-lee*) [-n (*fah-mih-leen*)] – family

feind (*find*) [-e (*fine-duh*)] – enemy

fest (*fehst*) [-e (*feh-stuh*)] – festival

feuerdrache (*fewr-drah-kuh*) – fire dragon

Flammezunge (*flah-muh-zoon-guh*) – Flame Tongue's Zhulanese
    name

frau (*frow*) [-en (*frow-in*)] – woman

fräulein (*froy-line*) – young woman; miss

freund (*froynd*) [-e (*froyn-duh*)] – friend

Frieda (*free-dah*) – the demigoddess Peace

gasthaus (*gahst-house*) [-häuser (*gahst-hoy-sehr*)] – inn

geist (*ghyste*) [-er (*guy-stehr*)] – nonphysical part of a creature:
    mind, spirit, soul, ghost; *Der Geist (dehr ghyste)* – The
    Ghost

geisternetz (*guy-stehr-nehtz*) [-e (*guy-stehr-neht-zuh*)] – mental net;
    web of Mindspeakers

Geisterstück (*guy-stehr-stewk*) [-e (*guy-stehr-stew-kuh*)] – Spirit
    Play

Geistmagie (*ghyste-mah-ghee*) – mental magic

Geistmagier (*ghyste-mah-gheer*) – Mindspeaker

Gift Clans (*ghift klahns*) – Poison Clans

Gleichrat (*glyke-raht*) – formal meeting held between the
    erstehäuptling, the Drache Krieger, and the häuptlinge of
    all the Unified Clans; literally "equal council"

glück (*glewk*) – luck; *viel glück (veel glewk)* – good luck

gör (*ghehr*) – brat

gott (*ghoht*) [götter (*ghehr-tehr*)] – god

gouverneur (*goo-vehr-newr*) [-e (*goo-vehr-newr-uh*)] – governor

gratuliere (*grah-too-leer-uh*) – congratulations

grossmütter (*grohs-mew-tehr*) – grandmother

gute nacht (*goo-tuh nahkt*) – good night

guten morgen (*goo-tehn moor-ghehn*) – good morning

guten täg (*goo-tehn taygh*) – good day

halbgott (*hahlb-ghoht*) [-götter (*hahlb-ghehr-tehr*)] – demigod

hallo (*hah-loh*) – hello

halt die klappe (*hahlt dee klah-puh*) – shut up; harsh form of
    "be quiet"

Hass (*hahs*) – the demigod Hate

häuptling (*hoypt-ling*) [-e (*hoypt-lin-guh*)] – clan leader

hauptmann (*howpt-mahn*) [-männer (*howpt-may-nehr*)] – title of
    military leaders in Zhulan's cities

Hauptplatz (*howpt-plahtz*) – main square; city's central plaza

haus (*house*) [häuser (*hoy-sehr*)] – house

Heilemagie (*high-luh-mah-ghee*) – Healing Magic

Heilemagier (*high-luh-mah-gheer*) – Mage Healer

Heilig (*high-lihgh*) – Holy Man

heiligetier (*high-lihg-uh-teer*) – sacred animal

herr (*hehr*) [-en (*hehr-rihn*)] – sir, mister

hexe (*hehk-suh*) – derogatory word for a female

himmelfeuer (*hihm-mehl-fewr*) – sky fire

Hoffnung (*hohf-noong*) – the demigoddess Hope

ja (*yah*) – aye

jahr (*yahr*) [-e (*yahr-uh*)] – year

katastrophe (*kah-tah-stroh-fuh*) – catastrophe

katze (*kaht-zuh*) [-n (*kaht-zihn*)] – desert cat

katzenauge (*kaht-zihn-ow-guh*) – cat eye (gemstone)

komm (*kohm*) [-e (*koh-muh*)] [-t (*kohmt*)] – come!

kopfabdeckung (*kohp-fahb-deh-koong*) [-en (*kohp-fahb-deh-koong-inn*)] – head covering; square of spider silk worn over the head to protect wearer from the sun and hair from senf seeds

köter (*kehr-tehr*) – cur

Kräftetier (*krayf-tuh-teer*) – Power Animal; the animal with which an Animal Mage's magic connects most powerfully

Kreis (*kryse*) – those river-dwellers who are friendly to nomads

krieg (*kreegh*) – war; *Krieg* – the demigod War

Krieg mit Fayral (*kreegh meet fay-rahl*) – War with Fayral

kriegrat (*kreegh-raht*) – war council

Kriegschrift (*kreegh-shrihft*) – war script

Leben (*leh-bin*) – the demigoddess Life

lebenfrau (*leh-bin-frow*) [-en (*leh-bin-frow-inn*)] – female lifemate

lebenmann (*leh-bin-mahn*) – male lifemate

Liebe (*lee-buh*) – the demigoddess Love

liebling (*leeb-ling*) – darling

Luftmagie (*looft-mah-ghee*) – Air Magic

lügnerin (*lewgh-nehr-inn*) – female liar

magie (*mah-ghee*) – magic

magier (*mah-gheer*) – mage

Majestät, Eure/Seine (*mah-yeh-state, oy-ruh/ sigh-nuh*) – Your/His Majesty

mann (*mahn*) [männer (*may-nehr*)] – man

Marktplatz (*mahrkt-plahts*) – Market Place

mein (*mine*) – my

mit vergnügen (*miht vehrgh-new-ghehn*) – with pleasure

Mitte Jahreszeit (*miht-tuh yahr-eh-zite*) – Mid-Season

mitternacht (*miht-tehr-nahkt*) – midnight

mörder (*mehr-dehr*) – murderer

morgen (*mohr-ghehn*) – morning

mütter (*mew-tehr*) – mother

Mylady (*mye-lah-dee*) – Milady

Mylord (*mye-lohrd*) – Milord

nacht (*nahkt*) [nächte (*nayk-tuh*)] – night

nein (*nine*) – nay

noch nicht (*nohk niksht*) – not yet

nomade (*noh-mah-duh*) [-n (*noh-mah-dehn*)] – nomad

oase (*oh-ah-suh*) [-n (*oh-ah-sehn*)] – oasis

Oma (*oh-mah*) – Grandma

Parshen Gut (*n*) (*pahr-shin goot*) – Parshen Estate

perle (*pehr-luh*) – pearl

pferd (*fehrd*) [-e (*fehr-duh*)] – horse

Pferdetanz (*fehr-duh-tahnz*) – the Horse Dance; a song created
 by Animal Mages that bears magic powerful enough to
 make a horse dance

Pflanzenmagier (*flahn-zihn-mah-gheer*) – Plant Mage

Phönixfest (*fehr-nihks-fehst*) – Mid-Summer Festival; literally
 "Phoenix Festival"

politik (*poh-lih-tik*) – politics

recht (*rehkt*) [-e (*rehk-tuh*)] – right

Regierhaus (*reh-gheer-house*) – home of the city's governor

respekt (*reh-spehkt*) – respect

Rotvogel (*roht-voh-ghehl*) – red bird; name of Berg's inn in
 Machtstadt

Ruhe! (*roo-huh*) – Silence!; Quiet!

saiten (*sigh-tehn*) [-s (*sigh-tehns*)] – stringed instrument similar to
 a guitar

scharfmond (*sharf-mohnd*) [-e (*sharf-mohn-duh*)] – Twin Moon
 Blade; literally means "sharp moon"

Schattenrenner (*shuh-tehn-rehn-nehr*) – Shadow Racer's
 Zhulanese name

scheisse (*shice-uh*) – curse word

Schicksale (*shihk-sah-luh*) – the Fates

Dorothy Tinker

schlampe (*shlahm-puh*) – immoral woman

schlange (*shlahng-uh*) [-n (*shlahng-ehn*)] – snake

Schlangenfest (*shlahng-ehn-fehst*) – Mid-Spring Festival; literally
    "Serpent Festival"

schlingel (*shling-ehl*) – street runners; children, often thieves,
    who roam the streets of cities in Zhulan

Schutzmagier (*shoots-mah-gheer*) – Protection Mage

schwester (*shwehs-tehr*) [-n (*shwehs-tehrn*)] – sister

senf (*sehnf*) – desert plant whose seeds do not need earth or
    water to grow; these seeds will latch onto anything,
    including living creatures, and grow; travelers must be
    wary of these, and often require 'deseeding' after a long
    journey

siebentäg (*zee-behn-taygh*) [-e (*zee-behn-tay-ghuh*)] – sevenday

skorpion (*skohr-pee-ohn*) [-e (*skohr-pee-oh-nuh*)] – scorpion

spinne (*shpin-nuh*) [-n (*shpin-nehn*)] – spider

stadt (*shtahdt*) [städte (*shtayd-tuh*)] – city

statusgürtel (*shtah-toos-gewr-tehl*) – status belt; thick spider silk
    belt dyed at one or both ends, it declares a nomad's clan
    and status

täg (*taygh*) [-e (*tay-ghuh*)] – day

tante (*tahn-tuh*) – aunt

tanz (*tahnz*) – dance

tempel (*tehm-pehl*) – temple

Tieremagie (*teer-uh-mah-ghee*) – Animal Magic

Tieremagier (*teer-uh-mah-gheer*) – Animal Mage

Tod (*tohd*) – the demigod Death

unwetter (*oon-veh-tehr*) – desert rainstorm

vater (*fah-tehr*) – father

verdammt (*fehr-dahmt*) [-e (*fehr-dahm-tuh*)] – damn

Vereinte Clans (*fehr-ine-tuh klahns*) – Unified Clans

verliebt (*fehr-leebt*) – in love

verwöhnt (*fehr-vehrnt*) – spoilt

Violettauge Nomade (*fee-oh-leht-ow-guh noh-mah-duh*) – Purple-
Eyed Nomad; a rare title used for James Caffers
wache (*vah-kuh*) [-n (*vah-kehn*)] – guard
Wanderung (*vahn-dehr-oong*) – migration; a clan's journey
across the desert from one oasis to another
wasserdrache (*vahs-sehr-drah-kuh*) – water drake
wille (*vih-luh*) – will
witz (*vihtz*) – joke
wolf (*vohlf*) [wölfe (*vehrl-fuh*)] – wolf
Wölfefest (*vehrl-fuh-fehst*) – Mid-Winter Festival; literally "Wolf
Festival"
wunderbar (*voon-dehr-bahr*) – wonderful
wurm (*vurm*) – worm
Zhulan (*jhoo-lahn*) – middle province of Evon
Zhulanbürger (*jhoo-lahn-bewr-gehr*) – citizen of Zhulan

Dorothy Tinker grew up dreaming of fantastical worlds and creatures, of plots in space, and of strange new cultures. Certain she needed something else to support her through life, she spent her time at the University of Texas at Dallas focusing on math and computer science. Two years after graduating with a BS in applied math, she rediscovered her true passion and rededicated herself to her literary dreams.

Since then, Dorothy has published an ongoing series of young adult fantasy novels, including *Peace of Evon*, *Gift of War*, and *Lost King*. Her short stories have appeared in HWG Press's *Riding the Waves* and *Out of Many, One*, Inklings Publishing's *Eclectically Cosmic* and *Eclectically Heroic*, and Writespace's *In Medias Res*.

Dorothy is also the owner of D Tinker Editing and works as copy editor and formatter for Inklings Publishing.

Excerpt
from
Lost King

Frenz Kanti woke with a groan. He hated mornings, and this one seemed to be particularly hot and bright.

Wrinkling his nose, the farmer squinted open one eye and quickly closed it when all that met his gaze was overwhelming sunlight.

Too bright for bed. I must have camped outside last night.

It wouldn't be the first time he'd decided to sleep out in the fields. With the war now two years gone, Frenz was the only person available to tend the crops. It was often simpler to spend the nights outside, especially during harvest.

Determined to enjoy a few minutes of quiet before beginning his day, Frenz sighed and let his head loll to one side.

All too soon, he realized something wasn't quite right. Despite the sunlight beating down on his body, there was a distinct lack of birdsong, a constant around his home in the forest of Kensy.

"Odd." He opened his eyes and blinked against the incessant light. Once he'd sat up and could see past the brightness, he continued to blink, taking in his current surroundings.

"Where . . . ?"

Gone were the trees he had grown up knowing. Instead, Frenz was surrounded by a flat, barren landscape, broken only by a large camp nearby that appeared to contain a modicum of greenery.

Nothing compared to Kensy's old forest.

"How in Maur's Fire did I end up in Zhulan?"

The desert province may have been no more than a two days' ride south of his farm, but Frenz had never passed Kensy's borders, not even to escape the constant violence of the war. Both he and his father had fought in the war against Fayral, his father dying to protect their land. As far as Frenz was concerned, he had no reason to leave Kensy.

So why did I?

Climbing to his feet, Frenz scanned the mostly empty horizon, noting what looked like a mountain range in the distance on the other side of the camp. He'd made a full turn before he finally realized he not only did not remember how he had come to be in Zhulan but also was completely alone.

Uttering a curse, he spun around again. "Last Chance! Last Chance!"

Please let her be nearby.

His chest tightened, his breath sped, and he dug his fingers into his palms. To wake up in a strange place with no memory of it was one thing, but to do so without his Last Chance for Hope and Freedom . . . ?

Frenz snapped his head from side to side, hoping to dislodge the thought, and shouted again.

"Last Chance!"